From This Moment

CHARLOTTE EVERHART

NEVINLY PUBLISHING

FIRST EDITION

Cover design by Tugboat Design.

ISBN: 9781737988656 (print)

ISBN: 9781737988649 (ebook)

1. Women's Fiction 2. Small Town/Rural Fiction 4. Contemporary Romance

For Claire

You are everything I could have hoped for in a daughter. May you walk through life with close friends beside you.

I love you.

Also By

Hope for Tomorrow
books2read.com/HopeForTomorrow

Joy of Today
books2read.com/JoyOfToday

A Time and a Season
https://books2read.com/A-Time-and-a-Season

Coming Soon
When Someday Finally Comes
Sweet December

Contents

Prologue — 1

Chapter 1 — 5

Chapter 2 — 13

Chapter 3 — 21

Chapter 4 — 27

Chapter 5 — 43

Chapter 6 — 49

Chapter 7 — 57

Chapter 8 — 61

Chapter 9 — 71

Chapter 10 — 81

Chapter 11 — 95

Chapter 12 — 101

Chapter 13 — 113

Chapter 14 — 121

Chapter 15 — 135

Chapter 16 — 147

Chapter 17 — 167

Chapter 18 — 177

Chapter 19   181

Chapter 20   191

Chapter 21   205

Chapter 22   219

Chapter 23   229

Chapter 24   233

Chapter 25   243

Chapter 26   245

Chapter 27   255

Chapter 28   263

Epilogue   279

Next In Series   285

About Author   287

<h1 style="text-align:center">Prologue</h1>

Ethan Rockford was in shock, just like everyone else in the richly appointed boardroom. The silence was thunderous as they all waited for a response to the bomb that had just been dropped by Ms. Leland, the steely eyed estate lawyer wearing a blue power suit, a bad wig, and a smug smile. She was the lone female in a room full of men, but if she was intimidated, she didn't show it.

Ethan's boss and company head, Bruce Josten, leaned forward, resting his elbows on the polished mahogany table. When he spoke, there was a small, almost imperceptible shake in his voice. "I was her only son. You expect me to believe she left me nothing?"

A poker-faced businessman, Bruce Josten had perfected the ability to receive bad news without giving anything away. It was probably one of the reasons he was so successful. But today was different. This wasn't just a business merger gone awry. This was personal, and for once the CEO of Josten's Holdings was on the verge of showing his cards.

"That's correct, Mr. Josten," Ms. Leland quipped.

Bruce shot a glance to his left. "Bert?"

Bert Townsend, the company lawyer, shook his head regretfully. "That's the way of it, Mr. Josten."

Bruce pushed away from the table in disgust. "I read the Will six months ago! She was leaving me everything—shares *and* money! So, what the hell happened?"

As the leading financial analyst at Josten's Holdings, Ethan knew Bruce already had more money than he knew what to do with; he didn't need his late mother's too. What he did need, what he'd been banking on, was getting his hands on her shares of the family company he'd been running the last twenty years.

Ethan knew the story. When Harold Josten, founder of Josten's Holdings, had surprised everyone by keeling over in the home of his long-time mistress all those years ago, his son, Bruce, had taken control of the company. He'd been only twenty-eight years old at the time. While his mother, Lenora, held the controlling shares, it had been Bruce's blood, sweat, and tears that propelled an already successful real estate company into the multi-billion dollar organization it was today.

Ethan had heard enough company gossip to know what Bruce Josten thought of his mother. They hadn't been close. She disapproved of his womanizing, and he'd long grown tired of her reminders that he was turning out just like his father. Bruce resented the fact that she'd done nothing to grow their investments, nothing to secure important business connections, and knew next to nothing about the day-to-day running of the company that had made her a very rich woman indeed. She'd just happily held on for the ride with her inherited shares and ever-increasing wealth, showing up only occasionally for board meetings and reaping all the benefits of Bruce's hard work.

Ethan had only spoken to Lenora Josten once. It had been to ask her what floor she was going to in the elevator so he could punch the right button. She hadn't known who he was, and why would she? Back then, he'd been a relatively new no-name, and she rarely came to the office. He'd come a long way in a short time, and just before her death, Lenora had recognized him enough to address him as Eric. Close enough.

Being involved in this meeting at all was a testament to his success. Ethan knew he was being considered for treasurer, the intermediate step needed to become CFO one day. He was well on his way to making his dream a reality. He'd be financially secure. More than that, he'd be rich. Even better, so would his parents and sister.

Ms. Leland couldn't keep the satisfaction from her voice when she said, "Your mother had a change of heart, Mr. Josten."

Bruce lost the remainder of his cool. "Well, who the hell inherited all her shares?"

"Your daughters."

Bruce closed his eyes and exhaled slowly before standing up and barking out a laugh. He brought a hand to his chest to straighten his tie. When he spoke again, his voice was smooth as buttermilk. "Well, why didn't you just say so,

Ms. Leland? You might have given me a heart attack, and I never would have known that those shares would stay safely in the family."

"Not *those* daughters, Mr. Josten. She left the shares to your daughters from your *first* marriage." The lawyer smiled widely. She was enjoying this.

Ethan held his breath. Brent, the CFO, glanced at him and widened his eyes in silent communication. Everyone knew about *these* daughters. Their existence was whispered about plenty, but nobody spoke of them openly, and definitely not in Bruce's presence.

Bruce was eerily quiet as he sat back down. Only the leather chair dared make noise as it creaked under the weight of him.

Ms. Leland consulted her binder. "Your mother split the shares equally between one Sarah Josten and one Nadia Josten."

Bruce looked down at his hands and spoke without looking up. "And who got the money?"

"It was divvied up between the same two daughters. A large portion went to various charities, and a small amount was also left to a Mrs. Lydie Mae Josten." Shooting him a smug look, she added, "Your ex-wife."

At that, Bruce lifted his gaze. "How much?" he demanded.

"I won't be disclosing that information to you, Mr. Josten."

"How much!" he shouted.

Chapter 1

The music from the reception tent floated along on the warm breeze. "Sweet Caroline," one of Sarah Josten's favorites, was playing. Alone in the dark, seated on a park bench overlooking Nicolet Harbor, she languidly hummed along. The moonlight reflected in ripples off the surface of the water, and Sarah watched it dance.

She smiled. Even the moon was dancing tonight. And why wouldn't it be? There was reason to be festive and in high spirits. Her good friend, Olivia Reeves—now Olivia Lacombe—she reminded herself, was celebrating her marriage today with a grand reception under a white tent strung with twinkle lights in the green space of Nicolet Harbor. It was a perfect night for a party under the stars, with the gently lapping waves of Lake Superior only a handful of steps away. The air smelled like summer. Like clean water and warm, green grass.

Sarah had witnessed Olivia and Sean's nuptials at their gorgeous wedding just before Christmas six months ago. It had been a small affair. Only close friends and Olivia's nine-month-old daughter, Nora, had attended the sweet ceremony at Grace Church. Being that it was the holidays, the church had been beautifully decorated with reds and greens and golds, and the whole sparkling affair had left Sarah's heart close to bursting open. The Christmas tree glowed at the front of the church, and candles flickered all around them. It looked straight out of a fairy tale.

For that one hour in the church, Sarah was a tangle of emotions, mostly good ones, but not all. Her feelings, good *and* bad, were just too big, and the effort of holding them all in made her throat ache. All through the ceremony, she'd had to swallow around a lump the size of an asteroid, and yet her face actually hurt from the genuine smile she wore. And that about summed it all up right there. She was equal parts thrilled for Olivia and sad for herself. Pleasure and pain all mixed up together.

But by the end of the ceremony, pleasure had won the day, and by the time Sarah left the church, she'd made a decision. It was time to have a little courage. A little faith. It was time to put herself back out there again. If she had to pinpoint the moment of the shift, she rather thought it had been when Sean led Olivia to the piano where he sat her down beside him and surprised her with a song he'd written just for her. The words, the melody, Sean's voice, the looks of adoration that passed between the two of them—all of it had moved her to the point of tears.

Even Jackson Lang, full of machismo, had been affected. Sarah could have sworn she saw him quickly swipe at one eye halfway through the song.

That night, as she left the church arm-in-arm with her best friend, Erin, her cup was full, and it was still full when Erin dropped her at the airport forty-five minutes later so Sarah could spend Christmas with her mom and sister in Alabama. But it didn't stay full, not that Sarah had expected it would. Even though she'd known what was coming and had been prepared, it was still a rude awakening to find what was at the bottom of that cup of joy once it ran out completely. It was crazy how quickly things could change. In less than five hours, she'd gone from happy and hopeful to dreary and depressed.

Starting the holiday with the experience at the Lacombe wedding and ending it with Lydie Mae and Nadia was a bit like drinking a hot mug of sweetened coffee, only to choke on the last sip contaminated with bitter coffee grounds. That one sip could ruin the entire experience, but even bitter coffee grounds would have been preferable to the ground up bits of dread and despair she'd found when she'd knocked on the front door of the rental she'd once called home.

No Christmas decorations in the world could brighten that place, not that her mother had bothered to put any up. Sarah had done her best on that front, going out to Michael's at the last minute to purchase a pre-lit, table-top tree and some ornaments. Lydie Mae hadn't noticed, but Sarah doubted her mother really remembered much of her visit, and Nadia had been her usual moody self. There'd been no Christmas cheer. No love. Sarah had woken up on Christmas morning and wanted to just turn right over and go back to sleep. Who felt that way on Christmas morning?

Laying there in her childhood bed with the sunflower quilt pulled up to her neck, Sarah consoled herself that it would be her last trip home. Why continue to punish herself like that? She hadn't known then that she would have to return a mere three months later for another horrible visit, not that she'd minded the final outcome of *that* trip. Boy, had she received the shock of her life! She still couldn't believe it had happened.

A slow song came on, and Sarah turned to watch the couples pair up on the floating dance floor. Young and old, they took their places under the lights, and the emcee called out for Olivia and Sean to join them.

Sarah watched them begin to dance, the petite, red-headed guidance counselor, and the tall, handsome hockey coach, and smiled. To think that they'd gone from best friends, to enemies, to lovers the way they had—she shook her head—it was something.

Sean and Olivia had put off their formal reception until tonight, which had kept the December wedding planning to a minimum, allowing them to get married in a hurry. If Sarah remembered correctly, they'd planned the ceremony in under a week. Plenty of people watched for a baby bump in the coming months to explain the haste, but no bump appeared, and Sarah knew none ever would. If she thought about it too long, it really bummed her out. They were such a perfect couple, the kind that should have lots and lots of tiny feet pitter-pattering around their home.

People continued to wonder and speculate, but Sarah knew the real reason for the quick wedding. Sean and Olivia had simply been unable to wait a moment longer to spend the rest of their lives together. Okay, well that and they'd saved themselves for one another until their wedding night. Sarah would have to remember that little trick if she ever needed a husband lickety-split.

"What are you doing out here all by yourself?" a voice asked from behind her, jarring her out of her thoughts.

Sarah's hand flew to her chest as she whipped around. "Goodness, Erin!"

Erin chuckled. "Sorry." She moved around the far side of the bench and sat down. When she did, her short, black bodycon dress cinched up even higher on her thighs.

Sarah could only imagine how many of the male guests, which included an entire college hockey team, had been transfixed as they watched and waited for a glimpse of Erin Hennings' nether regions as she'd performed her little shimmy-shake out on the dance floor for the last few hours. Brian Benninger had been particularly mesmerized. Nearly every time Sarah had glanced over at Brian as she danced by Erin's side, he'd been looking their way.

Erin sighed and lifted her blond hair off the back of her neck to cool off.

"Looks like you've worn yourself slap out," Sarah noted.

Erin cast her a wry smile before she kicked her legs out in front of her for a quick stretch and relaxed them again. Seated as she was, pressed fully against the back of the bench, her feet barely touched the ground. "You Alabamians have some interesting turns of phrase."

Sarah laughed and deepened her accent. "My meemaw woulda said yer knee-high to a grasshopper."

Erin raised a single eyebrow, something Sarah had never mastered despite spending an entire summer of her youth trying. "And that means?"

"You're short." And she really was. Even in those ridiculous heels, Erin probably wasn't much over five feet tall.

"Hmm. *Knee-high to a grasshopper* sounds better. But what the heck is a *meemaw*?"

"A grandmother, although I never called mine that."

In a flash, Erin's smile fell and was replaced with a fierce scowl. "And why *would* you? She doesn't deserve any pet names, no matter how much money she left you."

"I was referrin' to my gammie, my mama's mama. I didn't call my daddy's mama anything at all." She shrugged. "Why would I?"

"Exactly. She can just be the old bag who died and left you a shitload of cash." Sarah flinched.

Erin pinched her lips together. "Sorry. But there's no way I'm giving you a quarter for your stupid swear jar. This time it was necessary."

Sarah grinned in spite of herself. The canning jar at her house was overflowing with Erin's quarters, but her friend wasn't any closer to being a lady now than she was when Sarah had first come up with the idea.

While Olivia had been Sarah's first friend in town, Erin was the one she was closest to now. Sometimes, she forgot Erin was technically her boss. She'd only been in town a year, and already she felt more connected to this community than she had anywhere else.

Having two people she could count on was two more than she'd had since her gammie had passed away. Maybe she even had three. Back in February, her furnace pilot light had gone out on the coldest day of the year when her landlord was out of town. He'd talked her through what to do from a beach somewhere in Florida. It hadn't sounded all that difficult, but Sarah had stood in front of that old furnace for a solid forty minutes, unable to look away from the caution sticker of the person being blown to smithereens. Deciding she wanted to keep all her limbs, she put down the lighter and called Sean. Within twenty minutes, he had her pilot light relit, and as a bonus, she still had two arms and ten fingers.

Erin broke into her thoughts. "It's just that, that whole situation makes me mad whenever I think about it, and don't even get me started on your mother."

"She's done her best."

Erin laughed without humor. "Well, her best sucks."

That much was true. "Let's not talk about this now, alright? It's just too happy a night to dredge it all up again."

Erin nodded, looking thoughtful. "You're right. Let's talk about your fading accent."

Sarah angled her head. "My what?"

"Yeah, I've been noticing it lately. For the most part, you've rediscovered your *g*s."

"What on earth do you mean, my *g*s?"

"Say *wedding*," Erin directed.

Sarah smiled quizzically. "Wedding?"

"There! See? A few months ago, that would've been *weddin'.* You still do it, but now it's a nice little mix. "

"Hmm. That's *interestin'*, Erin." Sarah grinned.

Erin rolled her eyes. "Whatever. It's true, whether you realize it or not."

"If it *is* true," Sarah said on a serious note, "then I reckon that makes me a little sad. It's inevitable, I suppose. A southern girl living up north with the yanks. *When in Rome*, as they say. Watch, soon I'll start adding an *eh* at the end of all my sentences to fit in with the rest of the Yoopers."

"Me too! Whenever I talk to Jillian, she tells me I sound like a character from that movie, *Fargo*."

"I haven't seen it."

"Don't," Erin advised with an exaggerated shiver. "It's terrible. You'll never be able to look at a wood chipper the same way again."

Sarah laughed. "I'll take your word for it." She turned to look behind them at the tent. "Should we get back to the party? I'm sure Benny must be in a panic lookin' for you right about now. I've watched him watch you all night."

Erin waved a hand dismissively. "That's over, not that it ever really started."

"That may be, but he only has eyes for you. Not that I can blame him. Could you have found a shorter dress?"

"Hey, if you've got it, flaunt it. That's always been my motto. And let's face it, I'm not getting any younger. I'll be thirty-one this year. How much longer can I get away with wearing something like this?" Erin gave an ineffectual tug on the hem of her skimpy dress.

Sarah didn't say it, but she was pretty sure that time had come and gone. Erin Hennings was Nicolet High School's building principal. She couldn't afford to dress like a trollop. That was Sarah's closely held opinion, anyway. Instead she said, "You're not old yet. You'll be thirty-one and havin' fun, and maybe if I had legs like yours, I'd wear a dress like that too."

"Girlfriend, I've seen you in a bathing suit, and so I know you could rock a dress like this even better than me. Maybe *I* should take up yoga."

"You should!" Sarah said enthusiastically. Erin was always wound so tight; yoga would do her a world of good. For Sarah, yoga had been a gift from heaven to help her stay relaxed over the roller coaster of the last several months. Without it, and without the support of her friends, she just might have come unglued. "Come with me to the studio tomorrow."

Erin mulled it over. "Yeah, okay. What time?"

"Seven."

"PM?"

Sarah smirked. "Uh, no."

"Seven in the *morning*? On a *Saturday*?" Erin shook her head. "You're crazy! Never mind!"

Sarah poked Erin in the shoulder. "You're comin' with me, and that's that. Don't argue."

"You know," Erin began thoughtfully, "Olivia likes to call you *honey* and me *vinegar*, but she hasn't seen this side of you. I swear, you save it just for me."

Sarah shrugged and grinned. "You're just lucky that way."

"Well, if I'm waking up at the ass crack tomorrow, you're closing out this reception on the dance floor with me. Enough moping out here in the dark."

"I'm not moping!"

Erin stood, pulling Sarah up with her. "Good. Let's dance. I'll even ask the DJ to play 'Sweet Home Alabama.'"

That earned Erin a wide smile. "Best song ever!"

Just as Sarah had suspected, Brian Benninger—or Benny, as the students at Nicolet High called him—was in the process of scanning the tent when they got back. She knew exactly who he was looking for, and she took the moment to study him unobserved. He looked the way she imagined an authentic Roman would have looked. He even had a Roman nose, or maybe they were called hawk noses. Whatever the name, it suited him, and his dark eyes and hair lent him an air of mystery that his aloof nature only added to. He'd probably been looking for Erin the whole time she'd been with Sarah on the park bench.

Last winter, Sarah had thought Erin and Benny might end up getting serious. He'd most definitely been interested, and while Erin had played it cool, Sarah thought her friend might have had some feelings for him too. It was the little things, like the fact that she'd been awfully protective of him once when Olivia had called him *creepy*. But for whatever reason, their relationship had never made it off the ground.

It was ironic that Erin had no trouble sticking her nose into other people's business, but when it came to herself, she was fairly tight-lipped. Olivia had asked a few times, but Erin was an expert dodger of questions, and Sarah appreciated privacy so much herself that she mostly left it alone.

Erin had let go of her hand when they reached the tent and was bee-lining it to the dance floor, beckoning Sarah to follow her. It was too loud, and she was too far away to be heard, so Sarah gestured she'd be just a minute. She needed to rehydrate first, so she headed over to the bar for a glass of water, passing behind Brian on her way there. He was chatting with Steven Davis, Olivia's neighbor.

"A water, please?" Sarah asked the young bartender. He nodded and moved to grab her a glass. When she had it in hand, she turned and leaned against the edge of the bar while she took a long, cold sip.

Benny and Steven were still talking, and they'd since been joined by Sean. They must be talking hockey, Sarah thought. Steven's son, Mitch, played for Sean at Nicolet State, but he'd also played for Benny at the high school level.

Sarah noted that Benny looked pretty comfortable at this party, and she was glad. At school, he mostly stayed to himself. He taught science in the class across the hallway from hers, so she'd gotten to know him a little, and she couldn't help but like him, despite how some of the other teachers felt about him. The students loved him, so he couldn't be all bad, and he'd been a real sweetheart to her, helping her out when the photocopier jammed during a copying frenzy a mere thirty minutes before the first bell rang on the very first day of school. Later that day, he'd called the technology department for her when the attendance program kept spitting her out of the system.

He'd even sat next to her during the first staff meeting, where she was certain everyone would be able to see right through her and discover that she was a total imposter. Who was she kidding? She was no teacher! That whole first week, she'd felt like she was playing dress-up the way she and her childhood friend, Lauren, used to do when they were little. She could still picture Lauren, red lipstick smeared around her mouth, red stilettos on her feet, and her mother's black, lacy bra hanging open over the top of her Care Bears shirt.

She took another sip of water and watched Benny out of the corner of her eye.

Being brand new to teaching and brand new to Nicolet, Sarah had felt hopelessly out of her element those first few weeks of September. Having Benny—or Brian—close by had given her some peace of mind. She'd lost count of how many times she crossed to his room, interrupting a biology lecture or chemistry lab, to ask for help with one thing or another. He'd never made her feel like a nuisance, and for that, she'd always be grateful.

Despite her own positive experience with him, Sarah could see how he might put other people off. He was socially awkward, and that was being kind. Actually, he was a bit of a disaster when it came to people skills. Well, *adult* people skills. With the kids, he was different. More at ease. While he was definitely more comfortable with her now than he'd been at first, he still tended to stare at a place just over her shoulder when he talked to her, and while sometimes he was really chatty, other times he was painfully quiet. Although now that she thought about it, that didn't happen as often anymore.

Earlier on in their acquaintance, she would ask him questions, and he'd give one-word, dead-end answers. He hadn't done it to be rude, at least she didn't think he had, but still, conversing with him when he was like that had been as frustrating as attempting to play tennis against someone who wouldn't even lift their racket. She'd lob those balls over the net, one by one, and never get anything back in return.

But things had changed between them over the course of the school year. For one thing, she was learning. She was strategic in her conversations with him now—careful not to ask yes or no questions. She was also strategic about the topics she brought up because some topics appeared to animate Benny more than others. Hockey, for example. In those conversations, he'd serve up ball after ball, so much so that sometimes it was hard for her to get a hit in at all. But now, more often than not, their conversations held a pleasing rhythm with plenty of volleying back and forth. It was gratifying to know she could accomplish that kind of ease with him. Not everyone could. In fact, most couldn't, and that was the problem.

But awkward or outgoing, withdrawn or animated, Benny was always kind. It no longer mattered to her if he gazed at a place behind her while they talked, or if he occasionally met her eyes with such an intensity that it felt almost . . . *too* intimate. He was a good man. She knew that much, and it was enough.

Chapter 2

A slow song came on, and Benny watched Sarah set her water glass down on the bar top. He'd lost her for a while there. Most of the night, she'd been stuck like glue to Erin's side, so he hadn't approached her yet. Now, she was alone. He excused himself from the conversation with Sean and Steven to say hello and felt himself begin to perspire. That's all it took. Just the thought of asking her to dance, and he was sweating like a Finn in a sauna. But Benny was used to feeling nervous and uncomfortable, so he flexed his toes inside his right dress shoe, a childhood habit that had always worked to soothe him, and forced himself to approach her.

"Hey, Sarah."

She whipped around. "Benny, hi!" she said, and then immediately flushed a pretty shade of pink. "I'm sorry. I've never called you that to your face before. It's just, that's what everyone else calls you, so . . ."

Benny liked that she'd called him by his nickname, and he considered how to tell her that. He must have taken too long to spit out a word because Sarah continued talking the way other people did when they were nervous. He'd never understood that. If a person was nervous, why would they keep talking? It seemed like that would just make it worse. Having to find more words to say to fill silence was exhausting work. It was for him, at least.

"I'm sure you know all the kids call you Benny," she was saying. "They just love you and talk about you all the time. I hear it so often, that I think of you as Benny now too."

He worked to find his voice again. "That's alright," he reassured before extending his hand to her. She grasped it with her own hand, but she met his eyes in confusion, and that's when he remembered he'd forgotten to actually say the words.

"Sorry," he muttered. "I meant to ask if you wanted to dance."

Sarah looked out at the other couples dancing and back at him again. "I'd love to." She smiled and allowed him to lead her out to the dance floor.

His heart raced as he found them a spot, and it beat even faster as he placed a hand on her waist. "Go ahead and call me that, if you want. I like it."

She looked at him with a question in her eyes. He'd confused her again.

"Benny," he clarified. "You can call me Benny."

She nodded and looked at him with that sweet smile of hers, and his breath caught. Sarah was maybe the most beautiful woman he'd ever seen. She wasn't too tall or too short; she was trim without being skinny, and she had the kind of hair that made a guy want to touch and run his fingers through for hours. It was soft and wispy with blond highlights that had either come from the sun or a salon, he couldn't tell. Her lips were always pink and shiny from lip gloss or balm or whatever it was girls wore. And she always smelled great, like something fruity he couldn't quite name.

What made her even more attractive to him was that she didn't seem to know how beautiful she was. Some women flaunted their stuff and acted like they were doing you some big favor if they gave you the time of day. Sarah wasn't like that. She made him feel . . . well, he didn't know the word for it. But he liked it. He liked being with her. They began to step and sway to the music, and as he turned her, he noticed Erin dancing with Jackson Lang. It figured that'd be the kind of guy she'd go for.

Following his gaze, Sarah asked, "Who's that dancin' with Erin? I recognize him from somewhere."

"Jackson Lang. He's the Nicolet State assistant hockey coach."

"Oh, that's right. He works with Sean. He sat just in front of me at their weddin'."

"Everyone knows Jackson." His mouth formed a grim line.

"Oh?"

Benny nodded but remained silent.

"Why does everyone know him?" Sarah pressed.

"He's from here, and he's . . . I don't know . . . a popular guy, I guess."

"You're from here originally too, right? Did you go to school together?" Sarah's breath brushed across his cheek like a soft feather. He wanted to lean in closer, but he kept his distance.

"He was a year behind me."

"Were y'all friends?"

"Probably not."

Sarah angled her head, which Benny knew meant she wanted him to elaborate. He met her eyes just for a second or two and looked away again before he answered. "There were a lot of kids I grew up with who I thought were friends, but they weren't."

"Hmm." Sarah nodded thoughtfully. "I grew up with kids like that too." She still looked at him expectantly, like he was supposed to say even more, but he wasn't quite sure what to add. She filled the silence for him, and this time she was the one who looked away, some place just behind him.

It gave him a chance to study her while she spoke. She had the most striking brown eyes, made even more so contrasted against the light color of her hair.

"I had a friend, her name was Lauren, and she was my closest friend in the whole wide world. We did everything together. She knew all my secrets. I had . . . well . . . I had a *difficult* family situation, and when we were in the eighth grade, she told the whole school about it. Every ugly little detail. After that, I didn't have anyone over to the house anymore. I kept people away all through high school too." She paused before looking at him again. "It got pretty lonely."

He held her gaze. It wasn't easy, but he could do it when it was important. "I'm sorry," he said. And he meant it. Benny hated to think of Sarah in a bad family situation. The idea of her being lonely or sad or in any kind of pain was distressing. Someone like her deserved only the good things in life. From that very first day of school, he'd known she wasn't like the others. She had a gentle way about her, soft and kind and full of goodness. And he could listen to her lilting, musical accent all day long. It relaxed him. *She* relaxed him. It was a new experience.

Last year had been tough for him. He'd been dealt a heavy blow last fall, and he hadn't handled it well. He was used to a certain level of loneliness and self-doubt, but what he'd experienced for those first few months had been on a whole other level. Every good thing he'd ever felt about himself was called into question, and there was no way he could handle any further rejection. So, he'd held back with Sarah, even though his attraction to her had been instant. For months, he played the part of helpful colleague, doing whatever he could to make sure she was comfortable in her new role as teacher, but working very, very hard to deny his feelings for her.

And then Erin Hennings, his boss, had shocked him by coming on to him completely out of the blue one day when they'd both been at the school late one night. He'd been a man thirsting for validation, and she'd given him a long, slow drink. He knew they weren't a good match, he'd known that from the first day she'd come on board as Nicolet's principal, but there was no way he was going to turn down a woman with an interest in him, and certainly not a woman as easy on the eyes as Erin was, not with his ego in the gutter like it had been.

It hadn't been easy, but he packed away his feelings for Sarah and focused on Erin, thanking his lucky stars all the while that he wasn't a complete loser, not if someone of Erin Hennings' caliber wanted him. But . . . she hadn't stuck around very long, which was just as well—given their completely incompatible personalities—even though he hadn't been able to see the good in it at the time. All he felt now was relief that they hadn't gone much beyond first base, or any kind of relationship with Sarah would be out of the question now. Women were a bit of a mystery to Benny, but he knew enough to know that a girl didn't date her best friend's ex-lover.

He and Sarah made a few more turns in silence, and Benny's eyes fell once again on Erin and Jackson dancing just a few couples to the left of them. As much as it had stung when Erin had essentially ghosted him three weeks into dating, he didn't hold anything against her, and he'd hate to see her get involved with Jackson. The guy had a new woman on his arm—and in his bed—every week. Erin needed to be careful. She was strong, and he knew she could take care of herself, but he was still worried about her.

He looked back at Sarah and saw she'd been observing him.

"Benny," she began and paused, hunting for the right words, "I get the feeling that you're still interested in Erin."

She couldn't have been more off the mark, and Benny's dark eyebrows rose a notch. "Why would you say that?"

"Just an impression I get."

He was quiet a full turn. Sarah and Erin were close friends. He was certain his name had come up in conversation. What if she'd said something to Sarah that would turn her off? He flexed his toes again, grateful that this was the only one of his childhood tics that had lingered into adulthood. "Has she said something to you?"

"No, not really. I just knew y'all were talking a few months back."

He frowned. The last thing he wanted was for Sarah to think he was still hung up on Erin. "We aren't *talking* anymore."

"What happened?"

Benny wasn't in the habit of sharing details of his personal life with people, but he'd never deny Sarah anything, so he answered, "I don't know. Everything seemed fine, and then suddenly it wasn't." He pinched his lips together, and added, "Obviously, I did something wrong, so I got her roses, lots and lots of roses, but instead of saying thanks, she just got mad and told me nothing was ever going to happen with us. So . . ."

Tiny creases appeared on Sarah's forehead. "Mad? Are you sure? Women love getting flowers."

He'd known that! Roses were supposed to win a woman over. That's why he'd plunked down over two hundred dollars on them. "She wouldn't accept the last delivery. She made the delivery guy take them back to the store, and then she called me and told me to stop being *creepy*." That had really bothered him at the time. Whatever else he might be, he wasn't a creepy kind of guy, at least he fervently hoped he wasn't.

A peculiar look came over Sarah's face. "Um, Benny, how many times did you get Erin flowers?"

He counted. "Three or four, maybe." It had been a solid four times, but he thought three might sound better.

"Three or four times in how many months?"

Benny scratched at his chin, leaving one hand on her waist. "Um, let's see—I guess about a month." Suddenly, he understood.

She stopped moving. "Benny, you bought Erin flowers that many times in one month?"

He was an idiot. Nobody bought that many flowers for a woman who wasn't interested in them anymore. The heat of embarrassment intensified. Erin must have found him so pathetic. Had she told Sarah? No, Sarah was hearing about this for the first time. Would Erin tell Jackson? Benny cringed. That's all he would need—Jackson Lang having something else on him. That jerk had made high school hell for him.

Sarah gave a slight shake of her head. "Why?"

Benny cleared his throat and forced himself back into the conversation. She wanted to know why he'd bought all those flowers. "Well, you know, I was trying to . . . you know. . ." He gazed off over her shoulder again. He needed this conversation to be over.

"You're trying to woo her?" Sarah supplied.

His gaze collided with hers. "No! Well, I mean, I *was* trying. I'm definitely not anymore."

"But you still like her, right?"

He exhaled deeply and ran a hand through his dark hair. This was complicated. He liked Erin fine. Not the way Sarah meant, but he didn't have a bad thing to say about her. She'd gone from his boss to something more to his boss again. She was professional, and he was professional, so it hadn't been a huge deal. Except that, for a second there, it had seemed to him that they'd really connected. Tough-as-nails Erin Hennings had been surprisingly vulnerable with him, sharing stories about her ex husband and her father. He'd shared a few things too. Not much, but a little. Going out with her during that time had been a salve to his fresh wounds, so he'd probably allowed himself to make more of things than he should have.

They were chugging along fine, and then one day, it was done. She turned cold. It was like one of those hot summer days in Nicolet where the south wind shifted to a north wind and the temperature dropped twenty degrees within minutes. A person hardly had time to react.

But he was over it now. Now someone else had caught his eye, or recaught his eye, but she was giving off the same "just friends" signal she'd given from the very beginning. Even *he* could pick up on that. And now she was asking if he was still interested in Erin. The answer was, obviously, no, but it might not be a bad idea to keep her wondering if he was. He wouldn't lie—because he literally couldn't—but he wouldn't bare his soul either. That way she wouldn't guess the truth until he was ready for her to know.

He shrugged in response, and Sarah nodded as if this reaffirmed something she'd suspected all along.

They were both quiet for several moments. "What happened here?" Sarah gently touched her thumb to his mouth along the small scar on his right upper lip.

Benny was so startled by the contact that he took a step back.

"I'm sorry!" Sarah hurried to say before reaching for him again to continue dancing.

He glanced across the dance floor to see Jackson laughing at him and shaking his head. He ignored him. "No, no. It's . . . fine." But was it? Was he? His heart was beating so erratically, he felt a little dizzy. All because her thumb touched his lip. What would he feel if her *lips* ever made contact there? He'd probably pass out cold! He stretched his toes and felt the beats slow as he answered her question. "I was bit by my grandparents' dog when I was little. It's actually not a bad scar considering the injury."

"Oh no! How terrible for you. You must have been so scared. How old were you?"

"Six."

"I'm so sorry. I assumed it was from hockey or something."

He gave a small chuckle as he met her eyes again briefly. "No. Not hockey. You actually have to play to get injured, it turns out, and I didn't play much. I wasn't very good." His words were light, but his tone must have given him away.

Sarah bit her lower lip. She seemed to do that when she was thinking hard about something. "Brian, what are you doing tomorrow?"

He looked at her, startled, once again. How had they gone from his scar to tomorrow's plans? "Your mind is hard to keep up with sometimes," he admitted.

"Sorry." Sarah shook her head and laughed. "I think and talk in circles. I heard once that men think in a linear pattern, and women think in a circular pattern. We always get back around to the point, but it takes us a while."

Benny was pensive. "You know, I've never heard that, but I think you must be right. It would explain a lot of the female miscommunications I've had over the years." He chuckled.

Sarah grinned. "Listen. I hope you don't mind, but I need a favor."

He leaned closer. "What favor?" Not that it mattered. If she asked him to walk on water, he'd give it a shot.

"I'm sure you've heard I bought a place out on the Steele River Basin."

He nodded. "I did hear that." Everyone wondered how she'd managed to score a place out there on a teacher's salary.

"It was a right place, right time kind of thing." Sarah waved a hand dismissively.

"That's . . . lucky." There was more to the story than that, he knew, but he could play along.

She lowered her gaze. "Yes. So, anyway, a dock came with the place, and I'm putting it in this weekend. Do you think you might be able to give me a hand?"

He didn't even have to think about it. Of course he would help her. "How many sections?"

"Three, and then a platform at the end."

"What's it made of, what material?"

"Cedar, so it's heavy, but I have this dolly thingy to get the sections down to the water." Sarah stared at him expectantly. "I know it's a lot to ask, but—"

His questions must have sent the message that he didn't want to help because her expression had grown apologetic. He'd asked about the material because he was worried she might hurt herself if it was too heavy. She looked strong, but a dock like that would be hard to move. A dolly was a must, so it was good she had one. "I'm happy to help," he reassured. "When were you thinking?"

"Ten o'clock tomorrow? I think we could probably hammer it out in a few hours. I'll treat you to some sweet tea when we're done. We can sit on the

Adirondacks I bought for the platform of the dock." She winked. "You know, enjoy the fruits of our labor."

He smiled. Not his usual smile, the one he'd had to practice a million times as a kid in front of the bathroom mirror with his mother. This was the kind that came to his face unbidden. A reflection of what he felt inside. This was sheer luck! He'd get to spend some time with her tomorrow. And not just working, by the sounds of it. If she wanted to sit and talk over tea, maybe she was in a different place now than she'd been at the beginning of the school year.

"Great!" He asked for the address and said he'd be there at ten o'clock sharp. And with perfect timing, the song ended and was replaced by "Cotton-Eyed Joe." Benny stepped back and gave her an awkward nod. He wanted to thank her for the dance, but he waited too long and missed the chance. Sarah bit back a smile before turning to join Erin.

He stayed another half hour. Sean sought him out for some more hockey talk, and as they compared notes on players, Benny tried not to look too obvious as he watched Sarah, rosy cheeked and smiling, dance with her friends.

Chapter 3

Morning came far too soon, and Erin hadn't been in the best of moods when she'd first walked into the yoga studio to meet Sarah. But once she'd worked out the irritation of being up so early on a Saturday, she really had enjoyed it, and she'd done pretty well for a beginner. She only stumbled over one pose, and by the time the class was finished, she felt as relaxed and limp as a boiled spaghetti noodle. Maybe there was something to this yoga thing.

Changing in the locker room, she and Sarah chit-chatted about the reception the night before. They talked about Olivia's blush-pink dress and how cute Nora had looked in her matching one. When Sarah sighed and remarked that Sean and Olivia were the perfect couple, Erin snorted. "There's no such thing as a perfect couple, Sarah."

Sarah paused in the act of putting her shoes in her bag. "Why do you always say stuff like that?"

When Erin only shrugged, Sarah shook her head. "One of these days, I'm going to figure you out."

"Likewise," Erin shot back. But the truth was, she was pretty sure she'd pieced together enough of Sarah's past to have her more or less pegged. Her friend had let little details slip every now and again, long before the rich grandma kicked the bucket, and without realizing it, she'd painted an abstract little picture for Erin to interpret.

The condensed version of her story was that she'd grown up essentially without parents—no dad, and a useless drunk of a mother. If she hadn't had the one good grandma, the dirt poor one, in her life for the first half of her childhood, she'd probably be even more scarred than she already was. And then there was the mystery of some ex-boyfriend from her college days. He'd done a number on her too, whoever he was.

Sarah was a passive people-pleaser, aggravatingly so, and yet she was stronger than she realized. Otherwise, she never could have made it as far in life as she had. She should be cold and jaded, but by some miracle, she wasn't. She was sweet, too sweet, but she had bite when she needed it.

There were some holes in Sarah's story that Erin didn't know, but those were just the finer details, and Erin was filling them in one by one. But Sarah would never be able to figure Erin out because Erin still couldn't figure herself out. Take Benny, for instance. Overall, he was a good catch. He was very nice and quite the hottie if you could ignore the fact that he was basically a mute half the time. Erin actually found that half preferable to the other half, where the guy literally could not shut up about hockey. But he'd been interested in her and, in spite of his many shortcomings, she'd felt something for him. And so she'd had to turn it off. Flip the switch. It was what she always did.

He was one of many men she'd deemed "too nice" to date. No, not too nice, too . . . *good*. It made her uncomfortable. Of all the things that could make her skin crawl with Benny, and there were plenty considering his near-constant social foibles, the fact that it was his goodness that turned her off was telling. It said a lot about her; she was sure of it. She just didn't want to know what. A therapist would probably have a field day psychoanalyzing her, not that Erin would ever let anybody close enough to do that because, honestly, who knew what they'd find?

So, that's where she currently found herself: turned off by a guy because he treated her too well, and yet wishing deep down—in a place she rarely allowed herself to explore—that she could have the kind of relationship Olivia had. She could only blame herself for the sense of loneliness she felt. All the bad decisions of her life had brought her to this point. She knew it wasn't too late with Benny, but it didn't matter, and it wasn't really about him anyway. He was just one in a line of many. Part of a well-worn pattern, and she wouldn't be able to muster even the slightest attraction to him now. The switch was off, and she knew from experience it couldn't be turned back on again.

Sarah spoke again, her tone casual as she slid her feet into a pair of black, rubber flip flops. Too casual. "Benny's comin' over today to help me put in my dock."

Erin stopped packing her bag and looked up. She'd just been thinking of Benny, and now Sarah was bringing him up? Sometimes she swore her friend was clairvoyant. "How'd that come about?"

Sarah's voice was even more chipper than normal when she answered, "Oh, you know Benny. I asked him last night when we were dancin', and he just couldn't say no."

That sounded about right. Benny would gift someone a kidney if they only asked. He'd just annoy them to death first on the way to surgery. "Why are you nervous to tell me this?"

Sarah looked at her in wide-eyed innocence. "I'm not nervous."

"Yeah, you are. Your accent just got thicker."

Sarah coughed delicately. "I don't know what you mean. Anyway, he's com-*ing* over at ten. I told him we could sit out on the dock when we're done. I'm makin' him some sweet tea."

An amused smile played on Erin's lips. "Some sweet tea, huh?" What the hell was the southern belle up to? "Sounds nice."

Erin could see the wheels spinning as Sarah searched for what to say next. She was testing her. She wanted to know if Erin would be jealous. In a way, she was. She was jealous that Sarah would likely have it all one day, once she got over whatever the what's-his-face from college had done to her. She'd have the career, the family, the doting husband.

Arguably, Sarah had had the harder life of the two of them, but she wasn't broken deep down inside like Erin was. She had herself figured out. Not that she didn't have hangups, but she knew *why* she was the way she was. Erin didn't. At nearly thirty-one years old, Erin was coming to terms with the fact that she might just be stuck this way. Alone. Except she wasn't quite alone anymore. For the first time in her life, she had not one, but two real friends. Not just acquaintances, or good-time friends, but two *true* friends.

Sarah zipped her bag and slung it up over her shoulder as she said, "You could pop by around noon if you want. You know, to say hi."

Erin lifted her own bag. "No. I won't be stopping by, and whatever you're doing with Benny, make sure it has nothing to do with me, okay? That's done now."

Sarah pinched her lips together and nodded. Her face revealed a lack of understanding, but she wouldn't press Erin further. Sarah was good that way, and Erin put an arm around her shoulder as they walked out of the locker room.

"I have to go in to get a few last-minute details taken care of for summer school, but maybe I'll come out later in the afternoon"—she gave Sarah a pointed look—"once Benny's gone, and we can take those paddleboards out."

Sarah brightened. "Yes! Fun! Come on out anytime. Once we get the dock in, I'll just be doing some yard work." She treated Erin to her sweet smile, and

Erin felt like an ingrate. No matter how much she snapped at Sarah, her friend always responded with grace. She was an impossible person to have a fight with, which was mostly maddening but also a tiny bit refreshing. Sometimes, when Erin held Sarah up as a comparison to herself, she felt ashamed at who she had become.

While Sarah was gentle and refined. Erin was bristly and, well . . . a little vulgar. She'd prided herself on that back when she'd been growing up and living with Jillian. Pushing her mother's buttons through her extensive vocabulary of four-letter words and frequent verbal lashings had been a full-time hobby, but now, they were just bad habits. They were worse than bad habits. Over the years, they'd been woven into her personality, and if Erin wasn't careful, they'd be permanent fixtures of it.

Next to her near-perfect friend, these and all Erin's other flaws were only magnified—to the point where Erin would have been in danger of not being able to stand herself if it weren't for the hope of self-improvement that associating with Sarah was bound to bring about, even if only a little. It was the reason she'd agreed to the swear jar idea Sarah had come up with a few months back. Her friend had probably only been joking, but Erin had kind of liked the idea. She grumbled about it and made all the right comments to appear vexed, but the swear jar gave her the perfect excuse to start making some much-needed changes. If anyone noticed, she'd just blame the dumb jar.

When Erin pulled into her driveway several minutes after parting ways with Sarah at the yoga studio, she was blissfully unaware that anything was amiss. Normally it might have irritated her to have to stop by the house before heading to work since it wasn't even remotely on the way, but she'd wanted to grab her suit in case she made it out to Sarah's later, and today she felt calm in her mind, strong in her body, and happy all over as she hummed the last song that had played on the radio.

After parking in the garage, she headed out to the road for the mail, and she began to put together a mental list of what she needed to accomplish at school that day, starting with the emails that needed to go out to all the summer school students. It wasn't until she was walking back from the mailbox with Saturday's mail in hand that she saw it. She stopped dead in her tracks, dropping all the envelopes and catalogues in her shock. One word was spray painted in large, red letters across her front door.

Bitch.

Chapter 4

After yoga, Sarah ran a few errands and grabbed some groceries at the store, and by the time she pulled into her driveway, it was already five minutes to ten. She'd cut it a little close. One of the beautiful things about her new place was that it felt like a getaway into nature, but it was only seven minutes from the supermarket. She'd timed it.

The house, at just over twenty-eight hundred square feet, wasn't nearly as stately as many of the others on the basin, but it had still cost her three quarters of a million dollars. The previous owners had built it only two years ago, and everything in it was new and high-end, from the granite countertops to the farmhouse kitchen sink to the beautiful wood-plank floors. For Sarah, it was love at first sight. She didn't know a lot about house styles and decorating, but she knew when a house felt like a home. It was light and airy and beautiful, and it almost made her feel that way too.

Erin's poor excuse of a mother, Jillian Hennings, was an interior decorator for all the movers and shakers in Santa Monica, California, and as a result, Erin had gleaned a thing or two about decorating herself. A week after helping Sarah get all moved in, Erin had come for a glass of wine, and as she looked around, she'd complimented Sarah on her "Scandinavian flare." Sarah had laughed at that because whatever style she'd adopted for her home had been achieved completely by accident. Looking it up later, she discovered that Scandinavian style meant the decorating was minimalistic and clutter-free, as well as cozy and warm. It was gratifying to hear that her decorating style was "cozy," but she had laughed out loud again—all alone in front of her laptop screen. There was a reason her house was "minimalistic." She simply didn't have very much!

Nice as it was, the house itself probably hadn't been worth what she'd paid for it, but Sarah figured she was paying more for the location than anything else, and it was definitely worth that much to her. Ever since she'd been a little girl, she'd loved the water. She used to slip under the surface and hold her breath as long as possible over and over again. Those moments underwater had felt like a gift. All noise was muffled and her cares were muted as she disappeared, if only for a brief moment, from life above.

When Gammie had been alive—her mama's mama—she used to tell Sarah she was half girl and half fish. Gammie had said it made good, solid sense since her daddy was so cold-blooded he might as well have had gills and scales. Having now met the man herself, Sarah had to agree with Gammie's assessment. Not that she spent a lot of time thinking about him.

She sighed.

That wasn't true. She spent a lot of time trying *not* to think about him, and she wasn't going to let him invade her thoughts now. Not on this beautiful day. This was the kind of day Gammie would have wanted to make the most of.

Her grandmother had loved being outside. Several times a week, when the weather was warm, she'd take Sarah to the quarry down the road, set up a chair in the sunshine, and watch her swim for hours and hours. She never came in to swim herself, not even when Sarah begged, but occasionally she'd bring an air mattress and float in the shallows. More often than not, she sat, relaxed in her beach chair with a cigarette in hand and her big yellow sun hat shading her face as she watched her oldest grandchild frolic in the water. Sarah could still see her sitting there with that small, contented smile on her brightly lipsticked lips.

And she was always game to rate Sarah's hand stands on a five-point scale, saying things like, "Do it over! That one was just a four and a half, but point those toes an' you'll git yourself a five." When Sarah would finally drag herself out of the water, all pruney and goosebumped, to warm up in the sunshine, they'd play in the hot sand together, making castles with motes and digging holes to reach the other side of the world.

The quarry was a place just for them. Sarah's mom and sister never came along, which was fine by Sarah. She was protective of those precious after-noons with Gammie. She'd thought it over one day, and if her mama or Nadia had ever followed Gammie out of the house with beach towels in hand, Sarah would have made room in the back of the small, stale Civic, but she would have been bitterly disappointed.

It never happened, even though Gammie never gave up trying to coax them into coming along. She'd walk down the front porch steps alone, shaking her head, and when she'd open the door and get in the car, she would say, "We don't git to pick our kinfolk, Sarah Sue. We just gotta love 'em like the good Lord loves us, warts and all." Sometimes she would add, "Lydie Mae'd rather fight her demons in that dark house than come out into the sunshine with us. One day she'll break up with Jim Beam and send him packin'. You'll see." She'd look at Sarah and smile sadly.

Sarah always nodded along wisely, but she had always wondered who Jim Beam was. She was fifteen when she figured it out, and in that moment she missed her grandmother so much that she physically ached with longing to see her again and to tell her she finally understood the joke.

When Gammie had been alive, all things felt possible, and when she died, Sarah wondered how she'd make it through even one day. Jim Beam hung around a lot more frequently after the funeral, and the darkness in the house only got darker. She'd been eleven years old and at school when she'd gotten the news that her gammie'd had a heart attack and was in the local hospital. Sarah was whisked from Copper Hill Elementary School by her gammie's best friend, Claire. When she got there, her mother greeted her with vacant eyes and slurred instructions to say goodbye, which Sarah had done with a racing heart and vision blurred with tears. Nadia had refused to go into the room, choosing to stay in a chair just outside the room next to their mother. But Sarah had held Gammie's hand and whispered words of pleading to please not leave her all alone in the world.

It had been some kind of cruel trick of fate that after Sarah had waited all those endless hours by her gammie's bedside, she chose to leave the world while Sarah was only a few steps down the hall in the restroom. She'd passed on to the other side all by her lonesome, and she left the world in the very moment that her granddaughter had needed her the most. Sarah would never forget her fear and confusion when she saw all that blood in the toilet and in her white Fruit of the Looms, and how mortified she'd felt when she realized where it was coming from. There in that bathroom stall, Sarah thought she might be dying too.

She'd dragged herself to the nurses' station and told Nurse Shelby in a whisper what had happened to her. The kind old nurse had just smiled a knowing smile and handed Sarah a pad. At her utter cluelessness, Shelby had clucked her tongue and muttered something about deadbeat mothers as she took Sarah by the hand and back to the restroom. There, she talked to her through the stall door, telling her what to do and explaining that this painful and messy experience would return to her every month for the rest of her young life.

Sarah had well and truly wanted to die then, but Gammie actually did. Sarah heard all the machines start beeping from her place in the stall, and she heard Shelby curse before she ran out of the bathroom. Sarah worked frantically to get the side flaps of the pad unstuck and wrapped around the edges of her panties so she could make it back to Gammie's side, but she'd been too late.

In the following days and weeks, Sarah had never felt such despair. Even now, standing in her kitchen, grocery bags waiting to be unloaded on the counter, she gazed out over the water of the Steele River Basin and felt the loss all over again. She wanted to put on her bathing suit and goggles and do hand stands with Gammie shouting at her to point her toes.

One thing was certain, Gammie would have approved. She would have loved this property and this house, and she would have loved even more that it was paid for with part of her father's inheritance, not that he'd miss the money. The man had hundreds of millions of dollars, at least according to that article they'd written about him in *Forbes* a few years back.

Sarah still wasn't completely sure how she felt about being given so much money from a side of her family she didn't even know. A family that had basically rejected her. It still stung to know that her father and grandmother had both lived only one hour away for the whole of her childhood and had never once tried to make contact. Sure, Lydie Mae had secured that promise from them in the divorce settlement, but they hadn't even tried. What kind of grandparent—or father, for that matter—would agree to something like that in the first place?

Sarah would have liked to think that the inheritance money was a parting gift from a grandmother who felt some remorse about abandoning two grand-daughters to an unfit mother, but Lenora Josten's awful lawyer had made it very clear. It had been more about sticking it to Sarah's father, Bruce, than it had been about any warm and fuzzy feelings Lenora may have had towards her foresaken grandchildren. Gammie would have been gratified by that too. She'd despised the whole family, but Bruce especially. Knowing that he'd been robbed of even a little of his money would have sent Gammie into happy fits of wheezing.

For the first time in her life, Sarah had complete financial security. Gone were the worries of how she would pay off her student loans and other bills each month, and she no longer kept a running tally of the items in her cart as she grocery shopped. She had enough, and it was a weight off her shoulders. She should have felt settled. Instead, whenever she thought about the money and how she'd come to obtain it, she felt the flutter of butterflies in her stomach, almost as if she'd done something wrong or someone would soon come by and tell her it had all been a mistake.

Maybe it would help her anxiety levels if she educated herself. She was clueless about investing. Other than her 403b at work—which she was pretty sure worked more to the benefit of her advisor than it did to herself—she didn't have any experience in how to invest. She needed to learn, and quick. Not just for her own sake, but for Nadia's too. She owed her sister at least that much.

The sound of tires crunching on the gravel driveway chased the butterflies away and alerted Sarah to Benny's arrival. Through the window, she watched his Dodge Ram make the turn to park just behind the garage. His side mirror brushed against the bright green leaves of the beech trees that lined her driveway on the right side, and the sun glinted off the black hood of the truck. She checked the microwave clock and grinned. Ten o'clock sharp. She wasn't surprised.

Sarah opened the door and waited for him on the porch, leaning one hip against the railing. She'd kicked her flip-flops off inside the house and stood barefoot in her cutoff jeans and red v-neck shirt. When Benny didn't get out right away, she let her gaze wander. Was it prideful to take so much pleasure in looking at her new home and all its trimmings?

The first thing she'd done to the house was buy and hang a wood-slatted swing at the far end of the porch. She'd always wanted a porch swing. She wanted to rock back and forth in the evening, a good book in one hand and a glass of Chardonnay or sweet tea in the other. The porch was wide and spanned the length of the house, and she loved it. As much as she enjoyed the lake side of the house, she figured some days she'd prefer to sit out here and look at the trees instead of the water. Technically, since this was a lake house, the front faced the water, and where she was standing now was considered the back. It seemed wrong to her that when guests arrived, they arrived "out back," but she'd get used to the verbiage in time.

The Steele River Basin was huge, a full nine miles long, and it was breathtaking. Her place was tucked away in one of the small bays, so she had the feeling of seclusion when she wanted it, but all she had to do was paddle for a few minutes and she'd join the rest of the boaters in the main waterway. Eventually, she'd get a small pontoon with a tow bar, just for kicks, and join the others out there with a cooler, some music, and some friends. For now, she had the dock they were about to put in, two paddleboards, and the rowboat that had come with the place. It was enough.

Benny got out of the car and smiled broadly, gesturing first to the lake and then to the house. "Wow!"

When he smiled like that, he was transformed, and as her heart did a quick double beat, Sarah reminded herself about why she'd invited him out in the first place. She really did need help with the dock, but she could have paid someone for that. What she'd really wanted was to show Benny that he had a friend. He seemed so lonely to her, and she didn't like to think of him like that. Originally, she'd also thought she could give him some pointers to win Erin over, but after speaking with her friend that morning, Sarah had nixed that plan. She'd let them figure it out.

Benny stretched to his full height, which must be close to six feet, and removed his sunglasses. He wore a crisp, white T-shirt and gray swim trunks. "This is perfect. You're living in my dream house."

Sarah felt her cheeks go pink with pleasure. "Thank you. Let me just throw on my tennis shoes and put a few groceries in the fridge right quick so they don't spoil, and then we can walk out front. You can tell me where you think the best place for the dock is."

"Sure," Benny responded absently, doing a slow turn to take in the property.

"Would you like to come on in and wait?"

"Naw. Thanks." He was already heading down to the lake.

"Oh. Okay, then," she said to his retreating form. Odd that he didn't want to come in. But then, Benny was odd.

He was scanning the house when she joined him in the front yard a few minutes later. The original owners had done it right, in more ways than one. They'd angled the garage on the right side of the house so it was out of the way. Anyone coming up the long gravel drive and into the clearing surrounding the house had an immediate view of the lake behind it. They'd used a siding that looked like wood, but wasn't. Sarah couldn't remember the name of the product, but it was low maintenance and gorgeous. She loved the slate gray color they'd chosen to paint it, and the white trim around the gridded windows gave the place a crisp, clean look.

"This is perfect," Benny said again. "I still can't believe you scored this place. How did you afford it?"

Sarah matched his bluntness. "You're very direct sometimes."

Benny let his eyes rest on hers for a fleeting moment before looking back at the house. "Sorry. I do know that. I forget I can't say everything that comes into my mind. My mom's been telling me to 'engage my filter' since I was ten years old." He shrugged.

Sarah smiled at the admission. "It's okay."

He turned to look at the lake. "Maybe someday I'll have a place like this. I wasn't joking before. It really is a dream."

Sarah turned too, and together, they looked across the sparkling water to the wooded shoreline across the bay. "You can come out here anytime you want. I hear the fishing is fantastic. I even have a little rowboat with a troller."

Benny's face lit up. "Seriously? I love to fish. I take my nephew all the time. We go on a big fishing trip every year, but mostly, we trout fish over at the Hurricane River. I know he'd love to come out here with me, if you mean it."

"Of course I mean it! It will be how I repay you for your help today. That and the sweet tea I brewed early this morning."

He squinted his eyes. "I've never had sweet tea."

"You're in for a treat then."

They began to walk the slope of the backyard down towards the water, and when they reached the far edge, just before the sand began, Sarah looked down at the beachy shoreline a few feet below. She'd been told the last owners had hauled in this sugarsand for their grandkids to play in. A month later, they'd been slapped with a hefty fine from the EPA when a resident on the basin reported them. Or maybe it had been the DNR. She couldn't remember which, and it didn't really matter. The end result was that she had her very own private beach, and it was so lovely, she couldn't muster up more than a teensy amount of guilt that she was now the beneficiary of something that had not only been illegal, but also a real headache for the previous owners.

Sarah backed up a step as she felt the ground below her feet begin to sag. The water didn't come up this high, but time and weather had still caused a jagged line of erosion here at the edge of the lawn.

Benny scratched his chin. "You know, you should probably put in a little retaining wall here."

Sarah frowned. "I wondered about that. "

"I could do it for you. I just did one in my backyard. It's not hard."

"Wouldn't I need a permit?" The last thing she wanted was to tick off those same tattle-tale neighbors, whoever they were.

"Yeah. A soil erosion permit, probably."

"Will that be hard to get? Aren't they strict with waterfront?"

"I'll check. My sister's best friend does all the approvals for Nicolet County, so I think our chances are pretty good." He smiled that same smile at her, and this time her heart stopped altogether for a second or two. What was wrong with her? This was Benny, the guy she'd taught across the hallway from all last year.

"I guess it pays to know people in high places," she finally answered. She watched him scan the ground at their feet, probably already making plans for the wall. "If it goes through, I'd insist on payin' you," she added.

He grinned again, and this time Sarah felt her stomach dip. Something was seriously wrong with her.

"That makes two of us, but I'll cut you a good deal." He rubbed his hands together. "So, where are you thinking for the dock?"

She showed him. It was slightly off to the right of center from the house, and she was pretty sure it was the best spot. Likely, it was where it had been placed for the last two summers. It seemed too perfect not to have been. The yard sloped more gently down to the water in that area, and two pine trees on either side gave the feeling of a ready-made path. In fact, Sarah envisioned pavers from the deck down to this spot eventually.

Benny surveyed the area. "Yeah, good spot." He turned his head to the right and pointed at the small outbuilding there. It matched the house. "Sauna?"

"Yes, but I'm fixin' to tear it down."

Benny's face registered an almost comical horror as he took a giant step back. "Tear it *down*? You can't do that!"

The corners of Sarah's mouth twitched as she fought a smile. "Why not? I've never taken a sauna in my life."

"You need to try it first. You can't just go and tear down a perfectly good sauna. I know plenty of people who would kill for one of these on their property."

She crossed her arms. She didn't think she'd ever seen Benny so animated, and she wanted to have a little more fun with him over this. "Oh, really? Like who?"

"Me, for one. And anyone else who lives in the 906 area code."

She stared at him blankly.

"That's everyone in the U.P., Sarah." He shook his head and studied the small structure. "You've got a real gem here, and you don't even know it."

Sarah gave him a skeptical look.

He put up his hands like a cop directing traffic. "Just promise me you won't tear it down right away. Try it first. You might like it."

"Why would I want to sit in a hot wooden box and sweat? I'm from the south, so that's basically how I grew up, and it's miserable, I'll tell you what!"

He shrugged. "Apples and oranges. It's dry heat, for one. And it's . . . relaxing. And there are health benefits too. You'll see. I'll convince you."

She lifted her eyebrows. "I bet you can't." Was she flirting?

"If I can't, I'll haul that sauna off your property and set it up on my postage-stamp of a backyard lawn back in town."

Sarah laughed. "Deal."

Benny smiled and nodded. "You ready to get started?"

"I'm ready. Let me just go get the dolly. It's in the garage."

"I can grab it."

They walked in silence for several steps while the birds chirped a symphony all around them. Sarah loved that sound. Winters were long here in Nicolet. And sometimes eerily quiet. Now the summer sounds were back, and it made her want to sing too. "So, you mentioned a retaining wall in your backyard. Where do you live?"

"Over on Front Street, near the university. It's not much to look at right now, but I've got big plans."

"Really? Like what?"

"I gutted the inside last summer. Ripped up the carpets and found hardwood floors original to the house, which is a hundred years old. I resurfaced them. Knocked out some walls to open it up. I'm still fixing up the kitchen and bathrooms."

She opened the man door to the garage and pushed the button to lift one of the garage doors. Light flooded into the dark space. "You're doing it all yourself?"

He nodded. "It's slow-going. Looks more like a construction zone than anything else right now."

Before leading him to the back corner where the dolly was parked, she faced him and marveled, "Still, that's impressive. How did you learn to do all that?"

"YouTube, mostly," he said with a smirk. "This summer I'm repainting the siding, and next year I'll upgrade the windows. When I'm finally done, it'll be really nice." He shrugged. "Then, I'll probably sell it."

"Sell it? Why? That's a lot of work to put into something you're not going to be able to enjoy."

He shrugged again before following her to the back corner of the garage. "It's a lot of house for one person. It'd be great for a family. Might as well make a little money on it."

"But what if *you* have a family one day?"

He shot her a startled look and opened his mouth to say something before seeming to think better of it. Stepping around her, he reached for the large red dolly. "I'll just grab this here, and we can get started."

"Okay." Apparently, the topic of a future family was not something they would be discussing. Sarah fought a smile as she followed Benny out of the garage.

In just under two hours, the dock was put in and ready for the Adirondack chairs, which Benny carried out to the end for her. Standing at the shore and looking out at them, side by side with the bay just beyond, Sarah smiled. It was postcard pretty. Benny angled the chairs, making minor adjustments until they were just right, and then came to stand beside her on shore to admire their work. They'd done a lot of heavy lifting, and Sarah wondered if his arms ached as much as hers did. Surreptitiously, she looked over at the lean, muscled biceps of his right arm. Probably not, she decided.

Originally, Sarah had worried they wouldn't have much to talk about while they worked, but Benny started them out by enumerating the many virtues of daily sauna-taking, which surprisingly included benefits to the heart. Sarah never would have guessed that.

After a solid fifteen minutes on the topic, at least, he'd persuaded her to take a second look at the practice. She'd promised to give it a shot, if only to get him to stop talking about it.

Once Benny ran out of steam on the topic of saunas, she peppered him with questions about his coaching methods and found that his strategies weren't all that different from her teaching strategies. She assumed he was a lot like her in the classroom then too: stingy on criticism, generous with praise, and exacting in expectations, all while leaving plenty of room for fun.

In the end, he did most of the talking while they worked, but that was because Sarah kept lobbing him questions. He didn't ask many questions of her, but that was okay. She wasn't in the mood to talk about herself anyway.

It had taken some time to level out the dock, but it turned out perfectly, just as she'd hoped. It was so serene. So peaceful. Out there in those chairs, with the water all around her, that was where she'd drink her morning coffee all summer long. And when autumn came along, she'd sit out there with the wool blanket her gammie always used to use.

It was the one thing Sarah would never part with. She'd long since divested herself of Gammie's favorite teacup, the gold-rimmed one with the pink etched roses and tiny chip on the rim, and just before the move to the basin, she'd pitched the Raggedy Ann doll Gammie had given her on her eighth birthday that she'd slept with for years. Although she'd cried, it comforted Sarah to know that Raggedy Ann had at least gone to the dump with company. She was joined in the small box by the soft rabbit's foot Gammie had always carried with her on her key chain. Sarah had rubbed it for luck so many times, it was nearly bald when she'd kissed it goodbye and laid it on top of the doll.

She was far from a pack rat, but those keepsakes had been special to her, and it was hard to part with them. At least she still had the southwest blanket. It was made of such heavy-duty wool that it would probably outlive her.

With Benny still beside her, Sarah looked out over the water. This was her little slice of heaven, and even though Gammie would never see it, Sarah felt close to her out here.

Benny gave a contented sigh. She turned to him, and they shared a smile. "Thank you for helpin' me with this."

He nodded. "You're welcome."

She instructed him to sit down awhile to rest while she got them their sweet teas and some towels. He didn't need to be told twice. By the time she got up to the patio, he was already seated out on the dock with his head back and his legs stretched out and crossed at the ankles.

It took her only a few minutes to round everything up, and when she returned, towels around her neck and tray in hand, Benny, who had been staring out over the quiet lake, startled.

"Sorry about that. I wasn't trying to sneak up on you. I was stepping carefully so I wouldn't spill anything."

He stood and took the tray from her, setting it down on the wide armrest of his chair before accepting the striped beach towel she handed him. "Thanks."

"I'm sorry your shirt got a little wet. I didn't think it'd be that deep here at the end. It stays nice and shallow for a ways out, doesn't it?"

"Yeah. Good swimming spot for kids."

If only she had any. Sarah sat down, and while she poured from the pitcher into his glass, she asked, "What were you thinkin' about?"

Benny looked at her blankly.

"When I startled you." She handed him the glass.

He didn't answer right away, but she thought she knew what he'd been thinking about, or rather, whom. He surprised her when he answered, "You."

"Me?"

He didn't answer, just nodded.

Oh, heaven's to Betsy. She was blushing. "Uh, what about me?"

"Just . . . that you're easy to talk to."

About saunas and hockey? "Oh. Well, I'm glad you think so."

He searched her face, and she saw the moment he decided to move forward with his next question. "Why did you ask me to come out here?"

Sarah poured her own glass of tea and kept her eyes downcast. She poured very slowly, hoping that if she took long enough, he'd forget his question. It was too much to wish for, however, and when she finished pouring, she found him staring at her intently. What was she supposed to say? *I thought you might need a friend?* Or *I wanted to help you get Erin back?* Even the idea of saying either of those things made her hands sweat. In the end, she settled for the most obvious answer, which also happened to be true.

"I needed help with the dock." She took a sip from her glass to save herself from having to say anything more and waited for Benny to speak. The flavors on her tongue distracted her from the unease of the moment. She loved sweet tea, and she'd missed it. Somehow, it seemed wrong to make it unless it was warm outside. And since Nicolet had been buried in snow all winter and had experienced a very chilly spring, she'd gone months without it.

Benny gulped half his glass down before setting it on his armrest.

"I'm always glad to help a . . . *friend.*" He looked at her with a question in his eyes.

Was he looking for clarification? Clarification that she wasn't making some kind of move on him by having him out here? If he was, she could give him that. It was true, after all.

She worked to affect a teasing tone. "You're a good *friend* to know. Very handy."

He pursed his lips and nodded slowly. "Well, I'm always happy to help."

He was quiet for several moments, his face expressionless as he stared out over the water. Sarah had the terrible sense that she'd just hurt his feelings.

Maybe he'd hoped she was making a move. But wasn't he still sort of pining away after Erin? It was so hard to tell with him. As uncomfortable as it might be, she should set the record straight, just in case. "Benny, I'm not sure if you're . . ." She cleared her throat. "Um, I don't really date."

He raised his eyebrows at her words, but he didn't ask questions. If he had, she just might have explained it all. There was something about Benny that invited trust. Instead, he gave a single nod. "Well, good. We've cleared that up."

Had they? She still had no clue if he was interested in her. And honestly, she wasn't sure how she felt, herself. But really, it didn't matter all that much, Sarah decided, because she wasn't ready regardless of who felt what. Still, the relief she thought she'd detected in his tone irked her. She might not be as pretty as

Erin, but she wasn't ugly, and it might be nice to know *someone* out there was attracted to her.

She met his eyes, and he smiled. "You remind me of my sister, you know. You look a bit alike, and your personalities are similar too. You'd like her."

Her pride recovered slightly. What guy would be interested in dating someone who reminded him of his sister? "My stars! I have a doppelgänger?"

"Mmm, not *that* similar," he clarified.

"Younger or older?"

"Than me? She's four years older."

"Where does she live?"

"Here in Nicolet. She runs a hair salon in town—the Dancing Sun."

"Over by the old theater? I know the place. Erin goes there."

"Yeah. Kay—my sister—she works hard, and she's doing really well. Got a good reputation. She just expanded to a full-service salon and spa. I think she has six or seven employees now."

"And she's a stylist, right?"

"Uh-huh."

"I'm in need of a good haircut. I've just been going to the discount place since I got here."

"And now you don't need the discount?" His deep brown eyes stared intently into hers, and for once, he didn't look away.

That was when Sarah got the sense he knew. "No," she answered slowly, "I don't."

He nodded. "I'm happy for you."

"How did you . . . ?"

He let out a deep breath. "It's a small town, Sarah. I don't talk much in general, except to you and a few other people—but I do hear things, and when you have a photographic memory, you don't forget anything, not even small details."

Sarah was thunderstruck, and she leaned closer to him. "Are you kiddin' me right now?"

He chuckled again. "It's honestly more of a curse than a blessing."

"So wait, you remember everything you hear?"

He nodded. "And everything I see. All of it. It made school a breeze, I'll admit."

"So then why didn't you study to do somethin' else? Why become a teacher? You could have done anything."

"I wanted to teach. And I wanted to coach, and I wanted to do both of those things right here at home. So, here I am." He shrugged. "I like my life. My family's all here . . ."

"Wow!" Sarah sat back in her chair, still shaking her head and trying to imagine what it might be like to have everything committed to memory. At some point, didn't the mind fill up to capacity? Wouldn't some things start to spill over to make room for more?

"Anyway," he went on, "I noticed things, and Erin let a few things slip here and there, and then I heard stuff in the lounge at school. I just put two and two together."

Sarah's stomach performed a somersault. "What do you mean? What stuff?"

"You had a death in the family—a grandmother—in March, and in May you were buying this place. Erin, without meaning to, gave me the impression your grandmother was well-off. Then, when you bought this place, a few of the teachers looked it up on the internet to check the list price. You should have seen them all huddled around the lounge computer." He shook his head in disgust. "You know how people are. They can't help themselves."

Sarah pulled a face. She did know, and she got the sense Benny also knew he had sometimes been the topic of conversation in the lounge. She'd heard all kinds of things in there about him. Several of the teachers were from Nicolet, born and raised. From what she'd gathered over the course of the last year, Benny had run with the cool kids in high school, many of whom still lived in Nicolet, but he'd never really been one of them. They kept him around, but always on the outside.

He'd loved the game of hockey just as much back then, but he hadn't been good enough to make the high school team, so he served as the manager, and he took a lot of abuse from the rest of the players who'd thought they were all that and a can of beans. Ironically, Benny was still managing that very same team, though in a much different capacity, and certainly with a lot more respect.

All those years he'd spent watching the game and observing the coaching had paid off, and he'd taken those kids to the state championship four times in the last five years. The current players, unlike their predecessors, loved Benny. He was popular as could be with his team and all the other kids at Nicolet High. In a way, he was getting a do-over in life, but only with the next generation. His contemporaries, those he'd gone to school with, still hadn't really changed their opinions. People needed to grow up.

"You know, Benny, people like that will always exist in life. They live like they're still in high school, graspin' at popularity like their lives depend on it, social climbing and trying to jockey their way to the head of the pack, begrudging people their success and basking in their failures . . . But I don't care about people like that, do you? People like that are shallow and pathetic."

He nodded slowly, thinking.

"And back to your earlier question, I suppose I don't mind telling you if you'll keep it between us." She shared the story of her paternal grandmother's passing, leaving out the more sordid details of her parents' failed marriage and the nasty divorce that followed. She'd allow him to assume she'd had a relationship with this grandmother and was simply inheriting a little money from a loved one who remembered her in the Will.

It sounded normal enough.

Chapter 5

E rin had known the time would come, eventually. She'd known it from the day the family dog, Jimmy the Poodle, had died fifteen years ago: She'd be a dog owner again one day. What she hadn't expected was that this next dog would easily be twice the size of her first beloved pet. Erin looked in her rearview mirror at the already-enormous five-month-old Mastiff and experienced a sinking feeling. He turned circles in the crate she'd borrowed from Adele, her secretary who owned a Great Dane, and he let out small whines and yelps as he went round and round. "It's okay, Marvin. We're almost home. You're a good boy."

Apparently, this dog would max out somewhere around one hundred sixty pounds, maybe more. Marvin the Mastiff, his official name as of this morning, had checked out of the shelter at a whopping eighty-one pounds. She'd wanted a large breed, a lab mix or a German shepherd, or something like that. A Mastiff hadn't even been on her radar. What had she been thinking?

She hadn't been thinking. She'd been *feeling*. She'd looked at that dog through the bars of his cage, listened to his story, and made eye contact with him. That had been the kiss of death because, in that moment, she knew she had to have him. She had to give him a home. Some college kid had purchased him without realizing how huge the dog would get and then returned him a month later. It wasn't like Marvin was a sweater that didn't fit. He was a living, breathing animal! What kind of person did that to a puppy? And what kind of person would name a dog *Marvin*?

She supposed *Jimmy* wasn't much better, although the name had already been attached to that dog too, when they'd taken him in from their next-door neighbors, the Smiths. They were moving to New York City and didn't feel Jimmy would do well there, and while the parents had been indifferent about leaving him behind, their kids had been devastated. Erin had looked little Alex and Avery in the eyes and promised them she would take good care of Jimmy the Poodle, and she had. Little Avery, just six years old, made her promise not to change the moniker he'd come up with for his dog. Even though he never would have known the difference, Erin had kept that promise too.

Glancing in the rearview mirror at the ginormous fawn-colored puppy with the adorable black mask marking, Erin marveled at how something could be so ugly that it was actually cute. Maybe dog attractiveness wasn't measured on a linear scale. Maybe it was circular, such that if you traveled around all the way into the realm of *ugly* and then a hair beyond, you were actually back in *cute* territory.

Using that type of measurement, Marvin was way cuter than her poodle had been, but not nearly as smart. His name was the only thing the dog seemed to know. He wasn't housebroken, knew no tricks nor any basics of doggy manners—he'd immediately gone for her crotch when they'd been introduced—but he cocked his head in humanoid understanding at the sound of his name, so *Marvin* he would remain.

Adding "the Mastiff" to his name was like a sweet tribute to her old pet anyway, and that it was alliterative was a nice little bonus. Erin wasn't too worried about all that he lacked. She'd whip him into shape in short order. And really, his imposing size would work in her favor. She thought of her graffitied door for the hundredth time. This dog would be able to protect her, though she hoped he wouldn't need to.

The sound of her phone ringing over bluetooth interrupted her thoughts and startled Marvin into a few seconds of blessed silence as he cocked his head and listened.

Jillian was calling. This was a rare victory. Her mother hardly ever called her, and it bugged Erin so much that sometimes she'd engage in a juvenile version of *chicken* to see who could hold out the longest. Usually, Erin caved first, losing the game, and to add insult to injury, she was pretty sure she was the only one playing anyway.

She pressed the button on her steering wheel. "Hi, Jillian."

"Hello, darling! How are you?"

"Good. I'm driving, so I have you on speaker."

"Darling, I'm calling with the most exciting news!"

Lately, her mother had taken to calling everyone "darling." Otherwise, Erin would have been tempted to feel special.

"What's up?"

"Westridge Prep is hiring a new headmaster! I spoke to Elaina Ring, she's on the board you know, and she says to get your CV in right away. She says she'll watch for it and put it at the top of the pile. Isn't that wonderful of her?"

Oh, hell. Not again. "Jillian, I'm not interested in a move back to Santa Monica or anywhere else in California. We've talked about this."

Her mother clucked her tongue. "Please don't be stubborn. I've gone to all the trouble of speaking with Elaina. The least you can do is apply!"

Erin took a quick, deep breath. "I didn't ask you to do that. I don't need your help to find a job. I *have* a job, and I like my work. I like where I live, and if you'd come here for a visit sometime, you'd see—"

"Heavens, *what* is that racket?"

"What? Oh, that's, um, that's my dog."

"Your *dog*!? You have a dog now?"

Erin took a deep breath. "Yup."

"I just spoke to you a few days ago, and you said nothing of a dog then."

"We spoke a few *weeks* ago, Jillian, but you're right. This was . . . a recent decision."

"What's the matter with it? Why is it making that awful sound?"

Erin rolled her eyes and flipped on her blinker to make the turn into her neighborhood. "He's just whining. He's a little scared, that's all."

Jillian Hennings, the woman who had given birth to Erin but had refused to allow her to call her *Mom*, sniffed. "Jimmy the Poodle never made that noise."

Erin sighed. "I know. Jimmy the Poodle was perfect. Marvin the Mastiff is . . ." She looked in the rearview mirror and saw a line of drool hanging from his mouth. "Well, he's not."

"A *Mastiff*? Erin! Have you lost your mind?"

"You know, I think maybe I have." Erin giggled, as Marvin began turning circles at a dizzying rate in the back of her Yukon.

Her mother sniffed again. Jillian was a master *sniffer*. As always, it was loaded with meaning—namely, disapproval.

Erin took another deep breath and waited. Silence screamed at her from the other end of the line. After a few beats, she couldn't stand it anymore. "Listen, thank you for thinking of me for this job. I'm sure it will make someone else very happy. But I'm happy here, and I wish you could accept that." *I wish you'd come here and see how well I'm doing.* Erin had been in Nicolet for close to four years, and in that time, she'd seen Jillian exactly once. That had been two years ago when Erin had invited herself home for Christmas.

Her mother remained quiet, and Marvin the Mastiff took the opportunity to howl into the void of silence. When Jillian spoke again, her tone was frosty. "I can see this is a bad time. We'll talk later. In the meantime, Erin, I hope you'll reconsider and apply. It's a *very* prestigious position, and it will only be posted through the rest of this week."

Erin spoke slowly. "Again, good for someone else, but I won't be applying. Let's talk soon, but let's not talk about this again, okay?"

"Fine," her mother said tightly before signing off with a promise to call soon. Erin knew the only way that would happen was if another job opened up that Jillian thought had Erin's name written all over it. A job that would, more than anything else, benefit Jillian in her endless endeavor to climb that social ladder.

"Hush, Marvin," Erin scolded as she ended the call. "We'll be home in a minute, and we'll get you all settled in. Then we'll head up Mt. Joliet for a hike and get you good and tired out. How's that sound?"

Marvin cocked his head at her before resuming his neurotic circles. Maybe she had made a colossal mistake, but if she had, Marvin wouldn't suffer because of it. She was all he had in the world, and she wouldn't let him down. Honestly, Erin knew she needed him too, and not just as a guard dog. She needed someone to love. Someone to come home to and take care of. Someone who would adore her without demanding things of her she couldn't give.

Erin would have liked to think Jillian missed her on some level, and that was what had prompted the phone call, but she knew better. Westridge Prep was the *it* school for all the uppity families Jillian was always trying so hard to impress. While her father had been happy to play the game, Erin had always stubbornly refused. To say she was a disappointment to her mother was an understatement. But then, she and Jillian had never really had much of a chance. What child could attach in any meaningful way to a mother who refused to be called *Mom*? They didn't even have that most basic of foundations, so how could they build anything lasting? Anything real?

Erin had tried it once. She'd called Jillian *Mom* exactly one time and then never again. It hadn't exactly gone over well. She'd been five years old and desperate for the kind of warm relationship her classmates had with their moms. They got notes in their lunch boxes and hugs and I love yous when they were dropped off at school. Some days, they even cried big crocodile tears because they missed their mothers so much. Erin would pat their shoulders in a bewildered attempt to comfort them, but secretly she wondered what all the fuss was about. She didn't miss her mother one iota. Kindergarten was the best thing that had happened to her young, little self.

A few times, she'd tried to muster tears, just to try it out, but she couldn't pretend a sadness she didn't feel. Especially because she always experienced a springy-stepped joy when she walked into Mrs. Hershey's classroom every morning. Mrs. Hershey was what Erin always imagined a grandmother would be like. She was soft and round and just as sweet as the chocolate she was named after. She'd stroke Erin's head and call her *sweetie* and tell her how smart she was. Erin had truly loved her.

Being in Mrs. Hershey's class was as relaxing as the warm baths Erin took with her barbies every night. And just like the baths, Erin was always pulled out of the warmth and back into the cold long before she was ready. Her dad made it all bearable, at least. That is, when he was home. He was an airline pilot, and without the promise of his return from work most evenings, Erin had considered asking Mrs. Hershey if she could live at the school with her, which was where she had assumed her beloved teacher lived. Erin had always wondered where she kept her bed and why her toilet was so tiny.

Every day before school, Jillian pressed Erin's uniform and styled her hair in one of many ridiculous headbands with a big, gaudy bow on the side. She'd had one in every color. Even on the weekends, Jillian dressed her *just so*. She'd been nothing more than a doll her mother fixed up and showed off to the other parents—the ones who didn't have to scrimp and save to send their children to the elite private school she attended.

It wasn't until sometime in the ninth grade, when Erin switched to a high school that didn't require uniforms, that she put her foot down and came downstairs dressed in something other than the pre-selected outfit Jillian had laid out for her the night before. Oh, how tempers flew! It had been glorious, and that was the day Erin discovered her power. She finally had her mother's attention. It didn't matter that her mother was spitting nails at her. Attention was attention.

And from that day on, she did her best to push all Jillian's buttons, and she kept at it like it was a religion until the final stretch of her senior year. Her father was diagnosed with cancer, and she lost her drive after that, settling into an eerie sort of indifference toward her mother. That indifference toward Jillian was real. What she showed toward her father those last few months, well, that wasn't. She knew what it looked like to everyone around her. She seemed distant and unconcerned, but she was anything but that. She felt more love, more fear, more pain, more . . . *everything* than she knew what to do with, and it would have crushed her if she'd been anything other than stoic.

Because of Sam Hennings, Erin had known the love of a parent. Not every kid got that. She knew that more than ever now as a building principal. The kids she had the most interactions with were the ones without support at home. She'd been one of the lucky ones, even though his job kept him away most of the time. But when her dad was home, he was the glue that connected the three of them together as a family. Or maybe he'd been more like a bridge between herself and Jillian. Through him, she at least had some real access to her mother. Erin hadn't fully understood just how detached and cold their relationship had actually been until her dad had passed and that bridge was removed forever. After his death, nothing was ever the same again.

At fifty-one years old, Sam Hennings was diagnosed with malignant melanoma. It all happened so fast. From the time the biopsy was found to be malignant to the day of the funeral, barely three months had passed. Erin, eighteen years old at the time, was just weeks away from high school graduation when her world and everything in it had flipped and shifted into something she no longer recognized. Home, without the promise of her father coming back to it, felt as hollow as an empty cask. And without him there to soften Jillian, she was all sharp angles and razor blades towards Erin.

On the evening before the funeral, a night when they should have been comforting one another, they'd had their most intense fight ever, and Erin, like most teenagers who were prone to dramatic over-exaggeration, had shouted, "You don't love me, and you never have!"

Jillian, shaking at the bottom of the stairs, hadn't corrected her, and it was then that Erin understood the truth of her words. Her mother didn't love her. How was that even possible? It went against nature, didn't it?

But it was true. That antagonism and lack of affection that had always existed between them went far beyond that of a rebellious child and a detached mother, and Erin realized something was *very* wrong with her relationship with Jillian. She didn't stick around to try to figure out what that was.

Two days after the funeral, she met Seth out at The Pump House, a popular night club she and her friends had been going to for years with their fake IDs, and she'd used him as her ticket out of town. She'd latched onto him like a barnacle, leaving California with him shortly afterward. Erin had cannonballed into that relationship with no thought at all, so it shouldn't have come as a surprise when it all fell apart a few short years later. It was a miracle it had even lasted that long.

Chapter 6

"I can't believe how transformed this place is! Last time I was here, there was still a little ice out on the water. Now look at it!" Olivia exclaimed.

Sarah smiled. The three of them, Olivia, Erin, and herself, sat on the front patio with a bottle of Chardonnay and a platter of cheese and crackers on the glass-topped table between them. She looked out over the basin, which sparkled in the early evening sunlight, before replying to Olivia. "You'll have to come out and paddleboard soon. Erin was supposed to come out and try it last Saturday, but she stood me up."

Erin rolled her eyes. "I didn't stand her up. Duty called, and I had to stay at work." She popped a piece of cheese into her mouth, followed by a cracker.

Olivia leaned forward and rested her elbows on the table. "I'd love to try!"

"It's a good workout, but it's peaceful too. I actually did my yoga out there in the bay this morning."

Erin was incredulous. "You did yoga on a paddleboard?" When Sarah nodded, she added, "And you didn't fall in?"

Sarah shook her head.

"I barely managed to keep my balance on solid ground at your studio."

"I came close to going in a few times, but if I had, so what?"

Erin grinned. "You're right. I want to try."

"Get in line," Olivia said.

"Y'all don't need to squabble. I just got myself another one."

Erin raised her eyebrows. "Oh?"

Sarah rushed to explain, fibbing just a little so they wouldn't think she was spending money willy nilly. "Yes. I stumbled on one that was on sale, and I thought we could all go out together that way."

"Aw, that's so sweet you had the three of us in mind. We'll be like the three musketeers on paddleboards. I can't wait!" Olivia glanced back out at the water, her red hair glinting in the sunshine. "Sean needs to get out here too. He'd beg to take your little boat out fishing. He used to fish all the time as a kid, and now he wants to teach Nora."

Erin raised her eyebrows. "Isn't she a little young for that?"

Olivia looked thoughtful. "Maybe. But it won't be long. She's growing up so fast. I still can't believe I have a one-year-old, and her birthday was months ago. You should see her move! That girl doesn't just walk now, she runs! And yesterday, she said her third word, which is really advanced for her age."

Sarah and Erin smiled brightly at Olivia and then gave one another a knowing look. As much as they loved Nora, and Olivia too, Olivia's tendency was to talk about all of Nora's milestones with the pride and enthusiasm of a parent whose kid just got accepted to Yale or Harvard.

"So," Erin said, "tell us about your honeymoon. We want to hear everything. And I mean, *everything*." She waggled her eyebrows suggestively.

Olivia set down her wineglass, and it made a tiny *clink* as it hit the tabletop. "Oh, you guys! It was so great. We had such an amazing time. The weather was perfect, and the ocean—"

"No, no, no! We don't care about the ocean. I bet you two were like a couple of rabbits, huh? No baby to distract you, nothing else in the world to do . . ."

Sarah pressed her cool wine glass against her temple. She may never get used to Erin's tendency to say out loud whatever popped into her head. No topic was off limits for her. But Olivia didn't bat an eye, so she must be a lot more comfortable about this kind of stuff than Sarah was.

"It was the best," Olivia gushed. "We didn't come out of our room until, like, three o'clock that first day. It was like a reawakening, not that we really needed one, mind you." She winked before taking another sip from her glass.

Erin followed that up with a very specific question that Olivia gave a very specific and detailed answer to, and Sarah wondered why she couldn't be more at ease discussing sex and intimacy like her friends were. She was red to the tips of her ears by the time Olivia finished her description, and Sarah quickly changed the subject.

"So, how did you do being so far away from Nora? I know you were worried about that."

Erin rolled her eyes—she had Sarah's number—but if Olivia had noticed the abrupt shift, she didn't seem to mind.

"It was hard, especially the first night, but it helped knowing she was with Anna, and we called and video chatted a couple times a day, so that helped. She always looked happy, so . . ."

"I still can't believe you left her with a teenager," Erin mused.

"If you knew Anna better, you'd understand. She's not your typical teenager. Plus, she's nineteen now, and her dad was right next door if she needed anything."

Anna Davis was Olivia's next-door neighbor and very close friend, despite their age difference. Sarah had been Anna's English teacher last year, and she thought the world of her. Even then, still in high school, she'd been more of a grown-up than most adults were. "Yeah, and her aunt's a doctor, so she probably had her for backup too," Sarah added.

Erin sipped her wine. "I like her, the aunt. We talked a long time at the reception. Heidi, right?"

"Yeah," Olivia answered. "I've gotten to know her pretty well. She's next door at Anna's house a lot these days. I think things with her and Steven are getting pretty serious."

Erin shook her head. "That's so weird."

Olivia shrugged. "Maybe, but they're happy."

"Well," Erin said as she helped herself to another slice of cheese, "good for them. At least that horrible story has a decent ending."

Sarah was glad for that too. Olivia had filled them in on Heidi and Steven's long history and the tragedy they'd both suffered. Knowing the details of their past, Sarah didn't find it at all strange that they'd ended up together. It seemed fitting to her, and she even thought Heidi's late sister would approve. "They're a sweet couple. I've seen them out a few times."

Erin turned her focus on Sarah. "Alright, so we're caught up on Olivia"—she smiled a lopsided grin—"and the Davis family too, so what's new with you? I haven't talked to you in a week. Work's been kicking my butt." She gestured towards the water. "Obviously, you got your dock in. How'd that go?" She reached for two more crackers.

Sarah eyed up the platter before answering. She should have put out more food. "Fine. Looks good, doesn't it?"

Erin nodded, her mouth full.

"It's perfect," Olivia said. "We should be sitting out there."

"Next time," Sarah promised.

Olivia sat back in her chair and crossed her slender legs. "How was Benny? It's nice he helped you."

"Fine," Sarah repeated with a small shrug. "He's a really good guy. He's going to build me a retaining wall down by the beach as soon as the permit comes through. He thought he might be able to start as soon as next week."

"So, did he talk about me?" Erin asked.

"No, not really," Sarah replied. She tried not to let her irritation show. Sometimes Erin's need to have everything be about her was a little much.

"What did he say?"

"I'm not sure he said much of anything," Sarah said, truly not remembering if Erin's name had come up or not. Erin looked slightly miffed at that, so she broke down and added, "I get the sense he's disappointed it didn't work out between y'all, but he's doin' alright."

Erin smiled widely at that. "It was fun while it lasted, but you know me. I get bored easily."

Sarah gritted her teeth. "Don't worry about it. He's fine."

"You know, I'm starting to think I've been all wrong about Benny," Olivia broke in. "Anna could never understand why I didn't like him. But I always thought he was an odd sort of duck, weird even, but Sean's known him for years—you know how tight the hockey community is here—and he really respects him."

A protectiveness for Benny surged up inside Sarah. "I'm not at all surprised. He's a respectable guy. He's just shy." She worked hard to keep from sounding defensive, but she failed. Benny was so misunderstood, and it made her feel a little sick. He deserved so much more than what he got, and Olivia, of all people, should have known better than to judge a book by its cover.

Olivia had the grace to look sheepish. "I know, and I'm embarrassed I didn't see him that way from the beginning. I mean, I'm a guidance counselor. I'm supposed to be good at reading people. But every time I crossed paths with him at school, I always felt kind of uncomfortable. But I think now that what I sensed was *his* discomfort, and that's what made me feel that way. He's still awkward with me, but when I'm with Sean and the two of them are talking hockey, he's different. More . . . relaxed. More like a regular guy."

"You're psychoanalyzing him," Erin accused.

"Yeah. So?"

Sarah thought Erin might say something feisty in response, but she surprised her. "He's almost universally misunderstood, and that hurts him." She grabbed another slice of cheese, this time the gouda.

Sarah agreed, but she wondered why, if Erin knew that, she'd walked away from a relationship with him. He was good-looking, successful, he'd treated her like a queen . . .

"That makes me feel pretty terrible," Olivia admitted.

"Could be worse. At least you didn't dump him. I feel like I wounded a puppy." Erin took a nibble out of the gouda and smiled. Sarah wanted to shoot her with the blue rubber band laying on the table that she used to seal up the crackers. Instead, she looked pointedly at Erin and said, "Speaking of puppies . . ."

Olivia leaned in. "Yeah, what's that all about? I didn't even know you were in the market for one."

Erin shrugged and reached to pour herself another half a glass. "I like dogs. I had one growing up, and I wanted to get another one."

Olivia fought a smile. "But why that *particular* breed?"

"What, did you think I would get a froufrou dog?"

Olivia slanted her head thoughtfully. "Maybe not a *froufrou* dog, just not a behemoth. That dog is going to weigh twice as much as you do. How are you going to walk him on a leash? If he sees a squirrel, you're toast."

Erin, who couldn't weigh much more than a hundred pounds, appeared to be considering that for the first time. "Shit, you guys. I *am* toast."

Sarah giggled. The image was too perfect. "I can picture it."

"What? Our teeny-tiny friend being dragged across town by a monster dog named Marvin?" Olivia clarified with mock disapproval. Then she laughed along with Sarah. "Yeah, me too."

Erin sighed. "Not exactly feeling the love right now, girls, and if I'm teeny-tiny, Olivia, then so are you."

Olivia's eyes danced. "Touché, but I'm not the one who's going to have road rash up and down her arms and legs." Turning serious, she said, "You'll just have to make sure he's well trained, that's all." Her face lit up, and she added, "Hey! Take him to puppy school! I think there's one over by that furniture store on Third Street." She snapped her fingers. "What's the name again?"

"K-9 Kollege," Sarah chimed in. "I remember because the spelling of Kollege with a *K* bugs me. Why do people do that?"

Erin raised her eyebrows. "Because it's creative?"

"It's stupid and annoyin,' but whatever," Sarah said.

Olivia shot a look at Erin before addressing Sarah. "You're a little feisty today. You feeling okay?"

Sarah dismissed that with a wave of her hand, even though she had to admit that she *was* a little on edge. She just wasn't really sure why. For a second, she thought it might have something to do with Benny, but that couldn't be right. She let the thought go. Here she was on a beautiful summer day, drinking wine and eating cheese with her two best friends. She shouldn't feel negatively about anything. "I'm just rosy." She flashed Olivia a reassuring smile and turned to Erin. "I want to meet this Marvin the Mastiff. Bring him out next time."

Erin grabbed her arm. "Really? You wouldn't mind? Because I've felt *terrible* leaving him in his crate the last two days. I *had* to work yesterday, but today I had to listen to his sad yelps all the way out to my car, knowing I was *choosing* to leave him to come over here."

"Aw, bless his sweet little heart. Yes, bring him on out. I don't know that I want him in the house, but he could run around out here and swim in the lake."

"He'd sink."

Olivia looked at Erin, a question in her eyes.

Erin waved a hand absently. "Barrel chest and everything. You'll understand when you see him."

Late that night, long after her friends had left and long after the sun had set, Sarah sat at the end of the dock and looked out over the expanse of water. Except for the sound of the rustling leaves and the occasional jumping of fish, it was quiet. She felt a peace out here she wasn't sure she'd ever really experienced before. It was as if, for the first time in her life, she could fully relax. And that was saying something, given her present circumstances.

She was now getting almost daily calls from her sister with updates about their mother. She'd spoken to Nadia more in the last few weeks than she had in the last several years. They'd been close once, when Nadia had been little. Sarah remembered driving home from the hospital with Nadia in the car seat. She'd only been five, but she remembered sitting in the back seat and looking at her sleeping sister, with the pink cupid's bow mouth, and falling completely in love with her.

Lydie Mae had mostly slept and cried those first few months home with the new baby, and Sarah didn't really remember seeing much of her father. She had very few memories of him at all, to be honest. She just remembered she and Gammie had looked after the baby together. Gammie taught her how to make the formula, how to keep the air out of the nipple of the bottle during feeding, how to burp the baby, and all kinds of other things. She remembered those long strolls down the tree-lined driveway to the fancy gate and back to their mansion of a house, just herself, Gammie, and Nadia.

And then suddenly everything changed. Sarah found it hard to remember the details from her child's perspective. Things were fuzzy. Obviously, she knew exactly what had happened now, as an adult, but at the time, all she knew was that they'd moved from the mansion to a big house in another nearby town. The one time she could remember asking where her Daddy was, Lydie Mae had gone on a terrible screaming and crying jag. Gammie moved in with them to help out, so for a while she was around all the time. It was hard to miss her daddy too much with that kind of trade.

Some things changed, and some stayed the same. Their walks continued, though eventually the stroller was replaced by the red wagon Gammie bought them, and while the house was very nice, there was no gate. Sarah would pull Nadia behind her, pretending she was the Mama and Nadia was the baby. Nadia would laugh and giggle, and Sarah would smile, and Gammie would say they were the sweetest little girls in all of Alabama.

Lydie Mae continued to live life in her pajamas, and she'd still screamed and cried a lot, but Sarah got pretty good at ignoring it. Those might have been the best years of her childhood, come to think of it. But then they moved again, this time to a house roughly the size of a shoe box, and Gammie went back to work at the local grocery store, something Sarah's younger self couldn't understand. Even at the tender age of seven, she knew something wasn't quite right about Gammie going to work for nine hours a day and Mama staying home in her slippers. She found it terribly unfair—mostly for herself. To say she preferred Gammie was an understatement. And Nadia, for her part, began to prefer sitting with Lydie Mae over heading out in the wagon with Sarah. Over time, they drifted further and further apart, and by the time Gammie died, Nadia had felt like a stranger.

They might not ever be close sisters, but at least they were talking now, and the hostility in Nadia's voice was fading. And while it had taken some time and effort, Sarah could now think about her mama and sister without all her muscles tensing up. For years, Sarah popped Tylenol with the regularity of daily vitamins to treat her frequent headaches. Now she couldn't remember the last time she'd popped a pill.

She felt free and hopeful for the future, sitting here on a piece of property that was so beautiful she could almost cry. It was a "lake forty," which meant she had about thirty-four acres of land along with however much of the water—not that she owned it—and a thousand feet of frontage. Most of her property was to the south of the house, which was perched a few yards away from the property line on the northernmost edge of her land. The south side was beautifully wooded and graced with a winding trail system put in by the previous owner. Apparently, he'd spent months making those trails. It was a shame he and his wife had had to move, but one of their adult children had developed some type of illness, and they'd felt the need to be close by.

Sarah walked those trails with her realtor before putting in her offer. She'd imagined herself hiking them in the summer and fall and skiing them in the winter. This place really was an outdoor enthusiast's dream, and sometimes, like now, she felt the need to pinch herself to make sure it was all real.

Sarah did have neighbors to the south, abutting the trail system—a nice retired couple whose names she couldn't remember. But with all that land between her house and theirs, she felt they may as well be miles away. A neighboring house, a cabin that her realtor referred to as a *camp*, sat to the north of her place, and when she'd walked through her house as a prospective buyer back in May, she'd been able to see it clearly out one of the living room windows and through the leafless trees. With everything in full bloom now, she could no longer see it, but she knew it was there, and she knew it was still vacant. Little did she know, within a week, that would no longer be the case.

Chapter 7

Ethan Rockford had never been this far north in Michigan. For the last fifty miles, he'd been seeing signs for Mackinac Island, a popular tourist destination he'd never visited. It was located in the straits separating Lower Michigan from Upper Michigan. He cruised along I-75 at just under eighty miles per hour in the car his company had waiting for him when he'd landed in Detroit just a little after dinnertime yesterday. It was flashy and not at all his taste, but it did zero to sixty in four-point-four seconds, and the engine actually purred as he raced along the expressway.

He'd stopped in Flint to see his family for a quick overnight. Regrettably, he'd only had a few hours with his dad, who'd had to work the night shift. Arthur Rockford had been a hard worker all his life, and recently he'd been promoted at Flinn Chemical. Ethan's mom couldn't wait to fill him in as they'd all sat together in the tiny living room.

"They finally seen your dad's potential, Ethan, and it's about time." She'd said once they'd all been seated on the faded living room furniture with cans of Pabst in hand and potato chips and sour cream on the coffee table.

His sister, Sonya, had been given a ginger ale, and she took a sip from her spot on the floor. She rested her arms on the coffee table while they visited, snagging occasional chips out of the bowl. During family gatherings, she'd always preferred the green shag carpeting to an actual chair, but in her current condition, he'd insisted she take his. Stubborn as ever, she wouldn't hear of it, but they were cut from the same cloth, and he couldn't let it go. After glancing at her for the tenth time with a disapproving frown, she smiled and stuck her tongue out at him.

Ethan rolled his eyes, but he returned her smile with one of his own. Some things never changed, no matter how old you got.

"Congratulations, Pop," Ethan said heartily, even though he hated the thought of his aging father heading off to work at the same chemical plant he'd given four decades of his life to. "What's the new job?"

Arthur sat up a little taller. "I'm a production finisher now."

"Wow, Pop, that's great!" He exchanged another look with Sonya. They had a shared dream for their parents: an early retirement where they could finally relax and enjoy one another without the worry of money or the stress of factory work. Sonya was a year out from graduating nursing school, and Ethan knew she hoped to be able to start helping him support their parents. He didn't really need the help now, and if things went as planned for him, there'd be no need whatsoever. In fact, he could continue to support her too.

Sonya was smart, and her ultimate goal was to become a nurse practitioner. If anyone had asked him before, he would have said nothing would stand in her way of achieving all her goals, but now he wasn't so sure. With a baby coming, he just didn't know what to expect.

It didn't sound like she'd be getting any help from the father, and with their mother, Denise's, worsening rheumatoid arthritis, he didn't know how much help she could be in caring for a baby. Mentally, he began to calculate daycare costs. He could swing it, he was pretty sure. It might be a little tight with one more year of Sonya's tuition to pay for, but he'd convince his sister to take it. Yes, they were cut from the same cloth, but he was definitely the more stubborn of the two of them.

"Tell him about your raise, Arthur."

"Aw, Denise. He don't need to know that."

"Tell him. He's always worryin' about us. Go on," she prompted.

"Aww, hell." He shook his head, and Ethan could see his father was equal parts proud and embarrassed to tell him. "Well, son, I seen what you drove into the drive, so I don't s'pose the amount will impress you all that much, but I got raised to twenty an hour. That's a three dollar raise overnight, and it sure will help me and your mom start to save for the future."

Ethan worked hard not to cringe. Saving for the future shouldn't begin in one's fifties, but his parents hadn't had much choice. He reminded himself he didn't need to be too concerned. He was going to cover them. They'd be alright. And so would Sonya, regardless of how her plans turned out.

"That's really, really great, Pop. I'm happy for you."

His mom beamed. "Don't you ever forget where you come from, Eth. We're hard workers in this family, whatever we do. We don't need fancy things, just honest work. Isn't that right, Arthur?"

"That's right."

Ethan squirmed.

Shaking her head, Sonya asked, "Remember your time at Kerns, Mom?"

"How could I forget? Miserable work."

"You did it for fifteen years," Ethan reminded her.

"Don't I know it." She looked down at her gnarled fingers. "And I have the hands to prove it."

Arthur chuckled. "I'll never forget the first day she come home from that job. She was a temp at first, if I recall. Come home all covered in grease and cryin'. I says, 'Denise,' I says, 'You don't have to go back to that place. We'll find you somethin' else.' And you know what she told me?"

Ethan knew. So did Sonya. They'd heard the story a hundred times. It was the kind of story that told the whole tale about their mother. Some stories were like that. They revealed a person's character more clearly than anything else could. "What, Pop? What'd she say?"

"She says, 'It's alright. I ain't too proud to get my hands a little dirty.'"

Ethan watched his father gently reach for his mother's hand. "She did that job fifteen years until the pain got too bad."

And things had gotten very, very tight. Ethan remembered that too. His parents had refused the disability his mom had every right to claim. "We're not livin' off the dole," his father had said sternly when Ethan asked, "and that's that."

"How are you doing, Mom? Still doing that drug trial?" Ethan asked.

Arthur scoffed in disgust. "She was one of the people in the group that gets them sugar pills and not the real stuff."

Denise nodded. "I just found out yesterday, but let's not talk about that now. We're celebrating."

Ethan shot his mother a small, understanding smile. She never wanted the focus to be on her. One of her favorite things was having the family all gathered together, and it rarely happened anymore with him living so far away. Whenever the potato chips and sour cream came out at his house, there was no doubt about it: it was a party. He reached for a chip and turned his attention back to his father. "Well, Pop, great news on the promotion. I really am happy for you."

"And we're so happy for *you*!" Sonya chimed in. "Tell us about the car."

Ethan grinned sheepishly. "It's just a company rental."

"But you get to drive it all the way up to Nicolet and keep it for the whole summer?"

"Yeah."

"What're you goin' up there for all summer, honey?" his mother asked.

Ethan cleared his throat. "Uh, just a small project the CEO wanted me to handle for him personally. It has to do with company stock and some potential . . . investment money."

"Soon you'll be runnin' that company, hey son?" his father asked with a proud smile.

Denise gave him a playful, gentle swat. "Now don't go puttin' ideas in his head, Arthur. We don't need him to run no company. He don't need us pressuring him." She looked at Ethan. "You just do what makes you happy, Eth. There's more to life than all them"—she waved her hands as she hunted for the right words—"mergers and portfolios and such."

Ethan nodded and smiled, but something tightened in his chest, and he felt a corresponding sting in his eyes. He loved this family. They were honest, hard-working, and simple, and the business world didn't reward people like that. But he would. He absolutely would.

The conversation ebbed and flowed until the shadows grew, then faded into a gray dusk and Arthur had to leave for work. They exchanged hugs and promises for another visit soon. After waving his father off, Ethan sat with Sonya and Denise and listened as they talked about how they'd never been up to the Upper Peninsula before and how they'd all like to go someday.

And now here Ethan was, in a car that embarrassed him, going where his family had never gone before, and wishing like hell he didn't have to do it.

Chapter 8

"Are you sure I can't help you?" Sarah asked again. "I'm really not doin' anything else." She trailed behind Benny, who expertly maneuvered a wheelbarrow full of concrete block to the waterfront. The permit had come through the day before, and once Benny had called to make sure she wanted to move forward, he'd wasted no time rounding up the materials needed for the job.

"I guess if you really want to help, you could grab the stuff out of my truck. It's nothing too heavy, but it'll take you a few trips."

"What do you need?"

"Everything in the back seat needs to come down here." He looked at her with worried eyes. "But I can get it in a minute myself."

She clapped her hands and held them. "Don't be silly. I'm on it." Sarah ran back to the driveway where Benny's black Dodge Ram was parked. The truck's bed was filled to the brim with the decorative block she'd chosen for the wall. She'd told him he could back it up to the water, but he didn't want to drive on her lawn. She hadn't been able to persuade him, and he planned to haul the blocks to the waterfront one wheelbarrow at a time.

It took Sarah three trips to get the shovel, broom, mallet, garden stakes, mason's line, work gloves, level, and a funny plate thingy on the end of a stick that Benny told her was called a *tamper*. It would be used to make sure the gravel he'd already brought in yesterday was compacted in the trench before he started laying the blocks. The gravel used for backfill also needed to be tamped down.

There was a lot more to this process than just stacking bricks, Sarah was coming to realize. She was grateful for Benny's expertise, and she had the sneaking suspicion he hadn't asked for nearly enough money. She'd give him extra and demand he accept it. She had the means to pay him what he was worth, not that she would carelessly spend money away on frivolous things. She wasn't built that way. But paying Benny a fair price wasn't frivolous. Fair was fair.

While she carried supplies to and from the truck, Sarah thought about the money. Regardless of her beefed up bank account, she would still teach. Since she was well aware she could be a rooster one day and a feather duster the next, she'd live as she always had. Simply. Honestly, she really didn't need much in life to be happy. She had a job and students she loved, good friends, and a beautiful place to live.

What more could she ask for?

Immediately, her sister and mother came to mind, followed by an image of Joe, laughing and looking as handsome as he always had at the front of the lecture hall, and she quickly pushed the image aside.

Sarah finished her task well before Benny finished his, so donning her own work gloves she'd bought yesterday at the hardware store, she climbed up into the truck bed and helped move the bricks towards the tailgate for Benny to load into the wheelbarrow. They worked in silence, mostly, each seeming happy to be in their own heads. She was, at least.

Once they moved the last load of brick and had everything down at the building site, Sarah made Benny take a break. He protested that he hadn't even started the wall yet, but after at least six wheelbarrow trips from the truck to the worksite, he'd sweat through his white T-shirt, and droplets hung from the tip of his nose. It was at least eighty degrees, and the late morning sun shone hot and bright.

"We'll get back to it directly. I'll just grab us each an iced coffee and a scone, and we'll sit for fifteen minutes, tops, alright?"

Benny reluctantly agreed. He was a completionist. Sarah had known that about him almost from the beginning. He didn't leave his classroom for the day until everything for the next day was set and ready to go. He had the cleanest desk and most orderly classroom of anyone else at that school. She should have known that once he'd started this task, he'd want to get it done as expeditiously as possible. But Sarah didn't want him to work like that for her—that intensively. There was no rush, as far as she was concerned. *Plus, the longer this takes, the more time . . .* Sarah's stride faltered a moment as she headed up to the house. What was the end of that sentence? The more time she'd get to spend with Benny?

Well, yes, she admitted. Everyone liked spending as much time as possible with their friends, didn't they?

Hmm.

She stepped into the house without answering her own question. One thing she did know was that she wanted him to feel relaxed at her house. Or as relaxed as someone hauling heavy blocks in the hot sun *could* feel. She grabbed the tray and loaded it up with the coffee fixings, scones, and butter and headed out to the patio.

It hadn't taken her long, but in the amount of time she'd been inside, Benny had already begun excavating the area where the wall would go. He used nothing but a shovel and muscle power, and she watched, mesmerized, as his biceps bunched and rippled beneath the sleeves of his T-shirt. Sarah found she couldn't look away, and he must have felt her eyes on him because he abruptly stopped and looked up.

Quickly, she scrambled to make herself look busy. She moved the coffees off the tray and onto the glass patio table and set their plates with the scones next to their coffees.

"Thanks again for doin' this for me," Sarah chirped when his shadow fell over the table.

Benny pulled a chair out and sat down. "My pleasure."

She seated herself directly across from him.

"I actually like this kind of work." His lips formed a small smile. "You know, when I was little, I used to like watching the Zamboni refresh the ice. I was a little . . . obsessed with it. I liked seeing the instant results of the work. Building and construction are kind of like that."

"Right," she agreed as she poured some creamer into her glass and stirred. The ice made a refreshing *clinking* sound. "As opposed to teaching, where sometimes you don't know the impact you've made for years, right?"

"Yeah, that's true, I guess." He looked around as he chewed his first bite of scone. After washing it down with a sip of black, iced coffee, he said, "You know, out here, it feels almost . . ."

"What?"

He shook his head. "I don't know. Like everything's okay in the world." A loon chose that moment to sound its call, and he chuckled. "I mean, the world might be totally crazy, but out here, you'd never know it. The loons don't know it."

"Is your world crazy right now?" She stopped buttering her scone to look at him.

He angled his head, thinking. "Not any more than usual, I guess. I've got stuff like anyone else. Family stuff, work stuff. You know."

She did know. "I have some stress lately myself. Some decisions to make."

He raised his eyebrows.

"Without getting too specific, I'm in charge of my sister's inheritance, which is . . . a substantial amount of money. My grandmother set it up so that Nadia won't have access to it unless I sign it over to her, which I can't do until she turns eighteen. In my grandmother's letter, she strongly recommended I wait until Nadia turns twenty-two. It's our decision to make—well, mine really—but our grandmother *incentivized* it by reducing my sister's amount by twenty percent if Nadia takes control of it early."

"When does she turn eighteen?"

"End of August, and I'll bet you can guess what Nadia wants me to do."

He grinned briefly, then sobered. "She wants the money now, penalty and all."

Sarah nodded. "Penalty and all."

"And you don't want her to have it yet?"

"No."

Benny reached a hand up and stroked at the stubble on his chin. "Other than the obvious reason, why not?"

"She'll give it all to my mom, and I think my grandmother must have known that."

His brows lifted once again.

Sarah blew out a deep, long breath. "My mom's an alcoholic, Benny. She's also highly manipulative. The way she pulls the marionette strings to get Nadia to do exactly what she wants, it's disgusting. I want to protect my sister. I've always wanted to protect her, but I haven't been able to do that until now. She'll hate me if I don't give her what she wants, not that it would change things between us a whole lot. She already hates me for leavin' Alabama."

Sarah shared the rest of the story with Benny. The fact that Sarah had tried to take her sister with her didn't seem to matter to Nadia. She still accused Sarah of abandoning her. Of not caring about her family. But Sarah cared. She cared a lot. She just knew she couldn't stay. She would have lost herself completely if she had. Even though her first instinct after graduation had been to hop a bus, she'd stayed several months arguing with the courts. After her attempts to take over the guardianship of Nadia failed, Sarah left without looking back.

There was nothing else holding her there. Nadia was barely speaking to her, and Lydie Mae had long since kicked her out of the house in a fit of rage over the court battle. So she'd packed up, emptied her bank account, said goodbye to Gammie at the cemetery, and left. She'd never been more relieved or more terrified. The next day, she exited the bus in Duluth, Minnesota, and that's where she'd stayed. Wanting to get as far away as possible, she'd gone almost as far north as a person could go in the continental United States without hitting Canada. In Duluth, she'd found a job as a waitress at a popular diner and put herself through school on tips. She'd also found Joe, not that she'd be discussing him with Benny.

Benny ran a hand through his thick hair. "Wow. I didn't know you had all that going on. You always seem so . . ." He cleared his throat.

"So what?"

He turned pink. "Uh, serene, I guess."

Sarah smiled, flattered. "I hide it well. When you grow up keepin' secrets, you become an expert in coverin' feelings up."

He kicked gently at an ant hill built up in the cracks of the patio pavers. "I'm sorry."

She shook her head. "Don't be. I'm okay, and it'll all work out somehow. I just have to stick to my guns with my sister. To protect her. She's got loads of gumption, she just doesn't know it yet. And as far as our mom goes, who knows? Maybe she'll turn out in the end too." It was wishful thinking, and Sarah wouldn't hold her breath, but she couldn't discount the possibility either. Miracles did happen.

"Maybe she will," Benny agreed.

"She's actually doing a stint in rehab right now. It was another stipulation in the Will. My grandmother left my mom a little something, but ninety days at Calista's Place—that's a rehab facility down there—was a condition for receiving it. Paid for by my grandmother, of course. It took Lydie Mae, my mama, a few months of cursin' and carryin' on, but I knew she'd go eventually. She'll take that money and spend it all, like she always does, and then she'll start putting the pressure on Nadia again."

"She won't pressure you?"

"No." Sarah didn't provide an explanation. Instead, she took a bite of scone. They both chewed in silence for several seconds before she inquired about his family. "You mentioned you've got family stuff," she added.

He laughed. "Compared to your story, my family situation is downright boring."

She grinned. "Tell me about them. You already mentioned a sister."

"Yeah, so she's my only sibling, and my parents are still alive and well. They're both retired now, just within the last few months. About the only problems I have with them are that my mom won't stop letting herself into my house to clean and leave me dinners in the fridge, and my dad refuses to act his age. The other day, I pulled into their driveway, and he was standing on the top rung of a ladder, trimming a tree limb with a chainsaw. I about had a heart attack!"

"Oh my goodness gracious! That's really dangerous!" Sarah held a hand over her heart as the image of an old man running a chain saw high in the air took shape in her head.

Benny chuckled and stared at her with a wide smile before briefly looking down and giving a small shake of his head. "Yeah, tell me about it. Anyway, other than that, I don't have any complaints. They're great parents. I got lucky, I guess. My sister and I are close. Her husband's a great guy. They have two amazing kids."

Sarah had never experienced Benny like this before. He was relaxed and talkative, and she was so gratified to be learning these things about him. About his family. "What are their names?" she asked.

He grinned fondly. "You'll love this. They named them Jack and Jill."

"Hush your mouth!"

He treated her to that same look he'd given her a second ago and began to laugh.

She narrowed her eyes. "What's so funny?"

"Uh . . . nothing," he said through his laughter. "I just like the things you say."

Sarah felt her cheeks turn pink with pleasure.

"Anyway," he went on, "you'll get it once you meet my brother-in-law. He's hysterical. Always playing pranks on Kay and the kids."

There was no trace of the awkward Benny in this moment. Even his face, normally sort of . . . expressionless, was animated. He'd assumed that she *would* meet him, and she found that she really wanted to. She wanted to meet them all. "How old are they? Your niece and nephew, I mean."

"Jill is eight, and Jack is six."

"What are they like?"

"Jill's a real talker. She's eight going on eighteen, but in a good way. She's an old soul. And Jack is . . . Jack is really great too. He's a pretty special kid." He looked like he was about to say more but then changed his mind. Finishing his last sip of coffee, he wiped the back of his hand across his mouth. "Should we get to it?" He stood and pulled uncomfortably at his damp shirt, which clung to his skin and revealed the hard muscles underneath.

Sarah wondered if he might take it off. She kind of hoped he would, but when she answered, "Let's," she couldn't quite meet his eyes.

They worked together for several hours. It was back-breaking work, and by the time they called it a day, Sarah's own muscles were screaming at her. All they'd accomplished was site prep, and Sarah hadn't expected that. Sadly, it didn't look like much, but Benny had explained that preparing the earth was the most important part of the process and the one most often skimped on or skipped *over* altogether. If she wanted this wall to last, they had to do it the right way, and that would take time.

Who was she to argue? She knew nothing about this kind of thing, having grown up without anyone to show her. She had friends from college whose parents had taught them things, like how to change a tire, balance a checkbook, or even how to sew on a button. She'd had to learn all those things on her own. Now she was learning how to build a retaining wall, but this time, she had somebody to teach her. It felt nice. Exhausting, but nice.

She couldn't have asked for a better teacher. Benny was patient, methodical, and confident—and currently in the process of removing his sweat-soaked shirt.

"Oh!" Sarah exclaimed in surprise. "Are you—?" The words stuck in her throat as she took in Benny's bare flesh. His shoulders were broad and developed. In fact, everything on Benny was developed, including his abs. Sarah swallowed, and even though her face was hot with embarrassment, she couldn't look away.

Thankfully, Benny didn't seem to notice. "Is it okay if I take a swim?" he asked. "I told myself that would be my reward for working in this heat. I even wore my swim trunks," he said, nodding at his shorts, which Sarah could now see were, indeed, swim trunks, although not the same ones as the last time. These were orange with gray stripes.

Sarah rubbed the back of her neck. "Go ahead."

He sat down in the grass to remove his shoes. "What about you? Don't you want to cool off? I can wait for you if you want to grab your swimsuit."

A swim sounded heavenly, but did she really want to swim half naked with Benny right now, feeling the way she did? Her body screamed yes, but her head said no.

Absolutely not. No way.

But what if she didn't wear her bathing suit? Maybe she could go in as she was. She was wearing a tank top and shorts, and that was almost like a bathing suit, and what she was wearing definitely covered more of her skin than the black bikini hanging in the laundry room would.

Sarah considered it a moment and decided. She was wearing a sports bra under her tank anyway, and the fabric was a deep purple, so it wouldn't be see-through if it got wet. Same for her black shorts. She threw down her gloves and sat next to Benny to remove her shoes and socks. "A swim sounds great, actually." He smiled, and Sarah noted his perfect teeth. They were straight and strikingly white. "Did you have braces as a kid?" she asked.

"No. I got lucky. You?"

"No, but I needed them. My bottom teeth are really crooked."

"Huh. I've never noticed." He peered closely at her.

Sarah pinched her lips together, and Benny laughed. "Don't hide your smile. It's a nice smile. So friendly."

"That's . . . so nice!" Who was this guy, so easygoing and personable? Where was the reserved, taciturn Benny? He must be one of those people who needed time to warm up to others, Sarah decided. Like a shy child who begins a play date holding his mother's leg and ends it by leading everyone in a game of hide and seek. Except in Benny's case, it hadn't taken an hour or two to get comfortable. It had taken a whole year.

He grinned again and hopped to his feet. He held a hand down to her and hoisted her up. "Let's go."

Benny ran across the small beach and splashed through the water. Sarah followed, the sand hot and gritty on her sweaty feet. Within seconds, he'd disappeared under the surface, and she dove under too, just to the right of him. The water was cool and refreshing as she swam underneath the surface. She loved the feel of it gliding across her skin. When she came up for air, the hot breeze greeted her along with Benny's laugh from far behind her.

"What are you, half fish?" he called.

Half fish. Sarah immediately thought of Gammie, and her eyes stung.

Treading water, she turned and they shared a smile just before he dove under again. When he popped up once more, he was right beside her out in the deep.

He gave his head a shake, and droplets flew from his hair. "You can't beat this, Sarah. This is your backyard. How many people get to say that?"

"Not many. I'm lucky, I know."

Movement on shore caught their attention at the same time, and they both trained their eyes on the cabin next door. A car, a black sedan with tinted windows had pulled in, and a man was getting out.

"Didn't you say that camp was empty?" Benny asked.

"Yeah, it was." Sarah would never get used to the tendency Yooper's had to refer to all cabins and cottages as *camps*. She found it so odd. Watching the man disappear behind the cabin, she added, "I guess it's not now." A second later, the sound of a screen door slamming shut echoed across the water.

They treaded water in silence, watching and waiting. The door slammed again, and he reappeared a moment later to grab a large box out of the car. Sarah couldn't make out any features with the distance between them, but she could see he was quite tall and had hair as dark as the sedan.

"I didn't realize how close your place is to his," Benny remarked with a frown.

Sarah squinted at him in the bright sunshine, the light from which caused the beads of water to glisten in his hair. "Actually, it's a rental, but I didn't think the owners were renting it to anyone this summer." She gave him a playful splash as he continued to frown. "Hey! Why so serious?"

"It just looks like he's alone."

"And if he is?"

"Then it's just the two of you out here. He turned in the water to survey the woods to the right. I can't even see any other neighbors in this cove. It's just the two of you," he repeated.

Sarah felt her belly warm when she realized he was worried about her. Benny was revealing all kinds of things about himself. He was sweet as sugar. "I have neighbors just on the other side of that point yonder way," she said, pointing. "You can't see their place, but they're not too far off."

Benny continued to look mildly peeved. "He drives a Rolls Royce. That's a brand new Wraith."

Sarah glanced back at the dark, two-door sedan. "How can you tell what kind of car it is?"

His lips twitched. "I'm a guy."

"What's wrong with driving a Rolls Royce?"

"Nothing, but do you know how much a car like that costs?"

"No," Sarah admitted.

"Three hundred grand, easy."

"Oh!"

"What kind of guy comes up to the U.P. with a car like that?"

"I guess we'll find out." Sarah made a mental note never to buy a Rolls Royce. Not if she wanted to impress Benny, anyway. She swam forward towards the shore several strokes before turning back. "I'll grab us some towels," she called out to him. "No rush."

"Thanks," Benny said distractedly, still looking at the car next door.

Chapter 9

Erin was pretty sure she was losing it. She'd been sleeping alone a long time, and she'd never been scared of the dark before, not even as a kid. Yet here she was in her king-sized bed, Marvin splayed out beside her, wide awake with a baseball bat wedged between her and her new bedmate. She'd awoken to a crashing sound several hours ago, which had only been the fridge making ice, but she was on high alert, and lately every little noise in the night made her heart skip a beat.

It was surprising just how many noises there were. She imagined it had always been like this in her old, creaky house, but she'd never noticed before. Now she felt like each creak could be the bogey man armed with more paint (or something worse) coming to get her. And Marvin, snoring away beside her, didn't even seem to care. Some guard dog he'd turned out to be! Erin doubted he'd know how to protect her if she ever was in any kind of danger. Unless death by licking was a thing. If that were the case, he could take down a three hundred-pound sumo wrestler with his tongue alone.

Erin glanced at him and watched the rise and fall of his enormous chest, and she smiled in spite of herself. Her boy might look imposing, but he was all love and no fight. It was amazing how quickly she'd come to care about him, and with an intensity that made her a little sad if she thought about it too hard. It said a lot about her situation in life that the person she loved most in the world, and the one who loved her the most back, wasn't a person at all, but a jowl-faced, drooly dog.

Erin glanced at the stack of books on her nightstand. They were all about dog training and caring for a puppy, and so far, they'd been invaluable. Marvin had already mastered *sit, stay,* and *come* after just a few days. Tomorrow—she looked at the clock—or rather, today, she was taking him out to Sarah's for the first time. She planned to spend the day out there.

Maybe she'd head over in a few hours. Sarah was one of those annoying people who woke up before their alarms ever had a chance to go off. She was an early riser, even on weekends and summer break. Erin, on the other hand, could easily sleep until noon if she didn't set two alarms—one main alarm beside her bed that she always managed to turn off without waking up, and one backup alarm on her phone that she left way over on the dresser. That way she couldn't shut it off without physically getting up, and she had the added bonus of not being radiated to death by it, something she'd read about in an article but still wasn't quite sure she believed.

Now she had three alarms since Marvin awoke at first light, which—at this time of year at least—meant he began whining at her and licking her face well before five-thirty in the morning. She feared her days of sleeping in were over forever, and she sighed. And while he didn't emit any radiation, what he did emit were horrible, fowl, awful farts that woke her up from the deepest sleep with their smell. Lucky her. Lucky *him*, was more like it. He was lucky she loved him, or he'd be back at that shelter waiting for someone without a nose—or eyes for that matter—to adopt him.

Erin turned to lie flat on her back and stared at the dark ceiling. There was no way she was falling back asleep now, so she might as well put on the coffee and get the day started.

Swinging her legs out from under the covers and letting them dangle over the side of the bed, she stretched her arms up over her head and yawned. Marvin stirred briefly, farted loudly, and then resumed his snoring.

Hmm. Not much different from Seth.

And so it was, with her ex-husband on her mind, that Erin sipped from her oversized mug of coffee at four o'clock in the morning. Seated on the sofa in the living room with the cold steel of the baseball bat resting against her bare thigh, she shivered. She still missed Seth, even after all these years. As messed up as she knew their relationship had been, she'd have stayed in that marriage forever. It had felt safe to her.

As a petty officer in the navy, most of Seth's time was spent at sea. He'd come home for brief stints and then take off again on long assignments. His job kept him at a literal distance, so it had been easy to keep things surface deep. If there was a problem, and there'd been plenty, all she had to do was hang on until the next deployment date. And every time he came home again, it was like hitting the reset button and getting to know one another all over again. It had worked, for a time, but she'd always known he'd grow tired of her. And he had.

It should tell you something, Erin, that I'd rather go live on an attack submarine with a bunch of dudes for six months than be home with you.

And that was when she knew it was over. Seth was done trying, and she supposed she couldn't blame him. Their marriage had been a sham from the beginning. It was actually kind of surprising it had taken him so long to realize she wasn't worth the effort. She was pretty sure she'd loved him—in her own way—and when he left for good, she'd cried barrels of tears. Oddly, though, the person she thought of most in those crazed moments of weeping was her father.

He had loved her. She'd never once doubted it. Not once. Jillian got most of his attention when he was home, sure, but that was only because she demanded it. Sam Hennings had his work cut out for him when it came to keeping Jillian happy, and Erin had always secretly wondered if that was why her dad had never tried very hard to get stateside flight routes. He was always flying to one exotic place or another, and when he did finally make it home, he was usually exhausted. Erin loved him too much to put any extra pressure on him. Still, she lived for the small moments they shared together—just the two of them, hiking or grabbing an ice cream. In those moments, she'd felt almost ridiculously special.

A small *tap* interrupted her thoughts and made her tense. She listened closely and heard it again. It was coming from the back of the house. Erin jumped to her feet, her heart beating faster than a drum roll, and the head-to-toe rush of hot dread made her feel momentarily dizzy. She placed her hand on the armrest of the sofa to steady herself.

Investigating the noise was the last thing in the world she wanted to do. But who else was going to do it? She lived all alone, and not even her dog seemed to care that a psychostalker was right out back, just waiting to do her in. Retrieving the blaze-orange bat from the sofa, she gripped it the way her dad had shown her all those years ago before her first little league practice. After taking a deep breath, Erin slowly tip-toed her way to the back of the house.

Tap.

She stood in the dark hallway, just outside the laundry room, and worked up the courage to peer through the doorway. She raised the bat higher, heart in her throat, as she looked into the room.

Tap.

Sighing with relief, Erin's shoulders sagged, and she lowered the bat. A small tree branch was hitting the window above the dryer.

How long was she going to let this go on? She was falling all to pieces over a small breeze when she was supposed to be tough. She'd always prided herself on that. She thought again about getting some help, but it felt too much like admitting weakness, and she just couldn't be seen as weak. Not by anyone.

It had all started two weeks ago with the spray painted door. Then, a few days after that, she found a curt note stuffed in her mailbox and mixed in with the rest of her mail. The three words had made her blood run cold.

I'm watching you.

She'd gotten Marvin the next day, but when more than a week went by with no further creepiness, she thought maybe the person had grown tired of harassing her. But then another note had arrived in the mailbox just yesterday that said, *Nice dog. Protection?* A graffitied front door and hand-written, postage-free threats in her mailbox were just a little too up close and personal, and Erin was losing sleep. This guy knew where she lived and appeared to be watching her.

She had to do something. Calling the police was the obvious course of action, but what could they do? She didn't have the first note any longer—in a moment of stupidity she'd thrown it away—and she'd already paid someone to repaint the door. And nothing had really happened.

Yet.

Nothing had happened yet, but something *could* happen if she didn't come up with a plan. During the day, she was mostly okay, but alone at night and in the wee hours of the morning, Erin was afraid.

"I'm really glad you texted this morning," Sarah said from her paddleboard a few feet away. She addressed Erin upside down from her downward dog position. "I've been wanting you to try this. I think it will really center you."

"Oh, I feel centered alright," Erin grunted. She held her pose, but she knew it was precarious and at any moment, she'd be in the drink. "Sorry about Marvin. It's not very relaxing with him carrying on like that."

"He's fine. I've tuned him out."

Erin hadn't. And with each bark, she felt her blood pressure climb. She watched her upside-down dog strain at his tie-out in the middle of Sarah's yard. "Marvin! No bark!"

"Do you think that'll hold him?" Sarah asked doubtfully.

"I bought the biggest, strongest one they had at the pet store, so it better."

"Will he run away if he breaks free?"

"He's not going—"

In perfect comedic timing, Marvin did just that. His collar must have snapped open, releasing him, and he ran around the yard in gigantic circles at top speed.

"Sugar-Honey-Iced-Tea," Erin muttered. She broke her pose and grabbed her paddle. "Be right back."

"Look at him go!" Sarah marveled behind her. "That dog's crazy as all get out. What's he doin'?"

Erin didn't trust herself to keep her balance if she turned around, but she tipped her head back to answer. "When he does this, I call it *the crazies*."

"He has the crazies alright," Sarah agreed. "Do you need help?"

"No. Stay here. I'll be right back."

Erin made it to shore in seconds and pulled her board up on the beach. After quickly unfastening her ankle lanyard and laying her paddle down, she made her way up to the grass.

"Marvin!" she shouted, maneuvering around the wall construction site.

Marvin halted mid stride and turned at the sound of her voice. Tongue hanging out, he bounded towards her happily.

Erin crouched down and gave the loose skin on his head a small pat. "What're you doing, dummy?" He gave her face a single lick in answer, coating her in slime. "Blech!"

She still wasn't used to the persistent and copious amounts of drool that clung to his jowls. Marvin's salivary glands produced spit at such a fast rate, it was a wonder he didn't dry out completely. She wiped the wet goo off her cheek. "You're so gross, but I love you too. Now, come on. Let's get your collar back on."

She stood and moved towards the tie-out laying in the grass, but Marvin had other plans. He took off like a dart towards the sound of a slamming screen door through the trees. In a flash, he was gone.

"Marvin, no! Come!" Erin yelled as she took off after him. "Sit! Stay!" She'd reached the limits of his knowledge in under three seconds. He didn't seem so smart to her now as he had yesterday in the front yard.

Whether truly dumb or simply choosing to play deaf, Marvin raced through the woods. She'd never catch him in her bare feet and bathing suit, but she ran anyway, and in her haste, she whacked herself in the face with a rebounding tree branch she'd tried to clear out of the way. It was at that moment, with the sting of a forming welt below her left eye, that she heard a man shout out in alarm.

Marvin responded with a series of playful barks. At least, to Erin they sounded playful. To the large man, who Erin could see through the trees was winding up to kick her sweet, stupid Marvin, they must not have sounded so harmless.

"Stop!" she yelled, coming into the clearing.

The man froze mid kick as Marvin danced around him.

"What's the matter with you? He's just a puppy!"

Marvin couldn't have looked happier to see her than if she'd been out of sight for days instead of a few seconds. He ran to her and rubbed himself along her bare, wet legs before lying directly on top of her feet with a loud grunt.

"A puppy?" The man pointed at Marvin as he closed the distance between them. "This dog is a menace! He tried to attack me!"

"He's only five months old! You were about to kick a *baby*, you asshole!"

He shot her an incinerating glare. "Lady, I don't care how old he is! He's a hundred pound animal who charged me!"

"He's an eighty-pound puppy who wanted to play! He doesn't know how big he is!" Marvin gave a cheerful bark and thumped his whip of a tail off the ground before he jumped up. Erin grabbed at his scruff and told him to sit. He obeyed promptly, and she praised him.

The man, not nearly so impressed with Marvin's obedience as Erin was, took a giant step back. His eyes still showed a trace of fear, but his lips curled into a sneer. "Get that dog off my property and keep him off."

What a jerk! This wasn't even his property. He was a renter. "My friend, Sarah—"

Sarah chose that moment to crash through the trees and into the yard. Marvin broke free of Erin's loose hold and trotted over to her with his tongue hanging out. Sarah gave his head a small pat without breaking stride, and she was grinning when she reached Erin's side. "Well, now. I see y'all have met. Erin, this is Ethan. Ethan, this is my friend, Erin."

Ethan, the impossibly handsome stranger she now loathed, scowled at her. Erin scowled back.

Sarah looked back and forth between them and put a hand on one hip. "Alright now, quit bein' ugly, both of you." To Ethan, she said, "I'm sorry if Marvin scared you. He's a puppy in training, and he broke free from the tie-out in the yard."

Ethan turned a light shade of pink and shook his head in denial. "He didn't scare me."

Erin crossed her arms and scoffed.

Throwing her a murderous look, he repeated, "He didn't!"

"You were about to kick him when I got here. Do you normally kick dogs you aren't scared of? Just for giggles and grins, maybe?"

Ethan's cheeks went from pink to red, but this time from anger, not embarrassment. "If you think you can just come over here and—"

Sarah broke in. "Alright. I can see you both have your backs up. Let's just take a break." She put her hand on Erin's arm and tugged her gently. "Erin and I will take Marvin back," she said to Ethan. "And again, I'm very sorry. We both are. It won't happen again."

Ethan ran a hand through his thick hair and held it there on the back of his neck. He thanked Sarah before resting his dark eyes on Erin. "Look . . . I'm sorry if we got off on the wrong foot."

Erin raised her eyebrows incredulously. "*If?*"

His face hardened. "Whatever."

"And which foot?" Erin couldn't help but add. "The one you kick with?" She had the pleasure of seeing his nostrils flare before she turned on her heel and gave Marvin's rump a small pat. She loved having the last word. "Let's go, boy."

Marvin didn't need to be told twice, and he ran ahead through the trees back towards Sarah's place. Sarah hung back, probably to apologize some more, the traitor.

When Sarah emerged through the trees several minutes later, Erin already had the dog secure and happily chewing a bone she'd brought for him. Erin sat on a patio chair, legs crossed, with one foot bouncing out an angry rhythm as she waited.

Sarah walked towards her with a purposeful stride. While her gaze was direct and unwavering, Erin thought she could detect a glint of amusement in her eyes. "Wall's looking good." Erin pointed her thumb to her friend's incomplete retaining wall.

The corners of Sarah's mouth lifted when she answered, "Yeah, it's coming along."

Erin nodded towards the small cabin. "And nice neighbor you've got there."

Sarah shot her a rueful grin. "He *is* really nice, as it happens."

Erin snorted.

"He's a financial something-or-other from Flint who came up here for a little getaway and some peace and quiet."

"Ah, he's from *Flint*. Well, that explains it."

Sarah rolled her eyes and ignored the cheap shot. "Can you blame him for bein' a little startled by Marvin? He is a big dog."

"*Startled* is one thing. Kicking my puppy is another."

Sarah gave her a stern look, and Erin got the sense it was the same one she used on misbehaving students. "Erin, did he actually kick Marvin?"

Erin stayed stubbornly silent, but her foot bounced more rapidly.

Sarah answered her own question. "He didn't kick him, so it doesn't amount to a hill of beans now, does it? Next time you see him, I hope you'll be gracious."

Erin shook her head, smiling in spite of herself. A hill of beans must not be worth much in Alabama. But her smile caught when she digested Sarah's words, and her foot stilled. "Wait, how long is he staying?"

Sarah shrugged. "All summer, I think."

Well, didn't that just suck! Erin hadn't broached the subject with Sarah yet, but she'd decided on a plan that morning, and she'd been about to bring it up just before Marvin got loose. That jerk next door was going to ruin everything because now, after this little fiasco with the dog, Sarah might just say no.

Erin took a deep breath. The only way to know for sure was to ask, and now was as good a time as any. She was a "rip off the bandaid" kind of girl anyway and always had been.

"Listen. I have to ask you for a really big favor."

Sarah slanted her head. "A favor?"

"Yeah, a really big one. Um . . . so, I'm having some work done on my house, and I wondered if I might stay with you for a little while."

Sarah's eyes grew wide. "Oh!"

"And now I'm afraid you might say no because I hate your neighbor's guts, and I'm pretty sure he hates mine. Plus, I do have Marvin."

Sarah hesitated. "Oh, Erin. I'm—"

"Sarah, *please* don't say no!" Erin blurted in a voice so pleadingly pathetic, she'd grimace every time she remembered this moment for the whole of the summer. But the panic she felt must have shown through because Sarah's face softened as she crouched down to Erin's level.

"You really need this?" she asked gently.

Erin felt her eyes sting with tears she would never let fall. She nodded.

"Because you're . . . having work done on your house?" Sarah lifted her eyebrows dubiously.

"Uh-huh," Erin answered without hesitation, but she wouldn't meet Sarah's eyes. Instead, she rubbed at the welt the branch had left and stared into the distance while she waited for Sarah to give an answer. She couldn't stand lying to people, especially to Sarah, who was so darn *good* she made everyone around her look like ugly, wretched sinners.

The perfect southern belle nodded. "Alright, then."

She didn't ask when Erin would be moving in, and she didn't ask how long she'd be staying. And she definitely didn't ask why.

Erin loved her for it.

Chapter 10

"**H**ere? She's moving in here?" Benny held the mallet in hand and stared at Sarah in surprise. "Why?" It was the Fourth of July, and Benny was wearing yet another pair of swim trunks. These were patterned after the American flag.

"She's having some work done on her house," Sarah answered, setting the level down on the brick Benny had just pounded down.

Benny studied the level with narrowed eyes. "What work?"

"She didn't say."

He lifted the level and handed it back to Sarah before grabbing another brick. "Erin's house is pristine. What work could she possibly be having done?"

"I don't know. I didn't ask."

Benny paused with the brick in hand and gave her a knowing look. "You don't believe her, do you." It wasn't a question.

Sarah sighed. "I don't know."

"But you're letting her stay anyway?"

"She needs to be here right now. Does it matter why?"

They held each other's gaze a little too long, and she looked away almost at the same time he did. This was happening more and more between them. Their friendship was growing, shifting. But into what, exactly?

He placed the brick, and they repeated the process all over again. At this point, Sarah had the steps down so perfectly, she could probably assist Benny in her sleep. They'd been at it about a week, and they'd developed a comfortable rhythm, and not just with the work, but with one another too. Conversation flowed easily between them now, and Sarah had begun to notice and appreciate his unique mannerisms and little idiosyncrasies. For instance, when they weren't talking, often he would whistle, and so far every tune he'd whistled had been a country song, except for yesterday's "Don't Worry be Happy." Today it was John Denver.

Normally, she found whistling a little irritating, mostly because she could barely whistle herself, but when Benny did it, it made her smile. It meant he was happy, and that made *her* happy. When they took their breaks and sat down to a snack on the patio, he'd sometimes twirl his hair absentmindedly while she talked, which Sarah found so endearing she had a hard time maintaining her focus. And then there were his swim trunks. The man had more of those than Erin had shoes, and that was saying something.

These were just a few of the things she'd come to notice and love about him, and each day she found herself looking forward to the mundane task of stacking bricks just so she could spend time with him. Honestly, she hadn't expected to see him at all today. It was the Fourth of July, and there were parades and barbecues to go to. But here he was, and here she was, and she had the sense that it was where both of them most wanted to be.

After several minutes of working together in silence, he stopped and eyed up the wall. It was really coming along. Sarah figured they were about halfway done. They'd been putting in about four hours of work each day, starting at eight o'clock and ending at around noon to avoid the hot afternoon sun. At this rate, it would be finished by the end of next week, and then Benny wouldn't need to come out anymore. The thought sent a wave of disappointment rolling through her, which was telling. It was time to start being honest with herself.

It had been a long while, but Sarah knew the signs. Lately, Benny would just randomly appear in her thoughts, and when her phone rang and his name popped up on her screen, her stomach did a weird little dip. As if that weren't bad enough, every time he looked at her, even if it was just to ask for the mallet, she experienced a body-wide reaction: a flash of heat, another flip of the stomach . . .

Without lifting his eyes, Benny said, "You're a good friend to her."

She stared at him blankly. What had they been talking about?

"To Erin," he clarified.

Right, Erin. "Well, she's the best friend I've ever had, so . . ."

Benny looked up. "Really?"

She laughed. "Why the surprise?"

He shrugged. "You guys are so different."

"Yeah, but it works. We're real with each other. Like sisters."

"May I?" He held his hand out for the level, which she handed over, careful not to let their fingers touch.

Flip.

"I ran into her the other day at school," he said casually.

Sarah watched the bubble of the level rest at center. With Benny in charge, this wall would be perfect. "Oh, yeah? She didn't say anything."

"Why would she?"

He was right. Benny meant nothing to Erin anymore. He was just a coworker. "How was it?" she asked. "How did it feel?" She held her breath as she waited for his answer.

"Fine. It was fine. Felt like it always used to."

She kept her voice casual. "Does that mean you're over it?" *And her?*

"Yeah, I think so." He seemed distracted as he counted their remaining bricks.

It wasn't exactly the answer she'd wanted to hear, but it was close. Sarah pressed further. She couldn't help herself. "But if she were interested, would you be interested?"

He was still counting, but he paused briefly to answer her. "I don't know."

"Oh." That was most definitely *not* the answer she wanted.

He stopped and shot her an inscrutable look. "Why?"

"No reason." She grabbed the level off the wall and set it down with the rest of their supplies.

His brows drew together. "You okay?"

"Mm-hmm." She busied herself with organizing the rest of the tools sitting on the finished part of the wall to her left.

"You sure? You're acting weird."

A surprised giggle escaped. She couldn't help it. Benny was the kind of guy a girl needed to be very careful with. Through their time together, she'd discovered he was honest to a fault. If the truth was, "Yeah, your butt does look a little big in those jeans," then that's what he'd say.

The sound of breaking twigs drew her attention, and she turned her head in time to see Ethan emerge from the trees. He was limping heavily. "Hi!" she called out.

"Remind me not to wear flip-flops when I come over next time," he hollered back. "I just stabbed myself in the foot with a stick."

"Oh, no!" Sarah abandoned the tools and moved towards him. "Can I do anything? Get you a bandaid?"

He looked sheepish. "Thanks, that'd be great."

"Oh, look at you! You're really bleeding." Blood dripped from his big toe. He must have jabbed it but good. "Let me grab the first aid kit from inside." She was already rushing towards the house before she finished talking, but remembering her manners, she called over her shoulder. "Benny, this is my neighbor, Ethan Rockford. Ethan, this is Brian Benninger."

Leaving the men to get to know one another, Sarah grabbed the first aid kit out of the bathroom cabinet and was back outside in a jiffy. It wasn't until she'd gotten Ethan all fixed up that she realized Benny was a little stiff and quiet. Remembering how awkward he'd been with her at first, she sought to ease his discomfort.

"Benny, Ethan works in finance. He's from downstate, but he's up here on a working vacation for the summer. Ethan, Benny teaches science and coaches hockey at our high school. He's kind of a jack of all trades, so he's helping me with this retaining wall."

"Yeah, he was telling me you guys work together. It's good to meet you, man," Ethan said affably.

Benny, looking at the retaining wall, mumbled, "You too."

The two men were actually quite similar in appearance. Ethan was taller. He probably had Benny in the looks department also, but not by much. They were both dark haired and brown eyed and even had the same olive complexion. They looked like a pair of Italian brothers.

If Ethan found Benny to be rude, he didn't show it, and he turned to Sarah with a smile. "I decided to take today off work since it's the holiday, and I thought maybe we could have some lunch, but"—he glanced at Benny—"it looks like you're busy."

Sarah caught Benny's scowl before she glanced down at her watch. "Oh, wow! It's almost one already."

Benny shrugged.

Boy, was he moody! She made her voice extra chipper when she said, "I'll go prepare us something to drink and make up some sandwiches. Does that sound okay to y'all?"

"That sounds great. Thanks!" Ethan said easily.

Benny grabbed another brick from the pile and placed it on the wall. "Sure."

Ethan looked at Sarah and raised his eyebrows as if to say, "What's with this guy?" Sarah pretended not to notice and motioned for him to follow her up to the house. He'd popped by the day before, later in the afternoon, but he hadn't come inside, and he whistled when he stepped across the threshold of the slider door. "This place is beautiful."

"Thanks. I really like it."

"I can see why." He looked around the open floor plan and nodded with approval. Then he turned and looked out the window towards the lake. "We don't have views quite like this in Flint." He laughed.

"I've never been there."

He lifted his shoulders. "You're not missing anything."

Sarah got to work behind the island counter to prepare lunch, first grabbing the cutting board and utensils. "So what exactly do you do in finance?"

"I'm an analyst."

"What does that mean, like, on a daily basis? What does it look like?"

"On a daily basis? Well, I research potential investments and make recommendations for my company, and I keep tabs on our financial position, maintain our budget, that kind of thing."

"What's the name of your company?" She took bread out of the refrigerator and set it on the counter before turning back and grabbing the mayo and mustard out of the side door. Ethan still hadn't answered, so she popped her head out and repeated her question.

"It's a small company. I'm sure you haven't heard of it." He didn't quite meet her eyes.

"Oh." He didn't want to give her the name of his company? Why? "What does your company do?"

"We're . . . in real estate."

"Oh," she said again. Just like her father, although her father's company was huge. Ethan's company in Flint probably didn't come close in size or in prestige. "Well, I'm sure it's interesting work."

He grinned at that. "For nerds like me, it is."

She laughed, relieved that whatever it was that had made him uncomfortable a second ago had passed. "You know, my mind doesn't hold on to numbers for some reason. I had a really hard time in my math classes back in high school. College too," she added, trying not to cringe. She did her best not to talk about college, so why she'd mentioned it, she wasn't sure. "I used to stay behind almost every day in tenth grade to get help with algebra two."

"Did you pass?"

"I got an A, but that's only because I had a teacher who took the time to help me. She's actually the reason I became a teacher."

"Nice."

"Yeah, she was the best. You know, I remember weird words, like *tergiversate*, but I couldn't tell you what's in my bank account, even though I just checked it yesterday, or what my monthly cell phone bill is."

Ethan grew more alert. "You can keep a binder with all that information in it. That might help," he suggested.

"I have it all in a folder, so I can reference it when I need to. It's not as organized as it could be, though." Now that there was more money at stake, Sarah should take the time to really go through everything. She needed to get a good grip on her finances, but to say it felt overwhelming was as big an understatement as calling a tornado a wind storm. But it had to be done, and if she was going to manage Nadia's trust for the next few years, she owed it to her sister to be a whole lot more organized than she'd been so far.

She couldn't be a *complete* numbers moron. She could learn. Whether she could do it without yanking out her hair in the process, well, that was a different question.

Her thoughts, as usual, must have registered on her face because Ethan said, "You know, I could help you if you want."

His tone was casual, but his eyes stared into hers with an intensity that caught her off guard. Was he hitting on her? She didn't think so, but why else would he be looking at her like that?

She waved a hand. "I couldn't ask you to do that. You're on vacation. Sort of. The last thing you want is to do extra work while you're here."

His eyes crinkled at the corners, and whatever tension they'd held disappeared. "Hey, like I said, we nerds love this kind of thing. Analyzing finances and making recommendations is fun for me. It's like doing a puzzle."

"Oh my goodness, I *hate* puzzles!"

He gave her a quizzical look and laughed. "I love 'em. I guess you and I are real opposites. English brain, math brain. What was that word you said earlier?"

"Tergiversate?"

He shook his head and grinned. "I'll never remember that. What's it mean?"

"It's a verb. It's the act of changing your mind or opinions all the time. Flip-flopping."

"See, I'd just say that instead. Flip-flopping. It's a whole lot easier."

Picking up the knife, Sarah grinned. "But a lot less fun."

She'd begun slicing the cheese when Ethan asked, "And what the heck is a verb?"

Sarah looked up from the cutting board with wide eyes.

"Just kidding," Ethan joked, and then he surprised her by singing, "Verb, that's what's happening!"

Sarah laughed loudly. "Oh my lands! You know Schoolhouse Rock?"

"Yeah, I remember the songs, but I can't say English was ever my strong suit in school. Numbers, though, those are a different story. Seriously, Sarah. I can help you. Just say the word."

"Thanks, I'll think about it." And she really would. She needed help, but the thing that had kept her from getting any was not really knowing where to start or who to start with. *With whom to start*, she silently corrected and then performed a mental eye roll. She was such a geek! "Could you grab the pitcher of lemonade out of the fridge for me?" she asked Ethan, bobbing her head towards the fridge behind her.

"Sure," Ethan pushed off from the counter and made his way to the refrigerator with only a small limp.

He'd just pulled it open by the handle when the front door flew open and Erin appeared like a whirlwind. Her hair was gently tousled, and her cheeks were flushed pink. She looked like summertime come to life with her blond highlights and sun-kissed skin. Her white tank top and jean short cut-offs showed off her golden tan beautifully, and Ethan stood, hand on the handle of the open refrigerator, transfixed. Sarah could understand why.

Erin was the kind of woman who did that to men without even trying. She was petite, pretty, and vivacious. In contrast, Sarah was average everything—average height, average looks, average personality. As much as she tried not to, sometimes when she stood next to Erin, she felt like a real dog.

Dropping her bag near the door and setting her keys on the small table in the entryway, Erin announced, "So, I guess this is where all the men are. You've got 'em wrapped around your little finger, by all appearances." She laughed. "I just saw Benny out front, slaving away for you in the hot sun, and you have your neighbor here working for you in the kitchen. And on a holiday too. You'll have to tell me what your secret is." She sauntered into the kitchen with a saucy grin.

Mastering the art of sauntering. That was next on Sarah's list. She kept her voice light when she joked, "You know Benny would build you an entire house from the ground up if you only asked, so don't go askin' me what my secret is. Plus, I'm payin' him."

Erin pulled out a counter stool and hopped up onto it. "I'm sure you are," she replied with a sly smile.

Ethan snorted.

Her friend turned her attention to Ethan, who appeared to be functioning again. He'd just set the pitcher down on the counter next to Sarah when Erin addressed him. "So, disgruntled neighbor, we meet again."

"No ill-mannered dog with you today?" he shot back.

"No, he's outside with Benny. Marvin took to him right away. Good instincts, that dog."

Ethan scowled but wisely remained silent. Sarah wondered why Erin felt the need to antagonize her neighbor. It was as if she were out looking for a fight. "We're about to have some lunch. Can I make you a sandwich?"

Erin smiled brightly. In her mind no doubt, she'd bested Ethan on this occasion. "Sure, but I can't sit too long. I need to unpack. I had no idea Marvin and I would come with so much stuff. You should see my car right now. Boxes up to the roof."

"Wait," Ethan said slowly. "You're moving in here?"

"Just for a little while," Sarah said quickly.

Erin shot her a look that, roughly translated, said, *Thanks a million, traitor.*

"You *and* the dog?" Ethan clarified.

"Yep," Erin sang out happily as she hopped off the counter stool and headed to the bathroom to wash up. "We're going to have so much *fun*!"

Ethan watched Erin's retreating form before turning to Sarah with raised eyebrows.

She took a deep breath and released it. "I hope this is okay, Ethan. I know you don't like Erin's dog."

"I don't much like Erin, either." At Sarah's worried expression, he hurried to say, "That was a joke. It'll be fine. I actually like dogs. I just don't like untrained dogs the size of gorillas."

Sarah giggled. "She *is* doing a good job with Marvin. He's learned a ton in a short time, but she's still thinkin' about enrolling him in puppy school."

"Oh, good. Maybe there's a manners school Erin could get enrolled in."

Sarah grinned. She couldn't help it. "Wishful thinking, I'm afraid."

Ethan grinned back.

"But I have to tell you something, Ethan. She has some prickles, but Erin's just about as loyal as they come. If you give her a chance, you'll see that."

He looked doubtful, but he answered, "I'm sure you're right."

Lunch was painful. Benny would have preferred to continue to work on the wall. He didn't like Ethan—the guy was definitely his competition—and he wasn't all the way back to feeling comfortable with Erin yet. But one look at Sarah's face when he'd tried to decline lunch was all it took to get his feet moving toward the patio table and the two people he'd really rather avoid. Once he was seated, Sarah hovered and fussed over him until Erin told her to sit down and stop being so "southern," which was disappointing because he was kind of enjoying all the attention.

"So, Ethan, do you have a family?" Erin asked in a voice that, to Benny, seemed a little too sweet.

"Yes Erin, I have a family. Do *you* have a family?" He spoke with exaggerated slowness.

Benny took a bite out of his sandwich and chewed. Maybe this lunch wouldn't be so bad after all. He was already entertained.

Sarah rolled her eyes. "She's trying to ask you if you're married."

Erin shot Sarah a murderous look.

Raising his eyebrows briefly, Ethan answered, "I'm not married."

Erin shrugged as she tore a piece of bread off the corner of her sandwich. "I'm not all that surprised."

"You *would* say something like that," Ethan fumed.

Sarah flashed an overbright smile. "Ethan, could you please pass the lemonade?"

Ethan ignored her. He looked pointedly at Erin. "I knew *you* weren't married the moment I met you."

"And how would you know that?" Erin challenged.

He lifted his shoulders in a careless shrug. "Sometimes you can just tell that about a woman."

Benny came out of his seat to pass Sarah the lemonade her already-full glass told him she didn't really need and sat back in his chair to enjoy the fireworks. Erin was moody—he'd learned that the hard way—and she wouldn't stand for any insults. She could dish it, but she couldn't take it at all. Man, he'd really dodged a bullet there. Why he'd ever thought she would be good girlfriend material, he had no idea.

Actually, that wasn't true. He knew why. He'd been lonely, she'd been cute, and—at least for a short time—she'd been interested. He'd jumped at the chance. It's not like women were lining up to date him.

He looked at Sarah. She was keeping her hands busy. He'd noticed this about her. If she got nervous or uncomfortable, she moved things around. At first glance, it might look like she was just doing some organizing, like with the tools earlier, but all she really did was move objects here and there. Sometimes they wound up exactly where they'd started.

She was adorable. He liked everything about her. He just wished he knew what she was thinking. He wasn't quite sure if he was being a clueless idiot, which he now knew was very possible, or if she was the one sending mixed signals.

"What, I don't look like I could be married?" Erin blustered, playing right into the new neighbor's hands. "I'll have you know I *was* married once."

"Did he slit his wrists?"

Okay, that was too far, and Benny leaned forward in his chair, ready to help if Erin needed him to.

She chewed her lip. She'd painted herself into a corner, and now she was going to have to talk about Seth. She hadn't told Benny a lot about her first husband, but he knew enough to know the wound was deep.

Benny hesitated. His first instinct was to come to her defense, but with Erin he could never predict what would annoy her, and for now, she was holding her own. He'd give her a minute, but he'd remain on the edge of his seat, ready to pounce.

"We divorced!" she snapped.

Ethan smirked. "*Aw.* I'm so *sorry.*" The words were right, but they were laced with such deep sarcasm that even Benny picked up on it. He saw Erin flinch.

For a few seconds, nobody spoke. Sarah's wide gaze flitted around the table while Erin's rested on her plate.

"Don't be a jerk, buddy," Benny said quietly but firmly. He stared Ethan down, and the other man fidgeted under the intensity of his gaze. Good. Let him be uncomfortable.

Despite his unease, Ethan looked armed with a comeback. He opened his mouth to speak but closed it again, thinking better of it. He lifted a hand. "You're right." He looked at Erin. "My apologies."

Erin studied his face, maybe looking for any leftover sarcasm. She must not have seen any because Benny watched the fight leave her as she sagged back into her chair. It wasn't in her nature to let things slide completely, however, and she said, "You don't know anything about me."

Ethan nodded. "You're right, I don't. I'm sorry. Truly."

"But you will soon enough," Sarah chirped. "With Erin living out here for the summer, there will be plenty of opportunity for y'all to get to know each other."

God bless her, the woman was trying to pretend these two might actually become neighborly. She looked at Benny like she wanted him to say something to back her up. He thought fast, but not fast enough, and she moved on to address Ethan. "Maybe y'all could go paddleboarding sometime."

Ethan forced a smile. Erin's scowl deepened.

Sarah prattled on about the paddle she'd gone on the day before, and how she wanted to take the boards out on the big lake sometime over the summer. She was trying to talk enough to make up for the quiet, Benny realized. He wouldn't have thought it was possible, but she worked some kind of magic over that patio table, and soon tensions eased enough to allow them to resume their lunch. Ethan was the first to engage, discussing his own plans to explore the area. Benny chimed in a time or two, giving his two cents about what Ethan should check out, and even Erin was coaxed out of her mood to add to the conversation a few times.

When the topic reverted back to Erin's move out to the basin, Benny turned to her and spoke to her directly for the first time. It might not be the right moment, but he wanted to know. "So, why are you moving out here?"

Erin didn't meet his gaze, but she answered. "I'm having some work done on my house."

He should have let it go, especially since he was still feeling sorry for her. But he was pretty sure she was lying, and Benny had a *thing* about lying. He hated it. "Really?" he challenged.

"Yes," Erin answered slowly, making brief eye contact. "Really."

Sarah shot Benny a warning look, but he ignored her.

"What kind of work?" he pressed.

Erin shifted her gaze to study her nails. "Um, electrical work."

"Electrical? Why, what happened?"

"Uh, well, I had an inspection, and things aren't up to . . . uh . . . code."

Now it was clear. Erin *was* lying, and they all knew it. Still, Benny pressed on.

"Didn't you tell me you just moved into that house a few years ago?"

"I don't know."

"That's what you said."

She set down her glass. "Fine. I moved in a few years ago. Who cares?"

"I'm sure it passed inspection then."

Erin released an exasperated breath. "I don't know, Benny. I wasn't there. All I know is they inspected it and told me I had to have it fixed." She pushed back her chair and stood. "Okay? Any more questions? Anyone?"

"You don't have to get all defensive. He was just making conversation." This came from Ethan. Benny shook his head. This guy must have an even lower social IQ than he did.

Erin's eyes flashed, and she pointed a finger at Ethan. "I know *exactly* what he was doing. Okay? I'm not an idiot. Now, if you'll excuse me, I need to finish unpacking." She called to Marvin, who was lying asleep under the large white pine to the left of the dock. He didn't budge, and Erin let out a loud, agitated sigh.

"He's fine," Sarah soothed. "I'll keep an eye on him. You go on."

Erin bit down on her lip, and for a brief second, Benny wondered if she might cry. But he was mistaken because when Erin spoke again, her voice sounded like it always did. "I don't know how he can be so tired. He snored like a freight train all night. I'm the one who should be napping." She turned and went inside the house before anyone could respond.

Benny had noticed the bags under Erin's eyes. Whatever was going on with her was robbing her of her sleep, and he didn't think it was a snoring dog. Now that she was out here, she'd be okay. Regardless of why she was here, being near Sarah would help. It worked for him, at least.

He hadn't felt this happy in a long time, which was saying something considering he'd spent the last week waking up early to do hard labor in the hot sun. But he'd build a hundred walls if it meant he could be close to Sarah. She made everything better. Take now, for example. Normally, confrontations made him so uncomfortable he wanted to sink into the ground, but he wasn't even fazed at the moment.

Nobody spoke for at least a minute. Finally, Sarah said, "Gentlemen, that was . . . unfortunate."

Wait, was she lumping him in with the jerk neighbor?

Ethan ran a hand through his hair. "You're right. I'm sorry, Sarah. I'll apologize to Erin next time I see her. I was an ass."

Sarah nodded. "You absolutely were." She turned to Benny. "And you shouldn't have pushed her."

"But she's lying," he said stubbornly.

"Benny, I've known that from the very beginning."

Her words were gentle, but he was definitely being admonished, and he began to feel a little sheepish.

Sarah shrugged. "She has a reason, and whatever it is, she's losin' sleep over it."

"But is there ever a good reason to lie?"

Ethan shifted in his seat and looked at the ground. Benny thought he was probably well-versed in lying. He was a businessman. It also seemed he might have a thing for Sarah, and why wouldn't he? She was beautiful and good and kind, and Benny wanted this guy to stay far away from her. Businessmen knew how to close a deal, and if he wasn't careful, Ethan would scoop Sarah up in no time at all, and right from under his nose. Maybe he should slow down his work on the wall so he could spend more time out here. Maybe he should make his move sooner rather than later. He didn't want to miss his chance with her, but he was still trying to get a read on what her feelings might be.

"I don't know," Sarah said in response to his question, "but I hope you'll let this go. She needs to be here right now, Benny. And that's all we need to know."

Chapter 11

E than focused on putting one foot in front of the other as he ran the final mile of the five-mile loop he'd mapped out for himself even before he'd made the trip up to Nicolet. Running was his therapy. Normally, it was really good therapy, but he was back on Steele Basin Drive and didn't feel any better about himself now than he had when he'd first started out.

When had he sunk so low? When had that happened? In high school, he'd been voted *best looking* and *best personality*. Obviously, he'd gone downhill from there. Winning a contest because of his looks had embarrassed him, but he'd been proud of being voted best personality. He was a nice guy, dammit! At least he used to be.

Now he was the guy who made women feel small for being divorced and helped dead-beat dads cheat their daughters out of dividends that were rightfully theirs. He was a puppy-hating sleazeball. Nobody would vote that guy best personality. No, that guy sucked.

Right, left, right, left . . . His feet pounded out the familiar rhythm while he continued beating himself up.

With respect to Erin, all he could say was from the very beginning, from the first moment he met her, she'd brought out the worst in him, and he resented it. He was already feeling like a dirtbag because of what he was there to do, and then she stormed into his yard and accused him of being some kind of animal abuser. How was he supposed to know that the enormous dog was just a playful puppy? It was true he didn't have a lot of experience with dogs—his family had never been able to afford one—but he could have sworn Marvin wanted to eat him for lunch. He'd felt like an idiot, and she'd made it ten times worse.

He wiped sweat from his eyes as he slowed to a walk. He wanted a do-over with her, but it was way too late for that. He was pretty sure he'd insulted her far beyond anything recoverable, and he still wasn't sure what had gotten into him. He wasn't *that* guy, but she pushed his buttons in a way he wasn't really used to.

What was he going to do? He wanted that position. He was born to be the CFO of Jostens Holdings. Despite Bruce Jostens being a shady character in his personal life, professionally he'd always been above reproach.

Until now.

But Ethan's future was bright, and by extension, his family's future was bright. He was so close to the type of success he'd always dreamed of. All he had to do was find out if Sarah understood Bruce's fiduciary duty to both her and Nadia.

That was it. Ethan stopped to stretch and think.

Bruce hadn't asked him to do anything more than a little digging. He hadn't even told him why he wanted to know, but Ethan wasn't dumb, and Bruce must have known Ethan would be able to connect the dots. It's why he'd asked that this be kept between the two of them. He'd also made very casual mention that they were seriously considering Ethan for the promotion to treasurer. They weren't ready to announce anything yet, but they were close.

For Ethan, the expectations were clear. If he delivered on this, it was in the bag. The position would be his, and it would come with a hefty raise and the promise of CFO in the future. It was all he'd ever wanted.

Every day since that conversation with Bruce, Ethan worked to rationalize what he was doing so he could finally rid himself of the sinking feeling he carried around in the pit of his stomach. It wasn't like *he* was the one withholding anything from Sarah. That was on Bruce. But Ethan knew about it, and he was helping, so didn't that make him just as guilty?

At least Sarah wasn't lacking for anything. He felt good about that. She was living the dream life in a place so beautiful, Ethan was sorry he couldn't live here himself. She was doing just fine . . . more than fine. She had far more money than he'd ever have—probably more than she could ever spend. And wasn't there an expression that what you didn't know couldn't hurt you?

If Sarah didn't understand that she had dividends coming to her, and it didn't appear that she did, she wouldn't miss those payouts. That meant Bruce could hang on to that money and reinvest it in the company, squeezing her and her sister out in the process. Or he could dilute the shares. With enough time, he could get rid of them that way. If they didn't have a basic understanding of what it meant to be a shareholder, and why would they, they wouldn't know about their right to review corporate records, and Bruce could easily do either of those things. They would be none the wiser until it was too late.

Ethan knew that Bruce had to finesse this just right, or it could blow up in his face. If Sarah understood how much power she had at the moment and how badly her father wanted to prevent her from participating in the management of the company—something her shares definitely entitled her to do—she could sell them back at an exorbitant price. Either he'd end up shelling out a fortune for them, or he'd end up risking his stake in his own company to two daughters he refused to acknowledge. But if he played his cards right, he could delete them from his company, and from his life, forever.

Ethan still wondered why he'd been chosen for this unsavory job. Why hadn't Bruce asked someone else? Someone more senior? Sure, Ethan had as firm a grasp as anyone on the company's financials, but that wasn't really necessary for this type of fishing expedition. He thought it had more to do with the fact that he was single than anything else. Being that he had no family to tie him down, he was probably the only one who could take off to the North Woods for the whole of summer. And then there was Bruce's completely mistaken impression that Ethan was some kind of ladies' man. Where he got that idea, Ethan didn't know. As if he had time to date!

A deep, loud bark broke into his thoughts, and Ethan turned in the direction of the noise. Behind him, Marvin strained at his lead while the diminutive Erin worked hard to hold him back. At one point, she literally dug her heels in, but Marvin continued to pull her as easily as if she wore rollerskates.

"Marvin, heel!" she yelled.

Marvin paid her no heed, and he dragged her along behind him until he reached Ethan. The dog's tail was going a mile a minute, and his tongue lolled happily. Ethan reached down to stroke his shiny coat. Marvin looked even bigger than he had a few days ago, Ethan was certain of it, and all that loose skin and those four enormous paws signaled that he was far from being full grown. Erin didn't have a prayer in the world of ever being able to out-muscle him.

"I tried, sorry." Erin was speaking to him, but she was looking off somewhere behind him, refusing to make eye contact.

"It's fine," he reassured.

"No, we promised to keep him away from you, and I didn't." Her voice was hard.

He moved his head to catch her eye before responding. "Erin, it's fine. You might not believe it, but I actually do like dogs. I like Marvin, now that I know he's not going to devour me." Ethan smiled, but he wasn't sure it came off quite right because Erin stared at him with a scowl.

He needed to fix this. He'd probably never like this woman, but he needed to be able to bump into her without sparks flying—not the exciting variety, although he got the sense those could have flown too if they hadn't gotten off to such a rotten start.

"Listen," he said, "I really do like your dog. Please don't worry about him on my account. And I need to apologize to you. I've been a little . . ."

"Jerky?" she supplied.

Ethan pursed his lips. He would not react. "Sure. *Jerky.*"

"Alright," she said. With her nose in the air, she moved to pass him, but Marvin wouldn't budge and she ran out of leash length.

Ethan tried not to smile. The dog had ruined the effect. She'd intended to breeze past him, all hoity-toity, but instead she was grunting and tugging on a leash that might as well have been attached to a large boulder.

Ethan gave the dog's head another friendly pat. "Good boy."

Erin narrowed her eyes.

Grinning, Ethan took a step. "I'll walk with you. We're heading to the same place anyway."

Erin sighed in defeat. "Fine."

He matched her pace before asking, "Where's Sarah today?"

Erin eyed him up distrustfully. "Are you interested in her?"

"What? No!"

"Hmm." She continued to peer at him.

"What? I'm not!" And he really wasn't. Sarah was pretty, sure, but he found her a little too . . . well, he wasn't sure what. Not boring exactly, just a little too . . . sweet. He liked his women sweet *and* salty—with a touch of feistiness. Not too much, or they became a handful and more trouble than he was willing to deal with.

He studied Erin. Case in point. Not that she wasn't attractive, or that he wasn't attracted to her. He was. He'd have to be dead not to be. But she was trouble, and he had enough of that going on in his life for the time being.

"Good, because I'm pretty sure she has the hots for Brian."

"Brian?"

"Benny."

"Ah. The landscaper slash teacher slash hockey coach."

Erin grinned. "Do I sense a little competitive streak there, Ethan? Is our Benny just a little *too* talented?"

Ethan laughed. "Whatever."

Erin looked thoughtful. "You know, you guys could be brothers."

"We don't look anything alike."

"You have the same hair," she pointed out.

"I see. Same hair? Must be brothers," he joked.

"Shut up."

They walked several steps in silence, but he could feel her stare fixed on him.

"What?" he asked with a laugh.

She looked quickly away. "Nothing."

Chapter 12

Because of her work schedule, it had taken Erin several days to fully unpack, but she was finally all settled in, and she let out a long, contented breath from her new favorite spot at the end of Sarah's dock. It had been a while since she'd felt this relaxed. She'd been a bundle of nerves for far too long.

Sarah and Olivia had asked her to go to the fireworks on the Fourth a few days ago, but she'd declined. It had been the first fireworks display she'd missed since moving here, but she just hadn't been up for it. All she'd wanted to do was slide into her pjs and binge watch season six of *Friends* with a bag of Cheetos in her lap, so that's what she'd done.

She'd said no thanks to their plans tonight too. Normally she loved a good night out on the town, but lately she craved downtime as much as a downhill skiing enthusiast craved the snow. She was glad to be alone in the quiet with her dog instead of watching some stupid laser show down at the ore dock with a huge crowd of spectators, half of which would recognize her as their kids' principal and want to ask her questions or give her tips for improvement.

Sarah was meeting up with a bunch of people, including Benny, interestingly enough. They were all going to dinner first and then out for drinks once the show was over. They'd probably have a great time, but Erin had no regrets about staying back. This was where she wanted to be tonight.

She sat, alone with her thoughts, watching the sun go down with Marvin the Mastiff at her feet and her dad's old whiskey flask resting in her lap. It had been gifted to him by his best friend, Antone, on his twenty-first birthday, and it had become Sam Hennings' most prized possession after Antone had died in a motorcycle crash a few years later.

Erin ran a thumb over her father's initials, which were etched into the stainless steel. She wished he were here right now. He'd ask her about her day, just like always, and she'd ask him about his. Even as a busy airline pilot, he'd been plugged into her life in a way Jillian hadn't been. So long as he wasn't in the air and actively flying a 747, he'd call to check in when he was away, and he knew all the names of her teachers and friends. He knew things like who was dating whom and who had just broken up, and all because he cared enough to ask.

She'd always appreciated that about him. He'd listen with interest as she'd tell him how Erica Johnson had cheated on Jordan Peters and how Jules and Andy, co-captains of the football team, had hung a dead chicken from the flag pole on senior prank day. Of course, he probably hadn't really cared much about a bunch of teenagers he didn't know, but he cared about her, and because it mattered to *her*, it mattered to him.

They'd had such an easy, effortless relationship. Erin was glad, for both their sakes. Tough and capable in every other area of life, for whatever reason, when it came to Jillian, her dad had been a real pushover. He'd let Jillian run all over him. How he'd become one of *those* men—the sweet, doting husband with the bitchy, domineering wife—Erin had never been able to sort out. Jillian was constantly nit-picking at him. Always finding fault. Her dad would just kiss her on the cheek to pacify her and wink at Erin as he dutifully went off to do Jillian's bidding.

As easy-going as he was, Erin knew it had to have taken its toll on him. To compensate, she'd tried to be as low-maintenance and unneedy as possible—with him, at least. Not with Jillian. Any chance she had to get under her mother's skin, she'd taken it, and she'd done it with a satisfied smile. She'd tried not to get into it with Jillian too much when her dad was around, saving the worst behavior for when he was out of town, but he'd ended up playing referee a time or two, and Erin still felt guilty about that.

Even though she'd made plenty of mistakes along the way, her dad would still be proud of who she was today. Erin knew that. And he'd have known just what to do about her little problem with the unnamed, unseen, psychostalker that had driven her out of her house and over to Sarah's.

Erin knew coming out to the basin was just a temporary bandaid, but it had definitely helped settle her nerves. Pulling into the driveway four days ago in her packed car, she'd immediately felt more at peace than she'd felt in weeks.

Whenever she drove out here, she made plenty sure nobody was following her. She was like a female James Bond, but without all the cool gadgets.

At least she could get herself one of those porch cameras. She was going to call the local tech company who did work for the school and have one installed. Whoever he was, Erin had a feeling he'd go to her house again, and when he did, she'd get a glimpse of the creep and recognize him. *Or her*, she corrected. Plenty of females hated her guts too.

It was crazy to think that at sunrise almost a week ago, she'd been a bundle of nerves, ready to beat a would-be intruder to death with a baseball bat, and now tonight, at a beautiful sunset, she was as light and airy as the dollop of whipped cream she'd put on her strawberries after dinner. It helped that she had a nice little buzz going. Not that she was drunk. Erin never got drunk. There was something about that feeling that scared her. It was a loss of control she couldn't allow. But she didn't at all mind being *one* sheet to the wind—that place where her limbs felt slightly disconnected from her body, and her thoughts blurred just a touch around the edges.

The sky streaked oranges and pinks across the horizon, and with her father's flask in hand and Marvin stretched out on top of her feet, Erin sighed in contentment. She was unscrewing the cap of the flask for another small sip when the platform gave a little jump. Marvin hopped up and trotted down the length of the dock, and Erin turned to see Ethan walking out towards her. He was barefoot, having kicked off his green sandals at the beginning of the first section, and looked to be in solid vacation mode in his faded jeans and gray hooded sweatshirt. At first she didn't notice the large manila envelope he had tucked under one arm.

For a split second, Erin thought about being snarky—rudely asking him what he wanted or warning him that her dangerous puppy might try to play with him again—but she didn't want an argument tonight. She felt too soft and fragile to win one anyway. Plus, they'd sort of made their peace when she'd bumped into him on the road. That had been three days ago, and she'd seen him a few times since then, just in passing. For a guy who wasn't interested in Sarah, he sure did hang around a lot.

They'd been cordial with one another, but still cool. A tension had hung in the air between them during those brief encounters, and Erin found herself wishing she could disappear, just *poof*, evaporate into thin air, which wasn't at all like her. She never backed down from a fight.

Maybe she'd just reached her limit. She felt exhausted and worn down by all the negativity in her life. She had a mother who didn't love her, a stalker who hated her, and a stranger of a neighbor who'd managed to tear open a wound so old she'd thought it couldn't hurt again.

Marvin greeted Ethan with a wagging tail and lolling tongue, and Erin felt her resolve to dislike Sarah's neighbor crack a hair when he stopped for several seconds to stroke the scruff of Marvin's neck. She tried to make out what he was saying to the dog, but she only heard the low hum of his voice followed by, "Good boy."

He straightened and looked at her warily. "Hey. Is Sarah around?"

Erin shook her head. "She's in town."

"Alright. Thanks, I'll come back tomorrow." He was turning to leave when she added, "You can stay awhile, if you want."

He pulled back in surprise. "Really?"

Now, why had she gone and done that? She blamed the alcohol. It had always turned her into a nicer version of herself. Smoothed out all her edges. That or living with Sarah was causing that famous southern hospitality to rub off on her.

He hesitated before closing the distance between them, and when he sat down, Erin noticed the envelope.

"Is that for her?"

He nodded.

"What is it?"

"Just a few pointers on how to get her finances in order."

Erin studied it. "But it looks so thick."

"I might've gotten a little carried away. It's a packet I put together from a bunch of stuff I had saved on my hard drive from my first job." At her questioning look he added, "I worked at a personal investment firm. Anyway, I thought she might like to have it."

Erin's brows knit together. "Sarah's talked to you about her finances?"

He shrugged. "Some."

"Huh." She'd have to speak with Sarah about being too trusting. The last thing someone who'd just come into money should be doing was blabbing about it indiscriminately to strangers from Flint.

"*Huh?*" he echoed. "What's that supposed to mean?"

"Nothing. I guess I'm just surprised. I mean, you barely know each other."

He squared off with her. "You know, contrary to what you might think, I'm not a bad guy."

She held up her hands, even the one holding the flask. "I didn't say you were."

"You didn't have to," he muttered.

Erin slid back into her chair, which seemed to swallow her up. Why couldn't she be even just two inches taller? She faced the water and didn't turn her head when she spoke. "Listen, I don't want to fight, okay? It's too perfect a night, and I don't want to ruin it. Stay if you want; leave if you don't. Your choice."

Out of the corner of her eye, she could see Ethan studying her. Then he nodded and settled into his chair. "Fine," he agreed. Unlike her, his feet still touched the dock when he slid all the way back. He stretched out his legs, crossing them at the ankles.

His feet were large but cute somehow, with little dark hairs sticking up on his two big toes. It should have grossed her out, but it didn't. Then again, she thought Marvin was the cutest dog alive, so she was pretty sure she'd relaxed her standards.

The Mastiff, as if realizing she'd just paid him a compliment, hopped up and stared at her in blatant adoration, his tail giving a tentative wag. She leaned forward and scratched him behind one ear. He leaned into her hand briefly before rewarding her with a slick-tongued lick on her knee and bounding down the dock towards shore.

Ethan turned and watched him go. "So, where *is* Sarah tonight?"

"She went into town to watch some laser show thing."

His brows lifted in interest. "Lasers? Cool. You didn't want to go?"

"To watch a bunch of lasers flash around in the dark? No."

He laughed.

"It's a better show out here anyway," she said, pointing to the vibrant sky. Shades of purple, orange, red, and yellow streaked across the horizon, stacked one on top of the other like layers of a trifle.

"That, I totally agree with."

"The colors are so bright and bold. I don't think I've ever seen them like this."

"Reminds me of that toy from when we were kids. Brite Lite? Lite Brite?"

"Hmm, you're right." Erin couldn't remember, but she knew the one he was talking about.

They sat together in silence and took in the view.

Marvin lapped at the water behind them before jumping back up onto the dock. It shook with each footfall as he made his way back towards them, and the dock heaved when he threw himself down again, this time at Ethan's feet.

Ethan chuckled.

Erin grinned. "Looks like he's won you over, maybe."

The smile lingered on his lips. "Or I've won him over." He leaned forward to stroke Marvin's back, and for Erin, it was enough of an apology to move on and leave the near-kick—or the kick that wasn't—in the past. She'd have to work on forgiving Ethan for implying that marriage to her would cause a man to slit his wrists, though. Yeah, that one might take a little longer to forget.

"Sarah said you haven't had him all that long, just a few weeks?"

Erin did the math. She'd picked him up from the shelter on June twenty-first, and today was only the eighth of July. Seventeen days.

"It feels like I've had him a lot longer than that," she remarked with some surprise. How could she love someone so much in such a short time? Erin watched Marvin lay his head down on Ethan's right foot and close his eyes. She let out an amused giggle. "You know, I got him as a watch dog, but I swear, all he does is sleep."

He shot her a quizzical look. "Why would you need a watch dog?"

"Oh, you know. I'm a high school principal, so I've got haters by the hundreds." She tried to sound cool with that and failed.

"That can't be much fun."

It wasn't. It didn't use to bother her, being the most hated woman in town, but Erin had to admit that it was starting to get old. She never heard from parents unless they had a complaint. The only students she got to interact with face to face on a regular basis were the ones who were always in trouble, and since she was in charge of their discipline, they didn't tend to like her a whole lot.

She craved relationships with her students, but she was pulled in a million different directions all day, every day. Her responsibility footprint was enormous, so connecting with the student body at large the way she wanted to wasn't possible. There wasn't enough time in a day to do the job the way she wanted to do it. To make the connections she wanted to make in order to have a real impact.

Even relationships with her own colleagues were difficult because they weren't just straight up co-workers. She was the dreaded boss who did all their performance evaluations and made all the tough decisions.

Until Olivia and Sarah had come along, the only real friend she'd had in her building was Adele. Her secretary had been a constant and loyal presence in her life for the last several years, and she kept Erin sane. Really, Adele was more of a mother figure than a friend. A kick-ass, no-nonsense mother figure who could have run that school all by herself. She was both revered and feared by everyone in the building. Whatever needed doing, she was the one who could get it done.

Adele, originally from Savannah, had once said that Nicolet was the "whitest" place she'd ever lived. "White people and white snow," she'd said. During

Adele's first few months living in town, back in the late nineties, she'd come across another woman of color in the downtown, and the two of them had squealed and laughed and carried on right there on the sidewalk as if they were long lost sisters. When she'd retold the story to Erin, they'd both had a good laugh.

At first, Adele hadn't liked it here. She'd felt conspicuous. But over time, she'd come to love their white little town, to the extent that she encouraged her brother and his family to move here when a professorship position had opened up at the university. Erin was glad Adele had stayed. She couldn't imagine the high school without her. She couldn't really imagine her *life* without her.

Next summer, she was retiring, and Erin would miss her like she'd miss her right hand. She didn't even want to think about what the day-to-day would look like without Adele there running interference for her and sharing all her one-liners—some designed to impart wisdom, and others for a little comic relief when things got too heavy. A few months back, after Barry Sandstrom's delinquent uncle had come in and accused Erin of "planting" weed in his nephew's locker, Adele had set an apple down on Erin's desk and said, "An apple a day keeps anyone away if you throw it hard enough. Next time."

The hard truth was this: There would always be a next time, and Erin was tired of being used as a punching bag by disgruntled students and parents all day, every day. She used to be able to let it slide, but lately the attacks were sticking, and she was beginning to wonder if it was even worth it. Maybe she should return to classroom teaching where it was still hard work, but she could at least have that relational piece back again. That had been her whole reason for getting into education in the first place. She wanted to be someone's Mrs. Hershey.

Erin had been quiet too long, and when she finally met Ethan's concerned eyes, she offered him a small smile and shrugged. What more could she say?

"I'm a good listener," he said simply.

For a split second, she was tempted. But no. She didn't like this guy. Or at least, she didn't trust him with her secrets. And she certainly didn't need his help or his sympathy. She was Erin Hennings. She could handle anything. She pinched her lips together and looked away.

"Suit yourself." Ethan cleared his throat before he changed the subject. "What's that you got there?" He nodded at the flask. "Whiskey?" He looked so impressed that for a second, Erin wished it were.

"No. It's brandy." She held the flask out to him. "Want some?"

He accepted it, and she watched as he unscrewed the top. After taking a swig, he let out a satisfied *ahh*, and she swore she could see the tension leave his shoulders. "That's good stuff. Smooth."

She smiled. "My dad used to drink a little brandy before bed."

He turned the flask in his hands and looked at the engraving on the front. "Is this his?"

Erin nodded. "He passed away a while ago."

His gaze settled on hers. "I'm sorry."

She nodded, accepting his sympathy this time. She reached for the flask, which he relinquished, and she took another small sip.

"Do you have other family?" He lifted his hands. "Honest question, this time."

She smiled in spite of herself. "Well, as you know, there's no husband." She handed the flask back to him and was gratified when he looked like he might want to bite off his tongue. He might have apologized again, but she kept going. "Just Jillian, my mom. She's still out in California."

"Do you see each other much?"

"No. Jillian isn't exactly what you'd call *warm*. She's been a cold fish since the beginning of time. We aren't close."

He pulled a face. "That stinks."

Erin shrugged. "What about you?"

"My parents are both in Flint, and my younger sister, Sonya, still lives there. Everyone's really excited. Sonya's expecting. Due the end of November."

Erin couldn't help but tease him. "Uncle Ethan! Makes you sound old."

He shook his head with a smile. "Nice. Real nice. But I suppose it *is* true. I'm almost thirty-five, which in math terms means I'm basically turning forty on my next birthday." At her raised eyebrows, he added, "Rounding."

Erin laughed. "I knew I hated math."

Ethan grinned and his teeth flashed white. He really was very easy on the eyes. Erin didn't think there was anyone in this town better looking than he was. Too bad they'd gotten off on the wrong foot. Not that it seemed to matter anymore. At least not at the moment.

"Is your family close?" she asked.

He nodded. "Maybe too close. Everyone is always in everyone else's business, but we all mean well. My parents wish I'd come back closer to home, and they don't make a secret of it. But at least my sister's still there."

Erin tipped her head. "But I thought you lived in Flint too."

He looked startled. "Right. I just meant that I'm up here right now, and they're all down there."

Huh. After years of working with teenagers, Erin knew when something was off. For now, she let it go, but she made a mental note to revisit the topic later. She'd probably missed her calling. Nosy as she was, she really should have been a detective.

Ethan handed the flask back to her, and she took another pull. It went down smooth and warmed her from the inside out. Unlike Ethan, she was still dressed for the daytime heat. Little goosebumps had appeared on her skin well before he'd shown up, but she hadn't wanted to leave her spot on the dock. She wanted to soak in the evening in its full glory.

Ethan rested his head on the back of the Adirondack and closed his eyes briefly. When he opened them again, he said, "So, you're a principal."

"This is true," she deadpanned.

"What's that like?"

"Pretty similar to herding squirrels, I imagine."

He broke into a broad smile. "You're funny."

"I try."

"You seem young for a building principal. And you're, you know, not bad to look at. Do the boys ever give you a hard time?"

Erin's lips twitched in amusement.

He shot her another boyish grin, full of mock innocence. "What's so funny?"

"I think you just called me pretty."

He wiped the smile off his face and shook his head in denial. "I don't know what would give you that impression."

She gave him her best *drop dead* look, and he laughed.

"Okay, fine. I called you pretty."

"Thank you." She beamed. "I haven't had a compliment in a while, so that one will keep me well fed for a month, at least."

He looked her up and down, the way men do when they like what they see, and Erin's goosebumps tripled in number. "I'm sure I could come up with some more between now and then."

"Better make them good." Although she'd attempted to keep it light, her voice broke, giving her away. Suddenly, she felt nervous.

His smile widened, and for a moment, they just stared at each other. Erin didn't know if she wanted to jump into the lake and swim far, far away, or jump into his lap and kiss him senseless. Her cheeks burned.

Ethan had mercy on her and returned to their earlier thread of conversation. "Seriously, though. Is it hard to oversee all those kids?"

She took a deep breath and blew it out slowly. Not only did the action have the effect of calming her, but suddenly she wanted to confide in him. Later, she'd figure out why she'd changed her mind. "It is hard, and sometimes it really sucks. Some of the kids are pretty tough to deal with. Some of them break your heart because of the hell they have to live in every day. Others come from solid homes, but they're just bound and determined to make bad choices. They have their reasons, but you still wish you could shake some sense into them, you know? Try to get them to see that they're only hurting themselves." She thought briefly of herself and Jillian. She used to think she had come out the winner, but more and more, she realized they'd both lost.

She looked at Ethan and lifted her shoulders. "But then, you don't have to look very hard to see where you've made a difference, and that's what keeps me going."

He nodded. "What you do is important. Thankless, maybe, and definitely tough, but it's the kind of work you can, you know . . . feel good about."

Erin heard the wistful quality of his voice, and she frowned. "Do you not feel good about your work?"

He let out a long breath. "Mostly, I do. I guess . . . well, lately it just seems more about the money than anything else. Profit."

"Isn't that, like, the whole point of your work?" She'd used a teasing tone and had expected him to laugh. He didn't.

"Yeah," he answered slowly, "but I think it's more . . . I think maybe . . ." He ran a hand through his hair, causing several strands to stick up on end, and Erin found herself wanting to comb her fingers through it to tame them back down again. Suddenly, he appeared more boy than man—a man whose age rounded up to forty.

"I've been promised a . . . promotion, a really big promotion, if I deliver on a big ask by our CEO. By fall, it'll be mine. If I want it. You know, if I can deliver."

"If you can deliver? Is that why you're here? To try to figure out if you can?"

He squirmed. "Oh, I can. I'm just not sure I want to."

Erin was dying to know more. Normally, she'd just ask. She had a way of getting information out of people that they didn't want to share. But for whatever reason, this time she let it go. Instead, she tried to relate. "You know, this might not be the same, but I used to work for a restaurant in college that had absolutely terrible food. One day, a family came in, and the dad asked me what was good on the menu. I wanted to tell him, 'Nothing. Nothing is good here. Quick, leave while you can!'" She laughed. "I quit the next day because I realized I didn't want to work at something I couldn't be proud of."

Serious and alert, he stared at her for a long, drawn-out moment. Even unsmiling, he was hot—she couldn't deny it—and she was beginning to think she might be in trouble. An attraction was brewing. She could feel it in the pit of her stomach.

"May I?" he said finally, reaching for the flask and taking another sip. After screwing the cap back on, he spoke. "That's not different at all. That's exactly how I feel. One of the things, anyway."

He offered back the flask, and Erin took one final pull herself before replacing the cap for good and setting it on the armrest of her chair in the space between them. Sharing the flask the way they had been was practically like kissing, but without any of the fun. The thought gave her pause. Did she really, truly want to kiss Ethan?

Maybe.

Probably.

Oh, who was she kidding? Definitely. She definitely wanted to feel Ethan's lips on hers. But where would it all lead?

To nowhere. To her pulling the plug before it got good. It was like getting up and leaving the theater right when the movie began building to the climax. Right before she began to care about what might happen. It was unsatisfying, sure, but it was safe, and for a while, it had worked just fine for her, but it wasn't working anymore. It left her feeling hollow. Or shallow. She wasn't sure what had changed.

Erin looked out across the bay. The sun had set, and the colors were less vibrant now—softer and more wispy, almost dream-like. The two of them sat together in silence, taking it all in. She felt herself smile. It was one of those undefined moments where a person just existed outside all the noise and demands of life. A profound feeling of well-being took hold. Undoubtedly, she was screwed up. But even knowing that, in this moment, she felt nearly perfectly happy. She wanted to say something to Ethan. She wanted to thank him for sharing the moment with her.

She was trying to put together the words when Marvin woke himself up with a fart that just might have been heard all the way across the bay by the silhouetted person in the canoe on the other side. Why did he always fart in his sleep like that? He whipped his head around in astonishment, looking for the source of the noise, and Erin and Ethan looked at one another in suspended surprise before breaking into gales of laughter that were so powerful and lasted so long that her abdominal muscles were sore the next morning.

Marvin the Mastiff looked back and forth between the two of them as if he thought they'd lost their minds. It was the perfect ending to the day, and when they gathered their things and headed for their respective homes ten minutes later, Erin was still smiling.

Chapter 13

"Y'all, I feel like I'm on a date. Am I on a date right now?" Sarah looked into the mirror at the reflections of her two friends as they washed their hands at the sinks. They'd just arrived at the historic Waterfront Inn, and they'd gone directly into the ladies' room while the men grabbed them all a table.

She knew her eyes revealed her panic. How had she ended up on a date without even knowing it *was* one? It had just . . . *happened* somehow. Benny had mentioned the laser show to her in passing, and she'd mentioned it to Sean and Olivia, who in turn had invited Steven and Heidi, and from there it had become this plan to all go together. Regardless of intentions, three men and three women out on the town looked and felt like a triple date, whether they'd meant it to or not.

When she'd been making the plans to go, she'd thought of it as something fun to do with a group of friends, and she'd assumed Erin would go too. Even when Erin had given the invitation a hard pass, it hadn't completely registered with Sarah that she'd essentially be partnered up with Benny for the night. Not that she didn't want to be, but she'd felt out of sorts and unnatural all evening . . . like her arms were too long and heavy and her smile was too big.

Olivia and Sean were always touching—holding hands and stealing quick kisses when they thought nobody was looking. Steven and Heidi were nearly just as bad. They'd brought along a blanket and sat snuggled up together during the show, effectively removing themselves out of range for any kind of conversation. Olivia and Sean kept themselves at a distance too, so Sarah had stood there, shoulder to shoulder with Benny in almost complete silence for the entirety of the interminable show. Erin had been right: lasers were boring, but standing beside Benny, feeling the heat radiating off of him long after the sun had gone down, well, it had been an exquisite form of torture.

Sarah thought she could sense a certain rigidity in his posture that hinted he might be feeling just as awkward as she was, but she wasn't sure if that had made it easier or harder. All she knew was that the show seemed never-ending, and she'd been in agony the entire time as she simultaneously worried and hoped that Benny would reach across the two-inch space that separated them and take hold of her hand.

He hadn't, and now here she stood, in the restroom of one of the most historical and ornate buildings in all of Nicolet, a hotel that housed the best pub with the best mojitos, and all she wanted to do was stay in the ladies room and hide.

"Looks like a date to me," Heidi said as she applied a fresh layer of tinted lip gloss to her lips after drying her hands. She was a pretty woman. Sarah had figured her to be somewhere in her mid to late forties. Even though she was quite a bit older than they were, she was a lot of fun, and Sarah could see why she and Olivia had grown so close over the last few months.

Sarah put her head in her hands and muttered, "Oh, no."

Heidi turned from the mirror to look at her directly. "What? Don't you like him?"

"No, I mean, yes. I like him fine, but we're just . . . friends."

"Hmm. I'm not so sure he feels that way." Heidi winked and tucked her lip gloss back in her purse.

"Why do you say that?" Sarah asked, hoping Heidi wouldn't pick up on the hopeful quality of her voice.

"Sarah, you're so sweet," Olivia interjected as she wiped her hands with a paper towel. She met Sarah's eyes in the mirror. "Haven't you noticed the way he's been looking at you tonight?"

"No!" It was just the opposite. To her, it had seemed like Benny was avoiding looking at her at all. There was a distance between them tonight, an emotional distance that was a vast and disappointing departure from the ease they'd had with one another since the beginning of summer.

"She's been blinded by the lasers," Heidi joked. "I know I'm still seeing colors when I close my eyes." She blinked hard twice. "That can't be good."

Blinking several times, Sarah checked her own vision and was relieved to find all was normal. She turned to Olivia. "What do you mean? How is he looking at me?"

"Like he wants you for dessert," Heidi supplied before Olivia could answer. She waggled her eyebrows and laughed.

"Stop. You'll scare her," Olivia scolded with a grin. She grabbed another paper towel from the dispenser on the wall. "You should just go with it, if you want my opinion. I know I wasn't too keen on Benny at the start, but he's really grown on me. He's a terrific guy, and as I'm sure you've noticed, he's not too hard to look at."

Sarah experienced a small flutter in her stomach as she allowed herself to entertain the idea. Just for a second. "Y'all really think so? It wasn't so long ago he was pining away after Erin. I'm not sure it would be smart to start somethin' with him now."

Heidi placed a hand on Sarah's shoulder. "If I've learned anything from my own experience, it's this: The heart wants what it wants when it wants it, and it can't really be changed or controlled by the head. You can't rationalize it, and you'll drive yourself crazy if you try."

"Hmm." Sarah chewed on a nail. It was a bad habit, she knew, but it had served her well all these years, and she figured if she hadn't kicked the habit yet, it was here to stay at this point.

Olivia put her hands on Sarah's other shoulder. "Just take a deep breath and have fun tonight. Whatever else you might be, remember, you and Benny are friends. You're just having a fun night with friends. That's all. Okay?"

Sarah nodded. "Okay."

When they got back to the table, Sarah flashed Benny a small smile. She needed to behave as she always had. Whether Benny was interested in her or not was irrelevant. Nothing would happen between them. Nothing *could* happen. She wouldn't allow it. Whatever Heidi might believe about the head and the heart, Sarah knew how to use the one to control the other. She'd been doing it forever, minus one small lapse in college. Okay, one *big* lapse in college. She'd let her guard down then, allowing herself to believe that she could be loved by somebody amazing. That she could be cared for. Cherished, even. And just look how that had turned out. She was lucky the whole affair hadn't derailed her entire career path. As it was, it had taken a major detour.

Sarah was driving him to distraction tonight. As she walked back to the table, Benny could see a tiny sliver of her midriff showing between her white halter top and those low-rise jeans that hugged her curves in all the right places. And not that he was looking, but she'd been cold most of the night. He found it difficult to look her in the eye at all, knowing that every time he did, his gaze would be pulled about twelve inches south of there.

As she sat in the vacant chair beside him, she smiled at him shyly. He'd been so riveted, he'd forgotten to get up and pull her chair out for her, but he returned her smile and found he was still smiling like an idiot a full thirty seconds later. Quickly, he made his face go neutral.

"So, what do you think, Sarah?" Olivia asked. Benny had no idea what she was talking about.

Everyone was looking at Sarah now, not just him, and she squirmed in her chair. "Sorry, y'all. I was just doing a little woolgathering, I guess. What was that?"

They all grinned, and Heidi, who was seated to Sarah's left on her other side, reached over and patted her hand. "You're an absolute delight, you know that?"

Sarah looked confused, but she laughed. "Oh, I don't know about that. My mama would probably say otherwise."

Heidi gave her hand a squeeze. "Well, she must be a fool."

"As a matter of fact, she is," Olivia said, somewhat darkly.

"*Anyway*," Sean said, casting his wife a sidelong glance, "Olivia was just saying we should help you throw that housewarming party you mentioned wanting to have. It could even be a housewarming-slash-retaining wall celebration. Benny says he'll be all finished up within the next few days." He looked at Benny for verification, and Benny nodded. "We could help you throw your party and have a beach day out on the basin."

Benny had drawn out the project as long as he could, and the idea of not being out there with Sarah on a regular basis made him feel a little sick. How was he going to keep seeing her? School wouldn't be starting up again for weeks, and the idea of waiting until then to see her again didn't really feel like an option.

He was going to have to tell her how he felt, only he *still* couldn't gauge her feelings for him. One minute he thought she might be into him—like earlier tonight, when he'd gotten the sense that she might want to hold his hand—and the next she'd throw up a wall as strong as the one he was building for her.

About halfway through the laser show, he'd worked up the courage to reach for her hand, but a split second before he made his move, she stepped away from him. Did she like him or didn't she? This couldn't be all on him. Yes, he might have defective radar, but she had to be sending at least *some* mixed signals. He'd never had this much trouble reading a woman before.

"Oh, no!" Sarah said, taken aback. "I don't want y'all throwing me a house-warming party. I'm supposed to do that, and y'all are supposed to be the guests!"

Olivia leaned forward. "We want to do this for you," she assured her. "Please let us. We'll take care of everything. We'll get the food, and we'll bring some chairs so that it can be an outdoor party, more or less. You wouldn't have to do a thing. We can even put our housewarming gift to use in the evening."

Sarah blinked. "Y'all got me a gift? That's so sweet!"

The gift had been his idea. He'd ordered it weeks ago, not that Benny needed her to know that. He wasn't even thinking about it. All he could think about at the moment was how much he wanted to reach out and stroke her slender arm, from the top of her shoulder to the inside of her wrist. He wanted to tell her that *she* was the sweet one. His hand tingled as he imagined what her skin would feel like. Soft and silky-smooth.

"And we'll be able to put our boat to good use, too," Sean added with a twinkle in his eye.

"Wait, what? What boat?" Sarah asked.

Sean smiled proudly. "Livvy's birthday gift. I got her a ski boat."

Sean got his wife a boat as a birthday gift? Benny fidgeted with his silverware. His gift seemed a little . . . less-than in comparison.

"Wow, Olivia! I didn't know you skied," Steven remarked. He sounded impressed.

Olivia rolled her eyes. "I don't, and my birthday isn't for another three months, but Sean wanted a boat, so he figured he'd buy one, name it after me, and give it to me for my birthday so he wouldn't get in trouble."

Steven whistled and gave Sean a high-five. "That was genius, man."

"She's putting you guys on. She's just as excited as I am. Right, Livvy?" The two of them exchanged a smile.

Benny hadn't said very much to the group tonight. He'd been more content to listen and observe, and daydream about Sarah. But now he leaned forward and rested his elbows on the table. He could talk about two things all day long: hockey and boats. And Sarah. Make that three things. "Tell us about this boat," he commanded.

Sean was happy to. "It's a twenty foot MasterCraft, a hundred twenty horse pow—"

"Yes, fine," Heidi interrupted, "But what *color* is it? Is it pretty?"

"It's *so* pretty!" Olivia answered excitedly. "It's red and white, and has *LIVin' Life* written on the back. Get it? *Liv?*"

"Oh, that's so sweet," Sarah and Heidi gushed at the same time.

Benny looked at Sean and Steve. Words weren't necessary. How had the women hijacked this conversation so quickly and taken it down such a trivial path? Colors? They wanted to talk colors?

"I guess if anyone wonders about the difference between men and women, here's a prime example." Steven lifted his mug of beer as if he were giving a toast. Benny raised his glass too before drowning his smile with a large gulp of beer. He was drinking the house stout, which he had to admit, was even better than the stout he enjoyed over at 906 Pizza. He felt disloyal for even thinking it.

Sean shook his head with a grin. "See, I knew you'd love the boat, Livvy."

"I actually really do," she admitted before turning to Sarah. "So, what do you say? We could bring the boat out and have some fun on the water."

Sarah appeared to be warming to the idea. Benny sure was. It was another chance to see her without having to formally ask her out on a date. Maybe he'd get a better sense of what she wanted after spending another day with her. He wished, not for the first time, that he were better at this kind of thing.

"You know," Sarah answered, "that sounds really fun. When are you thinking?"

Heidi took out her phone. "Let's check the weather." While she looked up the extended forecast, Benny tuned in to Sean and Steven's renewed conversation about the boat. A few months ago, he would have waited anxiously for an opportunity to jump in and add something to the discussion, but after what Erin had told him, he was taking a new approach to social situations. One day, maybe he'd thank her, but not yet. He really could have done without being called a "tryhard" and a "creep," especially with everything else he'd been trying to process. For now, it was much more comfortable for him to spend his time listening and observing and less time trying to find something clever to say anyway. It took the pressure off, and for the first time in his life, he thought he might actually be enjoying large gatherings of people.

"It looks like next Saturday will be clear," he heard Heidi say. "It'll be in the eighties too, so that's perfect, and I just happen to be off that day. What do you think, ladies?" She eyed Sarah and Olivia.

Olivia opened her phone and tapped the screen a few times before answering, "Works for us."

"Me too!" Sarah said excitedly after tapping at her own phone.

Me three, Benny thought. He didn't need to check his calendar. Nothing could keep him away.

"Alright gentleman," Heidi announced, interrupting Sean and Steven. "Next Saturday it is."

"That was quick!" Steven exclaimed.

Heidi dumped her phone back into her purse. "*Quick* is my middle name."

"That is *very* true," Steven replied with an easy smile, and then Benny watched his eyes grow wide, as if he'd said something he hadn't intended to say.

Heidi stilled in the act of hanging her purse on the back of her chair and turned as pink as the maraschino cherry resting on her napkin. She hissed something at him that Benny couldn't quite make out, and Steven held up his hands, his grin broadening. "At running!" he insisted. "I meant at running." He looked around the table at everyone. "Honest. She's really fast at . . . running."

Benny checked around the table, looking for social cues to understand the joke. As usual, he'd missed it, but over his lifetime, he'd discovered that nine times out of ten, in situations where words had double meanings, it had something to do with sex.

"Thank you, Steven, for that . . . over-the-top clarification. Everybody believes you now," Heidi said with exaggerated formality and a roll of her eyes. Sarah was biting down on her lip to keep from laughing, and Olivia's shoulders were shaking as she stared down at her lap. When Benny saw Heidi's mouth twitch, he knew he'd guessed correctly. This was about sex.

Sean let out a loud snigger that he'd tried and failed to hold in, and then the whole table lost it. Everyone was in hysterics. It didn't matter that Benny had missed it in real time. He still laughed. He couldn't help himself, and he remembered the idiom about laughter being contagious. It really was. He didn't often laugh, which his mom had always thought was a shame. It just didn't come easy for him, but in spite of that, he'd always considered it a balm. Especially when it was this kind of laughter. The kind that came from deep in his chest.

Benny sensed Sarah looking at him, and he turned his head. Her gaze was riveted on his, and her eyes sparkled. He returned her bright smile, and for the moment, at least, all his insecurities fell away. She was the most beautiful woman in the world, and she was smiling at him.

Chapter 14

Erin heard the crunch of tires on gravel and put down her laptop. She was working upstairs in her bedroom, sifting through dozens of resumes. They had two open positions to fill. She needed a ninth-grade Spanish teacher and a health teacher for next year. While she was sad to see the health teacher go, she hadn't been able to get rid of the last Spanish teacher fast enough.

There'd been red flags all over the place when she'd hired him, but Maria Jacobs, a Nicolet High School teacher of twenty years, had retired unexpectedly a week before school began last fall. Jason Bender had been their only applicant, and even though Erin hadn't gotten the best vibe from him, he'd lived in Spain for a year and was fluent in Spanish—or so he said. By November it was obvious he didn't really know much Spanish at all, and he definitely didn't know how to teach. As if that weren't bad enough, Erin began to suspect he just might be nuts to boot.

The only two Spanish words Jason Bender ever uttered in class were *Hola clase*. Once that greeting was out of the way, he spent the rest of the class period storytelling. Every hour, the students sat, transfixed and enthralled, from bell to bell. According to his students, Señor Bender was a total badass who, at the age of twenty-three, had by far and away led the most exciting life of anyone on the planet. He'd been struck by lightning, shipwrecked, robbed at gunpoint, and he'd even survived a plane crash. He'd traveled the world, working a vineyard in Italy and meeting the Dalai Lama in India. He'd also won some major surfing competition in Australia. Erin wouldn't have been surprised if he'd claimed to have fought off a great white shark while he was at it.

He told these stories, and countless others, all class period long—in English. How did a person say, "You are so full of shit" in Spanish, she wondered.

Predictably, the kids loved him, but the head of the foreign language department, Brandon Kottila, had Jason's number from the very beginning, and Erin should have too. Brandon, a sixty-something teacher of German and Finnish, had an adjoining door to Jason's classroom, and he could hear everything. By the end of the first week, he was in Erin's office to inform her, with intense disapproval, that she'd hired a monolingual, compulsive liar into his department.

It took longer than it should have, but Erin was finally able to convince the board to get rid of Jason before the start of second semester. It should have been enough that he was completely unqualified for the job and that he threw a weekly *fiesta*—the third Spanish word he knew—at the end of every week. Like clockwork on Friday mornings, young Mikey Perry, who lived a few houses down from her, trotted past her office carrying his mother's oversized electric skillet. That baby cooked up cheese quesadillas all day long until the heating element had finally quit in protest just before Christmas break.

Mrs. Perry had shown up on Erin's doorstep the morning of Christmas Eve, dead skillet in hand, and demanded the district buy her a new one. She seemed more upset about the skillet than she did about the "porn" she accused Jason Bender of showing students during the parties. It had taken some coaxing and a payout by Erin for a new skillet to get Mrs. Perry to agree to make a formal complaint to the board, but it was worth it.

Thankfully, it wasn't actual pornography being shown to students during the *fiestas*, but it was pretty darn close. Jason had allowed students to watch movies like *Desperado* in class while they nibbled at their quesadillas and tortilla chips, and although definitely inappropriate for school with its R-rating, at least it *had* a rating. Most of the movies Jason had shown were foreign films with no rating at all.

It was finally enough to get the board's attention, and they fired Jason Bender. He'd threatened to file a grievance or lawsuit, but so far, nothing had come through and Erin didn't think anything would. In fact, she felt pretty confident they'd never see or hear from him again. Last she'd heard, he was living in Chicago. Good riddance!

Unfortunately, hiring a replacement was proving to be a little tricky. She had plenty of applicants, but most of them had only minored in Spanish. She wanted a Spanish major, preferably a native speaker or one who truly had lived abroad for a year, but Erin had the sinking feeling she might be forced to hire one of the two Spanish majors who'd recently graduated from the local university.

She had nothing against hiring brand new teachers. She'd hired recent graduates before—Sarah, for example—but neither of the top two applicants had completed a study abroad, and Erin didn't think a non-native speaker of a foreign language could be all that strong without an immersion experience in the target language. She really needed this next teacher to be good. After a semester of Jason and another semester of multiple substitute teachers, she owed it to the kids.

But for now, she was calling it quits on her job search. She wanted to find out how Sarah's night had gone and see if she could squeeze some information out of her about Ethan. She climbed out of bed and headed down the stairs with a yawning Marvin trailing behind her. Sarah was just coming in from the garage when Erin took the last step on the staircase. "Hey, you."

Sarah brought a hand to her chest and flipped on the light. "Goodness! What are you still doin' up? It's late."

Erin looked at the clock on the microwave. It *was* late. It was after one o'clock. "I had work to do."

Sarah *tsk*ed. "I swear, your job is never done. And here I thought English teachers were overworked. You never quit workin'."

She'd never admit to having no life, but honestly, what else would Erin do with her time if she wasn't working? She had no family, and until recently, she hadn't really had any close friends. "I don't mind it. How was your night?"

Sarah walked the rest of the way into the house. "It was . . . good."

"Yeah? What was good about it?"

Sarah threw her purse down on the counter. "Well, not the lasers, that's for sure." She laughed as she turned to grab a glass out of the cupboard. "But if you asked Benny, he'd probably tell you it was the best thing ever."

"I figured that part would be boring. Figures he'd love it. What about the rest of the night?"

"It was . . . good."

Erin tipped her head. "You already said that."

Sarah filled her glass from the faucet. "That's 'cause it was."

Erin flounced over to the sink and stood next to her. "Sarah! Tell me about your night!"

Sarah sighed. "Fine. If you have to know, I felt kind of awkward most of the night. It felt like the date that wasn't. You know? But it ended well, so . . ."

"The date that wasn't?"

Sarah walked to the sofa, and Erin followed. "Yeah. Two other couples, and me and Benny. We were the third couple, except we're *not* a couple. It just felt . . . weird. I'm not usually uncomfortable with Benny, but all of a sudden, I felt nervous to even look at him. And call me crazy, but I think he felt the same way. We'd look at each other and then look away right quick, like a pair of middle schoolers. What does that even mean?"

Erin thought the answer to that question was pretty obvious. "Do you like him?"

"Of course I like him."

"No, stupid. Do you *like* him?"

Sarah made a face at the playful insult, but she remained serious. "I do, but I'm not really in a good place to go jumping into something with someone, and . . ."

Erin spread her arms wide and did a full circle in the room. "Not in a good place? Sarah, look at your life! You're in a *great* place!"

Shaking her head, Sarah grabbed a coaster and set her water down on the coffee table. "You don't understand."

That was the truth. It was time to start pushing for the rest of the story, so she sat down beside Sarah and made herself comfortable. "Then make me understand. I know you've been holding back. Something big must have happened to make you so gun-shy with men."

"I don't know what you mean."

"Of course you do. Jackson Lang was putting out all the signals, making all the moves at Olivia's reception, and you shut him down. And we both know it's not because he's ugly."

"Makin' moves on *me*! You're the one he was dancin' with."

"Only after he gave up on you. Sarah, if you're happy being alone, then great. I'm not one of those people who thinks you need a man to be happy. But you're *not* happy alone. I can tell. And I can tell you're into Benny. So, what gives?"

"I'm going to make some tea. Want some?" Sarah got slowly to her feet.

Erin threw up her hands. "Seriously?"

"I'm not changing the subject, but if we're going to go digging into my past, I need a cup of hot tea in hand."

Erin felt a small jolt of excitement. She *loved* hearing people's stories, and while she knew most of Sarah's, she was finally going to learn the rest. "Okay! Tea sounds great!"

Several minutes later, the two of them were seated on either end of the couch again, legs tucked up underneath them and Sarah's wool blanket over their laps.

"Okay, spill the tea, as they say," Erin directed with a smile.

Sarah didn't hesitate. "You already know my life wasn't exactly rosy growin' up."

Erin nodded.

"I had a hard time making connections with people because I didn't want anyone to know about my mama's problems. It was like a big secret I tried to keep hidden. Nadia and my mom, they had each other, even though it was a weird, co-dependent thing. But after Gammie died, I had nobody. Well, I stayed close with Gammie's friend, Claire, until she moved away, so that helped. Anyway, after graduation, I got out of Copper Hill as fast as I could. I tried to take Nadia with me. She wouldn't leave, but she didn't want me to leave either. She's held it against me a long time."

"That's not fair."

"No, it's not," Sarah agreed. "I ended up in Duluth, don't ask me how. A southern girl in such a northern town. I guess I wanted to get far, far away."

"Mission accomplished," Erin said with a chuckle.

Sarah smiled. "I worked a few months before starting college. I had some money saved from workin' in high school, plus Gammie had left me a little. I got a job at this cute diner near my apartment, and I made great tips. It was amazing. For the first time, I had a space of my own that I could have friends back to. I even dated a little."

Hesitating, she cast Erin a glance. "Finally had my first kiss, even, and *don't* make fun!"

Erin fought down a grin. "I wouldn't dream of it."

Sarah rolled her eyes. "I know you must think that's crazy. Nineteen and never been kissed. But I was having a wonderful time. It felt like the world was open to me. Then ... *bam*! Junior year, in my elementary methods coursework, I had a math professor who took a special kind of interest in me."

Erin's eyes darkened. That couldn't be good. "What do you mean, *special interest*?"

Sarah played with the tassels of the large pillow she was partially propped up against. "Just what you think it means. At first, I didn't recognize what was happening. He offered to help me—"

"Wait, *elementary* methods?" Erin interrupted in surprise.

Pressing her lips together, Sarah nodded. "Yes. I was on the elementary education track."

"Whoa! How did you end up—"

"I'll get there."

Erin mimed the zipping of her lips. "Okay, keep going."

"Math and numbers don't come naturally to me, and I was struggling. He offered to help me. He'd have me come back to his office to get extra help. I went twice a week for a month before he told me to call him *Joe* instead of Dr. Elder, which should have tipped me off right then. It didn't. It wasn't until he started asking if I had a boyfriend that I started to wonder. He was so sweet to me, Erin. It was like he wanted to take care of me. I know it sounds a little gross, but he was like a cross between a father and a friend."

"How much older than you was he?"

"I was twenty-one. He was thirty-six."

A pretty big age difference, but not necessarily gross. And it wasn't unusual that a girl without a father would look for a facsimile of one in other men. Weren't psychologists always saying that? Erin could think of a handful of high school girls who were doing the same thing: Looking for love in all the wrong places. It was sad to watch. They'd seek attention wherever they could get it, even if it led them to the backseat of some loser's truck who would never talk to them again afterward.

"Before I really knew what was what, I had a pretty solid crush going. Joe started greeting me in his office with these great big hugs, and Erin, those hugs. They were . . ." Sarah looked sheepish.

"Of course you loved his hugs. You'd been starved of affection for years!"

"They were amazing," Sarah agreed. "I started to live for those hugs. Started goin' into his office even when I didn't really need help anymore. Pretending not to understand this or that. Pathetic, I know."

Erin smiled sympathetically.

"Anyway, the day he kissed me, well, that was probably the happiest day of my life. Two weeks later, we said we loved each other. He was busy and I was busy, so I only saw him about once a week outside of school, but for a year, I had a man who loved me, and that's what I focused on. It was all that mattered. That's why I missed all the warning signs."

Erin experienced a sinking feeling. "What warning signs?"

"He never had me to his house, for one thing. We always went to mine. That was probably the most obvious one."

"Oh, no! Was he married?"

Sarah's jaw dropped. "See! You came to that conclusion in less than a second! Why did it take me a year to figure it out?"

"Oh, Sarah!" Erin knew her friend well enough to know how devastating this would have been for her, and on so many levels. "How did you find out?"

"We took a day trip to Two Harbors at the end of August. We were laying on the beach together, holding hands, havin' a moment, and I looked down and saw a tan line on his ring finger."

Erin could feel her blood pressure rise. What a slime! "Did he fess up?"

"Not right away, but I kept at it. I ended up wailing like a banshee and kicking sand in his face. I was madder than a wet hen. Havin' myself a colossal hissy fit right there on the beach with families lookin' on. I was madder than I've ever been in my life. Completely crazy, really."

"I get the idea," Erin said wryly.

"I'm not sure you do. You wouldn't have recognized me. I didn't even recognize myself." Sarah shivered. "And when I cooled down and the tears came, I realized what a total fool I was. What a fool I *am*. I can't trust my instincts, Erin. And a woman who can't trust herself can't trust anyone else."

Erin shook her head vehemently. "No, that's not true. You can trust people. You trust me, right? And Olivia?"

"That's different. You're my friends. You're women. I'm talkin' about men."

"You trust Sean?" At Sarah's nod, Erin continued, "He's a guy."

Sarah rolled her eyes. "You know what I'm saying."

"I know what you're saying," Erin agreed. "You just trusted the *wrong* man, that's all."

"Erin. I was carryin' on with a married man for a year, and I didn't know it. Didn't even suspect it. How could I not have known something like that?"

Erin thought for a moment. That was tough. It would unsettle her too. "I don't know. I'm sorry."

"He broke my heart and dashed my dreams all to pieces. I dropped his class from my fall schedule the next day, and that messed up my entire course of study. I ended up having to go secondary ed after that. Otherwise, I would've had to wait an entire year for that course to be offered again, and he'd probably have been the one teaching it anyway. As it was, I had to finish up my secondary education courses in the summer of my senior year. Basically, I lost a semester."

Erin pulled a face. "That sucks. And you would have been an amazing elementary school teacher, but you know what? I do think you landed in the right place. Career-wise."

"I know. I've thought about that too. I was meant to teach high school. I just wish I'd figured it out some other way. Some other less painful, less ugly way." Her lips flattened into a serious line. "I'm so ashamed, Erin. Even now."

"I know, but you shouldn't be."

"How could I not be? That was some unsuspecting woman's husband." She paused, remembering. "I saw them out once, you know. She was beautiful. And gloriously pregnant. I was on the other side of the street, and I ducked into a store before they saw me. But I watched them through the window, like some crazy ex-girlfriend. I watched Joe put his hand at the small of her back, so gentle and so protective. He used to do that to me too. I loved how it felt. I can't believe I fell for it," Sarah admitted with shiny eyes.

"Was that the end then? After that day at the beach, did he ever try to reach out again?"

"Oh, yes! Tons of times. He called. He showed up outside my apartment. He wrote a letter, even. I never responded, of course. I never spoke to him again. I wouldn't let myself because there was a part of me that wanted . . . well, it feels awful to say it out loud, but a small part of me wanted to ask him to choose me. Pick me. You know? I still loved him, even though I hated him." Her voice grew earnest. "It was real love, Erin, and you can't just turn that off at will, but I knew I couldn't have looked at myself in the mirror knowing I'd broken up a marriage on purpose. That's not me. That's not who I am."

"I know it's not. Anyone who knows you at all would know that."

Sarah went quiet. A loon called from the bay. Such a beautiful, haunting sound.

When Sarah spoke again, her voice was subdued. "So, you can see why I haven't been real eager to get back into the saddle."

Until now, Erin thought. Sarah might not realize it yet, but she'd been polishing up that saddle all summer. She was close to giving it a go with Benny.

"Anyway," Sarah went on, "that was my first real relationship, and it was a total disaster. I don't want to ever feel like that again."

Erin nodded. "I get it."

"Do you really?"

She reached out and gave Sarah's hand a pat. "I really do."

Sarah stared at her. She seemed to debate something with herself briefly before saying, "I still don't know *your* whole story, Erin. Just that you were married to Keith and that he was in the military. I've tried not to invade your space, but are you ever going to talk to me about it?"

"Seth."

"What?"

"I was married to Seth."

Sarah nodded and waited expectantly.

"I said I understood, but I suppose I don't completely," Erin admitted, "because you were all in with Joe, and I'm just . . . incapable of doing that."

"Why do you think that?"

"Why do I *know* that?"

"Whichever."

"I just do. I can't feel it. It's just not in me."

"You can't fall in love?"

Erin shook her head. "Not all the way. I stop it."

"Why? There must be a reason."

Erin shrugged. "I'm sure there is."

"Don't you want to know? To understand yourself?"

"Not really."

"Hmm." Sarah took a long, slow sip of tea before remarking, "We're really quite different, aren't we?"

Erin laughed. "And you're just realizing this now?"

Sarah smiled.

Erin stretched out one leg and tickled Sarah's foot with her big toe. "One thing I do know. I love you like the sister I never had. And maybe that's enough."

Sarah's eyes shone bright, and Erin shifted uncomfortably.

"I love you too, but don't fool yourself, Erin. As wonderful as it is to have good friends, it's not the same as finding that one person you can't live without." She shook her head and smiled. "I read the books. I watch the movies. I see it in Olivia and Sean. Steven and Heidi. I want that. And I think you do too."

The next day, Erin woke up to the sun shining through her open window. A warm breeze floated in with it, and carried the sound of the piliated woodpecker going to town on that same damn tree it seemed unable to leave alone. At first, she'd found it to be almost magical. The piliated woodpecker, with its red and white markings, was such a beautiful creature. She'd wake up and peer out her window at it, marveling at its ability to peck such enormous holes in the bark of that big beech tree just outside her window. Now she was ready to shoot it.

Erin groaned. She would never be a morning person, no matter how many years it had been since she'd slept until noon. It was unnatural to wake up this early. She grabbed her phone off the nightstand and checked the time. Five-twenty. At least she was waking up with the sun. That helped a little. It was a lot easier to crawl out of bed when it was light outside than it was in the middle of February when she drove to work in the dark, cold hours of the morning.

Her alarm wouldn't go off for another ten minutes, so she laid there in her brightened room and thought about the conversation she'd had only hours ago. She and Sarah had stayed up well past two o'clock. Erin had told her about Seth. She'd told her everything, and it was a kind of funny thing, but after saying it all out loud, she felt like she just might understand herself a little better now.

Seth had been an escape for her. He'd been a ride out of town and away from Jillian, as well as a nice distraction from the grief she felt over losing her dad. She'd always known their relationship had been made on the cheap, but he'd still been her husband, and she'd wanted him to adore her the way her father had adored her mother. Well, okay. Maybe not exactly like that.

Her entire problem with men might boil down to the fear that nobody could truly love her, and that perhaps she didn't really even deserve to be loved at all.

Erin glanced at Marvin, snoring away peacefully beside her. She was her dog's number one, at least. She reached out and stroked the loose scruff on his neck. He woke up with a start, and just like that, he was pawing at her and licking her face. She giggled, which only spurred him on, and before she knew it, she had at least ninety pounds of exuberant puppy laying on top of her and a face so wet she might as well have just washed it.

She wiped at her cheeks as she struggled to get to a sitting position. Marvin backed off, but he continued to look at her expectantly, his tail smacking the mattress sporadically as he cocked his head from one side to the other. He'd declared himself, and he was waiting for her to do the same. She grinned. "I love you too, boy."

During her shower, Erin thought about Ethan. As much as she hated to admit it, she liked him. Thinking about him made her skin tingle, even as the hot water rained down over her. But despite how much she might like him, she still didn't think Sarah should be giving him information about her finances just yet. These days, a girl couldn't be careful enough. Especially a girl who'd suddenly found herself in possession of a small fortune.

Sarah was pouring herself a cup of coffee when Erin came into the kitchen, fully dressed and ready for work. Sarah still wore her pjs—a pair of boxer shorts and a white, cotton camisole. She wore her hair in two loose pigtails.

"Morning came early," Sarah said in a gravelly voice.

"Why are you awake? You should have slept in."

"I got up to pee at five, and I couldn't fall back asleep. My mind woke up." She shrugged and took a sip of coffee.

Erin set her messenger bag down on the closest counter stool and grabbed an oversized mug off the mug tree. "Thanks for making this," she said as she poured herself a cup. "I thought I was going to have to wait until I got to work. I keep meaning to buy ground coffee. Why you get whole bean, I'll never know." She moved to the fridge to grab the creamer. "Who wants to listen to coffee beans grinding first thing in the morning? It's so loud."

Erin cast a glance back at Sarah in time to see her roll her eyes. They'd had this conversation before.

"It's an itty-bitty price to pay for good coffee," Sarah insisted.

Slowly stirring in the creamer, Erin watched the coffee lighten to a perfect, rich almond color. "I honestly can't tell the difference."

"That's because all you can taste is creamer," Sarah replied with a grin.

Erin looked at her coffee. Sarah might have a point there. "Hmm. Well anyway, happy Monday. What are you up to today?"

"I'm fixin' to run out and grab a few things for the party on Saturday, just as soon as I finish wakin' up."

"What are you buying? Olivia, Heidi, and I are taking care of the food, remember?"

"I know. I just can't have a party and contribute nothing to it."

"Sarah—"

"I know, I know. I won't get much. Just a few things, and I do want to buy a few more beach towels and a sand castle set for Nora to play with."

Erin smiled. "She'll be fun to watch out here."

"That child melts my heart. Every time I'm around her, the tick of my biological clock is deafening."

"That makes one of us," Erin said, forcing a laugh. "How about you and Olivia have the babies, and I'll be the fun auntie." At Sarah's pinched expression, Erin realized what she'd said. "Oh, sh—I mean . . . crap. I've got to be so careful I don't slip up and say something like that in front of Olivia."

"She's come to terms with it, I think, but it's still not fair. They should have half a dozen kids, at least."

"I wish they could."

The two of them stared down at their coffee mugs. Poor Olivia. She was a terrific mother. It came so naturally to her, and it was a shame she and Sean wouldn't have any other kids to raise. Nora had been born by emergency cesarean, and something about the way she'd been delivered made any future pregnancy too dangerous for Olivia. At least she was a mother. She'd always have that.

Erin, on the other hand, would never be a parent. She'd be terrible at it, just as Jillian had been, and there was no way she'd do that to a kid. But to say it didn't hurt that she'd never experience motherhood would be a lie. To say she hadn't lain awake at night thinking about it more times than she cared to count . . . well, that would be a lie too.

"Anyway," Erin said, reaching for her messenger bag before pausing and giving Sarah a quick hug first. "I'm off."

Sarah set her mug down and wrapped both arms around her. "Have a good day. You holding some interviews?"

"Not till next week." Erin pulled away. "I'm in meetings all day with Gabe the Babe."

The corners of Sarah's mouth lifted. "Better stop calling him that, or you'll slip up in front of him one of these times."

Erin smirked. "I wonder what he'd do."

"Aren't you supposed to be on your summer vacation now? You said you had July off."

Erin gave her a pointed look. "Gabe's not going to let me have a summer vacation. He's too busy trying to prove himself to the board."

Gabriel Wright had just been hired as Nicolet's superintendent in late spring. Prior to that, he'd been the high school principal in Bayshore, a small town east of Nicolet. Erin had known him as an acquaintance prior to his coming on board in Nicolet. He was a nice guy, but very intense. After years of working with George Wiitala, the easygoing and grandfatherly superintendent Gabe had replaced, working with the high-strung Gabriel Wright was going to take some getting used to.

A frown knit between Sarah's brows. "I know it can't be easy being the youngest superintendent in Nicolet's history, and it probably doesn't help that he looks like a Calvin Klein underwear model, but this is ridiculous. He's using you to make himself look good to the board. All the data points he keeps asking you for, he knows how to find himself. He's been a principal. And he knows this is your time off." Sarah shook her head. "You need to put your foot down."

"If it keeps happening, I absolutely will."

"I'll hold you to it," Sarah warned.

"Alright, bossy pants." Erin grinned and slung the bag over her shoulder. She lifted her coffee mug in a silent toast. "See ya."

"Where's Marvin?" Sarah called after her.

"Crap!" Erin turned back, hand on the doorknob. "I forgot to let him out."

Sarah waved her along. "I'll take him out. You go."

"Thank you! I did feed him, though."

Sarah smirked. "That should hold him for about an hour."

Laughing, Erin opened the door, but she paused before stepping outside. "Hey, Sarah?"

"Hmm?" Sarah answered over the rim of her coffee mug.

"Thanks. For last night and for everything else. I mean it. I'm really grateful."

"You're welcome, sister."

Erin smiled. "Later."

Chapter 15

"You could just put that table over there, Ethan," Sarah suggested, looking up from the cooler she'd just filled with ice and pointing to the spot on the patio just to the left of the sliding glass door. "That way, the food will be in the shade a bit."

"Sure thing," Ethan said. He set the long table on its side and worked to release the folded legs.

"You're so sweet to help me. Thank you."

He slammed a hand against the second set of legs to get them in place and flipped the table right-side up. Then he turned to her and smiled. "You've thanked me plenty already, and like I said, it's my pleasure." He wiped imaginary dust off the tabletop. "You know, I've been looking forward to this party since you mentioned it. Gives me something to do other than stare at my computer screen and crunch numbers."

"You'll really like everyone."

"Well," he said, looking around, "you couldn't have chosen a more perfect day."

He was right. There wasn't a cloud in the sky, and the surface of the water glittered like diamonds. Sarah hadn't hosted many gatherings, and she felt both nervous and excited about what the day would bring. She glanced at her watch. This housewarming party was just a few minutes away from kicking off, but so far, Ethan was the only one there.

He'd seen her check the time, and he asked, "When's this boat going to get here?"

Sarah looked out over the open water. "The boat launch is out yonder way, but I'm not sure how far off. Olivia texted twenty minutes ago and said they were putting in, so I reckon they'll be here anytime."

"I'll get ready to help them dock if you're good up here."

She glanced around. Everything was set. The drinks were on ice, and the tables were ready for the plates and trays of food. She'd already set chairs down in the sand and in small groupings around the yard, and she had a stack of folded beach towels ready and waiting on a small table near the patio. From its perch on the kitchen windowsill, her Bluetooth speaker was blaring a summer playlist through the screen. All they really needed at this point were people. "Go on," she told Ethan. "I'm just fine here. Thank you so much for helping me. You're a real gem."

Marvin barked from his spot under one of the pine trees near the water, and Sarah moved to let him off his tie-out for a few minutes before guests started arriving. But Ethan remained rooted in place, and something in his face made Sarah stop and give him her full attention. "What is it?" she asked.

He turned himself to face her more fully. "Sarah, I . . . Well, it's just . . . I've had a chance to . . ." he shifted his gaze down to his feet before peering back up at her. "You know what, it's nothing."

Sarah frowned. "Is somethin' wrong?"

He forced a brief smile. "No, no. It's all good." His face said otherwise.

Sarah's stomach did an uncomfortable dip. "Is it my finances?" she pressed. "You've had a chance to look, right?"

He appeared pained. "I have. And it's not that, really. You're sitting pretty. Everything looks in order. For your sister too. We can have a sit down tomorrow if you want, and I can explain how the custodianship is set up for Nadia. I have some ideas for investments for her. For you too."

Sarah relaxed. "Oh, Ethan, thank you! You have no idea how much this has all been weighing on my mind. I've been afraid I'll mess something up, but with you steering me, I feel so much better already. I insist on payin' you, of course."

His face looked even more pained.

Something wasn't quite right. Normally, Ethan was a pretty chill, happy guy, but at the moment he looked almost . . . tormented. "Ethan, *what* is the matter?"

"I don't want you to pay me," he blurted.

"Of course I would pay—"

He held up one hand. "No. I mean it. I'm happy to advise you, but you can't pay me. Those are my terms."

Sarah didn't understand. He'd just delivered great news, but he looked like he was heading into a funeral, and his tone just now had been almost harsh. "Aright then," she said gently.

He nodded, and for a moment, they just stared at each other.

"Look, Ethan. I'm sorry if I said something—"

He sighed loudly and rubbed one hand along the back of his neck. "You didn't. I'm just . . . I'm having an off morning. I apologize."

"Alright," she repeated doubtfully. She might have said something more, but the sound of an engine in the bay made them both turn and look. Olivia and Sean waved to them from a white speed boat with a red stripe that ran along the side. Sean sounded the horn with three successive beeps.

"I'd better help," Ethan said, moving down towards the dock.

Sarah fell into step beside him. "I'll come too. And Ethan?"

"Hmm?"

"No more long faces. This is a party."

He glanced at her and grinned. "Deal."

They helped dock the boat, working out the best places to put the two white, rubber fenders, and then they began unloading the things the Lacombe's had brought along, including another large cooler—this one full of food—a half-inflated, two-man tube, and an electric air pump.

"Anna and Landon have Nora. They're driving Sean's truck with the rest of the food and some extra chairs, and"—Olivia waggled her brows above her aviator sunglasses—"your housewarming gift."

Sarah smiled. "I can't wait."

Olivia put her hands on Sarah's shoulders and squealed. "*I* can't wait! This is going to be such a fun day."

Sarah pulled her into a hug. "Thanks for making it happen."

"Of course!" Olivia looked around. Sean and Ethan were standing over the outboard motor, discussing horsepower. "Let's leave these boys to their talk, and you and I can get some of this food set up." She grabbed one end of the cooler, and Sarah took the other. They made it only a few steps before Olivia remembered something. "Sean?" she called back to the boat.

He turned at the sound of her voice. "Yeah?"

"Can you two blow up the tube so it's ready to go?"

"Yeah. We'll take care of it." He eyed up the heavy cooler they were carrying. "We can get that too."

"Nah," Olivia answered good-naturedly. "We've got this." The two women maneuvered the cooler off the dock and up to the patio. It wasn't all that heavy, but it was cumbersome. Halfway up the yard, Olivia glanced back at Sarah. "We bought a wakeboard too. It's in the bow. Sean's determined to get up on it today. But that leaves me driving the boat, and I don't want to."

"Maybe one of the other guys will know how," Sarah suggested.

"Let's hope. Because I kinda like my husband."

They reached the patio, and Sarah laughed. "Stop. The worst that would happen is you wouldn't be able to get him up."

Olivia's eyes sparkled as she set down the cooler beside the other one. "That's never been a problem."

When Sarah realized what she'd said, she choked on a laugh. "Oh my gosh! I didn't mean *that*! I meant up out of the water!"

"Yeah, that makes more sense," Olivia joked. She began to pull items out of the cooler and handed them to Sarah to place on the table. "Making you blush is just too much fun."

The two of them were still laughing when they heard someone arrive at the back of the house. They rounded the corner in time to see Landon and Anna climbing out of the front of Sean's truck. Sarah greeted the young couple with hugs and Olivia showed them where to unload and set up the food and chairs they'd brought with them.

Sarah stayed back and gently removed Nora from her car seat. She managed to do it without waking the little one-year-old, and the feel of the small child's warm body pressed against hers, her head resting on Sarah's shoulder . . . well, it was a wonderful feeling. A wonderful, sad, aching feeling. She carried Nora towards the patio and to her mother.

Olivia watched Sarah approach the patio as she directed the placement of the food and sent her an understanding smile.

Not ready to part with the baby yet, and seeing how Olivia had taken over as party planner, she said, "I'm just going to take her for a short stroll down the drive, if that's okay."

Olivia nodded. "That's fine, but I'll warn you. She'll get heavier by the minute."

"I won't go far."

"Go as far as you like, just know your arms will be burning before too long." Olivia winked.

Sarah smiled. She didn't care. Her arms could burn all they wanted. It wasn't every day she got to hold a little one. She turned and headed toward the front—oops, the back—of the house and was surprised to find Benny's truck parked just in front of the garage. She hadn't heard him come up the driveway.

He was getting out of the driver's side when he spotted her, and he hung suspended in the act of stepping down.

She stopped moving too, and they stared at one another in silence.

Benny was the first to speak. "She looks good on you." He nodded at the sleeping child.

Sarah approached him. "She's so precious, isn't she?"

"She is cute," he agreed before hopping down from the truck.

So was he. Benny's thick hair was slightly mussy, as if he'd forgotten to brush it after his shower that morning, and he wore sporty black sandals with black swimming trunks and his signature white T-shirt. He must have a dozen of those, at least.

In addition to his wide variety of swimming trunks, every morning he'd worked on her wall, he'd shown up in a crisp, white T-shirt, each one looking as though it had been taken fresh out of its packaging and ironed to perfection before being pulled on. He'd been deliciously sweaty and dirty by the end of every workday, but each morning, he started off squeaky clean and Sarah had always had the bizarre urge to bury her face in his chest and inhale his scent. She wasn't close enough now to get a whiff, but she already knew what he smelled like: a mixture of Old Spice and Downy dryer sheets. Heaven.

How many times during the last few weeks had she wished she could do that? She wanted to breathe him in. She wanted to hold him close, and she wanted his arms wrapped around her, holding her so tightly against him that she'd know he'd never let go of her. Making her feel like she wasn't alone in the world. She longed for it. She craved it with such an intensity that the frustration over the lack of it sometimes brought tears to her eyes. And yet, she was afraid to want it. She was at war with her own feelings.

Sarah watched him as he opened the back of his truck. He retrieved a towel and threw it around his neck before grabbing two grocery bags with each hand. He'd brought food for the party. By the looks of it, it was all store-bought and not homemade, but so what? It was the thought that counted. He hadn't wanted to come empty handed, and wasn't that just like him? He was so thoughtful. And more and more, she was of the opinion that he was the most good-looking man she'd ever met. She loved everything about him.

Sarah's heartbeat picked up speed as she remembered that Benny would be seeing her in her bathing suit for the first time today. Would he like what he saw? She didn't have a perfect body. She was strong and toned, but she was no model. Her breasts were too small and her thighs were too big, and yesterday she'd noticed a little cellulite where her butt met her legs. It had been enough to make her drive to the store and purchase board shorts to try to cover it up.

If Erin wore her new hot pink bikini, Sarah would be completely overshadowed. She'd never measure up. No doubt, Benny was still attracted to Erin, even if he'd said he'd moved on. The thought deflated her.

Before long, the guests all arrived, and Sarah's housewarming gift was strategically placed beside the sauna building. The younger guests were down on the beach, but everyone else stood with Sarah around the black steel fire ring they'd all chipped in to buy her. It stood on three legs and had cutouts of stars and moons, and she absolutely loved it.

Chairs had been set up around it, and Benny was already working on getting some kindling set inside the ring for the bonfire they'd have later that night. He'd picked up some firewood on the way out and had already set that down in a neat pile beside it. They'd also gotten Sarah some slightly scandalous roasting sticks for hot dogs and marshmallows.

There were four in total: two "male" sticks to roast a strategically placed hot dog, and two "female" sticks for strategically placed marshmallows. The picture on the box showed the placement of the wieners and marshmallows, and it was graphic enough to make Sarah blush. Olivia was right. It didn't take much.

"Let me guess whose idea these roasting sticks were," she said to the group as they laughed uproariously. Only Benny was subdued, likely over the same embarrassment she felt.

"Okay," Olivia said on a giggle. "But you only get the one guess."

Sarah shook her head, still smiling.

"Speaking of Erin," Heidi chimed in, "where is she?"

Ethan perked up at the question. Had Benny too? "She'll be on her way out soon. She had a meeting with the new superintendent this morning that she couldn't get out of."

Olivia shot Sarah a bemused glance. "On a Saturday?"

Sarah wrinkled her nose. "I know. He expects her to be at his beck and call. I've lost count of how many meetings she's had with him just this week."

"Is he on some kind of power trip with her or something?" Olivia asked with a frown. "I haven't even met him yet, and already, I don't like him." She watched Benny finish preparing the ring for the fire they'd have later. "And now I feel bad. We probably should have waited to give you this until she was here. I wasn't thinking!"

Sarah reassured her that Erin wouldn't mind, and then she looked at each of them in turn. "This is such a great present. Y'all are the best."

They smiled widely at her, pleased she was happy with her gift.

"Alright," Olivia said. "Well, when she does get here, the party's officially started."

Steven grinned. "Oh, it looks pretty well on its way to me." He and Heidi stood side by side, shoulders touching. Steven wore a blue sun shirt and flip flops, and Heidi had on a black tankini with hot pink board shorts. Sarah could only hope she looked that fit when she hit her forties. Heidi was a runner, she remembered. Steven too. Maybe that's what kept them looking so young.

Glancing around, Sarah saw that Steven was right. The "kids," as everyone liked to call them, even though they were all out of high school, were already down on the beach, and they were laying out towels and taking turns watching Nora. Sarah knew Anna and Jess, having taught them both in senior year English, but she'd only met Anna's boyfriend and brother, Landon and Mitch, at the wedding reception. They'd seemed like nice boys and definitely dreamy—by anyone's standards.

"I'm glad the kids could come," Sarah remarked. She glanced at Olivia and Sean. "They'll be able to help with Nora so you two can relax a little."

Olivia sighed. "God knows I love her, but it's so great to let someone else chase after her for a while." Addressing Steven, she added, "I don't know what I'd do without Anna."

"We don't know what Anna would do without you and Nora," Heidi returned with a smile.

Sean chuckled. "Anna already knows what to expect, but those boys are going to get a crash course in parenting today. Might make them think twice about certain . . . activities."

Olivia rolled her eyes. "Nice, Sean!"

Benny coughed. "How's Mitch doing these days?" he asked Steven.

Steven rocked back on his heels. "Really good. His ankle's all healed up now."

"He's a good kid," Sean said decisively. "I can't wait to get him back on the ice. You know, he was phenomenal last year, even when he had the weight of the world on his shoulders. With his load lightened, he'll fly across the rink. Honestly, he's every coach's dream."

"I sure was sad to see him go," Benny admitted. "They don't make them like that anymore. I'd say he's the best player I'll ever have."

"Maybe mine too," Sean agreed.

Steven set his shoulders back and beamed.

"You know," Heidi lowered her voice to a whisper, "he and Jess are dating."

Olivia almost dropped the water bottle she was holding. "*What?*"

Heidi just grinned in response.

Sarah glanced down at the beach in time to see Mitch put his arm around Jess's shoulders and pull her close as he spoke into her ear. She laughed and gave him a playful shove.

Olivia's shocked expression was comical. "How did I not know this?"

"It's a new development," Steven explained. "To tell you the truth, I'm surprised it took them this long to get together. Those two have been two peas in a pod for well over a decade. They're both young and attractive, and I sort of always wondered why it hadn't occurred to either of them to give it a go."

Sarah knew Jess and Anna had been best friends since elementary school. Maybe that was why. It would be a little awkward to date your best friend's brother. You'd have to be very, very sure before taking that step.

Heidi swatted at a lone mosquito. "I'm glad they waited. Mitch wouldn't have been ready for something real until just recently anyway."

Olivia nodded. Sarah knew that being a close confidant of Anna's kept her very much in the loop when it came to the lives of the Davis family. "Anna tells me he's still doing really well."

"He's in a good place," Steven confirmed. "He's come to terms with Shelly's death, which isn't to say he's over it, but at least the nightmares have stopped. I think he's finally been able to accept that there really was nothing he could have done to save her. He's been able to unload the guilt he's carried all these years. And"—he looked pointedly at Sean—"he's given up the drinking completely. He told me the other day he's not the kind of guy who can have just one."

As a young boy, Mitch had witnessed his mother's accident at the breakwall on a stormy day when Shelly had been swept off by a powerful wave and into the frigid, churning water of Lake Superior. Sarah didn't think anybody would ever be able to fully recover from something like that, but she was glad Mitch was learning to cope with it.

Both Steven and Mitch had gone into a tailspin after her death, which had lasted years and years, and Steven's relationship with Heidi, Shelly's twin sister, had fractured. It had taken a health scare with Steven's daughter, Anna, to unite the family again and spark much-needed changes in both of the Davis men.

Even Anna, who had already been stronger and wiser than her years, had learned a few things about herself and about life. Sarah was glad Olivia had been there for them all during that time. She and Anna had a very special bond, and it was even stronger now.

Sean looked thoughtful. "Maybe that broken ankle was a blessing, eh?"

"I don't know that I'd go that far," Heidi said sardonically.

"It slowed him down and gave him some time to think, at least," Steven said. "It gave him a fresh start. Let's just hope it sticks when school resumes and the parties start back up again."

"Landon will watch out for him," Sean reassured. "That kid has a good head on his shoulders."

"He'd better," Steven said with mock gravity. "He's dating my daughter."

Sean shook his head and laughed. "I give you a lot of credit, buddy. All I can say is nobody's dating my daughter. Not ever."

Steven turned to look at Nora playing in the sand, and when he turned back, he was smiling wistfully. "I think you have a little time to get used to the idea. Enjoy these years, Coach."

"Speaking of Nora," Olivia said, already moving towards the beach, "I need to get some sunblock on her."

Even from a distance, Sarah could see the sand that was stuck to every inch of the toddler's exposed skin. Olivia would have her work cut out for her.

Slowly, they all dispersed from their circle—Sean and Olivia to the beach, and the others to the patio to graze on food and grab drinks from the cooler. Sarah glanced at her watch. It was already after noon. Where was Erin?

Hearing movement behind her, Sarah turned and found Benny had stayed behind too. Her breath caught.

He nodded at the fire ring. "You like your gift?"

"I *love* it!" she answered a little too brightly.

He smiled. "I'm glad."

While he looked at her expectantly, her thoughts raced for something more to say. Gone was the ease that had existed between them before. She'd ruined it with her stupid crush. It had been a few days since she'd seen him, and she'd missed him. He'd finished up the retaining wall two days ago on Thursday. It felt like forever ago, and in that time, it seemed she'd forgotten how to talk with him like a normal person.

"The wall looks great, Benny," she said. "Thanks again."

Briefly, he looked at the wall. "Yeah, it turned out."

It had more than turned out. It was beautiful and professional looking and had far exceeded her expectations, but she could see Benny didn't want to chat about the wall.

All of a sudden, he was tense. He looked like the young boy she'd seen the other day out at Sable Rocks, fighting with himself as he worked up the courage to leap off the edge and into the water fifteen feet below. He took a step towards her. "Listen, Sarah, I wanted to talk to you about—"

"Hey, Sarah," Ethan interrupted from the patio, "Can I let Marvin out of the house? He's standing at the door, whining."

Sarah shot Benny a look of apology before she answered. "Yes, thank you. I guess he woke up from his nap early."

"He takes scheduled naps?" Ethan said dubiously as he came up beside her.

"He *is* just a baby," she reminded him.

Ethan grinned. "Coulda fooled me."

"Go ahead and let him out, but can you put him on his leash? I don't want him to scare Nora."

"You bet," Ethan said as he turned away.

Sarah watched him walk back towards the patio door before turning back to Benny. He also was watching Ethan, and with an expression of such disdain, it took Sarah by surprise. She knew Ethan wasn't Benny's favorite person, but his reaction was a little much. "So, what were you saying?" she asked him. Whatever it was, she had a feeling it would be profound, and she held her breath as she waited for it.

"He knows where you keep the leash?"

The *leash?* "Uh . . . yeah."

"And Marvin likes him now?"

"They've gotten to know each other, and—"

"So, he's over here a lot then? Inside?"

What on earth? Sarah thought. And then it clicked: Benny was jealous. It was so obvious; she didn't know how she'd missed it. Ethan was taking care of Erin's dog and was familiar with Erin's space—her temporary space, but still, her space.

Benny had been out here for weeks on end working on the wall, probably in hopes of catching a glimpse of Erin in her pink bikini. Sarah had noticed him slowing down his work, and for a time, she'd entertained the idea that he was deliberately drawing it out so he could spend more time with *her*. But he'd just wanted more opportunity to connect with Erin.

Her heart sank, and she quickly smiled to make sure her face didn't show it. She felt silly for having held on to the hope that, just maybe, Benny might be interested in her.

She swallowed hard. "Ethan's a really great guy, Benny. I know you got off on the wrong foot before, but you'll get to know him today, and you'll see how awesome he is."

His eyes narrowed. "*Awesome*, huh?"

"Well, yeah." At his wounded expression she added, "Just like you. You're pretty . . . um . . . awesome too."

His scowl deepened.

"I mean, you're both *so* great. Really, really great." For heaven's sake, could she be more idiotic?

"Thanks," he replied flatly, pinching his lips closed before he turned on his heel and walked towards the dock.

Sarah stood there, completely dejected and totally flabbergasted. What had just happened?

After her late-night talk with Erin earlier in the week, Sarah had given her situation a lot of thought. She liked Benny. She liked him *that way*, and there was no reason to pretend otherwise. One of the things she most appreciated about him was how direct he was. He had a blunt honesty about him, which made for some awkward moments and conversations, but because of that, she'd decided she could let herself trust him. He was one of the good ones. And she'd told herself, she deserved one of the good ones.

She watched him walk out to the end of the dock. He really *was* awesome, but awesome or not, she'd wasted her time—and her emotional energy. In all of her thinking, she hadn't considered that Benny might truly still be pining away after Erin. After all the hours they'd spent together working and swimming and going to the laser show, Sarah had half convinced herself that he cared for her but was just too shy to make a move. Instead, all along, it had been Erin he preferred, and for a split second, Sarah resented her.

Chapter 16

The party was in full swing when Erin arrived. She parked behind a car she didn't recognize. Maybe it was Mitch's, she thought. She'd had Steven's son as a high school student. He'd been a senior at her school a mere two years ago. Now he was a hockey star for Nicolet State. He'd shattered his ankle last year after a drunken mishap, but it turned out it might just have been the best thing that could have happened to him. The Davis family had experienced two health emergencies over the last year. One with Anna, and one with Mitch, and both had served to reunite a family that had been desperately in need of healing.

She got out of her car and saw a boat leaving the bay, pulling a tube behind it with two people lying flat on their bellies on top of it.

Tubing—how fun!

It had been a long time since Erin had been towed behind a boat. She used to water ski and tube at summer camp back in California. Every summer until the eighth grade, Erin's parents had sent her to camp. It wasn't just any summer camp, though. It was a camp for the children of the rich and powerful. How her barely upper-class parents had afforded it, Erin would never know. All she knew was that it was of utmost importance to her mother that she attend. For appearances, of course.

The funny thing was, Erin had actually really enjoyed it, but once she realized she could use it to her advantage in the endless power struggle with her mother, she'd stopped going. That first refusal had put her mother in a real state. It used to make Erin smile to think about it. She must be growing up, or something, because now it just made her sad. She had never seen Jillian so angry as she'd been that day. Her dad actually had to physically come and stand between them as they shouted at each other. Sometimes Erin wondered what would have happened if he hadn't been there. At the very least, her mother would have slapped her. And then what would she, Erin, have done?

"You're here!" Olivia shouted from the beach. She was sitting in the sand in a green one-piece with Nora climbing all over her. The little girl was completely covered in sand, save one of those swim diapers Erin had seen commercials for, and she was bare on top. Even from the driveway, Erin could make out her cute little pot belly. Unfortunately, it was the only time of life that society at large found leg dimples and pot bellies cute on a female. She smiled at the thought.

"I'm here!" she hollered back. "Let me run inside and unload my stuff. I'll get my suit on and join you in a sec."

"Hurry up! You're missing all the fun, you big party pooper!" Olivia shouted back.

Erin grinned and stuck out her tongue. A second later, Sarah poked her head around the corner of the house.

"Oh!" she exclaimed. A leashed Marvin jerked her forward as he bounded towards Erin with exuberant barks. In a smart move, Sarah let go of the leash, and within seconds, he was at Erin's feet, rubbing his body against her as she laughed and greeted him. "Hi there, boy. Did you miss me?"

"He really did," Sarah answered when she reached them. She bent down and handed Erin the leash. "He was whining earlier, so I let him off his lead, but after he ran up to everyone and sniffed, he started howling. It was like he knew you were missing. Erin, it was the sweetest thing."

"Aw," Erin said. Her eyes misted over, and for once, she didn't try to hide it. "That is so sweet."

"He loves you," Sarah said, putting an arm around her shoulder as they walked to the door together. Marvin, still leashed, walked ahead of them, turning back periodically to make sure they were still there.

"How's it going? The party."

"Great! But where've you been? It's almost one thirty."

Erin shrugged. "Meetings."

"*Humph!*" Sarah expressed her disgust. "I may just need to write Gabe an anonymous letter letting him know what a tyrant I think he is. Anyway, you're here now, so the real fun can start. Everyone's having a good time, I think. I know I am. You missed it, but Sean tried to get up on the wakeboard. Benny was driving the boat. It was funny as all get out. Olivia was in stitches, and Sean was gettin' madder and madder in the water. Not at Olivia, of course. He's going to try again later, so you'll get to see the sequel."

Erin grinned. She wasn't sure she'd ever seen Sarah this animated. And she was absolutely certain she'd never seen Sean upset away from the ice arena. That would have been fun to witness. She imagined him smacking at the water in frustration and decided she definitely needed to be on that boat the next time he tried to wakeboard.

"Sounds like fun," Erin said. Marvin preceded them into the house, which broke one of the rules she'd learned at puppy school. He was supposed to sit and wait, knowing his place was always dead last after people, but that didn't seem all that fair to her. Why couldn't he be first sometimes? Taking his leash off on the other side of the door, she asked, "How's he been with the baby?"

"So sweet. Very gentle," Sarah reassured.

"Was Olivia nervous?" Erin moved towards the cupboard in the kitchen and took out a glass for some water. Likewise, Marvin got himself a drink. She could hear him lapping from his dish in the laundry room.

Sarah trailed after her. "Honestly, a little. But don't hold it against her. She's fine now."

Erin tried not to take it personally. "I can keep him in for a bit."

Sarah shrugged. "Whatever you think." She grabbed a glass for herself and filled it up from the tap. "How were your meetings?"

Erin was glad Sarah wasn't looking her in the eyes right then, or she would have known immediately that Erin was lying when she answered, "Oh, you know, about as good as meetings with Gabe can be."

"So you've said." She placed a hand on Erin's shoulder and gave her a few small pats. "Time to kick back and relax now."

Erin laughed. "Kick back and relax? Hell no! I'm going skiing, or tubing, or wakeboarding, or whatever else they've got going on out there."

Sarah smiled brightly. "That's the spirit!"

Water in hand, Erin turned to head up the stairs. "Just give me a minute to slip into my suit. Get ready," she warned with a wiggle of her hips. "I'm going to strut my stuff out there."

Sarah froze. "Strut your stuff?" she repeated slowly.

"Yeah," Erin said with a playful smile. "Remember my motto."

After giving a small shake of her head, Sarah asked, "In which one will you be . . . *strutting*?"

Her tone oozed judgmental disapproval, and it stopped Erin in her tracks on the very first step. "What?"

"What suit are you plannin' on wearin'?"

Erin tried to shake off her irritation. Sometimes Sarah could be such a prude. "My new one, obviously."

Sarah put a hand on her hip. "That pink one? Erin, there are kids here! And Benny's—" She pressed her lips tightly together as if she'd said too much.

Erin backed down off the step. "What? What are you talking about—kids and Benny?"

Inexplicably, Sarah turned the color of a McIntosh apple. "It's nothing," she answered defensively.

Erin let out a taut sigh. "Sarah, what's wrong with my bathing suit?"

Throwing up her hands, Sarah unloaded on her. "Let's see a minute! Besides the fact that it's made only of strings? Nothing. Nothin' at all. My gosh, Erin! You'll be parading around here practically naked!"

Erin felt like a faulty pressure cooker that was seconds away from exploding. What more could go wrong with this day? She forced her voice to remain calm and even, but the sarcasm was thick when she said, "Whoa, did you just say *gosh?*" She lifted her brows into mocking arcs. "You must be really, *really* mad!"

As a matter of fact, Sarah did look really, really mad, but Erin was well on her way too. Who was Sarah to tell her what she could and couldn't wear? To judge her?

"Fine!" Sarah spat with a hostility that nearly charred the air.

Erin was shocked. Honestly, she didn't know Sarah had it in her to get this ticked off, and she was torn. Was she outraged, or was she impressed? Maybe she was both. Or neither. There wasn't time to decide.

"Wear what you want, then." Sarah turned on her heel and stormed out of the house.

Erin stared after her for several seconds before taking to the stairs once more. As she climbed, she looked over the railing at Marvin who was laying, all splayed out, near the sofa on the floor. Obviously, he'd missed the whole thing. It might not be a big deal to him, but to her, it was huge. Sarah had just yelled at her for the first time ever.

By the time she reached the top of the staircase, she remembered something, and it all made sense. When she'd first worn her new bikini the week before, Sarah had made a comment. At the time, Erin hadn't really thought much of it, but now, it echoed in her ears:

"Wow! Remind me not to stand anywhere next to you at the beach. I'd be trampled to death by all the men that come runnin' to get a closer look."

It was clear: Sarah felt threatened. She was afraid Erin would steal Benny's attention.

It took Erin more than ten minutes to find it. She had to hunt through a few unpacked boxes she'd shoved to the back of her closet before she located the miserable thing. It was quite possibly the ugliest bathing suit known to mankind. Honestly, she didn't know why she'd hung on to this one and pitched the other one that only had a bit of shot elastic on one side of the bottoms. If she'd held on to that one, she'd have had something halfway decent to wear. Now, she was stuck.

A few years back, they'd piloted a swim program for severely impaired kids at the high school, and Erin had needed to take the place of one of the aides last minute. Since there was no way a bikini would be appropriate in that setting, she'd had to go shopping. There had been only two bathing suits for sale in the whole of Nicolet that October: the one she was staring at, which was yellow with white daisies and had a ruffled scoop top with no breast cups since it was made for a ten-year-old, or the women's size sixteen swimdress with cups sized large enough to hold over-ripened cantaloupes with room to spare.

It had been no choice at all, and Erin had definitely taken her share of teasing for those weeks the program had run. She'd handled it fine, probably because all the adults in that program had been very large women with their own wardrobe problems. But this was different. Now she was going to walk out there in front of everyone, Ethan included, looking like a pre-pubescent girl headed to the pool with her mother. She might as well throw on a pair of water wings.

Quickly, she donned the ugly suit before she could change her mind, and she threw on a pair of gray terry shorts to cover the fact that the one-piece wasn't quite long enough to fit her torso. Gratifyingly, that meant she was taller than most ten-year-old girls, but it also meant that with every step she took, the suit would ride further and further up her crack until she was wearing an inadvertent thong. She'd be well and truly chafed by the end of the day.

When Erin opened the door to the patio several minutes later and stepped outside behind Marvin, the expression on Sarah's face was worth it. She'd shocked her. Good! And she was happy to see guilt register there too because Sarah *should* feel guilty. Erin would never have done this to her—not wanted her to wear something because it looked good on her. But then, she'd never been one of those women who felt physically *less-than* around other women who were prettier or taller or whatever else. Her insecurities were under the surface and always had been.

Olivia walked toward them with her mouth hanging open. "Erin," she asked slowly, "what in the world are you wearing?"

Erin yanked at her wedgie. "My bathing suit," she said matter-of-factly as she moved to select a sub sandwich for herself.

Olivia's mouth twitched for several seconds before she lost the struggle and a giggle escaped. "How long have you had that thing, since elementary school?"

"Actually, it's fairly new," Erin deadpanned.

Sarah drew closer and whispered, "Erin, *please* go change. I didn't mean for you to—"

"Hey," Erin interrupted, stepping back and forcing a bright smile, "I'm wearing my bathing suit at a beach party with my two best girls. It's fine. Alright?"

Olivia looked back and forth between them for a moment and threw up her hands before reaching into the cooler for a Coke. "Okay. I can pretend this is normal if you guys can." She shot them both an amused grin as she closed the lid and started back down towards the boat. Marvin followed her. "I'll be right back," she informed them from over her shoulder. "I just need to give this to Sean."

It was just the two of them on the patio now, and Erin was aware of her friend's eyes watching her as she continued to fill her plate. After several seconds, Sarah placed a hand on top of hers just as Erin was reaching for a cookie.

"Listen, I'm sorry. I don't know what came over me before. It's like the Devil got hold of my tongue, or something. Please, go put on your pink suit."

Erin shot her a sugar-sweet smile. "Nope. I want you to look at me in this thing all day and know that *I* was the bigger person for a change. Oh, and I forgive you." She planted a quick kiss on Sarah's cheek and grabbed a handful of chips for her plate. She felt Sarah close on her heels.

"Erin—" Sarah tried again.

"Nope," Erin repeated, scooping up a large slice of watermelon and plopping it on her plate too, right next to the chips. "You're not going to win this one, my friend, so don't even try. You know I'm more stubborn than you."

Benny appeared just as Erin began doctoring up her sub sandwich. "Hey, Erin," he said, barely sparing her a glance before rummaging through the cooler.

Erin couldn't contain her smirk. Sarah was a complete idiot. There was exactly zero possibility that Benny was interested in her anymore. He was one hundred percent smitten with Sarah.

"What perfect timing!" she exclaimed, unable to help herself. "Sarah was just saying she wanted to try out her sauna today. You should fire it up, Benny. Show her how it's done. You know, get a little *sweaty* together in there."

Benny's head popped back up in surprise, and Erin had the pleasure of watching Sarah's jaw drop before she stepped off the patio to join the rest of the party. There, now they were even. Although, if anyone were to ask her, she'd tell them she'd just done Sarah a huge favor. *Someone* needed to be the one to give those two a gigantic shove out of the "just friends" zone.

Erin stopped to talk to Heidi, who was standing in the middle of the lawn, watching Anna and Jess play with Nora. She hadn't seen Heidi for a while, and she'd enjoyed the few times they'd gotten together. She was still probably more of an acquaintance than a friend at this point, but she and Olivia were spending more time together, which meant Erin was getting to know her better too. "Lookin' good, Doc," she said, giving the radiologist a nudge with her shoulder.

A smile lit her face. "Erin!"

"What are you doing standing here and staring off?"

Heidi turned to give Erin her full attention. "Just watching little Nora."

"She's a cute kid, huh?"

Heidi nodded, looking back towards the beach. "Sometimes, like now, I really wish I'd had kids of my own." She hesitated. "Do you ever wish for that? Motherhood, I mean?"

Normally, Erin would have given some kind of flippant answer, but this time she answered honestly. "Yeah, I do sometimes."

Heid's smile turned wistful. "I'm glad I have Anna and Mitch. I couldn't ask for a better niece and nephew. One day—and believe me, it can be a *looong* time from now—they'll have families of their own, and I'll get to be a grandmother."

Erin was about to agree before she fully understood what Heidi had just revealed. She shifted her plate to one hand and reached out with the other to touch Heidi's arm. "Wait, are you saying . . ."

Heidi's eyes widened as she realized what she'd just given away, and her hands flew to her mouth. "Oh, no!" She looked around to see if anyone was listening, but nobody was close enough to hear. Still, she whispered when she said, "Crap! You can't say anything. We haven't even spoken to the kids yet."

Erin clutched Heidi's arm. "But you and Steven?" she whispered back.

Heidi kept her voice low. "He proposed two days ago. We went up Mt. Joliet, it's kind of our place, and he got down on one knee."

"And?" Erin prompted.

Heidi laughed. "I said yes, of course!"

This kind of news was the hardest for Erin to keep under wraps. Usually, with secrets like this, she *had* to share it with one other person. Just one other person in the know, someone she could talk to about whatever it was, helped bring down the rush of adrenaline she always felt at knowing something nobody else did. But looking at Heidi right then and seeing how she glowed, how happy she was, Erin was determined to keep this one to herself. No matter how difficult it might be, she would *not* tell Sarah. Erin mimed the zipping of her lips. "I promise I won't say anything, but I am *so* excited for you!"

Heidi placed a hand on her heart. "Thank you. We're pretty sure the kids have seen it coming, but we wanted to tell them together. They should be the first to know. We're taking them to dinner tomorrow night, so we'll do it then."

"Hey, Aunt Heidi!" Anna called from the beach. "Can you watch Nora for a while? Jess and I want to grab some lunch, and then we're going to tube once the guys are done."

"Sure!" Heidi hollered back.

Olivia chimed in as she walked toward them from the dock. "I've got her, Heidi!"

Behind Olivia, on the end of the dock, Erin noticed her dog standing and watching Sean navigate the boat full of guys into the bay, towing the tube slowly behind it. It was as if Marvin wanted to go for a ride too. Erin could understand. She couldn't wait for her turn. She watched him slowly lay down, even though she could tell by the way he held his ears that he was still on high alert.

"Nora should probably get out of the sun anyway," Olivia added loudly enough for Anna to hear.

Erin returned her attention to Heidi, who looked disappointed. "Are you sure, Olivia? I don't mind."

Olivia reached their spot at the center of the yard. "Yeah. I'll feed her a little lunch and then put her down for a nap inside. I already have the port-a-crib set up in Sarah's room."

Olivia went to get Nora, but Anna requested a few more minutes at the beach with the baby, so the three friends made their way to the patio table where Sarah and Benny sat.

Erin pulled out a chair and set her plate down. Heidi followed suit while Olivia stood and waited for Anna to bring Nora up. "Sarah," Erin said, "Did you say Marvin already napped?"

"Yeah, but not for too long."

"Hmm. Maybe he'll go down again after his lunch. He's not used to so much commotion, and I think he's tired." She lifted her slice of watermelon and took a juicy bite.

Olivia chuckled. "I forget sometimes that Marvin's just a puppy. He's like a baby in a lot of ways."

"He is *such* a baby," Sarah remarked with a grin. "When Erin's not close by, he pouts." As if on cue, Marvin appeared and laid down on the ground beside Erin's chair, letting out a satisfied doggy grunt as he did.

Olivia grinned and squatted beside him to rub his chest.

"So, Benny," Erin began, taking notice of the fact that Sarah and Benny were not yet sweating it out together in the sauna, "why aren't you on the boat with the guys?" The answer was obvious: He wanted to stay back with her completely oblivious friend, not that he'd ever offer that up on his own. But today was the day. It was past time for one or the other of them to show their cards, and she was going to poke at them until that happened.

"I was hungry," he replied.

Erin rolled her eyes, and Sarah shot her a curious look.

"You built a nice wall for Sarah," Erin added before crunching on a chip.

He made a similar-sounding grunt to the one Marvin had just made.

She swallowed. "And didn't you help her put in her dock too?"

"He did," Sarah answered brightly. "He's really helped me out a ton. Thanks again, Benny." She threw Erin a warning glance.

Erin ignored her. "You know, you're being a *really* good friend to Sarah, and I think I know how she could repay you."

Benny met her eyes, and she could see the guarded curiosity there. "She's already paid me," he informed her.

Ignoring that too, Erin continued on. "Sarah makes this amazing peach cobbler. She should make it for you as a way to say thank you. I know she's *so* grateful." She glanced at Sarah. "When can you have him over for dinner and some peach cobbler out here on the patio, Sarah?"

Everyone was quiet. Erin used the moment to take a huge bite out of her sub sandwich. She sat back against her chair and chewed, looking at each of them in turn. Olivia straightened out, wiping non-existent Marvin hairs off her hands, while Heidi looked at Erin as if she'd grown horns. Sarah and Benny looked everywhere except at one another.

Erin swallowed her bite and wiped her mouth with her napkin. "Sarah?" She prompted.

"Um. Are you free tomorrow, Benny?" she asked, after shooting Erin a murderous glare.

Benny's expression was pinched. "Of course, but you don't have to—"

"But I'd love to!" Sarah interrupted eagerly, placing her hand over the top of his and then jerking it back again the moment she made contact.

Slowly, his guarded expression transformed to one of cautious optimism that spread from his mouth to the corners of his eyes, and when he finally spoke, he was wearing a full-blown smile.

Erin pushed herself away from the table. Her plate might still be full, but her work was done here. "Alrighty! Tomorrow night. It's a date, and I promise to make myself scarce." She glanced down at Marvin, who appeared ready to drop into a deep, doggy sleep at a moment's notice. "Come on, boy. Let's get you some lunch and see about that nap."

Olivia's eyes danced with contained amusement. "I'll be right behind you with Nora."

Inside, Erin scooped a cup of Marvin's food into his dish, and he inhaled the kibble, just as he always did. Then he looked at her, begging for more with his droopy eyes, just as he always did, and she tossed him a small Milk-Bone treat to pacify him, which was also a part of their routine. Once he'd licked up every last crumb, she brought him upstairs where it took only a few minutes to get him comfortable on the bed in her room.

Living on the water with a beach only steps away was definitely nice, but it did have one drawback: sand seemed to make its way into every nook and cranny of the house, no matter how careful they were. The majority of it came in on Marvin, and Erin had learned that placing a sheet down over the top of the comforter kept the bed from getting too sandy. She spread it out before sitting and patting the place beside her. Marvin needed no further prompting before jumping up and turning a few circles to get his position just right. She wondered why dogs did that.

She sat and stroked him with a small smile on her lips. She couldn't help but feel pleased with herself. She'd have to deal with Sarah's half-hearted annoyance that she'd interfered, but it was a small price to pay for helping out a friend.

How had this happened to her? Obviously, she'd had friends before. Growing up, she'd been popular, always surrounded by her peers, male and female. But there'd been a lot of land mines to navigate—heaps of drama actually—and she'd never been able to let her guard down. Sorting out the fake friends from the real ones had seemed like an impossible task, so she hadn't tried. It was a lot easier to keep them all at arm's length, so that's what she'd done. She'd had loads of good-time friends, but not one single person to call in her time of greatest need.

Now she had a circle, a friend group that felt more and more like a family with each passing day. And she had a dog who loved and adored her, who even moped when she was away because he missed her so much. It was more than she'd ever had before.

Jimmy the Poodle had been the canine version of Jillian. He was warmer and more reliable, but he'd been pretty stingy with his affection. Often, when she'd get home from school, he wouldn't even get up to see her. She'd have to go find him to give him a few pats on the head.

Marvin, on the other hand, gave love freely, with careless abandon, and asked for nothing in return. It made her chest burn and her throat ache as she thought about it. She may not have a family, and maybe she never would, but she had at least found her tribe, and the joy the realization brought her was overwhelming in its power.

Erin took a few more minutes to gather herself, petting Marvin's wrinkly forehead all the while, before standing and opening her door. Predictably, Marvin lifted his head and looked at her with eyes that pleaded with her to stay. "I love you too. Go to sleep, boy." He'd already laid his head back down before she closed the door behind her.

Downstairs, she crossed paths with Olivia who carried Nora in a towel.

"Aren't you just the bossy little matchmaker!" Olivia laughed.

Erin grinned. "I know how to get it done."

Olivia shook her head and continued on down the hall to Sarah's room. "I can't decide if Sarah is going to murder you or smother you in hugs later on," she called out behind her.

"I'll let you know."

Olivia turned, and with a sing-songy voice replied, "Not if you're dead."

Erin rolled her eyes. "Is Nora going down for her nap? I thought you were going to feed her lunch."

"I am. I'm just changing her first. I have a feeling she'll fall asleep in her booster seat. This way, she'll be all set to go."

Spoken like a seasoned mother. "I'll see you outside."

"Okay. And hey, Erin?"

"Yeah?"

Olivia stood in the doorway at the end of the hall, arms full of squirming child, wearing an expression of puzzlement. "Honestly, what's with the bathing suit? I thought you just bought a new two-piece."

Erin pulled a face. "I did. Let's just say Sarah wasn't a fan. "

Olivia opened her mouth to ask more questions and then appeared to think better of it. "Well, you still look hot. I saw that Ethan guy checking you out."

Erin snorted. "I sincerely doubt it. Have you seen what this suit does to my boobs? They're flattened like two tiny silver dollars. I look like a child."

"Hmm," Olivia said with a knowing smile. "I'm pretty sure Ethan wouldn't mind getting his hands on your silver dollars, Erin."

After laughing in surprise, Erin continued the joke, "That's only because he's in finance."

Nora reached for a lock of her mother's hair and tugged. Olivia winced, but she didn't miss a beat when she said, "He knows value when he sees it then."

Erin waved Olivia away. "Go change your baby," she ordered, but secretly, she was pleased. She'd only caught a quick glimpse of Ethan before he'd gotten on the boat, but she'd been looking forward to this party, and he was definitely high up on the list of reasons why. She might not completely trust him, but she sure wouldn't mind looking at him wet and shirtless.

When Erin got back outside, Jess and Anna were seated at the patio table with Heidi, eating some food. Benny and Sarah were examining the wall—*where their love story began*, she thought with an amused smile—and the guys were docking the boat and hopping off.

Steven was the first to make it up to them. "Time for some lunch?" he asked, giving Anna's hair a quick tousle as he rounded the table to Heidi's chair.

"Yep," she answered with a mouth full of food.

"How was tubing, and did Sean get up on the wakeboard?" Heidi asked, leaning in to receive the kiss Steven planted on her forehead.

"Great, and almost," he said, answering her questions in order. "He's close. It'll happen today."

"Did you drive, Mr. Davis?" Jess asked him.

"Not me, but your boyfriend did."

"I did what?" Mitch inquired, joining them on the patio and planting a kiss on Jess's head. A smile tugged at the corners of Erin's mouth. Like father like son, apparently.

"Pulled Sean," Steven answered. He walked over to the food table and grabbed a plate.

Mitch flashed a smile. "Can't say I didn't enjoy watching Coach face plant over and over again. I can't wait to tell the guys."

Sean came up behind him. "Just try it, and see how warm you can make that bench, buddy boy."

Landon was with him, and he grinned. "I've got your back, Coach. I'll tell everyone you were doing flips and three-sixties while Mitch was too chicken to even give it a try."

"Hey, I have a weak ankle!" Mitch protested. He grabbed Landon around the neck in a wrestling move, and they bumped into the side of the table.

"Alright, boys. Not near the food. Take it somewhere else," Heidi warned.

It was getting crowded up on the patio, so Erin excused herself and walked down to the boat. Ethan was still sitting in the bow, legs stretched out in front of him and face lifted to the sun. Since that night on the dock last Sunday, she'd seen him a few times while out walking Marvin, and they'd definitely moved on from their earlier animosity, replacing it with a thrilling, heart-fluttering flirtation.

Over the last week, preparing for a dog walk had never been more exciting. Would she bump into him, or wouldn't she? She never knew, but she definitely made sure she looked extra cute, just in case. Hot and sweaty from his exertions, Ethan always looked good enough to eat. So virile. He was as tempting as one of Sarah's baked treats, and just as bad for her. But as with the treats, Erin knew when she'd reached the end of her willpower and was ready to have a taste.

"You seem content," she said when she reached him. Bare chested, he looked just as she'd imagined he would. Strong, but not overly-muscled. Lean, but not skinny. God had finally perfected man when he'd made Ethan Rockford. She smiled at the thought.

He opened his eyes languidly. "I am."

"I'll join you." She kicked off her sandals and stepped over the gap between the dock and the boat and onto the vinyl bench seat. A second later, she was stretched out beside him in the bow. She closed her eyes and tipped her face up to the sun, but she knew he was watching her. She could feel his eyes on her.

"So, you were late to the party."

"You noticed." Her mouth curved in a slow, satisfied smile.

When he didn't reply right away, she opened one eye and then the other. He stared at her.

"I noticed," he finally said.

"Are you into me, Ethan?" She was careful to strike a teasing tone, but her gaze didn't waiver as she waited for him to answer.

He chuckled and looked away briefly. "You are something else." But when he refocused on her, he was all seriousness. "Yeah," he answered with a nod. "Yeah, I'm into you, Erin."

She grinned. "Good."

He laughed again and smiled broadly. "Good."

She lifted her face back to the sun and sighed. Ethan would be a fun summertime fling. It was perfect, really. There was already a built-in ending, so she didn't have to flip the switch this time. She could let her guard down and just enjoy the ride while it lasted. It felt like . . . freedom. A hot guy for the summer with no strings attached. What could be better?

"Do you want to grab dinner tomorrow night?"

"Yes," she said immediately without opening her eyes. The boat listed and the brightness of the sun was shadowed momentarily, but before she could react, warm lips pressed down on hers. Ethan was kissing her, and Erin felt her stomach go a little squishy—a very dangerous feeling. The kiss lingered just long enough to leave her wanting more, and when it ended, her lids fluttered open as if she was waking from a dream. Ethan, kneeling on the floor of the boat in the space between their seats, treated her to a wolfish grin.

"You don't waste any time," she remarked with a laugh before bringing her hand up to the back of his head and pressing his mouth down on hers again. The first kiss had been gentle and tender, but this kiss was hot from the outset, and Erin had the thought that she might just catch fire.

Ethan broke away too soon, and when he spoke, his voice shook. "Okay, well, I'd say we have chemistry."

She let out a breath of quiet amusement. "I knew we would."

He ran a thumb across her lips and his mouth curved into a slow, sexy smile. "Did you now?"

Briefly, she touched a hand to his jawline. It was scratchy under her fingertips. This man could definitely grow a full beard if he wanted to. "Didn't you?"

"Yeah, once I got over wanting to strangle you."

Erin rolled her eyes. "Way to turn down the heat there, Ethan."

His eyes smoldered. "Oh, I'm still hot." He moved his hand and trailed his fingertips down her arm, from her shoulder to her wrist, and she shivered. Then he moved to her ruffled top, lightly playing with it between his fingers. "You're gorgeous. Even in this ridiculous bathing suit."

"Thanks, and shut up," she whispered with a smirk.

He chuckled and leaned down for one last kiss, but the sound of footsteps approaching on the dock stopped him short.

"Erin, want to tube with me right quick?" Sarah called out as she drew closer.

Erin sat up, and Ethan reluctantly moved back to his seat. "Yes! Is it our turn?"

Sarah stopped beside them. "We're up next, after the girls. Sean's letting Landon and Mitch take them out."

Darn! She was going to lose her cozy spot next to Ethan when things were just getting interesting. "Does this mean I have to get off the boat?" she whined.

"Unless you want to be a fifth wheel," Sarah joked.

Erin turned and saw the two young couples making their way towards the boat. Landon carried a stack of four towels while Mitch hauled the tube on his back and shoulders.

"I guess that's our cue," Erin said to Ethan, standing up. "Time to hop off." Ethan had beaten her to standing, and as she stretched to her full height, she found herself eye-level with his bare, tanned chest. She could smell his sun-warmed skin—a combination of saltiness and Hawaiian Tropic suntan lotion, and it was yummy.

His voice was husky when he said, "You're just a tiny little thing, aren't you?"

She swallowed. "What I lack in size, I make up for in personality."

The corners of his mouth lifted slowly. "Lucky me."

The "kids" stayed out on the boat for the better part of an hour, and the adults swam, paddleboarded, and sat around visiting. Olivia stayed up on the patio with Sean, holding the baby monitor she'd gotten set up in Sarah's room.

Erin, doing her best not to behave like the smitten-kitten, had pulled herself away from Ethan's side and gone out for a swim with Heidi. Olivia called down to her. "Erin, I think I hear Marvin whining on the monitor. Do you want me to let him out?"

"Yes, please!" Erin yelled back.

Heidi was standing in water up to her waist. "I have to ask, Erin. Why did you get such a big dog?"

Peering at Heidi's face, Erin got the sense this wasn't just small talk. "I didn't really set out to, but he was the first dog I saw at the shelter, and once I made eye contact, I just had to have him." That was, more or less, the truth.

"So, he's just a pet then?"

Erin was dragging her fingers through the water and watched them leave a wake behind. "Yeah, why? What else would he be?"

"I just wondered."

Erin studied her. "You wondered what?"

Instead of answering, Heidi asked another question. "Erin, why are you here?"

"Because it's a party!" Erin replied, deliberately misunderstanding.

Heidi treated her to a *cut the crap* look. "You know what I'm asking."

Erin sighed. "What do you know?"

Shrugging, Heidi answered, "Nothing, but I have a few guesses."

"Which are?"

Heidi smiled gently. "You're lonely."

"Is that your first guess?"

Heidi was slow to respond. "No. My first guess is that you're in some kind of trouble."

Erin nodded wordlessly and resumed the movements with her hands, watching them slice through the water.

Heidi waited in silence.

After several seconds, Erin looked up and said, "You're not wrong. On both counts."

Heidi nodded. "I'm sorry. What's going on?"

"I have a stalker."

Heidi's eyebrows shot up. "Have you gone to the police?"

"Today, I did. That's why I was late." She filled Heidi in, starting at the very beginning and ending with what had happened just a few hours ago.

"That's awful!" Heidi exclaimed once Erin was done. "Have you told anyone else?"

"No."

For a second, it looked like Heidi might lecture her, but instead, she asked, "Erin, how can I help?"

"You can't."

Heidi took a step closer. "But you can't do this by yourself!"

"Why not? I've been handling it all summer."

"You've been handling it," Heidi repeated.

Erin worked to keep from sounding defensive. "Yeah. I'm doing just fine."

"And what happens when you move back home?" When Erin didn't answer she asked gently, "You do plan to move back home eventually, right?"

Erin sighed. "I don't know, Heidi. I really don't. I haven't gotten that far. For now, I just want to believe that everything's going to be fine."

"You're hoping this will go away by itself?"

"It's stupid, I know. At least today I made a move."

"That is good," Heidi agreed. "Are you being careful?"

"I am."

Heidi blew out an agitated sigh. "Will you please keep me updated at least? And let me know if there's anything I can do to help?"

"I will," Erin agreed. "But Heidi, please don't say anything to anyone. I'll keep your secret, and I'm asking that you keep mine."

Heidi hesitated. "Okay," she agreed. "I don't like it, but okay. Just . . . make sure you're being safe."

"I will." Erin sank back into the water, letting it fold over her body in a cool caress while she lifted her face to the hot sun.

Safe. She hadn't felt at all safe when the Facebook messages came through on her phone earlier. She'd been heading back to Sarah's for the party after her meeting with the superintendent when the first message came through. It left her so badly shaken, she'd had to pull over for several minutes. Then the second came through. After reading that one, her fear flipped to anger, and she turned the car around and drove directly to the police station.

The first message had just repeated and expanded on the sentiment written on her front door. The second read, "Did I scare you away, principal lady? Where have you run off to?"

The creep was playing with her, she realized, and he was having fun terrifying her. "I don't think he actually wants to hurt me," she'd told Officer James, the school's police liaison. She'd called him and asked him to meet her at the police department. "I think he's just having a little sick fun." Edwin James, a kind and jovial older man, rounded his desk and leaned against it.

He pinched his bushy eyebrows together and put his hand on her shoulder. "Young lady, you need to take this seriously." He went on to admonish her for waiting so long to tell him, and he gave her some common-sense pointers to keep herself safe, which included installing those cameras she still hadn't gotten around to buying. Sweetheart that he was, Officer James said he'd take care of that for her. Their meeting ended with him making her promise to stay at Sarah's until further notice. "And you need to tell Miss Josten about this, Erin. She needs to know so she can be on the lookout. For her safety as much as yours, you hear?"

She heard. But she didn't plan to heed. Erin would be careful not to put Sarah in any danger. Psychostalker would never know she was at Sarah's house. She'd make sure of it.

She'd continue to be careful. Obsessively, countless times each day, she checked from her office window to make sure no strange vehicles were camped out in the lot, and just like in the movies, she watched her rearview mirror to make sure she wasn't being tailed. She never went straight to Sarah's house from town; she always drove around for a bit first. Only once she thought someone might be following her, a gray, rusted out Impala. It had hung back far enough where she hadn't been able to make out the driver, but just when she'd started to squirm in her seat, it had turned off near the Crossroads. She hadn't seen it since.

Erin had spent the last weeks digging through the recesses of her mind to try to come up with someone, a parent maybe, who had something against her. Someone who was pissed enough—and crazy enough—to mess with her like this. She'd written down the names of every single person who came to mind.

She dove under the water and swam several strokes. The list was long. It depressed her to have a visual representation of the number of people who didn't like her, but that was the life of a high school principal, and she could take it. She had to.

Under the surface, Erin heard the hum of an engine, and sure enough, when she popped her head back out of the water, the boat was reentering the bay. "Looks like we're up," she told Heidi.

"Let's leave the kids behind with Nora," Heidi suggested. "We can get some adult beverages and take a slow ride when you and Sarah are done tubing."

"You don't think Sean will want to wakeboard again?"

"What do you mean, *again?* The man should quit while he's ahead before he pulls something."

Erin laughed.

"Landon got up, first try, Coach!" Mitch shouted from the captain's chair of the boat.

Erin turned to shore in time to see Sean shake his head and wave a dismissive hand before shouting back, "I'll believe it when I see it!"

It took a long while for the adults to get themselves organized. They changed out the skiing tow rope for the one used for tubing, and at the last minute, Sean decided the tube needed a little more air. Finally, after twenty or thirty minutes, Erin and Sarah laid side by side, belly-down on the tube, as Sean left the bay.

Heidi and Steven sat in the bow, and Ethan and Benny sat in the back of the boat. Sean looked like he was in his element in the captain's chair with his wife beside him. "You ready?" he shouted.

"Hit it!" Erin yelled back. And just like that, she was pulled back in time. She was twelve years old again, riding on the surface of the water at Camp Reina with the hot breeze rushing across her skin and whipping through her hair.

Water splashed occasionally into her eyes, making her squint, and she squealed and laughed as loudly as Sarah did beside her. "This is the life!" she hollered to her friend.

Sean had asked if they wanted a wild or tame ride. "Wild," Erin had answered immediately.

"But not too wild," Sarah had said. "I'm full as a tick on beer and picnic food. If I fall off, I'll sink."

"That's what life jackets are for, dummy," Erin had said with a laugh.

As promised, Sean began to maneuver the boat so that they swung, like a pendulum, back and forth over the wake. It was all great fun until it wasn't. Weren't all accidents like that? Her secretary, Adele, liked to say, "Nobody plans an accident." Boy, was she right. One moment, she and Sarah were laughing and shrieking, and the next, they were knocking heads so hard that Erin's vision went dark and it was all she could do to hold on to the handles. She let her pounding head sink down against the wet tube and tightened her grip.

Chapter 17

Benny watched it happen. They all did. The tube hit the wake just right, and the girls got at least three feet of air. At first, everyone in the boat cheered, but when the tube came down and they could see over the front of it, Sarah was no longer there, and Erin was bleeding profusely from her head. A brief silence took hold before total chaos ensued. Everyone was shouting at once, and Sean brought the boat to a stop—just on instinct—momentarily torn between hauling Erin in off the tube and going after Sarah.

It wasn't that Benny didn't care about Erin. He did, and he could see, just like everyone else, that she was hurt. But she was holding on, which meant she would be okay for the short term. Immediately, he scanned the water for Sarah. When he found her, he could have sworn his heart stopped beating.

"Sean!" he yelled, jumping to his feet and pointing to Sarah lying face down and lifeless in the water. "Hurry!"

Ethan's eyes followed where Benny pointed. "Oh, shit!"

Sean immediately brought the boat around.

"Sarah!" Olivia screamed, her face stricken with the same panic Benny felt. "Sean, do something!"

"Faster!" Benny shouted.

"Not too fast!" Ethan countered. "Erin's sliding off."

Benny glanced at the tube, and sure enough, Erin was starting to disappear off the back. Sean slowed down, uncertain once more, and that's all Benny needed to act. He hopped up onto the gunwale, with the boat still moving, and dove in. He had to get to Sarah. It might have only been a few seconds that she'd been face-down in the water, but it felt like an eternity, and a cold fear clawed at him, spurring him to swim faster and faster.

"Sarah!" he hollered as he closed the last few feet between them. "Sarah!"

She didn't move. Quickly, Benny flipped her over, supporting her head as best he could. "Sarah, wake up! Open your eyes!" Was she breathing? He couldn't tell. Could he rescue breathe treading water? Yes, for her, he could do anything. But it didn't come to that. The boat appeared, as if from nowhere, right beside them, and Benny worked with Sean and Steven to get Sarah out of the water and into the boat.

Once she was in, Benny climbed up using the ladder at the stern. His lungs burned and his arms and legs ached, but he made it up in a flash. Sarah needed him, and he wouldn't let her down.

It was as if the whole world was underwater. Voices were speaking, but they were garbled like a damaged recording. Everything seemed to be moving in slow motion. Sarah's limbs felt heavy, and the pounding in her head was unlike anything she'd ever experienced. Her eyes were open, but she wasn't really seeing, and although she was able to hear, she couldn't understand.

Days later, she would describe this moment of coming-to as a strange sort of brain reboot. She was like a computer that had been shut down and restarted again, and she regained her full senses one at a time. Her vision remained blurry long after she could understand the words spoken around her. The first voice she was able to make out clearly was Heidi's. She focused on it because hers was the quietest and the calmest. Everyone else was either shouting or frantic or both, and Sarah just couldn't handle that right then.

"Sarah? Can you hear me?"

"Yes," Sarah whispered. She could make out the black of Heidi's bathing suit and the honey curls of her hair, but her face was a featureless blotch.

"You're okay, Sarah," Heidi said softly. "You just hit your head, and you were knocked unconscious, but you're waking up now."

Sarah's ears began to ring.

"Everything's going to be fine, but you'll feel a little off for a few more minutes. Just lay still."

Sarah gave a small nod, but the movement caused an explosion of pain behind her eyes, and she whimpered. That seemed to set off a male voice, which began shouting some kind of gobbledygook. Was it Benny? Yes, Benny. What was he saying? She couldn't piece together his words in any kind of order that would make sense, but then she stopped trying when a deep, loud rumble drowned him out anyway. They were moving. That's when Sarah remembered. She was on the boat. She'd been tubing with Erin, and they'd been laughing. And now she was here, on the floor of the boat, feeling like she might vomit. And then she did. She threw up all over Olivia's lovely birthday gift.

As they slowly made their way back to the dock, Sarah began to see and hear more clearly, but her head felt like it might split in two, and the bright sunshine was almost unbearable. Heidi had given her a pair of sunglasses and told her to keep her eyes closed, if it helped, but Sarah needed to see to keep from throwing up again. And she needed to see for herself that Erin was okay, even though Heidi had already assured her that she was.

Benny, seated beside her, saw she was trying to sit up and lifted her off the floor and into his lap. He brought her up against his warm chest, and she allowed her head to rest against him. He wrapped both arms around her, and if not for the pain in her head and her worry for Erin, Sarah would have done a silent cheer. Finally, some real contact. She hadn't realized how desperately she'd wanted to be held by him.

Ethan, who'd been tending to Erin in the bow, finally moved out of the way enough for Sarah to see. He supported her friend with one arm, and with the other he pressed a blood-soaked towel against her forehead and temple.

"What happened to Erin?" she asked Benny in a voice so quiet he had to lean down to hear her. She repeated the question.

"The two of you knocked heads," he explained near her ear. His breath was warm against her skin. "She's okay, but she'll need some stitches."

It was scary how much blood was on the towel Ethan pressed against the wound, and there was still a fair amount trickling down the side of Erin's face. Her bathing suit was ruined, though no great loss. So was Ethan's T-shirt.

Heidi sat on the floor beside Sarah and Benny. "It looks worse than it is. Heads always bleed a lot, but she'll be okay. The gash is at her hairline, so nobody will even be able to tell this happened. She has a minor concussion, but she'll be just fine, don't worry."

Sarah had the vague sense that she'd already been told this before. Was there something wrong with her memory? Benny's hand reached for hers, and she gave it a little squeeze of thanks. He squeezed back. Even in her pathetic state, she felt a small thrill at that, and it only intensified when he swept his thumb over her knuckles in several soothing strokes. It took a second to compute, but she realized he was soaked.

"You're all wet."

She felt him nod, but he said nothing.

"He jumped in after you," Heidi informed her, leaning into her gently and giving her shoulder a brief, meaningful nudge. "The boat hadn't even stopped moving yet."

"Oh," Sarah said stupidly. She tipped her head back to see his face. "Thank you, Benny."

She saw him swallow once and nod. He'd rescued her . . . more or less. She couldn't help but smile.

Benny sat in his kitchen with his phone on the table in front of him. Heidi had promised to text him updates about Sarah. He'd been prepared to stay in the waiting room as long as it took, but Steven had pointed out there was nothing he could do for Sarah there. Instead, they all went back to her house to get everything picked up and put away so it would all be done by the time she got home. They'd finished over an hour ago, and now he sat, alone in his house, swim trunks still on, waiting for Heidi to text the results of Sarah's CT scan.

He should be at the hospital with her. That was where he wanted to be. That's where he could be if he hadn't been so slow to let Sarah know how he felt about her. If he were a normal guy, they might already be dating, and he'd be beside her now, holding her hand.

Seeing her face down in the water like that had shaved years off his life. And holding her in his arms on the boat had caused his heart to squeeze so painfully in his chest that for a second he thought he might be having a heart attack. It was a new sensation, but Benny knew what it meant. He wasn't just *interested* in Sarah. He wasn't just attracted to her, though he certainly was that.

He loved her.

Without a doubt, that's what this was. He loved her, and he'd loved her for some time. There was absolutely nothing he wouldn't do for her. So why hadn't he acted sooner?

He knew why. His confidence was shaken. Erin had hurt him some, it was true, but that wasn't really the reason. He'd discovered a lot about himself in the last few months, and it hadn't been easy to admit certain things. He felt defective. He was damaged goods, and he felt conspicuous, like everyone must know something was wrong with him. He wasn't like other guys, and he felt that Sarah deserved better than him.

But he wanted her. He wanted her to be his for a lifetime. He couldn't help it. She made him feel . . . whole. She made him feel alive. But could he possibly do the same for her? Could he be everything she needed? Benny was terrified that the answer to that question was no.

Sarah had been at the hospital for hours and hours. Erin had long since been cleared to go home, which was where Sarah longed to be herself. But she'd required tests to rule out a brain bleed, and it seemed that nothing happened very quickly at the hospital. Being a patient in the emergency room was an exercise in endless waiting, and she was miserable. She'd vomited several more times, and her headache persisted, even with the painkillers they dripped through her IV.

Heidi sat with her as she waited for the results of the CAT scan, and Sarah was grateful. Heidi knew almost everyone coming in and out of Sarah's room, and the doctor taking care of her, Dr. Leila Molina, appeared to be a personal friend. As it turned out, she and Heidi ran together several times a week.

"Okay, Sarah," Dr. Molina said cheerfully as she reentered the room an hour after Sarah's CAT scan was completed. She held an open laptop in her hands. "Your results are in, and I'm thrilled to say that everything looks normal."

Heidi stood and gestured towards the computer. "May I, Leila?"

Dr. Molina handed it to her. "Of course."

Sarah had been fairly certain she'd check out okay, but she still felt relieved. "Thank you, Doctor."

Dr. Molina nodded and smiled. She was a strikingly beautiful woman, Sarah noted. After wheeling the stool to Sarah's bedside, she sat down. Heidi remained standing on the other side, clicking the tracking pad of the laptop.

"It was good that we scanned you," the doctor informed her. She tucked a section of shiny black hair behind one ear. "You took a hard smack to the head, so it was important to check."

Heidi glanced up from the screen. "I'm glad we looked too. I watched it happen. I think I even heard it, and the persistent nausea made me a little nervous," she admitted. She handed the computer back to Dr. Molina, who set it on the desk behind her.

"Here's what you can expect over the next several days," Dr. Molina began. "You'll need to be monitored through the night tonight. Through the next twenty-four hours, actually. Every hour, someone will need to wake you up from sleep to check on you."

"I can stay through the night tonight," Heidi offered.

The younger doctor nodded appreciatively. "Wonderful, so we have that covered. You'll have a pretty good headache going for the next few days, Sarah, but I'd like you to refrain from taking ibuprofen and aspirin for the time being. Tylenol will be your best friend the next several days."

"Okay," Sarah said, but she was skeptical. If IV drugs weren't cutting it now, she doubted Tylenol could be much of a friend to her.

"And for the next forty-eight hours, you'll want to take it easy. Physically, you can do light activities as tolerated, but mentally, I'd like you to rest. Do you need a doctor's note to take off work for a few days?"

"No, I'm a teacher, so I'm off right now anyway."

Dr. Molina grinned. "I think I chose the wrong profession. My cousin is a teacher in Houston. She just finished her second year, and for the last two summers, she calls me to gloat from the pool at her apartment complex while I'm slaving away here at work."

"It's definitely a perk," Sarah agreed with a smile. "What does she teach?"

"Spanish. She's from Puerto Rico."

Sarah peered more closely at Dr. Molina. From the beginning, she'd thought she could pick up on a very slight accent, and the good doctor had skin the color of rich caramel along with the type of thick, wavy hair Sarah had always envied. She looked like a young Salma Hayek.

The doctor answered Sarah's unspoken question. "I lived there as well, until I was ten years old, but my cousin has only been stateside since college. She teaches world history too, but Spanish is her first love. What do you teach?"

"English." Normally, she would have had more to say on the subject, but Sarah was finding it harder and harder to keep her eyes open.

Dr. Molina patted her gently on the arm. "You're tired. Close your eyes for a time. We'll finish getting you sorted out."

Sarah was more than happy to oblige, but she continued to listen.

"Will you be able to stay with her through some of the day tomorrow, Heidi?"

"No, I have to work tomorrow, but I have someone in mind who should be able to. I'll make sure we have coverage for her."

"Excellent."

"How much longer do you think?"

Sarah heard a heavy sigh. "You know how it is. Nothing happens quickly around here, and we're short-staffed tonight. I'll get those discharge papers printed off myself and have Patty run through them with you. I'd handle it all as a favor, but I've got a toddler with a Lego shoved up his nose in room five, and mom's a basket case."

Heidi chuckled. "Good luck with that. Thanks, Leila."

Sarah opened her eyes. "Yes, thank you so much."

"My pleasure." The Salma Hayek look-alike rose from the stool and moved it back against the wall.

"You here tomorrow?" Heidi asked her.

"You know it. Seven to three."

"Me too. I can bring my running shoes for afterward. I'm going to dinner with Steven and the kids at six, but I could squeeze in a quick run first."

Dr. Molina brightened visibly. "Sure! I need to burn off some steam, and you always know the best trails." She turned her attention back to Sarah. "It was nice to meet you, Sarah."

"You too." Sarah winced as her head gave another painful throb.

She smiled sympathetically. "Listen, hang in there. You will heal from this." She winked. "And don't worry, you'll be tubing again in no time."

Sarah smiled weakly. "Or not."

Dr. Molina chuckled. "Alright, I'll get those discharge instructions. You'll follow up with your primary doctor in a few days." She was already halfway out the door when she added, "See you tomorrow, Heidi."

Heidi waved as the doctor left and then looked down at her phone. "Benny texted again. Poor thing's worried sick."

"Still?"

Heidi raised her eyebrows. "Are you surprised?"

"I guess not."

"Sarah, you should have seen him. That man was out of his mind."

Sarah felt a warmth wrap all around her. "Is it wrong that I'm tickled pink to hear that?"

"Not at all!" Heidi exclaimed with a laugh. "Doesn't every woman want to be the damsel in distress once in her life?"

Sarah pushed down a laugh of her own. Instinctively, she knew it would hurt, but she smiled and said, "I just wish it wasn't so darn painful, so I could enjoy the moment."

Heidi looked back at her phone and swiped at the screen. "Man, Sean's really beating himself up. He's been texting too."

Sarah worked to sit up. "But he shouldn't! It wasn't his fault."

"Olivia keeps telling him that."

"I'll tell him too."

"I'll text him. You just rest for now."

That sounded like a plan to Sarah. The lights in the room had been turned off from the beginning to help with her headache, but closing her eyes brought even more relief. "Just for a minute."

It was after midnight when Sarah and Heidi finally pulled back into the driveway at the basin, and Sarah breathed a sigh of relief at being home.

Erin and Ethan greeted them, and after several minutes of the two invalids fawning all over one another, Heidi ordered them both off to their rooms. She got Sarah settled in her bed with the promise of seeing her every hour through the rest of the night until six o'clock, at which time Benny would be taking over.

"Y'all don't have to do that. Ethan's here," Sarah protested, not wanting to burden Heidi or Benny. "He can just look in on me whenever he checks on Erin."

Heidi moved to the first of the four windows in Sarah's room. "Honey, I want to do this for you. And I had to give Benny something to do. You heard how many texts I got from him. He was adamant." She worked at the cord, pulling it right and then left until the cellular shades opened and stretched down to the windowsill. "And anyway," she continued, moving to the next window, "Ethan followed Erin upstairs, and I think that's where he plans on staying, if you catch my meaning."

"What?" Sarah stared at her blankly.

Heidi dropped the last of the shades and turned to face her. "Didn't you see them kiss earlier?"

"No!" Ethan and Erin? When had that happened?

"I thought for sure you would have seen. *I* did, and I'd say he's up there with her for the duration."

"Oh! Oh, my." Sarah hoped Erin wasn't planning on *exerting* herself. She needed to rest. She had a concussion too, albeit a milder one than Sarah's, which was odd because Erin was the one whose head had cracked open.

Heidi grinned and moved over to Sarah's dresser. "Do you want this turned on?" she asked, pointing to the black Honeywell fan that rested on the dresser.

"Yes, please."

She turned it on to the lowest setting. "It looks to me like you two girls have found two doting men. Ethan's stuck like glue to Erin, and Benny wishes I'd drop dead so he could be here in my place." She walked back towards the bed and glanced at her watch. "He only needs to be patient a few more hours. Not that I plan to drop dead," she clarified with a laugh.

Sarah groaned. "I'm going to have to get up and make myself pretty before he gets here."

Heidi *tsked*. "Don't be silly. You always look pretty, and besides, if Benny didn't run scared after you threw up on him, a little morning breath and bed head won't turn him off."

Sarah blinked. "After I *what?*"

"Oh!" Heidi froze in the process of pulling the covers up over Sarah. "I guess you don't remember that."

Afraid of the answer but needing to know all the same, Sarah asked, "I threw up on Benny?" She scooched down so her head rested on her pillow.

Heidi wrinkled her nose as she finished tucking Sarah in. "Well, just his feet."

"Oh, my gosh!" Sarah covered her face with both hands.

"Really, it was just his toes more than anything."

"No way! Stop, please. I'm mortified!"

Heidi sat on the edge of the bed and pushed Sarah's hair off her forehead the way a mother would. The gesture, or maybe the strain of the day, brought tears to Sarah's eyes, and she quickly wiped at one as it escaped from one corner and traveled across her temple. "I'm sorry," Heidi said gently. "I didn't mean to distress you further."

"You didn't. Sorry, I'm just havin' myself a day." She continued wiping as more tears leaked out. Like always when she cried, her nose got all runny too, and she wiped at that with the sleeve of her sleepshirt. She hated being a mess like this.

"I know the day didn't have the greatest ending, but the beginning and middle held a lot of promise, don't you think?"

Sarah shrugged.

"Listen, I was an observer today, and I have to tell you—concussion or not, things are about to get brighter for you."

"How do you mean?"

"Let's just say I read people pretty well. That's what decades of being a keen observer on the outside looking in will do for a person, if nothing else." She rolled her eyes. "So, like I said—brighter things ahead. Let that be what you think about as you drift off, hmm?"

Sarah nodded.

"Alright, then"—Heidi patted her head—"I'll just be on the couch if you need me." She got up, but she paused in the doorway. The light from the hallway behind her made it look like she had a halo of white around her head. It was fitting. But while Heidi might not really be an angel, she'd more than proven herself as a friend.

"Heidi?"

"Yeah?"

"Thank you. Really."

"You're really very welcome. Good night, sleep tight, and don't let the bed bugs bite, as my dad used to say."

Sarah smiled. "You either."

Chapter 18

"Are you still awake?" Erin whispered. She lay on her side, gloriously cocooned against Ethan, whose large form curled around her smaller one. She could get used to this. As a bedfellow, she'd take Ethan over the orange bat—or even the spatially unaware Marvin—any day.

He pulled her even closer. "Yes," his gravelly voice rumbled against her neck. "Thanks to your stupid dog."

Erin chuckled quietly. "He's so loud. At least we finally got him to lie down on the floor. He's used to the bed, poor thing."

Ethan lifted his head and leaned over her. "Poor thing? That dog leads a charmed life. In fact, in my next life, I'm coming back as your dog."

Erin laughed and then flinched slightly as a sharp pain traveled over the area of her stitches.

"You okay?" He touched her gently, carefully avoiding the sensitive spot near her temple as he smoothed her hair.

"Yeah. My head's still throbbing, but I can't do much about that."

"I can get you one of those pills," he offered. "They're down in the kitchen."

That doctor who had treated her in the ER had called in some painkillers, but Erin didn't want to take them. She shook her head. "It's not that bad."

She flipped onto her back to face him, careful not to break contact completely. He was so hot. Literally, he was like a furnace. Heat radiated off him in waves, so much so that she'd already kicked off all the covers. She normally ran cold, but even dressed in only a thin cami and tiny cotton shorts, she was toasty warm.

Not that Ethan wasn't hot in the figurative sense too. Actually, he was gorgeous, and even in the darkened room, she could make out all the features that made him so. Thanks to the full moon and clear sky, she could appreciate his high cheekbones and thick, dark hair. Looking at him, especially like this, stretched out beside her in bed, his hair all tousled, well, it did things to her insides. It made her want things she wasn't ready to admit that she wanted.

There'd been some truly magnificent kissing before Sarah came home, but Ethan had refused to take it further. "You're hurt," he'd said decisively, and nothing she'd said could weaken his resolve. He'd been insistent. "Let me just hold you."

He'd pressed her against him and wrapped her in his arms, and they'd lain like that for hours, just talking. She'd peppered him with questions about his family, and he answered them. He'd grown up poor. Dirt poor, by the sounds of it. His parents were high school sweethearts and had both dropped out of school when his mother got pregnant with him. They'd worked minimum wage jobs until his father had finally gotten night shift work at a nearby chemical plant. Even then, it wasn't nearly enough, and Ethan had grown up at the poverty level.

While his friends had all gotten cars of their own at sixteen, his family of four had just one vehicle, an old wood-paneled station wagon with vinyl seats. From the age of fifteen, Ethan had worked at the corner gas station to help the family pay rent and buy groceries. But as poor as they'd been, they were a tight-knit and supportive family, rich in love. Being rich and being wealthy were two different things, she realized, and she said so out loud.

Spooned together as they were, and letting the conversation ebb and flow wherever it wanted, Erin felt safe and protected and cared for, as well as opened up and laid bare. It both gratified and terrified her at the same time.

After an indeterminate period of silence where the only sound in the room was the even cadence of Marvin's snores, Erin snuggled in closer to Ethan, thinking he was asleep, and prepared to drift off herself, but then he reached out and gently stroked her hair.

"Erin," he whispered.

"Ethan," she whispered back before giggling.

He didn't join her in laughter. He was all seriousness.

She lifted her head off the pillow. "What is it?"

"I just want to say, I'm sorry for before."

She thought back. "For calling Marvin stupid?"

He did laugh then, but only briefly. "For that too, but I'm sorry for what I said on the patio that day. About your ex-husband."

He'd already made his apologies. Why was he making them again? She recalled the wrist-slitting comment and the sarcasm. At the time, she'd been livid—and hurt. And although it no longer made her angry, she did still feel a little wounded, not that she'd show it. "Oh, that," she said lightly. "It's fine."

He wasn't buying it. "No, it's not fine. I was way out of line, and I'm sorry."

The sincerity and remorse in his voice chased away any lingering hurt. She ran her fingers along his jawline, the stubble rough against her fingers. "You're one hundred percent forgiven. Don't give it another thought."

He shook his head. "I feel sorry for the guy."

Her eyes widened in surprise. "Why?"

"Because he's missing out. He lost big when he lost you."

She was pretty sure Seth didn't think he'd lost much of anything. "What makes you think *he* lost *me*?"

"What, you're saying *he* was the one to walk away?"

She hesitated. The truth would make her look pathetic, but she didn't want to lie to Ethan. She didn't want to lie to him about anything. In the hours they'd lain there together, she'd told him things she'd never told anyone else. Things about her childhood, about how lonely she'd been in that great big house with a mother who hated her and a father who was never home. She spoke about her father's illness and the moments she'd spent with him before he passed.

She'd shared everything with him. Everything except the finer details of her marriage. She'd glossed over those because, well, if she was being honest with herself, she was afraid he'd see her the way Seth had. She didn't want Ethan to know she was an emotional cripple. To see her as weak. That was the reason she'd also chosen to avoid talking about her stalker situation. She had thought about it. Considered confiding in him. She'd wanted to, but she'd held back.

Suddenly, she didn't want to hold back about Seth, so she took a deep breath and said, "He was the one who walked."

"Why?"

She heard the shock in his voice and pushed herself away from him, needing some space while she summoned her courage. "I drove him away. I'm emotionally unavailable. Cold."

Ethan didn't respond right away, and Erin held her breath. When he finally spoke, his tone brooked no argument. "That's not true."

"Oh, it's true alright." Erin laughed, but it sounded hollow, even to her own ears, and she turned her head away from him.

He closed the gap between them and cupped his hand under her chin. "Erin, look at me."

She did.

"It's not.

"How do you know?" she whispered.

"Because I *see* you."

"What do you mean, you *see* me?"

"You're not cold. I see you," he repeated. "As you are."

She swallowed. "What do you see?" Her words were tentative. She was afraid to know.

He played with her hair, running it through his fingers. Her scalp tingled, and she leaned into his hand. If she were a cat, she'd be purring.

"I see a woman who *feels* things. She feels things so deeply and so powerfully that she has to work extra hard to look tough on the outside, but on the inside, she's so sweet and gentle and soft. She's vulnerable, and it scares her."

Erin had stopped breathing again. She waited for Ethan to continue.

"She's so beautiful. So feisty. And she has so much capacity to give and receive love. It's all she wants, but she's afraid to chase after it."

"Why?" she whispered with wide eyes. "Why is she so scared all the time?"

He continued to stroke. "Because she's been hurt. She's protecting herself."

Erin swallowed again, this time in an effort to push down the large lump that had formed in her throat. It ached, and her eyes burned. Ethan continued to gaze at her, but his hand had stopped moving and now gently cradled the back of her head. He leaned down and pressed a slow kiss against her mouth. Again and again, he kissed her, and she felt herself growing more feverish in her response. When he ran a hand across her bare abdomen, Erin thought she might combust. She squirmed and writhed below him, breathless and needy and grabbing at his shirt to pull it up and over his shoulders. She wanted to be skin on skin. She wanted to be branded by the heat of him.

Ethan abruptly ended the kiss and gathered her against him, shushing her as she trembled. His own breathing was ragged and several minutes passed before he spoke. "Tonight, I hold you. Tomorrow, we'll talk."

She smiled against his shoulder. That worked for her.

Chapter 19

"**S**arah," a voice whispered once, then twice. She felt pressure on her shoulder. "Sarah."

"Hmm?" she answered groggily.

"Sarah, what's my name?"

All she wanted to do was sleep. This waking up every hour business was getting old, and it was always the same question: *What's my name?* Heidi must have already asked her this four or five times now, but . . . wait . . . this wasn't Heidi's voice.

Sarah's eyes fluttered open. "Benny?"

He stood awkwardly over her bed and nodded. "Okay, go back to sleep." He turned to leave the room.

Sarah scrambled to sitting and held her head as she did so it wouldn't split apart in the process. She'd never had a headache like this before in all her life. "Wait!" she whisper-shouted.

He remained in the doorway, but he turned around and waited for her to say something more.

"Um, hi. Hi, Benny." How dumb could she be?

He shoved his hands in his pockets. He was wearing yet another white T-shirt and a pair of well-worn jeans slung low on his hips. "Hi."

She squinted at him. "What time is it?"

"Six." He leaned a shoulder against the doorjamb and crossed his arms. She'd hoped maybe he'd come back in the room and they could talk, but he remained rooted there, fifteen feet away, in the doorway of her bedroom. He lowered his head and looked at the floor.

Heidi had told her he wanted to come, but he didn't look like a man who was all that excited to be there. "I'm sorry, Benny."

His head popped up. "About what?"

"You know—that you have to be here right now." *And that I upchucked on your toes.*

He took a step towards her. "I *want* to be here. I've wanted to be here all night. I was worried about you and I . . ."

Her face grew warm, and she couldn't tame the smile that tugged at her mouth. "Yes?"

But he didn't elaborate. Instead, he retreated to the safety of the doorway and repeated, "Get some sleep."

Sarah watched him turn and head down the hallway and back out to the living room. He was an enigma. Impossible to read. If he was so happy to be there, why did he seem so moody about it? In the boat, he'd held her hand. He'd held *her*. But now he wouldn't come within a few feet of her?

She tried to look at the bright side. At least she didn't need to worry about morning breath any longer. He'd never get close enough to smell it. She sighed and laid back down, staring at the ceiling. Her shades were room-darkening, but daylight snuck through the tiny cracks on either side of the window, and she could hear the birds chirping outside. Normally, those signs that the day had begun would have been enough to prod her out of bed, but not this time. Her eyelids had already closed, and before she even knew she was asleep, Sarah heard the question again.

"What's my name?"

She scrunched her eyes closed more tightly and ignored it, and she ignored it the second time and the third time Benny asked. Why? Well, she was dead-tired for one thing, maybe even more tired than she'd been the time she'd stayed up all night taking care of Nadia when she'd had what turned out to be appendicitis. Her ten-year-old sister had thrown up every fifteen to twenty minutes from sundown to sunup, and Sarah had eventually called Gammie's best friend, Claire, for help since her mama was out cold and no use to anyone.

She heard Benny approaching the bed, and when he said her name and shook her—somewhat frantically—Sarah smiled. She had to admit, the other reason had been just plain orneriness on her part. She hadn't wanted him to shout at her from the doorway again. She rolled over to face him. "Good morning."

He straightened and sighed in relief. "Why didn't you answer me? Could you hear me?"

"I could hear you."

"Then why didn't you answer me?"

She sat up. "I wanted you to come into the room this time."

Exasperation seeped into his voice. "Why didn't you just ask me to?"

Okay, now she felt downright silly. "I don't know. I wanted you to *want* to come into the room."

He scratched his head. "Alright. Well . . . I'll come in next time."

"That's okay. I need to get up."

He looked doubtful. "Are you sure? I think maybe you should sleep some more."

"And I will, but right now I need some more Tylenol, and I need to use the bathroom. Besides, I feel wide awake now."

"Alright. You can go . . . uh . . . do your thing, and I'll get the Tylenol ready."

Sarah smiled in amusement. "Okay. I'll be there right quick."

It took her well over five minutes before she met him in the kitchen. She peed, brushed her teeth and her hair, and applied some light makeup, just enough to where she looked refreshed but not enough where it would be obvious she was wearing any. At least, that was her hope. And she sure hoped this headache would abate before too long.

Lots to hope for this morning.

God willing and the creek don't rise. That's what her gammie would've said. It's what she said anytime she hoped for the best. Sarah peered at her reflection in the vanity mirror. She didn't look half bad considering how little sleep she'd gotten. "Maybe Benny and I can have ourselves a moment today, Gammie," she said out loud. "God willin' and the creek don't rise, of course. But whatever you—or He—can do to help things along, I sure would be grateful."

Sarah lifted her eyes to the ceiling and felt like she should cross herself. Gammie had never been all that reverent, even though she'd always claimed to be a good Christian woman. She'd said things like, "God hears us just as well prayin' on the pot as prayin' in a pew." Unconventional though she'd been, Sarah was sure Gammie was up there in Heaven, and she trusted she could hear her now, standing in the bathroom, barefoot and in her Winnie-the-Poo pajamas.

Even before she turned off the bathroom light, Sarah could hear voices coming from the kitchen, and she couldn't help the wave of disappointment that rolled over her. She wanted some alone time with Benny, and it felt like they might not ever get it. Sure, they'd been alone as they'd worked on the wall together, but that was over now, and even then, the focus had been on the work and not on each other. She wanted to sit across from him over dinner and just talk. Just the two of them. He was making her crazy with uncertainty. One minute she thought he wanted to be with Erin, and the next she sensed he might be interested in her, that he cared for her. Now he couldn't even come into her bedroom unless he thought she was comatose.

"There she is," Ethan said when Sarah rounded the corner. The kitchen seemed brighter than usual, and Sarah squinted to keep some of the light out of her eyes.

"How are you this morning?" Erin asked, before pulling Sarah into a gentle hug.

"My head hurts somethin' fierce," Sarah admitted. "How are y—?" Before she finished speaking, Benny had switched off the overhead lights in the kitchen. He was so thoughtful.

Erin pulled back from the hug and looked at Benny in confusion. "Why'd you do that?"

He moved to the switches in the living room and shut those off too. "The light hurts her eyes."

"It does? It doesn't hurt *my* eyes," Erin said.

"Well, it hurts hers," he insisted.

Sarah relaxed. "That does help a lot, actually," she admitted. "Thank you, Benny."

He rejoined them in the kitchen. "Sure," he said. He handed her the full glass of water she'd noticed on the counter and dropped two pills in her hand. "Here you go."

"Thanks," she repeated.

"You're welcome."

Erin stood in the center of the kitchen, looking back and forth between them with an expression of mild amusement.

Sarah swallowed down both pills at once and finished the water. "How was your night?" Sarah asked Erin.

"Fantastic," Erin said before casting a smile at Ethan, who sat at the counter with a mug of steaming coffee in hand. Rumpled and sleepy-eyed, he somehow looked even more handsome than usual, and Sarah could see why Erin, even sutured and bandaged and with a shaved hairline, appeared happier than she'd ever seen her.

"Fantastic, huh?" Sarah smiled weakly. "Sounds like your night was a whole lot better than mine."

Erin walked to the charging station near the microwave and unplugged Sarah's phone. "Your sister called last night and again this morning."

That was unusual. "She did?"

"Uh-huh. Last night, I told her you were at the hospital. She got *really* worried. It was kind of cute." Erin looked thoughtful. "You know, I had her all pictured in my head, but she's not quite the little monster I expected her to be. She just called again about a half hour ago, but I didn't answer."

As soon as Erin handed over the phone, it rang.

"Wow, there she is again," Sarah marveled. She'd gotten texts from her sister with updates about their mother as well as requests for money, but the last time she'd actually spoken to Nadia, it hadn't gone very well. More likely than not, Lydie Mae had put her up to making that call, but Nadia had done her part in demanding Sarah turn over her inheritance money early. Sarah had said no, of course, and then had to listen to some shouting on the other end of the line, and not just from Nadia. Lydie Mae was going off in the background too. It felt the way it always had—the two of them united together and Sarah all by her lonesome. In that moment, she'd missed Gammie something fierce.

She squinted at the screen.

"Aren't you going to answer it?" Benny asked. He'd stepped up close behind her.

"I'm sort of afraid to," Sarah admitted. "I'm not sure I can handle getting yelled at this morning. It might be the thing that finally does in my brain."

"Here." Erin scooped the phone out of Sarah's hand.

"Wait—" Sarah reached out, but Erin had already answered.

"Morning, Nadia."

Silence.

"Yep, she's right here in the kitchen, but listen, she's not feeling the greatest." Erin gave Sarah a quick once over. "And you know, she's not looking the greatest either—you should see how pale she is, and she's wearing these awful—"

"Erin!" Sarah hissed. She put her hand out for the phone.

Erin ignored her.

"Anyway, you'll need to keep your voice down. No yelling and no carrying on about whatever the latest bug is you've got up your butt that your mother planted there—"

"Oh my gosh!" Sarah whispered. She put her head in her hands before looking pleadingly at Benny, who put his hand on her shoulder in a showing of support. Both Benny and Ethan stood in rapt attention as they listened to

Erin handle her sister with an ease that was impressive, if not annoying. She shouldn't be inserting herself in Sarah's life like this.

"It's not jumping to conclusions at all. In fact, I'm sure there must be something bothering you, or you wouldn't have called last night in the first place."

Erin listened and nodded to whatever Nadia was saying. "Good, it's about time for you to see that. She deserves better. She always has."

She listened some more, and Sarah wasn't sure if she wanted to hug her or choke her. Either way, she definitely wanted to know what her sister was saying.

"Good," Erin repeated. "If that's the case, I'll put her on." Erin smiled proudly and handed Sarah the phone.

Holding it, Sarah looked around the room. There was no way she was taking this phone call while the three of them listened. "I'm going to my room."

"But—" Erin began.

Sarah held up a hand. "I'll leave the door open." She turned and swayed, but Benny was right beside her, and he righted her with one strong arm that he wrapped around her as they both headed back down the hallway. It was thrilling, and she found herself leaning into him long after she'd found her equilibrium.

"Hello?" she could hear Nadia saying.

"Thanks, Benny," Sarah whispered as he helped her seat herself on the edge of her bed. Leaned over her as he was, she caught his scent. Her new favorite: Old Spice and dryer sheets. Yummy.

He nodded and looked like he'd like to say something more before changing his mind and walking out of the room. Sarah shook her head. She'd pay good money to know what it was he was thinking at any given moment.

She brought the phone to her ear. "Sorry, Nadia. I wanted to get back to my room so I could have some privacy."

"Are you alright?" Her sister's voice cracked. "I've been worried all night long. I musta called a hundred times!"

Sarah ignored the accusatory tone and focused instead on the words. Her sister had been worried about her, and that felt like a breakthrough. "I'm alright," she reassured her.

"Erin said you had to have a CAT scan, and that they talked about a brain bleed."

"They ruled that out."

"Oh, good!" Her sister breathed in relief. "I was upset as all get out." This time, there was no accusation in her voice. Another breakthrough.

"I'll be alright."

"Okay. I mean, are you sure?" Nadia's voice sounded small, like she was a little girl again.

"I'm sure. I'll be right as rain in a day or two."

The sisters were silent. Sarah had no idea what to say next. She'd never been able to predict Nadia's moods. Never understood her even when they lived together. Now, with actual distance between them, it was even harder to make conversation.

Nadia cleared her throat. "Mama's still doin' good at Calista's."

"Oh?"

"She still calls every Saturday. I know it's only been a few weeks, but I think it's goin' pretty good."

"Well . . . great." They both knew the only reason Lydie Mae had agreed to go was for the money, but Sarah also knew they both hoped for change. Real change.

"Yeah."

Silence.

Sarah rubbed at her temple with her free hand. Since when was talking on the phone so mentally exhausting? She was fading fast. Although Nadia's next words had her sitting at attention.

"I guess Ronny's comin' to stay at the house."

Ronny was Lydie Mae's on-again, off-again boyfriend and a total bum.

"What?" Sarah sputtered.

"Yeah. He's gonna care for the place while Mama's at Calista's."

"Why? You're there."

She could almost hear Nadia's shrug. "Mama said so. I'm gonna find a place to stay while he's here."

"But that's a ninety-day program, and it's *your* house." Where was Nadia going to live for two and a half months?

"I'm eighteen now, Sarah. I mean, let's face it—it's mama's house, not mine. Well, technically it's the landlord's house, but you know what I mean. And I guess I'm an adult now and everything, you know? At least she said I can use the car . . . for now."

She sounded near tears, and Sarah could understand why. Nadia was in that awkward place between childhood and adulthood, and even Sarah, who out of necessity had always been independent, had a difficult time when she'd gone through it. It was scary to be on your own for the first time. The world had seemed so big, and she'd felt so small.

The dynamics between Nadia and their mother were interesting. Sarah hadn't studied up on it enough to know a lot about codependency, but she knew it was at play in the relationship between her mother and her sister. Nadia had taken care of Lydie Mae, yet she'd always been dependent on her at the same time. She took all her cues from their mother and allowed herself to be manipulated every which way. It had been the most unhealthy relationship in the world, but they needed each other in a way Sarah couldn't quite understand.

"You're not destitute, Nadia. Far from it. And I know there's a lot for us to sort out, but just know you don't ever have to worry."

"The money you're sendin' me isn't enough," Nadia pouted.

And there it was. The same old argument. Sarah was already sending Nadia a thousand dollars a month with the promise of more if she either got a job or applied to college. Sarah had even suggested Nadia start looking for an apartment and had promised to supply the rent money from her fund. But so far, Nadia hadn't made a move in any direction. Sarah could almost picture her sitting in that dark house and on that stupid, plaid couch, wasting away while she watched *Keeping Up with the Kardashians*, or some other equally banal show.

A thousand dollars a month was a lot of money for a girl who didn't pay for a single bill. Where was that money going? Or to whom? That was the better question. Sarah pinched the bridge of her nose. "We can talk about this further when my brain doesn't hurt, but for now, let me know how much extra money you need. You can always stay at a hotel for a while until we get this figured out."

"So, I have to ask you for permission to use *my* money?"

"Don't say it like that."

"I say it like that 'cause it *is* like that."

A sudden nausea came over her, and Sarah held back a gag. "Nadia," she warned weakly, "you're turnin' ugly, and I can't do this right now. I really can't."

Erin rolled into the room like a wave. She must have been listening in the hallway. "I'll take it from here," she said firmly.

Sarah handed her the phone without hesitating and crawled back under the covers. "She needs money, Erin. Legitimately. For a hotel."

"I'll hook her up." Erin patted Sarah's shoulder. "You rest." She turned and traveled across the length of the room, closing the door behind her, but Sarah could still hear her say, "What did I tell you, Nadia? For cripe's sake! You exhausted her, and now she's back in bed . . ."

Sarah slept. She slept for hours, but when she woke up, she didn't feel much better.

Chapter 20

Sarah rode in the passenger seat of Erin's SUV, eyes fixated on her lap. She couldn't handle looking out the window of a moving car just yet. Doing so made her feel like she was riding the Tilt-A-Whirl at the county fair, an activity she hadn't even enjoyed pre-concussion. She was more of a Ferris Wheel kind of person.

"This'll be good for you," Erin said for the third time. "Get you out of the house. Plus, you deserve some good pampering." She maneuvered her vehicle into a parking space right in front of the Dancing Sun Day Spa.

Normally, Sarah loved getting her hair done. She'd always considered it such a luxury, especially those few times she'd gone to an actual salon and not just a discount place. She still felt that way, but today, she was too out of sorts to get all that excited about it. It had been a little over a week since the accident, and she was still suffering an almost constant headache. Even worse, she was having trouble concentrating, and that come-and-go dizziness prevented her from driving.

Everything felt catty wampus in her life at the moment, but there was one good thing that had come out of this concussion, and that was that she and Nadia were finally making a positive connection. Nadia had nothing else to do, sitting alone in her hotel room all day, and Sarah was getting the idea that it was fear, not laziness, holding her back from getting herself a job or applying to schools. Her sister had an alarmingly low self-confidence, which Sarah was doing her best to try to boost.

Sarah had nothing to do either. She couldn't drive anywhere. She couldn't even watch TV without increased symptoms, and so the two of them talked, sometimes for hours. Often, they spoke of nothing. It seemed safer than discussing the things that really mattered, the things that bound them (painfully) together—their shared history or their shared inheritance, for example—but they were beginning to establish something new between them. Something almost . . . sisterly, maybe.

"What are you planning for your hair?" Erin asked, breaking into her thoughts.

Sarah considered her options. At just above her shoulders, her hair was already pretty short, and the sun had already given her a few highlights. She'd argued this with Erin when she told her she'd made this appointment—that she didn't really need one—but Erin hadn't listened, and now here they were. She might as well make the best of it. "Maybe some more highlights to brighten me up, but I'm not sure about the cut. Just a trim, probably."

"I love it on the longer side, like it is now, but I loved that sassy little bob you had going on when you first interviewed too."

Sarah smiled. "Thanks for surprisin' me with this, Erin. It'll be nice to get pampered a bit. "You said I'm seeing someone named Bethany?"

"Beth. I tried to get you in with Benny's sister, Kay, since she's supposed to be the best stylist in town, but she was booked, and Beth always does a good job on my hair. Plus, she's easy to get in to see on short notice, so—"

Erin looked down at Sarah's purse where her phone had begun to ring. They both knew who Sarah hoped it would be.

Sarah fished frantically around inside her bag. She always meant to keep her phone in the designated pocket, but without fail, it always ended up at the very bottom of her purse, underneath her wallet, pocket tissues, old receipts, and shopping lists. Her fingertips connected with the case, and she pulled the phone out just as it began its fourth ring. She checked the screen. "It's Olivia," she told Erin with false cheerfulness

Erin shot her a sympathetic smile. "Go ahead and take it. We're a few minutes early." She put the car in park and pulled the keys out of the ignition.

But Sarah sent Olivia to voicemail, and she saw Erin shoot her a look of surprise out of the corner of her eye. She didn't want to be rude, but she just didn't want to answer any questions right now. *How are you feeling, Sarah?* Or *Have you heard from Benny yet?* Because the truth was, she felt crummy half the time and wanted to cry the other half. And no, she hadn't heard from Benny. He'd left her texts unanswered for days now. All week. She hadn't seen him since the morning he'd come over to spell Heidi. Maybe it was the Winnie-the-Pooh pajamas that had scared him off.

"I'll call her later. I don't want to be late." Sarah dropped the phone back in her bag. No doubt it shot straight to the bottom again.

"I'll walk you in."

"Thanks," Sarah muttered. Two days ago, Olivia had driven her to her primary doctor's office for the totally useless appointment in which her doctor told her there was nothing she could do to speed her recovery along except to rest and be patient. The day before that, Erin had run all over town with a list of errands Sarah had given her while Sarah sat on the couch and fielded calls from Nadia.

With the exception of the meeting she'd had with Ethan yesterday to go over financial stuff, which honestly, she could hardly remember, sitting on the couch and talking to her sister were the only real activities she'd engaged in over the last several days. The sunlight gave her a headache, and so did the light from screens. In today's world, what did that leave? She felt utterly useless, and while Erin had meant well by making her an appointment today, Sarah couldn't help thinking she was being dropped off at the hair salon like some helpless little old lady in need of her monthly perm. She hated this dependency she had on her friends right now, but what could she do about it? "You don't have to stay," she said.

"I won't," Erin said cheerfully, ignoring the agitation Sarah hadn't been able to keep out of her voice. "I have a few things going on back at school. I figure I'll be done about the same time you are, but you can call me when she starts blow-drying you."

The two of them climbed out of the car at the same time, but Erin was faster and met Sarah on the passenger side just as she was shutting her door. She took Sarah's arm, and together they made their way along the sidewalk and into the salon.

The door jingled as they entered, and Sarah's nostrils were greeted with the loveliest combination of smells. She breathed in deeply and sighed. All salons smelled the same: like warm, blow-dried hair and beauty products. She'd been in middle school before she'd ever been inside of one, and she remembered that first experience well.

Gammie's friend, Claire, had a niece fresh out of beauty school who had rented a chair at a local salon, and she had done their hair for them one rainy Sunday for extra practice before her first clients came in the next day. Sarah had felt so special and so pampered. Never mind that Gammie walked out of there with blue-tinted hair and Sarah with freshly cut bangs that hit a whole inch above her eyebrows.

Gammie was the one who always cut Sarah's hair. She'd turn the little bathroom into a makeshift salon, lining the sink with a rolled towel and hauling in a folding chair from the garage. Sarah's favorite part was the shampooing and conditioning. There wasn't anything quite like the feeling of someone else washing your hair and massaging your scalp. She only wished Gammie could do it one more time.

This was going to be really nice, she admitted to herself. She squeezed Erin's arm. "Thank you for this. It was sweet of you to plan it."

Erin gave her a brief squeeze back and grinned. "There you are."

"Sorry?"

"You're back."

Sarah looked at her quizzically.

"*Sweet* Sarah is back. She rocks. I'm not sure what to do with *pissy* Sarah."

A voice called to them from the desk off to the right.

"May I help you?"

She and Erin turned at the same time and were greeted by a woman wearing a bright smile and a blond, layered bob.

"Hi, Kay." Erin touched Sarah's arm. "I have Sarah here for an appointment with Beth."

Sarah smiled. Benny's sister was pretty as a peach. She looked to be several years older than Sarah, but the smile lines around her eyes and mouth did nothing to detract from her prettiness. If anything, they added a certain something. An extra bit of friendliness, maybe.

Kay's eyes sparkled. "Brian's told me *so* much about you, Sarah," she said, moving around the desk to stand directly in front of them. "I hope you don't mind, but when I saw your name on the schedule, I switched a few things around so I could take care of you today."

Sarah felt herself blush, and Erin gave her a small nudge with her shoulder, which Sarah did her best to ignore. She didn't want to read into anything. "That's real nice of you, but you didn't need to go to all that trouble for me."

"Sure I did! Brian talks about you so much, I feel like you're an old friend." Kay beamed at her.

So did Erin.

"I'm ready for you now, if you'd like to come on back."

Sarah cleared her throat. "Um, okay. Erin, I'll call you when I'm close to done."

"Have fun!" Erin said, pulling her arm away with a small wink.

Kay took Erin's spot beside Sarah and locked arms with her. "My station's in the way back, so let me help you to the chair. I understand you're having some dizzy spells."

So Benny *had* gotten at least one of her messages. She'd left that one for him last Monday morning, a full week ago.

They walked down a tiled hallway with curtained-off rooms on either side. The sound of muted blow dryers and soft chatter with occasional outbursts of laughter created a nice little beauty parlor symphony, and it made Sarah smile. It might have been her first real smile in days.

She thanked Kay. "They don't happen often, but the trouble is I never know when one is coming."

"That must make it hard. I had a bout of vertigo a few years back, so I can relate. My husband had to take off work to take care of me and the kids a couple of days. I remember crawling on the floor at one point when it got so bad I couldn't even stand up without falling over. Felt like I was in one of those fun houses with the tilted floors and trick mirrors."

"Oh, dear! That sounds just awful!"

They walked into a back room, and Kay paused to close a door with frosted glass behind them. It was a large, yet cozy, space. The walls, painted in earthy tones, held Kay's framed certificates and pictures of her family interspersed with southwestern art, including several of the Kokopelli flutist.

"Here we are!" Kay chirped. She helped Sarah sit down before placing a cape over her and snapping it at the back of her neck. She lifted her hair out from under it. "There." Standing behind Sarah, she met her eyes in the mirror. "Well? You're booked for a cut and color, but what specifically were you thinking?" She began to run her fingers through Sarah's hair.

Sarah studied Kay. Her bob was adorable, and she was almost tempted to cut hers the same way, but Benny had once said they resembled one another, and the last thing she wanted to do was come out of there today looking like a carbon copy of his sister. "I think I'll keep most of the length, if you can just clean it up a bit, and I'd like to get some foils to brighten me up. I've been feelin' a little . . . drabby."

Kay clucked. "Poor thing. That's just on account of the accident. You don't look drabby in the least." She continued running her fingers through Sarah's hair, getting a sense of its texture. "Your hair is actually quite thick, but it's baby fine. How about a few longer layers to give it some movement? We can put some highlights throughout for some added dimension, and Iike you say, to brighten you up."

Sarah was under no illusions that layers would suddenly give her the beautiful, thick hair she'd admired on Dr. Molina, but anything that would give her *dimension* worked for her. "Sounds perfect."

Kay flashed her a happy smile and announced she'd be right back. After ducking behind a curtained-off area next to her mirror to mix the color, she was back in a jiffy, giving Sarah just enough time to decide she needed to get similar lighting around her own vanity at home. Something about the bulbs surrounding the mirror made Sarah's skin glow. It did wonders for her self-esteem, which was kind of in the toilet at the moment.

Kay rolled out a black cart that held all the supplies she'd need—foils, brushes, combs, and a blue ceramic bowl full of goo that smelled simultaneously of flowers and chemicals. She stopped the cart next to Sarah and pumped the chair's pedal to raise it to the right height.

"So, my brother tells me you teach right across the hall from him."

"I do, yes."

Kay reached for a comb. "I always wish I could see him in action. What's he like as a teacher?"

"He's a phenomenal teacher. The kids love him."

Kay smiled, but she pressed further. "What's his style, though? Is he strict or a pushover? Do kids hang out in his room after class? Does he hang out with the other teachers?"

Sarah didn't know which question to answer first. She figured she'd go in order. "He's . . . just right, I guess. Not too strict and not too lenient. Kids are always in his room. Mostly the hockey boys, but other kids too." She didn't mention anything about the other teachers. She wasn't sure how she could spin their standoffish behavior towards Benny.

Kay nodded and weaved strands of hair into a foil. A notch had formed between her eyebrows. She switched gears. "So . . . he mentioned helping you out with some landscaping this summer."

"Yes. He did a *wonderful* job! He built me a retaining wall, and it's perfect." She paused. "We worked on it together."

"He said that." Kay folded up the foil and pressed it against Sarah's scalp. "So . . . what kinds of things did you talk about while you worked?"

Kay, it would appear, was on a fishing expedition today. What she was trying to catch, Sarah wasn't exactly sure yet. "This and that. School. Hockey. He told me about growing up and about your kids, Jack and Jill." She gestured to a photo stuck to the mirror of two kids dressed in Halloween costumes. Jack was a ninja and Jill was a ladybug. "They're really cute."

Kay grinned. "They're little hellions." But she wasn't deterred, and she continued with the questions. "So, what did he tell you about growing up?"

Sarah squirmed in her chair. "Oh, I don't know. Stuff about sports. Things like that." And then, before she could stop herself, she added, "He said he had a hard time. In high school, but before that too."

Kay's hands stopped their work for several beats, and she met eyes with Sarah in the mirror. "Yeah. Yeah, he did. It was hard to watch. Middle school was the worst, but high school wasn't much better. Jackson Lang made his life a misery." She got back to work.

"Really? The assistant hockey coach at Nicolet State?"

"The very one," Kay answered with a roll of her eyes.

"What did he do?"

She scoffed. "What *didn't* Jackson do. I swear, I have a hard time looking at that man even now. Any chance he could, he tried to make Brian feel small. He was really good at it too. He'd tell Brian he was this thing or that thing, and Brian would believe it. In middle school, Jackson constantly told him he was a *retard*. Can you believe that?"

"Oh my lands, I *hate* that word!"

"Oh, me too. Believe me."

"But why would he call Benny, er, Brian that? He's so smart, with his photographic memory and all."

Kay's face registered surprise before she schooled her features and grabbed for another foil. "I couldn't say."

Sarah lowered her head as she felt her face heat up. Had she just pulled an Erin and pried a little too much?

Kay worked quietly and spoke again after several seconds. "Sarah, can I be frank?"

Sarah lifted her head with a jolt. "Of course."

"What are your feelings towards my brother?"

Sarah's eyes grew as wide as Gammie's green Christmas cookie platters. "My . . . *feelings?*"

Kay's face was grim and serious. "I need to know before I say anything more."

Sarah nodded slowly. This may just be the most surreal conversation she'd ever had, but she wanted it to continue. She considered her words before responding. "I see you do. I would just ask that what I say not go any further than the two of us girls."

Kay nodded once. "I agree and ask for the same."

Her face was so serious, and her words so solemn, it felt like they were entering into some sort of strange contract. Sarah bit down on her lip. "Okay, then. You asked if you could be frank, and I'll do my best. I haven't . . . told him this yet, but . . . oh, dear. How do I say it?"

"You like him?"

Sarah hesitated. "Of course I *like* him, but—"

Kay's hands stilled. "You *love* him?"

Sarah blew out a shaky breath. "I'll tell you what, if it's *not* love, it's sure got me fooled."

Kay broke into a wide smile. "I knew it!" She put a hand on Sarah's shoulder and gave her a light squeeze. "I just knew it. Thank you."

Sarah watched the blush creep up her face as she stared at their reflections. "Don't thank me! Nothing may ever come of it. Benny and I seem to be . . . incapable of moving to the next step, and I'm not really sure why. I can't read him."

Kay painted the strand of hair that rested on top of the foil she'd been holding in place. "You're not alone there. Brian's been, more or less, a mystery to me my whole life, but I'd still throw myself in front of a logging truck for him. He's—" her voice broke, and she cleared her throat. "Listen, he's not the best at talking about feelings, but he's told me enough about you to paint me a pretty clear picture. He's got it bad for you, sweetie. But you're right, something *is* holding him back."

"What?" Sarah held her breath as she waited for an answer. She was afraid Kay was going to say something like, "His unresolved feelings for Erin," or something.

But Kay didn't answer. Instead, she turned Sarah's chair to begin adding foils to the other side of her head before abruptly and jarringly shifting topics. "So, my son, Jack. He's a special kid. And Brian and him have a real special relationship. They're the same, those two. Jack is just like Brian was at his age, and that's why—" Kay's voice broke again, but this time she didn't recover herself as quickly. Her free hand flew to her mouth, and she held it there for several seconds, as she blinked rapidly over bright eyes.

Sarah leaned forward in her chair and turned around to look directly at her. "Kay?"

Benny's sister put out a staying hand. "Sorry. You must think I'm a conversational moron." She let her hand fall. "It's just, I'm so relieved to see Brian has made a success of himself, you have no idea. He owns a house. He's a teacher, and by your accounting, a good one. He's a terrific coach—I've seen enough games to know that—and to think that he might just find love too, it gives me hope for my son."

Sarah wasn't following, and the confused notch between her brows gave her away.

Kay rested the brush back in the bowl and pressed both hands to her cheeks. "I'm all over the place, I know. I just feel like a very disloyal sister right now, and I'm beating around the bush. But I *need* to tell you something. Maybe it's right and maybe it's wrong, but I need to, and I trust you not to repeat it."

Sarah's stomach performed a series of flips. She truly had no idea what was going to come out of Kay's mouth next, and it was more than a little disconcerting. Even so, she replied without hesitation. "I won't breathe a word. Cross my heart."

Kay nodded and took a deep breath. "My son, Jack, is the reason I now have to color my own hair because if I didn't, I just might be completely gray. Every single gray hair I have has been earned through worry over him."

This was bizarre. Were they talking about Benny or Jack here? Sarah worked to keep an open mind. "Why? What's been going on with him?"

"He's been so tough to raise, Sarah. So different from his sister, but not so very different from Brian. I remember things here and there, growing up as Brian's older sister, but mostly it's my mother who's noticed stuff. Parallels between Brian and Jack."

Okay, now they were getting somewhere. Sarah pulled her hands out from under her cape and rested them on her lap.

"She was the first to notice that little Jack walked on his toes as a toddler, just like Brian did. That lasted until Jack was about four or five. He was real bouncy and always bumping into walls and furniture and things. Honestly, I didn't think too much of it. He was a head-banger, too. To fall asleep, he'd bang his head against his crib, and then as a toddler, off the wall. Even in his car seat, it was how he fell asleep. It was soothing to him. We thought it was kinda sweet." She smiled.

"But then the tantrums started. They would go on for hours and hours. They still do, but they don't happen as much, and they're not so intense. Any time something happens he's not expecting, he gets set off. Like if I choose to drive a different way home from school. We used to *have* to take the same way home. No stops for groceries or gas. Nothing. It's getting better now, and we've been working with a therapist who's been a total blessing."

Sarah's nod encouraged Kay to continue.

"Anyway, I don't want to bore you with all the details. But long story short, or maybe the short story long"—she chuckled—"is that we got a diagnosis. My son has autism."

Sarah had been expecting as much, based on the description, but still, her breath caught. "Oh, Kay. I'm sorry!"

Kay waved a hand, but her eyes were bright once again. "It's still a little fresh. We just did the testing this last fall, but it's not as bad as it could be. We were told this would've been called PDD-NOS if that was still a diagnosis, which it's not."

"I'm not familiar with that."

"Pervasive Developmental Disorder - Not Otherwise Specified. It used to be in that DSM thingy, but now it's all just *autism spectrum*. Our pediatrician, another angel in disguise, has been taking care of kids for decades, and so he knows all the ins and outs and new and old names. He's tracked tons of kids into adulthood, and he said Jack is *on the shallow end* of the spectrum and will outgrow most of his autistic behaviors. He said when Jack's older, people will just think he's a little quirky."

"That's wonderful news!" Sarah really didn't know a whole lot about autism. They'd covered it briefly in the special education class she'd taken in Duluth, but as prevalent as she knew it was, she hadn't had any students on the spectrum yet, and despite her education and knowing better, when she thought of autism, the movie *Rainman* was what immediately came to mind. But autism really *was* a spectrum, and each person on that spectrum was affected differently.

And that was when she got it. She met Kay's eyes. "Benny?"

Kay nodded. "Yes."

This time, instead of a flip, Sarah's stomach twisted into an unpleasant knot, and she pressed a hand to it. "That's why he struggled so much growing up?"

"It's why he struggles a little bit even now," Kay added.

Sarah thought about his lack of eye contact with most people, including her at the beginning. She thought back to Olivia's first impression of him, as well as the way he was received by most of the high school staff. In some ways, not being obviously autistic might be even harder. People were so quick to judge and just call someone weird, not knowing anything about them. It wasn't fair. Everyone was quirky in their own way, and didn't everyone have something they wrestled with? Anxiety? Depression? Substance abuse?

Kay adjusted the cape so it covered Sarah's arms and hands again and reached for the bowl and brush. "This is probably why you say things aren't moving forward between you. He's awkward, socially, and when deeper feelings are involved, I could see why he might have an even harder time."

Sarah thought about that. "Hmm."

"And nothing against her," Kay went on, continuing the pattern of weaving the hair, grabbing the foil, painting the hair, and folding the foil, a pattern she could probably do in her sleep and was certainly doing now without having to think very hard about it, "but that Erin girl might have messed him up a little. He went way out of his comfort zone when he started dating her. He worked with his psychologist on it, and then he got burned. He might be even more cautious now."

Sarah knew her friend would never have deliberately hurt Benny. She could be insensitive, yes, and she probably had been, but the reason she'd run in the opposite direction had every bit as much to do with her and her baggage as it had him. But had Erin ever wondered about him? Had the possibility of autism ever crossed her radar? She supposed it really didn't matter.

As much as Sarah sympathized with Benny's struggles, she was kind of glad that he was the way he was. She couldn't help it. It made him . . . *him*. He was such a good person. So honest and so kind. Painfully awkward, yes, but who cared?

She didn't.

Kay worked in silence for a time, lost in her own thoughts.

Sarah was glad she knew this about Benny. She wanted to know everything about him.

A thought struck her. Kay had mentioned a psychologist. "Does he . . . does Benny know?"

"About Jack?"

"About himself. I assume he does, but receiving a diagnosis as an adult must be a little unusual."

Kay gave Sarah's chair a quick height adjustment before answering. "Me and my husband, we sat the family down a few months ago, just Brian and my parents and us. We took them out for dinner and told them about Jack's diagnosis. I don't think my mom was all that surprised, not that she wasn't sad to hear it. But she's the one who said it out loud as a possible explanation for Jack's behavior. And she's the one who drew the parallels between Brian and Jack."

"What did Benny say to that?"

"Not much. Not right then, at least. But he's gotten some answers for himself. I think maybe he was relieved in some ways. He started, you know, talking to someone, like I said. A psychologist who's really young, fresh out of school, but she seems really, really good. She's helped him a lot."

She. Sarah couldn't help but feel a touch of jealousy. Was this young psychologist pretty? How often did he see her? He must be able to open up to her, so she probably knew way more about Benny than Sarah did. Did she find Benny attractive too? She must. Benny *was* attractive. She shook off those questions, the ones she couldn't ask out loud, anyway, and asked one that she could. "What's she helping him with?"

"The first few visits," Kay said, turning Sarah's chair a few more degrees, "she tested him. Gave him some kind of special surveys and took the lead on diagnosing him, along with his doctor. Now, she's helping him come to terms with it. Helping him understand himself better. Maybe even working on a few things he still struggles with. I guess I don't really know."

They retreated back into their respective thoughts for several minutes. Sarah stared down at her black cape. Benny probably wouldn't be happy to know his sister had spilled these beans, but she was glad Kay had. She'd wanted to understand him better, and now she did. And she might just love him even more. Because what she'd admitted to Kay was true. She loved Benny. She felt it in her chest with each beat of her heart.

Kay broke into her thoughts. It was as if she'd been listening to them. "He has strong feelings for you too, Sarah. If he hasn't shown it, it's because he can't always guess people's intentions. You know, what they might be thinking or what they might want. That's what I'm learning with Jack. They call it 'theory of mind.'"

Sarah perked up. "That rings a bell from one of my education classes."

Kay nodded. "People on the spectrum have a harder time putting themselves in someone else's shoes to try to figure them out. And honestly, that's the biggest reason why I've told you all this. I don't want him to lose you because of a misunderstanding that he can't really help. It wouldn't be fair."

Sarah shook her head. "He won't lose me."

Kay visibly relaxed. "Good. I told myself I wouldn't say anything today, but as soon as I saw you, I thought, 'She can handle it. She won't run.'"

Sarah knew that was a compliment, and she smiled before she agreed. "I won't. But I have to say, it's possible Benny may not want to be with me. I've sent him three messages over the last week, and he hasn't responded to any of them."

Kay smiled. "They're on a two-week fishing trip."

"Who?"

"Brian, our dad, Jack, and my husband, Jordan."

So, he was fishing. Okay, fine, but he could still type a few measly lines into his phone and send them to her, couldn't he?

Again, Kay read her mind. "They're in a remote part of Canada. No cell service. They left their phones charging in my kitchen."

"Oh." Sarah inhaled a deep breath and blew it out slowly. That was a relief. He wasn't avoiding her. "But wait," she said with a puzzled frown, "he must have gotten my message about the dizziness, because you knew about it."

A blush crept into Kay's cheeks. "I have a confession to make. Before I powered off Brian's phone, I saw that message from you. It came through while I was plugging it into the charger, and I read it. I'm sorry." She threw Sarah a sheepish glance. "We're not great with boundaries in our family."

Sarah laughed. Benny had told her that once.

"Anyway, he hasn't seen it yet, so you don't have to worry that he's ignoring you. I can say without a doubt that he's yours all yours if you want him."

If she wanted him? That wasn't even in question any longer. Whatever had happened in the past was in the past. She wouldn't let it dictate her future. This was the rest of her life, and all Sarah wanted to do was call Benny because she *did* want him. She needed him. Unfortunately, she'd have to wait another week. Despite her impatience, she couldn't stop smiling.

Chapter 21

"I can see why you like this place." Ethan looked around 906 Pizza, and Erin could see he was impressed by Nicolet's top-rated restaurant. It had won that honor for the last five years. It was far from fancy, but it had a unique flair and fantastic food. Named after the area code that encompassed the entirety of the Upper Peninsula, the pictures that decorated its walls showcased all the best U.P. scenes. From Tahquamenon Falls to Lake of the Clouds, all the favorites were accounted for. Erin had pointed them out, frame by frame, to Ethan as they'd waited for their table.

The two of them sat in a cozy booth with a pitcher of beer between them, and they alternated between conversation and people-watching. After a long and busy week, it was great to finally relax. It was Friday night and crowded, and the pineapple, mushroom, and pepperoni pizza they'd ordered was taking twice as long as it should, but Erin didn't mind. She was in no rush.

Ethan poured himself a second mug of Summer Shandy from the pitcher as she waved to yet another person she knew. Fortunately, nobody had approached her yet to talk to her about their child's teacher, school curriculum, or whatever else they were concerned about at her school.

"So, where's this log chute you mentioned the other day, and when are we going to check it out?"

Erin leaned forward to rest her elbows on the table, but it was a little too high to be comfortable, so she rested her hands in her lap instead. She needed a booster seat like the kid sitting over in the next booth. He was covered in pizza sauce, and she shared a quick smile with the boy's mother before answering Ethan. "Anytime. It's over in Brule Harbor, about ninety miles from here."

He took a swig from the oversized mug that had *906* etched into the glass.

"We could go the end of next week," she suggested. "I'm going to try to take Friday off."

He set the mug down on his beverage napkin and began to spin it slowly around. "You can't go any earlier?"

"I wish I could, but work is kicking my butt, and next week is especially sucky with all the interviews on top of everything else." She shifted positions, pressing her spine against the back of the booth and relaxing against the soft vinyl.

So far, this summer had been the most work-centric she'd had since moving to Nicolet. She hadn't realized just how much she needed her four-week summer break to decompress. Gabe was new this summer, but he would no longer be new next summer, and Erin absolutely would not allow him to disrespect her personal time this way next year. One and done. This year, she was giving him the benefit of the doubt and trying to be a team player, even though she was getting no additional pay for all the extra time she was putting in. But that was the life of an educator.

Ethan made a low hum in his throat. "I'm beginning to think I don't like this Gabe very much."

"That's just because you heard Sarah call him by his nickname," Erin teased.

He grinned and held up his hands. "He can keep it. Trust me, no man with even a moderate level of testosterone wants to be known as a *babe*. Hot? Sure. Or a hunk even." He pulled a face. "Okay, maybe not a hunk either, but definitely not a babe."

Erin smirked. "Good to know. I'll never call you a babe to your face."

"You're the one exception," he informed her, treating her to one of his super-sexy smiles. "You get to call me whatever you want."

"How about mackadocious?" she asked playfully.

"Macka-what?"

"You know . . . gorgy, jiggy . . . finer than frog hair."

He laughed. "What's with you and Sarah and your made-up words? I don't know what any of those mean, but I do know frog comparisons are never a good thing."

"McDreamy or McSteamy then?"

He gave a decisive nod. "Now we're talking. I do know what those are, thanks to my sister's love affair with *Grey's Anatomy*."

"You're better than both those guys. Way hotter."

"And don't they both die?" He looked at her askance.

"Them and half the cast. I cried when Derek died, but honestly, Meredith should have seen it coming. That hospital is cursed. It's, like, the worst work place ever." She began ticking off her fingers. "Near-drownings, bombs detonating in operating rooms, planes crashing, getting burned alive . . ." She couldn't think of any others off the top of her head. "I'll never complain about my job again."

Ethan chuckled. "You can complain to me. You're working really hard. Gabe the Babe is lucky to have you."

She smiled in thanks before bringing her mug to her lips.

"So, you said you have some more interviews coming up?"

Erin leaned in towards him. They were seated near the kitchen, and it was a little loud. "Yeah. Shanna Lee, one of our math teachers, decided to retire last minute, so I need to fill her position along with the health and Spanish positions I already told you about."

He whistled. "Three positions, and it's almost August. Crunch time."

"It is. But did I tell you about the Spanish candidate I found? Or I should say, that Sarah found?"

"I don't think so, or if you did, I forgot."

"What, you don't hang on my every word?" she joked.

"Well, there have been so many of them," he shot back. "You talk more than my mother, and that's saying something."

Erin gave him a swift kick under the table. "Hey!"

The truth was, she *had* been doing a lot of talking. They'd had conversations late into the night almost every day this last week. She was more tired than she'd been in a long time, but it was worth it. They'd covered a lot of ground in a short time, but there was still so much more that she wanted to know about him.

She still hadn't told Ethan about Psychostalker. She'd almost told him last night, but nothing had happened since the day of Sarah's party, and that had been just shy of two weeks ago. Nothing unusual had shown up on her porch camera either. Maybe whoever it was had grown bored and moved on.

The way things stood now, Erin didn't see any reason to worry Ethan, and she knew him well enough to know he *would* worry. In fact, he'd do more than worry. He'd put it on himself, making her problem his problem. He seemed to feel an unusual responsibility to take care of the people in his life, his family in particular. She didn't want to add to that burden.

Ethan's eyes sparkled. "My apologies. Tell me again. Who is she, or he?"

"*She's* Dr. Molina's cousin." At his blank stare, she scoffed and added, "The beautiful, gorgeous, knock-out doctor who took care of me and Sarah in the ER."

Ethan was all playful innocence. "Oh, was she beautiful? I hadn't noticed."

"Yeah right, and I believe you. Anyway, her name is Elena, and she's a native Spanish speaker from Puerto Rico."

He looked impressed. "Sounds solid."

"I know. She actually lived here for a few years with her relatives, but she's been teaching in Houston, and she's not real crazy about city life. She wants to come back where it's smaller and quieter."

"And with a lot more snow. She'll be long gone by March," Ethan predicted.

Erin gave him another tiny kick. "Stop! She knows what she's getting into, and what do you know about it anyway? Live here through a winter, then we'll talk."

"Maybe I will."

She was pretty sure he'd said it only as a joke, but what if Ethan had meant it even just a little bit? Her stomach did a small somersault. What if he did stay in Nicolet? Was that so far-fetched? And if he felt even a fraction of what she felt, then . . .

Shoving the thoughts far from her mind, Erin plowed forward. "So anyway, if she takes it, we'll finally have a Spanish teacher who can speak the language!"

"There's an idea," he teased with a wide smile that lit up his whole face. Ethan was hot all the time, even in that scuzzy Beavis and Butt-Head T-shirt he'd had on the other day for the jog they'd taken together. Well, okay, it was more of a walk than a jog, but Erin had really tried. In her defense, her legs were so much shorter than his that she'd had to take two strides to match every one of his. She was pretty sure, when it was all said and done, she'd run close to a mile, and that wasn't too shabby for a beginner—in her opinion.

A few nights ago, Sarah told her she was "cathecting" with Ethan. Apparently, when you invested time and emotions into someone else by joining them in doing the things they loved to do, you were cathecting. That was fine with Erin. She could *cathect* with Ethan all day long.

Lately, she'd allowed herself to imagine where things with him might go. For the first time in a long time, it didn't scare her to consider a future with him. The only thing that scared her anymore was the thought of him leaving, which she'd originally viewed as a bonus. She tried not to think about it, and she tried not to think about what it meant that she wasn't looking for ways to pull the plug yet.

She studied him. When Ethan smiled, like he was now, he went from a solid ten to an eleven, even in a stupid cartoon shirt that should have been pitched a decade ago. At least he only wore it to exercise. He looked exceptionally striking this evening in a white, collared, button-down shirt. He had the sleeves rolled up to his elbows, revealing his strong, tanned, hair-dusted forearms.

He was such a *man*!

Erin loved it.

Surely, it was weird to find someone's arm (and toe) hair appealing. But she couldn't help it. She liked everything about him. It was just a bonus that when he talked, she got the shivers. And when he *listened*, well . . . it was hard to imagine there'd been a time when she'd thought she hated him. Especially now, when she was pretty sure he was the only man on the planet who could make her feel this way.

"When will you finally get some vacation time?" he asked.

She winced. "Technically, I'm supposed to be on my vacation now."

He raised an eyebrow. "Oh yeah? How does that work?"

"It doesn't." She laughed. "But it goes with the territory. I'll try to take some days, though, I promise." Maybe she'd be able to take Thursday and Friday off. The interviews would be happening earlier in the week, so that might actually work. They could take some day trips together to see some of the places hanging on the walls of the pizzeria.

Dinner arrived, and the two of them took time out of their conversation to dig in. After a few bites, Ethan wiped his mouth with his napkin and then dropped a bomb on her. "Listen, I need to go back home for a few weeks. I'm leaving in a couple of days."

Immediately, Erin felt her plans go *poof* as they evaporated into thin air. She'd been planning things for them while she chewed. Cliff jumping at Sable Rocks, hiking at the Sandstone National Lakeshore, the Log Chute, in Brule Harbor, and maybe even some nighttime swims back at the basin.

She swallowed down her bite of pizza, as well as her disappointment. "What for?"

"I need to check in with work."

"How long?"

He spoke without meeting her eyes. "Three weeks. Four tops."

Her jaw dropped, and she set down her slice of pizza. "A *month?*"

He inclined his head. "I hope it won't take that long."

There were just four days left in the month of July, and Erin had felt optimistic that she could take some time off in August, but now Ethan wouldn't even be there. School would begin before Labor Day this year, which meant the last week of August was going to be pretty nuts for her. Once school resumed, summer was officially over. And when summer ended, so would her relationship with Ethan. She'd known that, but she wasn't ready. She felt robbed of time.

Erin swallowed hard. Her throat felt impossibly dry, and she reached for her mug of beer, taking several gulps while her mind raced. There had to be some way to prolong this. "What about weekends?" she asked, setting down the glass. "Can you come back up on the weekends?"

He hesitated. "I'll be tied up on the weekends too."

She fiddled with her fork. She needed to stop, but she couldn't keep herself from suggesting casually, "I could always come to you. Flint's only about six or seven hours away, right?"

He squirmed in his seat again. "Yeah, it's about that far, and I wish that could work, sweetheart, but it won't. I'm sorry. This is important business, and I need to get it right."

The endearment was lost on her, which was too bad because for once it didn't make her want to cringe. Erin wasn't normally on board with being someone's *baby* or *honey* or *sweetie*, but with Ethan, she might not feel that way anymore. But any pleasure she might have had from being called his sweetheart was overshadowed by the strong sense that he was withholding information from her, just as she'd felt that first night on the dock. She needed to see his eyes.

"Ethan."

He looked up at her.

"You really have to go back for work?" She stared directly into his pupils to see if he would look away—the sure sign of a guilty conscience.

He didn't.

Ethan held her gaze and reached across the table for her hand. "Yes, and believe me, I don't want to go. There's nowhere in the world I'd rather be than right here with you."

Erin felt a rush of relief. He was telling the truth. He didn't want to leave. For a split second, she'd thought that maybe she'd been played. That he might have someone else back home or something. Or if not that, that he just wasn't into her anymore.

But this was Ethan, she reminded herself. Not Seth. Ethan could be counted on. He wouldn't change his mind. He wasn't indifferent to her. He was always calling or texting or just showing up at the door to see how she was doing or if she was free. He wanted to spend time with her just as much as she wanted to spend time with him.

"And listen," he continued, "when I get back, I need to tell you some other things. Things that I need for you to know."

The knot that had formed in her belly loosened a bit. "So, you *are* coming back?"

Surprise flickered in his eyes. "Erin, of course I'm coming back."

"But when does your summer end? When do you have to go back for good?"

"I'm . . . working on that."

Erin felt the hairs on the back of her neck stand on end. "What does that even mean?"

"It means, just trust me. Please."

"Ethan, I'm just asking—"

A shadow loomed over their booth, and a harsh voice spoke above Erin's head. "Well, well, lookee here! It's the wicked bitch of the North Woods!"

Erin recognized the speaker even before she looked up to see Jason Bender standing at the head of their table, wearing a ribbed, white tank top designed to showcase his muscles but only succeeded in making him look trashy. Beside him stood a tall, large-boned woman with blaze-orange hair sticking out in spikes around her head. She wore a smirk and a tube top at least two sizes too small. It was already beginning to roll on itself as it strained to cover a pair of the largest breasts Erin had ever seen. She wondered if the poor, stressed top would be able to keep those girls contained much longer. She fervently hoped so.

Ethan let out something that sounded remarkably like a growl and moved to stand up.

Erin's hands shot out to stop him. She shook her head.

His murderous look transformed to one of bafflement, but he stayed put when she gave another small shake of her head. She looked up at Jason and forced herself to stay cool. He wanted to get a rise out of her, and she was determined not to give him the satisfaction. Instead, she plastered on a wide smile and said, "That's not a very nice thing to say, Jason. What's the matter with you? Did you get struck by lightning again?"

Jason sneered at her. So did his ginormous date.

His eyes flitted to Ethan for a moment and then, satisfied that Ethan wouldn't be engaging him in a fight just yet, he turned his attention back to Erin. "Where ya been? Haven't seen you around lately." His ice-blue eyes bore holes into hers.

"I didn't realize you were looking. Aren't you supposed to be in Chicago?" She raised her eyebrows and then casually rested her chin in one hand.

He didn't answer her. Instead, he cocked his head and asked, "Hey, how's your dog? Interesting choice of breed."

"Erin maintained a bored expression, but it wasn't easy. How did he know she had a dog? She hadn't seen him when she'd been out with Marvin. Unless . . .

Jason gave her a look that gave nothing away but revealed everything at the same time. And then he smiled. Without taking his eyes off Erin, he addressed his companion, "Let's go, Jaska."

He turned, and as they walked away, Erin knew. It was him. Jason was her psychostalker. He had been the one messing with her, and he wanted her to know it. She wasn't sure what to make of that. She felt as though she'd just been sucker-punched. Jason Bender had vandalized her house and scared her so much she'd had to move in with Sarah. He'd robbed her of sleep! Stupid, pathetic *Jason Bender!*

And apparently, he was still trying to scare her. He hadn't *seen* her in a while? She wasn't really hiding. She'd been all over town. Where she hadn't been lately was home. Which meant he was watching her house. That's how he knew about Marvin.

He was a far cry from the scary villain she'd pictured in her head, but what kind of psycho staked out his old boss's house? "Hey!" she hollered after him.

Jason had nearly reached the door, but he turned around.

"Stay off my property, or I'll have you arrested."

His smile never faltered.

"I know it was you."

"Prove it," he replied before turning and leaving.

Erin thought she might pop a blood vessel, and she took deep breaths through her nose to calm herself down.

"Erin, what the hell was that?" Ethan demanded. He looked ready to jump out of the booth and chase Jason out into the parking lot. "And prove what?"

Erin took one more deep breath and reclined against the back of the booth. "*That* was a totally incompetent teacher I got duped into hiring last year."

Ethan's surprise was obvious. "That was one of your teachers?"

She nodded.

"I sure as hell hope you plan on firing him!"

She waved a hand. "I already did. And he's still a little peeved about that, as you can see."

Ethan stared at her. "Erin," he repeated, "prove what?"

She filled him in, and by the time she was done, Ethan looked ready to commit murder. Actually, so was Erin. Retelling the story brought it all back and reminded her of just how terrified she'd really been. But not anymore. Now she was ticked. She wanted Jason to come back in and show his face one more time just so she could land a punch on his Eagle's beak of a nose. Or at least let Ethan get in a shot.

Ethan was quiet as he observed her. He was upset, and not just with Jason. She could see it in the narrowing of his eyes.

She sighed. "Alright, I know. I should've told you."

He continued to stare. "Why didn't you?"

Ramrod straight, she sat up. "Because I was handling it."

"You were handling it," he echoed.

She lifted her chin. "Yeah, I was." This conversation seemed vaguely familiar until Erin remembered it was almost word for word the one she'd had with Heidi in the lake at Sarah's. Didn't anyone believe she could handle her own life? People needed to stop underestimating her.

He shook his head. "Erin, I know you *handled* it. You handled it really well, although I wish you'd gone to the police sooner. But you did it all alone. You didn't tell anyone? Not even Sarah? Why?"

Slightly mollified by his belief in her abilities, Erin relaxed. "Because I . . ." She lifted her shoulders in a helpless shrug. "I just . . . I guess I'm not used to, you know, telling people things like this. I've always just taken care of stuff on my own. I don't need someone to solve my problems for me. I never have."

"No," Ethan agreed, "you don't need anyone to solve things for you. You're strong and independent, and I love that about you."

Erin fought back a smile. So that's the phase they were in. Wasn't saying you loved *things* about someone a precursor to saying you loved *them*? She wanted to ask him, but she studied him instead. He looked so serious.

"I just think life is better, easier, when you go through the ups and downs with someone else. When you let people in. Carry each other's loads," he said.

"I didn't want you to have to carry my load. Your arms are pretty full as it is," she pointed out.

He grabbed her hand and held it. "Let me tell you something, Erin. I will always, *always* have room for you in my arms."

His words made her want to jump for joy and burst into tears all at once, but she did neither of those things. Instead, she squeezed his hand, and wished she could hold on to it forever. Suddenly, her chest felt uncomfortably tight.

What she felt towards Ethan was so new to her; she really couldn't explain it. Except that she could. Finally, staring at their joined hands and seeing how tiny hers looked within the solid warmth of his, Erin worked up enough gumption to admit something to herself.

She loved Ethan.

She loved him for every reason and for no reason, and she had to tell him.

The realization sent a small shiver of apprehension down her spine. It was too soon to feel these things, but it didn't matter. She could stick her head in the sand and pretend otherwise, but the truth was undeniable, and even though there was a risk he might not say it back, she was going to tell him. Tonight, when they were alone, she was going to admit to Ethan Rockford that she loved him and wanted them to carry each other's burdens for the rest of their lives. She was all in, and she thought—or at least she hoped—that he would be too.

An hour later, Erin was pulling onto Sarah's road. Ethan was going to meet her in a bit for a nightcap. She'd met him at the restaurant right after work, so they'd driven home separately, and in the silence of her car, she'd allowed her thoughts to roam wherever they wanted. Anywhere but on what she was about to do, that is.

She considered what Ethan had said about going through life's ups and downs with other people. At a very young age, without realizing it, she'd built an impenetrable wall around herself, and it had done its job. It had protected her, and in many ways, she remained grateful for it still. It had insulated her from the frequent lashings of her mother's tongue, helped her cope with the near-constant yearning for a father who was rarely home, and it had definitely blunted the searing pain of losing him completely to the ravages of a cancer so vicious, it had taken him in a matter of weeks. Even Seth's rejection had been survivable with the wall in place. She'd never let him inside its inner sanctum, so he'd never gotten close enough to do her any permanent damage. But that wall had also hindered the development of any close and meaningful relationships.

Until recently.

Looking back from her vantage point today, she could see that she'd begun dismantling it piece by piece when she'd moved to this small beach town.

From her very first day in Nicolet, Erin had felt like she could finally get a full breath of air into her lungs, and a brick came down. And then another, as she got settled. And then another as she put down roots. Little by little, without even realizing it, she'd changed.

Close friendships, like the ones she had now, would never have been possible before her move to Nicolet. She would have been too closed off with too many prickles and stings. Still, it had taken a long time, years even, for her friendship with Olivia to develop. It had been borne out of Olivia's need for support during a dark time, but arguably, Erin had been the one to benefit most. And then Sarah had come along, seemingly all alone in the world, and they'd taken her under their wing. The rest, as they say, was history.

And then came Ethan. She'd dated plenty of guys before him, Benny included, but she hadn't been ready. Now there were no bricks left. She felt exposed, wide open, but also liberated, and she craved more.

Erin flipped on her right blinker, even though nobody was behind her, and turned down Sarah's gravel drive. She loved the beech trees that lined the driveway. Honestly, she loved everything about this place. Lake Superior was majestic and gorgeous in a way that absolutely blew the mind, but the basin held a quiet, beautiful serenity that was all its own. How lucky she was to have both within only minutes of each other.

Just after the house came into view, Erin noticed an old Chevy Malibu parked off to the side near the garage. She didn't recognize the vehicle at all, and until she remembered her scary stalker was probably pathetic Jason Bender, she experienced a split-second shiver of fear.

Shaking it off, and reminding herself she needed to call Officer James first thing, she parked and hopped out of the Yukon. She really needed to get some running boards. It was like climbing in and out of a tree every time she drove anywhere. She'd thought about getting something smaller, but the Yukon's size made her feel safe driving on the icy, snowy roads during the long Upper Peninsula winters.

The air was warm and fresh off the basin, and Erin filled her lungs with it. Yes, she could breathe here. This place had become a part of her. It felt more like home than Santa Monica ever had, and she doubted there could ever be anything that would entice her to leave. She needed this place.

Through the window next to the door, Erin saw Sarah sitting on the sofa next to a young girl with fine, mousy-brown hair that was stringy in a way that spoke to it not having been washed in several days. She was twiggy, and not like the famous model from the sixties, but like an actual stick. Her cheekbones jutted out of her face like guardrails, and her eyes had the appearance of being far too large for the delicate bones of her face.

Erin let herself in and closed the door behind her. Hearing Marvin racing down the hallway toward her, she dropped her purse to the floor and bent her knees, lowering her center of gravity. Her great big dog rounded the corner a moment later and crashed into her legs, nearly knocking her over. This was the next thing they'd need to work on. A few more pounds and he'd level her completely every time she came through the door. But it was hard to fault him for his exuberant greetings because, honestly, they made her day. Erin stroked his soft, shiny coat. "Hey, boy! Did you miss me?"

"Erin!" Sarah exclaimed with a plastered-on smile. "Look who drove all the way from Alabama to see me!"

Keeping her face impassive, Erin moved from the entryway and into the living room, her gaze flitting back and forth between the two women. This must be Nadia, she guessed. There was definitely a small resemblance between the two sisters. Sarah's eyes were as wide as dinner plates when she added, "It's my sister, Nadia, and she's plannin' on stayin' a while. Isn't that great?"

Erin stopped at the kitchen counter and rested her purse there before slowly making her way towards the sofa, shadowed all the way by Marvin. She wasn't so sure Nadia's sudden appearance was a good thing. From what Erin knew of her, even for a teenager, Sarah's sister was a self-absorbed brat. Although, admittedly, she and Sarah had been talking a lot lately and seemed to be getting along. But Erin couldn't help but recall past stories Sarah had shared with her. She felt protective of her friend. The last thing she wanted was to see her get hurt again by family. She deserved better.

Erin finally spoke and agreed with Sarah. "Yeah, that's nice."

Nadia inclined her head. Erin's first impression of the girl had been dead on. She was a total waif. If she hadn't been so thin, she might have been considered pretty. The dark smudges underneath those striking violet eyes made Erin wonder if she'd driven straight here from Alabama without stopping. For a second, until she spoke, Erin felt sorry for her.

"So, you're Erin," Nadia said, staring down her nose at Erin and giving her a quick once-over.

Erin gritted her teeth and smiled. "In the flesh."

Nadia sniffed. "I pictured you taller."

"Oh, yeah? Well, I pictured you—"

"I thought I'd put Nadia in the extra room upstairs," Sarah broke in, shooting Erin a warning glance.

Erin groaned inwardly. Great. The extra room was right across from her room upstairs, which meant no more privacy. It also meant sharing the bathroom she'd had all to herself for the last month. She formed her lips into something she hoped resembled a smile, and the three of them looked around at one another in silence. Erin spoke first. "So why did you come all the way up here, Nadia?"

Sarah began to chew a nail, and Erin saw some of Nadia's bravado fade.

"I-I just wanted to be, you know . . ."

"What?" Erin asked when it didn't look like Nadia was going to finish the thought at all. "What did you want to be?"

Nadia looked at Sarah with an unreadable expression. "Close. I wanted to be close. To Sarah." She looked down at her folded hands.

"And I'm so glad you came," Sarah rushed to say, before shooting Erin a look that said, *Behave yourself!*

Nadia nearly smiled before becoming stoic once more. She addressed Erin. "Our mama's boyfriend's been livin' at the house, and I've been in a hotel."

Erin, of course, already knew that. She'd been the one to set her up in that hotel the day after Sarah's head injury, but she nodded along anyway. "Ah." It must be that the wretched girl had finally run out of money and come running to her sister. What a leach! Erin looked around the room. "I don't see any bags."

Nadia looked up. "They're in the car. I wasn't sure if you'd have room . . ."

"Of course we do. You'll stay here with us," Sarah said definitively.

Nadia sat up straighter, but she kept her eyes on the floor. "Thanks."

"Of course!" Sarah reassured with a smile that was just a little too wide.

Erin looked between the sisters and wondered how long they'd do this little dance. She supposed it would take time to get everything sorted out between them, assuming they'd be able to do that at all, which she kind of doubted. For now, the two of them looked wrung out. Sarah clearly needed to go rest, and Nadia was obviously exhausted from her trip.

"Let's go get your things, Nadia," Erin said. "Sarah, you look a little tired. Why don't you get ready for bed. I'll get Nadia settled in."

"Oh, no. I can show her—"

Erin shot her a sardonic smile as she affected a southern accent. "You're both worn slap out and need to rest. I'll make sure she's settled tonight, and y'all can catch up tomorrow when you're good and rested."

Sarah's tired eyes came alive with a small sparkle. "My goodness! You know how to speak southern!"

"I've had myself a grand teacher," Erin said, remaining in character.

Sarah's smile was replaced by a large yawn, and she shook her head. "Alright. I am feeling a bit tuckered out. Nadia, we'll talk in the morning?"

Nadia nodded.

"And you're sure you're not hungry? I can whip up some pancakes right quick."

Nadia shook her head. "I'm sure."

"Alright." Sarah wrung her hands together before stepping forward and wrapping her sister in a brief, awkward hug. "I'm glad you're here."

Nadia blinked a few rapid blinks as Sarah pulled away. "Thanks."

"Night y'all."

Chapter 22

All Erin saw when Nadia popped the trunk were three white garbage bags stuffed to the point of tearing. She looked at Nadia in surprise. "Where's your luggage?"

Nadia shrugged and looked away.

She didn't own a suitcase? Or a few duffel bags? Maybe they were poorer than Sarah had let on. "Is this everything then?"

"Yeah."

Erin heaved one bag over a shoulder and picked up a second one.

Nadia grabbed the third and shut the trunk. "So, I guess you'll be stayin' here too."

Erin ignored her perturbed tone. Clearly, Nadia had hoped to have Sarah all to herself. "Right across the hall from you."

"Why?"

"Because that's where my room is," Erin explained with exaggerated patience.

Nadia frowned. "No, I mean, why are you stayin' here?"

Deciding on raw honesty since she'd be telling Sarah tomorrow anyway, Erin replied, "Because I had a stalker." She tipped her head. "Maybe I still have one. I'm not sure." Erin chuckled at Nadia's horror. "Don't worry. He's harmless. So far, his only weapon has been a can of paint."

Nadia's eyes darted around the back of Sarah's wooded lot. "Are we safe out here?"

"Oh, totally. He doesn't know I'm here, for one thing, but I'm giving his name to the cops tomorrow morning."

Nadia eyed her suspiciously. "You don't seem scared."

"I'm *not* scared. The guy's a chump."

Nadia treated her to a long look of contempt. "*Hmph*," she finally said before sticking her nose in the air and flouncing off towards the house.

Erin felt a rapid rise in her blood pressure as she worked to catch her. Nadia was tall, and her stride stretched a lot further than Erin's. It didn't help that she was carrying only one bag to Erin's two. Quickly, Erin offloaded the extra weight and closed the distance between them. She reached a hand out to Nadia's shoulder and spun her around. "What is your problem?"

"I don't got one!"

"You don't *have* one," Erin corrected.

"Whatever!"

Nadia continued on towards the house, but Erin kept pace with her and finally grabbed at her bag, stopping her just before the porch steps. "What?" Erin demanded. "What is it?"

Nadia blew out an exasperated breath as she turned again. "Fine. I just think it was stupid and selfish of you to come here to my sister's house when you have some creeper after you. You put her in danger. And with her bein' hurt now an' all too."

Erin's jaw dropped. This was just too rich. "*I'm* stupid and selfish?"

Nadia took a step back. "What's that suppose' to mean?"

"Come on, Nadia. We both know why you're here."

Nadia placed her hands on her hips. "You know why I'm here? What are you, some kind of mind reader?"

"I don't have to be a mind reader to know you want something from Sarah."

"And what's that?" Nadia challenged. "What do I want from Sarah?"

Erin snorted. "Uh, hello!" She rubbed her thumb against her pointer and middle fingers in the universal gesture for money.

Nadia shook her head in disgust. "You don't know a damn thing."

"I know you owe Sarah a quarter," Erin spat, "and believe me, I know plenty more than that. And if you think I'm going to let you come here, to *her* town, *her* house, and pull that crap you and your train-wreck of a mother used to pull back home, you've got another thing coming."

Nadia looked as though Erin had just slapped her, and her eyes filled with tears. It might have been tempting to give her the benefit of the doubt, but then Erin remembered the countless stories Sarah had shared. This girl was an opportunistic user, and Erin was going to protect her friend from her, whatever it took.

When Nadia found her voice, it shook with indignation. "You have *no* idea what it was like for me back there! None! So don't stand here and pretend you know *anything* about us!"

"I know enough," Erin said coolly.

Nadia closed her eyes, and Erin imagined her counting to five. When she spoke again, her voice was calmer. "People can change." She pressed her free hand to her chest, and for a second Erin thought Nadia might push herself over. The girl needed to sleep. And eat. "*I've* changed," Nadia added.

"Right." Erin rolled her eyes.

"I have!" Nadia shouted. "And I don't have to prove anythin'—"

She stopped abruptly, and Erin watched the girl's eyes widen in surprise as she looked over Erin's shoulder.

When she turned around, Erin saw it was only Ethan walking towards them with a bottle of wine in hand. He'd changed into shorts and a sweatshirt, but somehow he looked even more delicious than he had at dinner. She decided then and there: She was going to tell him she loved him the moment they were alone and then immediately have him for dessert. Just as soon as she finished putting the prodigal sister in her place. Erin was about to do just that when she noticed Nadia gaping at Ethan.

"Ethan?" Nadia asked in confusion. "What are you doing here?"

Ethan stopped abruptly mid stride. It might have been comical if he hadn't looked so stricken. His face drained of color, and when his panicked eyes settled on her, Erin's stomach roiled even before her mind caught up. Something was very wrong here.

Ethan opened his mouth, but nothing came out. In a million years, he couldn't have predicted that this would happen. He was sunk. It wouldn't matter to Erin that he was going to tell her everything when he got back from Alabama.

"What are you doin' here?" Nadia repeated.

She'd lost weight. A lot of weight. So much so that he might not have recognized her in a different context. The girl he'd spoken to a few months back had been very pretty, much like her sister, in fact. This girl was bone-thin and looked like she could blow over in the gentle breeze coming off the water. And the girl next to her, well, she looked ready to blow him over! If he knew Erin, and he was pretty sure he did, this wasn't going to be easy.

"I'm . . . I'm, uh, staying next door." Ethan was addressing Nadia, but he was watching Erin, wondering when the moment would come when she'd make like Vesuvius. By the looks of things, it wouldn't be long.

"Right next door?" Nadia asked incredulously. "From my sister?"

He returned his attention to her and nodded.

"The one you were askin' me about a month ago on my mama's front porch?" She rested one hand on her hip, and she did it with such attitude that it must have cost her five calories, at least.

Erin straightened her back and crossed her arms. She was ready to do battle. "What a small world, Ethan!" she exclaimed, her words dripping with sarcasm. "Imagine finding the one rental right next door to a woman you were asking about more than a thousand miles away in Alabama." She shook her head. "Crazy!"

He held out his hands. "Erin, wait. Listen to me, I—"

And then she erupted, making Vesuvius look downright docile. Advancing on him, she yelled and pointed a finger at him until, eventually, she was poking him in his chest. Words spilled out of her at a rate so fast, he could hardly keep up until, finally, she ran out of steam. And then she broke his heart with two questions.

With wounded eyes, Erin asked, "Who even are you, Ethan? Was everything a lie?"

"No!" He tried to reach for her hand, but she wasn't having it. "No. And I admit, I came here to . . . to do some digging for my firm, but I told you I'm heading back to take care of something important, and I am. I'm resigning. I can't work for them anymore. I didn't do what they asked. I couldn't."

"What did they ask?" Nadia inquired curiously just as Sarah appeared on the porch. All eyes were on her as she quietly shut the door behind her and took two steps to the railing. She rested her hands there and regarded Ethan. He could see she'd heard everything, and he couldn't miss the accusation in her eyes when she asked, "What firm do you work for?"

Ethan regarded her warily. He needed her to know he hadn't sold her out. "Sarah—"

"What firm, Ethan?" Erin repeated in a flattened tone. "And don't tell me it's in Flint because you lied about that too, didn't you?"

He hung his head briefly, but when he spoke, he addressed Sarah first, looking her straight in the eye. "Josten's Holdings." Then to Erin, he said, "The firm is in Alabama, where I live."

Erin's eyes flashed, and Ethan could see her chest heaving, but she remained silent.

Sarah only nodded. "I see."

Nadia spoke up. "Our daddy's firm? Why? What is this?"

"He was sent here," Erin supplied.

"By who?"

This time, Sarah answered. "Our dear old dad."

Nadia's eyes bulged. "Why?"

Ethan didn't think he'd ever felt lower than he did right in this moment. He wasn't following through on what Bruce had asked him to do, but what kind of man would have let it go this far? He felt like his knees might buckle under the weight of his shame.

Erin had moved to the porch to stand with Sarah, and she answered Nadia's question. "Money. This is about money. Good old American greed, right Ethan?"

Ethan took a step towards her but stopped when she backed up. He held up his hands and stayed put. He wanted, no, he needed to make things right with Erin, but it was to Sarah he owed the explanation. Swallowing hard, he met her eyes. "I was asked to see what you knew. If you were aware that your company shares of Josten's Holdings entitle you to a yearly salary and dividends, as well as rights to participate in the running of the company."

Erin was outraged and began to bluster, but Sarah put a hand on her arm to quiet her. She looked genuinely puzzled. "But you told me about that already. I'm supposed to call that lawyer whose number you gave me yesterday to get that consultation set up."

"I know, but I didn't tell you that Bruce sent me here to see if he could get away with, uh, withholding that from you. He wanted me to find out how much you knew. One way or another, he was going to try and squeeze you out," he explained.

Nadia gasped. "He wouldn't do that to us! We're his daughters!"

Sarah shook her head. "We're nothin' to him, Nadia. We're worse than nothing. We're a thorn in his side."

"But why? I never did anythin' to him at all. I never asked him for a cent." Nadia's eyes were wild and her face was turning purple. "Why does he hate us? Why did Kelly Sue and Jenny Lynn get to be his real daughters and we got totally shit on with a shit mama and a shit life?"

"Nadia—" Sarah began in a placating tone.

"No!" her sister shrieked. "I see their Instagram. They get everything! And me? I got nothin' and no one!" She burst into tears and tore up the steps and into the house, slamming the door behind her.

"Nadia, wait!" Sarah called after her.

"See what you've done!" Erin shouted at Ethan.

Sarah corrected her. "He didn't do this, Erin. Our mama and daddy did this." She brought a hand up to her temple and began to rub small circles there.

Ethan moved towards the porch steps and then thought better of it. "Sarah, I'm so sorry. I . . ."

What more could he say? In the end, he just repeated himself. "I'm sorry."

Ethan's face was twisted with regret, and Sarah forgave him in that moment. She forgave him, but she was done talking for now. They could revisit this another time, and she could ask her questions then. For now, her sister needed her.

"Alright," she said simply, before nodding and turning away.

It was quiet behind her as she entered the house, but small sobs greeted her from within, and she traced them down the hall and to her bedroom.

"Nadia," Sarah said gently. Nadia looked at her from the edge of Sarah's bed where she sat, her face tear-streaked and pale.

"It's not fair, Sarah. Look at me. I'm a homeless nobody. Everything I own fits into the trunk of Mama's car, which she's goin' to want back just as soon as she gets out. I'm almost eighteen, and I haven't started livin' yet. I've done nothin' with my life. I've got no friends, no plans."

"What do you mean? What about all your friends back home?"

Nadia shook her head and turned red with shame. "I made it all up. I got no one." She hesitated. "Sarah, I didn't even graduate."

Sarah felt like she'd had the wind knocked out of her. "What?"

"I was too far behind. I quit after first semester."

"Nadia! That was in January! What did you do with yourself all of second semester?"

"Slept." She shrugged. "Watched TikTok videos. Sat with Mama watchin' *The Price is Right* and *Judge Judy* with the curtains drawn, day in and day out, until the days all blurred together in my mind. And I wasn't even the drunk one." Nadia wiped at her nose and met Sarah's eyes. "She started smokin' pot too, you know. After you left for college. As if she needed even less ambition. I'm pretty sure I got high a time or two just sittin' in the livin' room next to her."

Sarah was still feeling sick at the thought that her sister was a high school dropout, so the thought of her getting a contact high from their mother was just too much to process at the moment. Here she was teaching hundreds of kids who were completely unrelated to her, and her own sister had been left to languish in hell. And that was another thing. What was going on with her weight? She looked like she'd been starved for the last few months, but Sarah had sent plenty of money, hadn't she?

Guilt gnawed at her insides. Had she done the wrong thing, keeping her sister on a monthly allowance? She sat beside Nadia on the bed. "I'm sorry I left you there."

Except for some sniffling here and there, Nadia was quiet for a full minute. "You never said that before."

"I know. I shouldn't have left you behind, but I was young too, and so lost. But I did try to take you with me, Nadia, you remember that. I tried."

Nadia looked at her with shiny eyes. "I couldn't leave. You know I had to take care of her, Sarah. Somebody had to take care of her."

Sarah chose her words carefully. "I know it felt that way."

Nadia's eyes flashed. "Because it *was* that way! What would you know about it anyway? You were always gone. You were never home, even when you lived there. *I* was stuck doin' it."

Sarah put her hands up. "I don't want to fight with you, Nadia. You're right. We had a hard life. I handled it the best I could at the time, and so did you. We made the only choices for ourselves we could live with. I chose differently than you did, but that doesn't make either one of us right or wrong."

Nadia scoffed.

Sarah took a deep breath and let it out slowly. "Listen, Mama was an adult. We were the kids. We weren't supposed to take care of her. She was supposed to take care of us. And to me, it looked like you didn't want or need me around anyway. Half the time I wondered if either of you would notice if I didn't come home at night."

Nadia's chin trembled. "I would have."

It wasn't a declaration of love, but it was close enough, and Sarah felt her heart squeeze. She wanted to say something profound to her sister in that moment, but she found her tongue was tied.

Nadia filled the silence. "Mama's still doin' real good. I talked to her again today just before I got to the Mackinac Bridge. I told her I was comin' here."

"You did? What'd she say?"

Nadia hesitated, and she scrunched her nose. "You know Mama."

"She brought up the money?"

"Yeah, and other things. You aren't her favorite person right now."

That shouldn't have stung. Lydie Mae wasn't Sarah's favorite person either. In fact, she was downright disgusted with her mother at the moment. "Nadia, I don't want you giving Lydie Mae your money. And it is *your* money, okay? It's not mine. I'm just protecting it for you."

Sarah waited for some sharp retort from her sister, but none came. "We'll work something out," she continued. "Some system where you get what you need. Mama's got some of her own coming to her after rehab, but if history tells me anything, she'll burn through it right quick. It's sad, but it's her money and she can do what she wants with it. Burning through *your* money, though, that's different."

Nadia shocked her by conceding. "I know. It helps me that I don't control it and can't give much to her. She's mad as all get out at you, though."

The story of my life. "I can handle it," Sarah said.

"She tells me she would only need a little."

"Yes. I'm sure that's what she tells you."

"She's already taken a lot."

Sarah felt sick. "Alright, well, we'll fix that."

Nadia bit down on her lower lip. "What if we just gave her a set amount, and that's it? One and done."

"Nadia, she got a million dollars from our daddy when he left. It's the regret of her life that she didn't think to ask for more. She bought that big, fancy house—you probably don't remember it—and who knows what else. It was all gone in a matter of years, and then Gammie had to go back and join the work force. This time, Mama can get herself a job when she gets out. It'll be the best thing for her. It'll give her purpose. And she's going to have a real nice cushion from our grandmother while she gets on her feet."

Nadia nodded slowly. "I always wondered. Why didn't Daddy at least pay child support, Sarah? Didn't he care at all? I mean, I know he wanted nothin' to do with us, but why didn't he have to pay?"

Oh, how Sarah wished things could be different. If not for herself, then for this sad teenage girl in front of her who had never known the love of a father and desperately wanted to. She sighed and took Nadia's icy hand in her own warm one. "Because Mama played right into his hands. She negotiated a lump-sum alimony because she wanted the money right then and there, like always. She asked for sole custody to try to hurt him, but of course, it didn't. I don't know what kind of stupid lawyer advised her, but our daddy should have paid that guy's fees 'cause whoever it was did him a big favor."

Nadia stared down at their joined hands silently.

Sarah crossed one leg over the other. "I'm sure to Mama, a million dollars seemed like a lot of money."

With a lift of her eyebrows, Nadia asked, "A million dollars *isn't* a lot of money?"

"It can be in the right hands, but don't forget Mama's background. She didn't know how to handle loads of money. She started out as Daddy's secretary makin' beans."

"I don't know the story. Mama wouldn't talk about it."

Sarah studied her sister and decided to share a condensed version of the story. She knew it was important for Nadia to know their family history, but she didn't want to lose focus on what she wanted Nadia to take away from tonight, which was that despite all the family disfunction, she had a sister who would be there for her, come what may.

Quickly, Sarah recited the history. Lydie Mae had been Bruce's secretary, young and pretty, and they'd begun an affair. A *secret* affair since his parents would have put a stop to it immediately if they'd found out. But then Lydie Mae had gotten pregnant with Sarah, and the cat was out of the bag. Bruce was forced to *do the right thing*, and the wedding happened two months later.

"Why'd he leave Mama after I came along?" Nadia asked.

Sarah smiled ruefully. "Because another secretary came along. And Mama's drinkin' didn't help. He waited until his father passed on to walk out, though. The old man wouldn't have allowed a divorce to happen. Appearances, and all that."

Nadia nodded.

"But he'd been carryin' on with her a while, and Mama knew. Started drinking even more . . ." Sarah shrugged. "You know the rest."

Nadia sighed. "I do know the rest." The two sisters stared at one another for a long moment, and Sarah wondered if her eyes looked as sad as her sister's. Nadia was the first to look away. She fixed her gaze downward and began picking at a loose thread on Sarah's coverlet with her free hand. "Sarah?"

"Yes?"

"Don't you love Mama at all?"

Maybe Sarah should have been shocked by the question, but she wasn't. She thought carefully about how to answer. "Nadia, I don't *know* Mama. I don't have memories of Mama *mothering* me. Not a one. Plenty of Gammie, but none of Lydie Mae."

"So that's a no then." Nadia's voice was hard.

"I could say yes, Nadia. Lord knows I want to. What kind of daughter doesn't love her own mother? But I can't love a stranger. Not in the way you mean. I care about Lydie Mae, but . . ."

Sarah could almost hear the question that hung in the air between them now. *What about me, Sarah, do you love me?*

She didn't wait for Nadia to ask. She wasn't even sure Nadia *could* ask. What a question to have to ask your flesh and blood sister! But Sarah knew the answer. She was confident in it. A month ago, two months ago, she might not have been. But there could be no doubt now. "I love *you*, Nadia," she said. "We might not be close, but I love you all the same."

Nadia went very still. She stopped picking at the thread, but she didn't lift her eyes. "Thank you," she whispered.

Chapter 23

E rin hated Mondays. Why she'd chosen a day she already loathed to begin torturing herself with a three-mile run, she wasn't quite sure.

She stopped putting one foot in front of the other and doubled over to catch her breath. "You two . . . go on . . . without me," she said, gasping for breath. Heidi and Leila Molina both turned around and jogged in place.

"No, come on! You can do it!" Heidi encouraged with a voice so peppy and cheerful that Erin gritted her teeth. She grabbed at her side as she stood tall again. "I can't."

"You can!" Leila contradicted. "We'll slow down the pace. Whatever it takes, because you're finishing this run with us."

"I'm going to die," Erin panted.

"Not with two doctors running on either side of you," Heidi joked.

In a moment of insanity, after a full weekend of hating and missing Ethan, Erin had called Heidi to take her up on her offer to train with her and Leila for a race in September that was being put on by the local YMCA. "That way you'll have a goal," Heidi had said. "It's so much easier to stick with running when you've entered and paid for a race."

But this was far from easy. "How much further is it?" Erin asked. She caught Heidi's brief smile before she hid it behind her hand with a cough.

"Well," Leila said, squinting at her Apple Watch, "we've gone a quarter of a mile, so we have two and three quarters left to go."

Erin checked the four-letter word before it flew out of her mouth. "No frickin way. I'm done. I literally cannot go on. My side kills. You two go ahead."

Leila and Heidi looked at one another and came to a wordless agreement. "We'll walk," Heidi said. "We'll start slow and let your side ache recover, and then we can get a good brisk walk going. Alright?"

"I don't want to slow you guys down," Erin grumbled.

"It's alright," Leila reassured. "My shins could use the break, actually. I've had shin splints since the start of summer."

"Come on," Heidi said, grabbing Erin's arm. Leila locked step with them on Erin's other side.

They'd gone a hundred yards or so down the bike path along Lake Superior before Heidi asked, "How's everything out on the basin?"

Erin let out a hollow laugh. "Are you referring to Ethan or Nadia?"

"Nadia who, and what about Ethan?"

Erin shot her a quizzical look. "Olivia didn't tell you?"

"I worked all weekend, so I haven't seen her."

"Oh! Let me fill you in," Erin said flippantly. "A lot has happened in the last few days. On Friday, Sarah's miserable little sister, Nadia, showed up and moved in for the foreseeable future, Ethan left for good, and I confronted my psychostalker. I guess that about covers it."

She forced a smile at Leila, who raised her eyebrows and said, "Yikes!" before turning to Heidi to gauge her reaction.

"Okay, you're going to have to slow that story way down and give us a lot more details," Heidi instructed.

Erin shrugged and looked out at the lake. It must have been close to six o'clock, but the sun remained high in the sky, and the lake was still and tranquil, as it always was when the south wind blew. It seemed criminal to be so unhappy on such a beautiful day. She needed to snap out of it, but it wasn't that easy. Her heart hurt and her nerves were fried.

Heidi gave her a gentle punch on the shoulder. "You are going to tell us, right? Because otherwise, this is just cruel!"

Even though Erin had been the one to bring it up, suddenly she felt exhausted with the task of getting them up to speed, but she obliged them anyway because there was nothing worse than getting only half a story from someone. She started with Jason first, since that was the least emotional story to tell, and then moved on to Nadia, pausing every now and again to answer their questions.

Frown lines had appeared around Heidi's mouth as Erin spoke. "So, back to this teacher. The police are monitoring the camera now?"

"Yeah. The school liaison is reviewing it daily."

"It's nice when you know people. I wonder if they'd do that for just anyone," Leila remarked.

Erin shrugged again. "I don't know."

Heidi must have been satisfied that enough was being done to solve the Jason Bender issue because she moved on. "Alright, and what about Ethan?"

"I remember him from the hospital," Leila interjected. She whistled. "That man was fine."

"Very," Heidi agreed. "You said he left? I thought you two were, you know, kind of a thing."

A *thing*. Erin had practically married herself off to the guy. She'd never trust herself again. How she could have been so wrong about him, well, it disturbed her. "I suppose we were, but that was before I found out he was a liar and a loser."

She filled them in as they walked the shoreline, starting from the very beginning and ending with what had happened in Sarah's driveway on Friday night when she'd ordered him off her friend's property. He'd called and texted Erin several times until she'd finally blocked him. By Saturday, he was gone.

Heidi shook her head. "I'm surprised he could do that to Sarah. I usually read people so well, and I got such good vibes from him."

Leila spoke up, "But he didn't go through with it now, did he?"

Erin's mouth fell open. "Don't tell me you're taking his side!" Her voice held a warning, but Leila didn't back down.

They'd picked up their pace to the point where Erin had to do a little catch-up run every third or fourth step. Heidi and Leila were the same height—Erin guessed somewhere around five foot seven—which meant they had a seven-inch advantage with every step they took.

"I'm not saying he's completely innocent," Leila clarified, "but he did the right thing in the end, right?"

"He *lied* to me."

"To be fair," Heidi began, but Erin didn't let her finish.

"Are you seriously thinking about defending him right now?"

"Erin, all I'm saying is that he was evasive. He lied by omission, I suppose, but Leila's right. If what you're saying is true, then I'm not sure why you sent him packing permanently. Be mad, sure. Have him make it up to you a hundred different ways, but don't kick him to the curb forever over this. Not if you really like him."

Erin couldn't believe it. "You two are crazy!" She kept her voice light, and she followed that proclamation with a laugh and a change of subject, but all the rest of that day and through the week, Erin began to doubt herself. By the end of August, she was pretty sure she'd made a huge mistake.

Chapter 24

Benny unloaded his fishing pole and tackle box from the back of his truck. Fifteen days of fishing was too much, even for him, and that was saying something. He loved fishing, nature, and solitude almost as much as he loved Jack, his dad, and Jordan, but by the end of the first week, he was ready to head back to civilization. And to Sarah.

After the tubing incident, he'd nearly backed out of the trip until he'd realized that, at least for the time being, he wasn't anything more to Sarah than a friend. What would he have said to his dad and brother-in-law? "I'm backing out of the trip we look forward to all year because my teacher friend has a concussion?" That wouldn't have gone over very well, and Jack would have really struggled with any last-minute changes to the plan. So, he'd gone.

But he'd thought of her almost every minute of every day since he'd been away, and he needed to see her. He wanted to take care of her if she was still struggling the way her earlier texts had suggested. Benny felt the weight of his phone in his back pocket, and his fingers twitched. The moment he'd read her messages in his sister's kitchen, he'd wanted to call. He wanted to hear her voice on the other end of the line. He should have told her about the trip before he left, and he should tell her now how he felt about her. But everything felt confused in his brain. He loved her. He knew that much, at least. But he still couldn't shake the feeling that she deserved better than him.

Every bewildering moment of his youth could now be explained. Every uncomfortable social situation, all the teasing from his peers, it all made sense now. In a way, it was a relief. In another way, he was mourning. He was mourning the self he thought he'd known. Who was he now?

What if he passed his condition on to his hypothetical children? Because he did want children, which was definitely a new development. He'd never thought about kids before Sarah. But when he'd seen her holding Olivia's daughter, it had hit him hard, deep in the gut, and he'd pictured her holding *their* child. The image was enough to suck all the air out of his lungs.

Sarah.

Every time he looked at her—hell, every time he even thought about her—it made his pulse race. He wanted her by his side right now. He wanted her by his side forever. He could see them, old and gray, holding hands as they walked the bike path along the water's edge. In his mind's eye, he saw them at barbecues with their children and grandchildren all around them. But in reality, how would those kids turn out? There was at least some chance they'd end up on the spectrum too. His psychologist had told him he was worrying for nothing, but she had finally conceded that there could be a genetic component to this. If so, they'd be a backyard full of autistic people, and there Sarah would sit, smiling and wishing she had a normal family.

And maybe the fact that he was thinking so far ahead about a woman he hadn't even taken on a date yet was just another symptom of his autism. Maybe "normal" guys wouldn't be thinking things like that. Benny sighed in self-disgust and flexed his toes. How depressing. He couldn't even trust his own thoughts.

Sarah sat with Nadia at the end of the dock as the sun began to set. The days were getting shorter now, there was no denying it, and she could almost smell the coming of autumn. Yesterday, she'd spotted a few red leaves on her way back from the grocery store.

Marvin rested at Nadia's feet, and Sarah listened to her news as the water gently lapped against the shore behind them. Her sister, unlike the tranquility that surrounded them, was practically bouncing in her chair with excitement.

"And then they *enrolled* me, just like that! I walked in there to ask a few questions, and I walked out with a computer and my first class all set up and ready to go. Can you believe that? I only have five classes left to graduate, and they said some of their students, the ones who work really hard, can finish a class in two weeks. Usually it takes about four, sometimes longer, like if someone has to work or has a kid to take care of or something, but either way,

I might have my diploma before Christmas, Sarah, and doesn't that just beat all with a stick?"

Nadia had seen a billboard sign for a virtual learning program on her way back from the Secretary of State, where she'd gone to find out how to get herself a Michigan driver's license. Together, over the course of the last few days, they'd made the decision that Nadia would stay in Michigan with Sarah indefinitely. It felt right to both of them, and they'd gone out last night to celebrate with dinner at Nicolet's one fancy restaurant, Rebecca's Chop House. Nadia had shown more animation and enthusiasm than Sarah had known she was capable of, and she'd finished her filet mignon dinner with a gusto that was gratifying. Tonight, it appeared they'd be celebrating the continuation of her high school education.

Leaning over, Sarah swept her sister into a hug, and her voice cracked when she answered, "This is amazing news!"

"I still can't believe it!" Nadia continued once Sarah pulled away. "I thought my only option was a GED, but Sarah, I'm going to get, like, an actual *diploma* now! Do you know how much better that is? They said this is my second chance."

For a moment, Sarah thought she might cry. *A second chance.* It seemed like life was full of those all of a sudden. Lydie Mae was out of rehab and, for now at least, she was sober and working as a checkout clerk at a grocery chain. She hadn't spoken to Lydie Mae herself, of course, but Nadia had, and she'd filled her in. While Sarah might not have a relationship with her mother, and probably never would, she was still happy for her.

As if that wasn't exciting enough, it seemed that God had seen fit to give Sarah and Nadia a second chance at being sisters. True sisters, in the real sense. And now, Nadia was getting another shot at high school. About the only thing that could make this day better was some kind of communication—any at all would do—from Benny.

She'd written it on her calendar. Today was the day he was supposed to get home from that endless fishing trip he'd been on. When was he going to call her?

Nadia read her mind and switched gears. "He hasn't called yet?"

Flashing her sister a guilty smile, she said, "I'm sorry. I don't mean to shift the focus from you to me. I'm so happy for you, I could cry. But I guess, for just a second, my thoughts roamed away and landed on Benny."

Nadia wasn't in the least bit fazed. "Where's your phone?"

"Up at the house."

"Go and get it. Maybe he already called and you're worryin' for nothin.'"

Nadia knew all about Benny. She knew all about a lot of things. And Sarah had discovered plenty about her sister too. She wasn't the unmotivated couch mate of their mother that Sarah had always thought she was. The girl had dreams. She'd suffered for a lot of years with two warring needs: the need to help Lydie Mae and the need for freedom. To get off welfare and let life take her where it wanted. She'd resented Sarah's ability to go off and follow her passions because she saw herself trapped in a prison—stuck in that stale house. Stuck in that dark life forever.

Nadia loved Lydie Mae. Those moments beside her mama on the couch, those years taking care of her—cooking her meals to make sure she had at least some good nutrition, and keeping the house clean so she could have at least some dignity—they'd been depressing and anxiety provoking, yes, but they hadn't been all bad. There'd been glimmers of light sometimes. The little jokes here and there. The hugs and *I love you's* from Lydie Mae as Nadia helped her to bed. Those small moments had kept her sister going.

But now, Sarah could see she was ready to live in the real sense. She'd had a taste of how things could be, and she wasn't going back. She was completely out of the shadows and staring her future in the face. She was terrified, yes, and she missed Lydie Mae—also true—but mostly she seemed thrilled. There was a pep, a spring in her step, that Sarah had never seen. The last two mornings, she'd sung in the shower, and that was another discovery Sarah had made. Her sister had a voice! An incredible one. How had she not known that about her?

The money was still an issue. It probably wasn't going to go away completely, but it wasn't quite the sore spot it had been even a few days ago. They'd fight about it some more, of course. Sarah wasn't naïve. Nadia was still technically a kid, so she wasn't going to be able to understand or appreciate what Sarah was doing for her now, but she would someday, and Sarah hoped she'd be grateful then.

Yesterday morning, they'd met with one of the advisors Ethan had recommended, and she'd helped them come up with a monthly stipend for Nadia that would be fair and provide for her needs without disincentivizing her from working hard and planning for her future. It was more than Sarah had wanted to give her and less than Nadia had wanted to receive, but that was compromise for you. A person knew it had been done correctly when nobody was completely happy.

Despite having given a good chunk of her monthly checks away to Lydie Mae, something Sarah had suspected but still felt sick over, Nadia had saved the rest of it, and Sarah was proud of her. Unlike most teenage girls, she hadn't gone out and blown it all on Lululemon leggings. They'd opened a bank account for her, and it already had a nice little cushion. When it was all said and done, her sister was a good kid.

Nadia was still far too thin, but at this rate, with her renewed appetite, it wouldn't take long for her to look healthy again. She'd only been in Nicolet four days, and she already had a pink to her cheeks that hadn't been there when she'd first arrived, and those dark smudges under her eyes were fading. Things were looking up for her and for the two of them as sisters. They'd agreed to disagree about the stipend and revisit the topic only twice a year during their appointments with the advisor. It was really the only way to keep peace about it. And Sarah knew they both wanted to be at peace with each other. This was their second chance, and neither one of them wanted to blow it.

They'd also come to a decision, together, about how to handle their shares in Josten's Holdings. Jenna, their advisor, had told Sarah the same thing Ethan had. Both felt they should arrange a sale of their shares for top dollar through the lawyer Ethan had hooked her up with. Of course, Bruce would try to haggle down the price, but Ethan and Jenna had both advised that they hold tight to their asking price, because as unappealing as being active in their father's company was to them, their presence at Josten's Holdings would be untenable to Bruce, and as such, he'd go to great lengths to keep them far away from his company. "Remember, you have all the power here," Ethan had reminded her last night when she'd called him to relay the plan.

Sarah hadn't told Erin yet—she was going to wait for the right moment—but she'd called Ethan a few times now, and she planned to keep in regular touch with him. When she'd first called, he'd still been making his way back to Alabama. She told him she had no hard feelings, and she was glad she had because he was being very hard on himself. "People make mistakes," she said, "and you did the right thing in the end, so thank you. I'm grateful, and I know you sacrificed your career for it."

"I think maybe you're being too forgiving, Sarah. I don't deserve it, but I appreciate it. How's Erin?" he'd asked after a long pause.

"Still madder than a wet hen."

He laughed, but there was no humor in it. "I figured as much."

"Give her some time, Ethan. She'll settle."

He'd resigned as soon as he'd gotten back and texted her afterwards from his new phone number since his cell had been a company phone. She'd called him right away to see how it had gone. Her father hadn't been in, so Ethan had only spoken to his immediate supervisor, the treasurer who was retiring and whose job Ethan had been gunning for. Apparently, the older gentleman had demanded to know why his protégé was throwing it all away, and Ethan hadn't held back. He'd given him all the details, which left the devoted family man so disgusted that he made Ethan promise to use him as a reference for his next job.

"And what might that be?" Sarah had asked him, even though what she really wanted to know was *where* this new job might be.

He'd been vague in his response. "Something in finance, obviously, but I'm taking it one step at a time. First, I need to sell my condo. Then, we'll see."

Sarah wanted to help him, and the beginnings of a plan had already begun to take shape in her mind. Thinking about it made her feel giddy.

Nadia drew her back into the moment. "Okay, well if you're not going to get your phone, then at least look at the sky. It's pretty as all get out, isn't it?"

Sarah rested her head against the back of her chair and took in the pinks and oranges that streaked across the horizon. "It really is."

"I can't believe I haven't met him yet."

Sarah turned to Nadia and slanted her head. "Who?" For a second, Sarah thought Nadia might have been talking about Ethan, since he was the one who'd just been on her mind, but of course Nadia had already met him.

"Benny! You sure have talked about him enough." She rolled her eyes. "I want to meet him."

Benny was never far from Sarah's thoughts, so it stood to reason that she would talk about him a lot. "You would really like him."

"I *will* really like him," Nadia corrected. "This isn't a hypothetical. I am meeting this guy if I have to drive Mama's car to his house and knock on his front door. Don't think I won't do it."

Sarah smiled. She wondered what Nadia would make of him. She hadn't told her sister about him being on the spectrum. It wasn't that she was embarrassed about it or anything, but she didn't think it would be right to share such personal information with anyone. It was Benny's story to share if he wanted to.

"Speaking of Mama's car, how do you want to handle that?" Sarah asked.

"The only way I can. Like I told you, she needs it back now, so I'll have to return it." Nadia frowned, and Sarah knew why. It was a long trip, for one thing. But Sarah understood that as much as Nadia would love to see their mama and hug her, it was just too soon to go back to that house. She needed some more time. She needed to grow stronger. Plus, Ronny the boyfriend was still there, and he was a creeper.

Sarah had been thinking about the car situation since Nadia first mentioned it. "Is Mama real attached to that car?"

Nadia shrugged. "No. It's old, and it's got problems. I'm just glad it made it all the way here. I wasn't sure it would."

A few years back, the government had given welfare recipients cars and phones, and that was when Lydie Mae had gotten the Chevy Malibu. It had been at least five years old then, so it was ancient now.

"Why don't we buy it off Lydie Mae?" Sarah suggested.

Nadia looked at her with surprised disdain. "Ew, why?"

"Not to keep. We'll buy it from Mama to keep her happy and trade it in for something that's good in snow. That way, you don't have to visit just yet. I mean, unless you want to."

Nadia shook her head. "I don't. Not yet, and when I do, I want us to go together. I mean, if you'll come?" Her voice tipped up in question.

"I could do that."

Nadia's eyes lit up with momentary excitement before a notch appeared between her eyebrows, but her shifting emotions had nothing to do with their future visit. "You know Mama's gonna ask us to pay more than that car's worth. A lot more."

Sarah had already thought of that, but they had the money, and it was a small price to pay to protect Nadia for a bit longer. She wanted to see Lydie Mae sober for at least another few months before Nadia saw her in person.

"I know she will, but I think it's the best course of action, don't you?"

Nadia grinned. "What kind of car will I get?"

"What kind do you want?"

"I don't even know! I'll have to start lookin'!" Nadia pulled her phone out of her back pocket and got busy with her thumbs. "Are we talkin' new or used?" She looked up at Sarah with hopeful eyes.

A new car was the worst kind of investment, in Sarah's opinion. The moment you drove it off the lot, it tanked in value. Even *she* didn't have a brand-new car. But she didn't want to burst Nadia's bubble just yet, so she kept it vague. "We'll talk." Nadia pulled a face and got back to searching.

Sarah chuckled as she watched her sister's thumbs fly over the screen of her outdated phone. She'd have to move Nadia onto her cell phone plan. She added that to the growing list of things she needed to do for her sister, which included looking into insurance options and now, apparently, purchasing her a car. She was glad she was feeling back to her old self. Otherwise, these things would feel even more overwhelming to her than they already did. "Be right back. I want to check my phone and see if Erin called. I thought she'd be back by now." Sarah hopped up and headed down the length of the dock.

Nadia's head popped up over the back of her chair, and she turned to holler, "Checkin' to see about Erin or checkin' to see about Benny?"

"Both!" Sarah called back with a grin. She'd expected Erin home long before now, and because of her situation with Jason Bender, which Sarah still couldn't quite believe was happening, she would feel better checking in with her friend.

"Alright! I'll be right here"—Nadia lifted her phone and waved it in the air—"car shopping!" Nadia flashed her a wide, happy smile.

"You do that!" Sarah turned her attention to Marvin, who was watching her with his head cocked. She backtracked several steps so she wouldn't have to keep yelling. "Marvin, you stay with Nadia. Stay," she commanded.

"He wasn't leavin'. He loves me best, remember?"

Sarah laughed again. Poor Erin. She'd thought her friend might cry when her dog tried to sleep with Nadia the first night she was there. Good thing it hadn't lasted. For the last three nights, he'd slept with Erin.

Nadia seemed to hear Sarah's thoughts, and she craned her neck before saying, "Erin's not too happy about how much he likes me, is she?"

"No," Sarah admitted on a sigh. She crossed the remaining distance between them and rested a hand on the back of Nadia's chair. "It does hurt her feelings some. I'm glad he's at least back to sleeping with her again."

Nadia grinned sheepishly. "Can you keep a secret?" She didn't wait for Sarah's answer before turning the rest of the way around in her seat. "I've been hidin' treats under Erin's covers at night."

Sarah's jaw dropped. "What?"

Nadia nodded, and her smile grew.

"For how long?"

"Since Saturday."

"Why?" Sarah asked, even though she knew the answer.

"She needs him to choose her."

Sarah blinked. Her sister was more perceptive and had more depth and caring to her than she ever could have imagined. She shook her head in wonder. "You amaze me, Nadia. You really do." Impulsively, she leaned down and kissed the top of Nadia's head, which smelled like the lavender mint shampoo she'd purchased for her the day before. "I'm so glad you're here," Sarah added, her voice thick. "I mean it."

A smile took over Nadia's face, and she sat a little taller when she replied, "Thanks. Me too."

Nadia still hadn't told Sarah that she loved her. Every night before bed, Sarah said the words, and every night, Nadia thanked her. But right then in that moment, with her sister staring at her with such unbridled happiness, Sarah knew without a doubt that she did. She could see it in Nadia's brightened countenance, and she could feel it in the air between them, and she wrapped the knowledge around herself like a warm blanket. "Be right back," she said.

Chapter 25

Alone, Erin sat in her Yukon at Sunset Point out near Sable Rocks. The sun had already gone down, and the sky was quickly growing dark. Most of the people who'd been parked around her to watch Mother Nature's show had already started up their cars and left, but Erin wasn't ready to go home yet. Scratch that, she was beyond ready to go *home*, but she couldn't go there. Not while the police were still trying to get her situation sorted out. So far, Jason hadn't made any other moves. It was maddening because she *knew* he would. It was just a matter of time. But she was growing more and more resentful and agitated while she waited.

Where she wasn't ready to go was back to Sarah's tonight, even though Sarah had already texted to check on her. With Ethan gone and Nadia there, everything was different. Erin knew she was still welcome, but she felt like an outsider now, the odd woman out. Sarah and Nadia were trying to repair and build their relationship, and she was only in the way.

And even though she couldn't see the little cabin next door when she was at Sarah's, she often found herself staring off in that direction and at the thick trees that stood between it and Sarah's place. She wanted to hear the screen door slam shut, followed by Ethan's appearance in Sarah's yard a few minutes later. She wanted to bump into him on her walks with Marvin. She wanted to lie beside him in bed again, just to hear him breathe.

She choked on a deep sob and brought her hands up from the steering wheel to cover her face. Sometimes life could royally suck, like it did right now, so she was going to do something she never did and allow herself to cry as much as she wanted to. Her chest heaved as she let it all out.

She had been so angry at Ethan, and although she'd had good reason, the strength of her reaction hadn't really matched the offense. Leila was right about that, and the more time that passed, the more Erin could see it. Ethan had definitely screwed up, of course. Nobody disputed that, not even him. But she'd flown off the handle at him and completely kicked him out of her life. Why?

The things she'd said to him! The verbal thrashing she'd given him once Sarah and Nadia had gone inside. That was how he'd always remember her now. She'd never be able to take those words back. It was like she'd taken every hurt she'd ever experienced in life, placed the blame squarely on his shoulders, and then used him as a punching bag. Even if he *had* stuck around, there was no going back to the way things used to be. He probably hated her now.

And then there was Marvin. Erin felt like she was losing him too, stupid as it might sound. There was a new girl in town, and she'd caught his eye. The only reason he was sleeping with her again was because of those stupid treats either Sarah or Nadia kept tucking away at the foot of her bed. As funny as it was to watch Marvin crawl under the sheets, blindly sniffing out the tasty morsel, every night she had to clean up the crumbs, and the fact that it took bribery for Marvin to want to sleep with her, only made her feel worse, as well intentioned as the treat-hider might be.

And so she cried. She cried, and she cried, and she cried. And only when there were no tears left did she push the button to start the engine, back out of her spot, and drive away from Sunset Point.

Chapter 26

Benny thought he might just die of anxiety as he drove the last few miles that remained between his truck and Sarah's house. He took a right off the highway onto Steele Basin Drive. How many times had he made the trip to her house this summer? He felt like he could drive it blindfolded, and yet this time everything was different.

Every other time, he had known what to expect, for the most part. He'd be putting in a dock, building a wall, going to a party . . . but this time, he really didn't know what would happen. He'd started multiple texts to Sarah that night only to delete the words and start over. In the end, he'd sent nothing.

Instead, he'd hopped into his truck and headed for the basin, hoping for the best all the way there. It was time to tell her how he felt about her, come what may, and it had to happen tonight because he could not stand one more sleepless night not knowing how she felt. He only hoped she was still awake. Although a small amount of light remained in the sky off to the west, it was already after ten. He was taking a huge risk here, and he could only hope it would pay off in the end.

When he pulled up to her house, he noticed three things right away. First, her lights were still on, so she wasn't asleep yet. Second, Erin's car was missing, which meant, thankfully, he wouldn't have to do this with her standing around and listening. Instead, another car was parked in her spot in front of the garage, an old Malibu he didn't recognize.

That last observation made his heart pound loudly in his ears. What if the Malibu belonged to Sarah's date for the evening? She could be with someone else now. A lot could happen in two weeks, especially with someone as perfect as Sarah. He was surprised there wasn't a whole chain of cars down her driveway carrying men just waiting for their chance with her.

Despite these and other misgivings, Benny forced himself out of his truck and up the steps of her porch. She opened the door just as Benny raised his hand to knock. She looked so young and impossibly beautiful as she stared at him wordlessly for several seconds.

It was as if she'd conjured him up. Sarah had come up to the house to text Erin, and immediately after sending that one off, she'd begun a text to Benny. And now here he was, standing on her front porch looking so good in his jeans and white button down that she forgot to breathe for a few seconds. She forgot everything for a few seconds, even her manners. She didn't greet him, she didn't invite him in, she just stared. And so did he, though he was the first to recover himself.

"I should have called," he said apologetically, "but . . . I had to see you tonight."

"You had—you did?"

He nodded and shot her a gentle smile. "How are you feeling?"

"Fine, I'm fine . . . a lot better actually." Basic etiquette asserted itself, and she invited him inside.

"I hope I'm not interrupting anything," Benny remarked as he followed her in.

She turned around and saw him scoping out the house, looking for someone.

"I saw there was a car here," he explained.

She shook her head. "Oh, no, you're not interrupting at all. That's my sister's car." She corrected herself, "I mean, it's actually my mama's car, but Nadia used it to get herself up here. She's out on the dock with Marvin. She got here on Friday, and she's stayin' with me awhile." Sarah was babbling, but she couldn't help it. She brought Benny into the kitchen and offered him some tea.

He pulled out a chair and sat down at the counter. "That sounds really good. I've been craving your tea for two weeks."

She retrieved the pitcher of tea she'd made just that morning and got to work.

"So, how's it going? Your sister's visit?" he asked.

"Really well," Sarah answered, grabbing a pair of clean glasses out of the drying rack next to the sink, "but that's not to say there haven't been a few bumps." She poured one for him and one for herself, sliding him his glass before taking a sip from her own.

He thanked her, and they sipped in silence, eying one another up from over the rims of their glasses.

Sarah continued to stand across from him, but she set down her tea and rested her elbows on the counter. "So much has happened since you left."

He smiled at her. "Tell me."

She did. She told him first about Nadia showing up on her doorstep and about her plans to stay in Nicolet. He asked a few questions here and there, but she carried the conversation. A lot really *had* happened while he'd been away. The more Sarah talked, the more at ease she became. It felt like it had when they'd worked on the wall together, very laid back, and she could see from Benny's easy posture that he was as relaxed as she was.

He did tense up once when she got to the part in the story where Nadia had outed Ethan and his purpose for being in Nicolet. As if Benny needed another reason to dislike him! Nothing Sarah could say in Ethan's defense would change his mind, either, although he was partly mollified to hear that Ethan had left for good. He did express his surprise about Ethan and Erin's relationship. "I sort of thought he was, you know, looking at you," he admitted.

Sarah paused in the process of raising her glass to her lips. "Me?" she asked, genuinely baffled. "Why would you think he was interested in me?"

"Why wouldn't he be?"

"Well, because . . . Erin."

Benny shook his head. "Erin's very pretty, so don't get me wrong, but you're . . . Sarah, you're . . ."

She stopped breathing. "I'm what?" she whispered.

He gazed into her eyes before setting his glass down and standing up. Sarah's heart began to race as she watched him round the end of the counter and come to stand beside her. She turned to face him.

"You're perfect," he finished.

She wet her lips, which had suddenly become very dry, and shook her head in denial. "I'm not perfect, I'm—"

"You're perfect," he insisted. "And I have to admit something. You're the most . . ." A flush crept into his face as he tried again. "Sarah, I haven't stopped thinking about you for two straight weeks. Longer than that, even." He paused. "We've spent all this time together this summer, and I haven't said anything, but . . . you must know. It's not easy for me to—" he faltered and rubbed at the back of his neck. "But you must know how I—"

Sarah didn't let him finish. She balanced herself on her tiptoes and placed a gentle kiss on his surprised mouth. Slowly, she lowered herself back down again, not trusting herself to look at him just yet. She stared at her feet, suddenly shy, before his fingers raised her chin so she was looking him in the eye.

For a moment, she thought he was going to say something more, but instead, he gathered her up against him, taking solid possession of her mouth and sending a thrill of heat through her. Her equilibrium gave way, and her body molded to his as if her bones had turned to liquid. She fit perfectly against him, and her heart swelled as he wrapped her more tightly in his arms, surrounding her with all his warmth and strength.

The whisper-soft sound of the sliding glass door opening didn't register, but Nadia's startled exclamation did, and Sarah jumped back from Benny and turned to her sister with a sheepish grin.

Nadia stood, hand on the door handle, with an amused grin.

"Um, Nadia, this is—"

"Benny," Nadia finished for her. She closed the door behind her once Marvin was through.

"Benny, this is my sister Nadia," Sarah said, completing the introductions just as Marvin gave Benny an enthusiastic sniff of his privates.

Benny gave Marvin a quick pat before pushing him gently away and saying hello to her sister. He moved from the counter to shake Nadia's hand, and Nadia matched his formality by echoing that it was nice to meet him too.

As soon as he turned back to the kitchen, Nadia let her eyes go wide and mouthed, "He's so cute!" Sarah gave a quick nod of agreement. He *was* so cute. He was so cute, she could kiss him 'til the cows came home, and then some.

The three of them stood in silence for several moments before Nadia suggested, "You know, y'all should check out the super moon tonight. It's so bright, it's castin' shadows out there."

Sarah turned to Benny with a small shrug. "Want to?"

His eyes burned into hers. "Yes."

"Take that wool blanket of Gammie's with you. It's gettin' chilly."

Sarah used that blanket so frequently when she sat out on the dock late at night that it had found a permanent home folded on top of the hope chest next to the slider door. Nadia was closest to it, so she picked it up and handed it to her sister with a smile.

On their way out the door, Sarah's phone dinged with a message. It was back on the kitchen counter. "Nadia, can you just look right quick to see if that's Erin? I texted her earlier."

Nadia glanced at the screen. "Yeah, she says she's on her way."

Sarah breathed a relieved sigh. "Good." Now she wouldn't have to worry about her. No, she corrected, she wouldn't have to worry about her *safety*. Sarah was plenty worried about Erin in general. She'd been miserable since Ethan left and grew more miserable by the day.

Sarah had already pulled the door open before she thought better of sitting out lakeside. She turned to Benny. "Want to head out to the porch instead?"

They might not have the best view of the moon from there, but if they went out to the porch swing, she could sit closer to Benny than she'd be able to in the Adirondacks on the dock. And she wanted to be close to him. She wanted to share the blanket and feel his body heat mingling with hers.

His answer was yes, but Sarah thought he might say yes to just about anything right then. His pupils were still dilated, and she could see he was still as affected by their kiss as she was.

Outside, the air was crisp and fresh. It was the last day of July, but if someone had said it was the middle of September, Sarah would have believed them. It had been a much cooler day than normal, and she would bet they'd already dipped below sixty degrees now that the sun was gone.

"I love nights like this," Benny said as he closed the door behind them.

"Me too." Sarah sat, and Benny lowered himself down beside her, helping her open the blanket and settle it over them.

"Nadia looks a bit like you," he remarked.

"Really?" Sarah didn't see it, but the idea that they might resemble one another warmed her from the inside out. Maybe because it was yet another indication that they were sisters in the truest sense, something she'd never expected would happen.

"How do she and Erin get along?" he asked.

Sarah laughed. "They don't."

"Hmm." He smiled, but in the moonlight she could see the question in his eyes.

"They're too alike. Stubborn as all get out, the both of them, but I can see them warming up to each other bit by tiny bit."

"Two stubborn women in one house," he remarked with a shake of his head. "You've got your work cut out for you. How much longer will Erin stay, do you think?"

"I think she's fixin' to leave sooner than later, but she's havin' herself a struggle right now, and I think it's hard for her to think about going back to an empty house. She'll be lonely there."

"Are you worried about Bender?"

"For myself or for Erin?"

"Both, I guess."

She considered the question. "At first, I was nervous when she told me what he'd done, but Jason Bender always struck me as kind of pathetic, you know? It's hard to be afraid of a guy like that. So weak. I think writing little notes might be as freaky as he's going to get."

Benny frowned. "I think, just to be safe, he needs a little talking to."

Sarah's eyes grew wide in surprise. "And you're going to be the one to do it? How would you even know where to find him?"

"You know that woman you described?"

"The tube-topped chick with spiky hair?"

He fought a smile. "That's the one. I know her. She's from here. She graduated a year behind me, and my dad worked with her dad at the mine."

"So what? You'll just go to her house and hope Jason is there?"

"Well, yeah," he admitted.

"I don't know if I like the idea of you confronting him," Sarah fretted.

He reached for her hand under the blanket. "Are you worried about me?"

His hand felt warm and solid in hers, and she held on more tightly. "Yes."

He broke into a wide grin.

"What, that makes you happy?"

"Well, yeah," he said again.

She laughed. "Why?"

"Because it means you care about me. Unless . . ." He eyed her up playfully. "Unless you're really just worried about Bender. Do you have feelings for him I should know about?"

"Goodness no." She shuddered.

He paused and gave her hand a squeeze. "Do you have feelings for *me* I should know about?"

She met his eyes. "Yes. Yes, I do, actually."

The moment hung suspended between them, and Benny moved in to kiss her again. He was halfway there when Sarah blurted, "Have you talked to your sister?"

He stopped in his tracks. "No. Why?"

"She did my hair about a week ago."

"It looks great," he said automatically.

She laughed again. "Thank you, but that's not it. We talked about you, and I wasn't sure what she told you."

He straightened, looking wary. "Nothing. She told me nothing. Why? What did she tell you?"

"It's really more about what I told her."

He shot her a questioning glance.

"I told her how I feel about you, Benny. And she told me some things about you that helped me understand you better. Things that made me . . . like you even more."

He nodded slowly, staring off at some point in the distance. "So, you know then?"

She squeezed his hand. "I know."

He continued to stare off, still, except for the muscle jumping in his jaw. Maybe this hadn't been the best idea. Maybe she should have waited for him to tell her himself.

"Benny, look at me."

He did, and he looked so sorrowful that she felt her eyes sting. She blinked the prickles away as she sought to comfort him, moving closer and breaking contact with his hand so she could touch his face. She stroked his cheek, then his jaw, and felt those muscles twitch under her fingertips.

Leaning in, she kissed him there at that point of tension, and then she pulled back just far enough to look him in the eye. "Earlier, you said I was perfect, but I'm not." She shook her head. "I'm hopelessly flawed. But maybe what you meant—at least I hope what you meant—is that I'm perfect for you." Her voice tipped up in question.

He gave a small, almost imperceptible nod. Looking mesmerized, he waited for her to continue.

Sarah was so far out of her comfort zone, she had to work hard to keep her hands and voice steady. Taking the lead like this, being the initiator, well, it wasn't in her nature, but she owed it to Benny to lay it all out there for him. She didn't want him to have to guess at anything.

"I know you're not without your own flaws, and you might think being on the spectrum is a weakness, but I don't. I can't imagine a man more perfect for me than you. The things about yourself that you might consider a weakness, I consider a strength. And that's the truth. I love everything about you. Everything." She stroked his face again before moving her hand to his hair. Gently, she combed through it with her fingers. It was soft and silky. Somehow, she'd known it would be.

Benny was very still. It was as if he were waiting for something more, and since there was so much more to say, she continued on. "You're so handsome. So sweet, and genuine, and the way you make me feel, like I'm the most important person in the world to you, I just . . ." Her heart beat in her ears as she made the decision to lay it all out for him. She owed him that. She owed herself that. "It's not only that I love *things* about you, Benny." She took a deep, steadying breath. "I love *you*, the man that you are. I love—"

Benny didn't let her finish. He captured her mouth in a searing kiss, wrapping her so tightly in his arms, she felt all the air leave her lungs in a giant *whoosh*. His calloused hand caressed the side of her face, running the length of her jaw before cradling her cheek in warmth and roughness. He kissed her, slow and insatiable.

Minutes went by before Sarah pulled away. Shivering, she stared at him and waited. She needed to see him. Needed to hear him say those three words back to her. She didn't have to wait long.

"Sarah, when I saw you standing under the lights at Sean and Olivia's reception, I knew you were the most beautiful woman ever created, and I loved you then, even though I didn't know it yet. I couldn't keep my eyes off you that night. And building that wall with you . . . I can't believe it even turned out. You were such a distraction for me, I could hardly think straight. And when you were hurt, that's when I knew. I love you. I love you more than I've ever loved anyone. There's nothing I wouldn't do for you. I love you more than my own life. More than—"

"Hockey?" she broke in with a teasing grin.

His lips twitched. "I love you more than hockey," he said before applying a kiss to the hollow behind her ear.

The crunch of tires on gravel alerted them both to Erin's arrival, and they watched in silence as the Yukon continued up the driveway and parked in the space beside the Malibu. Erin must have spotted them snuggled together on the swing from inside of the car because the moment she got out, she shouted, "It's about time!" She grinned and slammed the driver's side door.

As she moved up the walkway, Sarah noticed Erin's bright eyes and puffy lips. Her friend had obviously been crying, but she was working so hard to affect a cheerful mood that Sarah decided to play along. She'd talk to her later. "Look who's finally home from fishing," Sarah said.

Erin continued to smile. "Benny, you can never leave Nicolet again. Sarah's been an absolute mope while you've been away."

"Don't look so happy about that," Sarah warned Benny with a shoulder nudge and a smile. When he met her eyes with a smile of his own, Sarah thought this might be the most perfectly happy moment of her entire life. Everything felt possible, and she finally understood what Louisa May Alcott meant when she said, "Love is a great beautifier" because, truly, life had never been more beautiful.

Chapter 27

For Erin, the first two weeks of August were a whirlwind. Not only had she and Adele finalized the master schedule, but they'd made the necessary tweaks to student schedules, planned the two district-wide professional development days that would be held prior to the start of school, and put together the in-service for new teachers that would include both the new mentee teachers and their assigned mentor teachers. Gabe had put Erin in charge of the new teacher training for the entire district, and between the four elementary schools, one middle school, and the high school, ten new teachers had been hired. Since most of the hiring had happened later in the summer, she'd had a hard time securing the venue for the day-long training, but in the end, the mess hall at a local day camp had become available, so she'd booked it. Next, she'd planned the day, and with Adele's help, the food, agenda, and speakers were set.

As if that weren't enough, she'd poured over the budget and finally found a way to order the livestreaming equipment the journalism advisor, Gary Cass, had requested two full years ago. She'd also completed the staff welcome letter, added the high school special events to the district calendar, and completed the necessary paperwork to wrap up summer school. There was still a lot left to be done, but she was ahead of where she usually was at this point in the summer, which was the one benefit to using work as a distraction from depression. The drawback? Incurring the wrath of Adele in the process.

"Alright girl," the imposing older woman said, closing the door of Erin's office behind her. "It's quittin' time, and I am not leaving this office until I see you march your skinny little bottom out to that parking lot. I'm even gonna watch you drive away, yes I am."

Erin looked up from her computer with a frown. "I'm not done yet."

"What are you doing that's so important you need to stay here on a beautiful Friday evening in the summer?"

"I'm going through the new EDP Google Form I modified last week."

Adele raised her eyebrows. "Kids aren't revisiting their Educational Development Plans until November, Erin. It can wait."

Erin began tapping at the keys on her keyboard again. "You know as well as I do that if I don't do this now, I'll be scrambling in November. I don't want that."

Adele sat down across from Erin's desk, and the chair creaked under the weight of her. "Erin, honey, how long have we worked together?"

"I don't know. Four years, I guess," Erin answered distractedly, as she scrolled through the electronic document.

Adele didn't reply to that, and after several seconds of prolonged silence, Erin looked up from her screen. Adele stared at her disapprovingly.

"What?" Erin asked, pulling off her blue-light glasses.

"There's something going on with you," Adele accused.

"What do you mean? Nothing's going on with me." She gestured at her desk, which had scattered papers and files end to end. "I'm just working."

"You're unhappy," Adele observed.

"No, I'm just . . . I'm—"

"Unhappy," Adele repeated.

"Why do you say that?" Erin challenged warily.

"Because, Erin, I *know* you. You're not yourself."

"That's just because I've been busy and stressed."

Adele shook her head. "No. I've seen you busy and stressed. That's not it. Or that's not *all*."

If it had been anyone but Adele, Erin would have held out with her denials, but Adele did know her, and it would be pointless to pretend that she wasn't right on the money. Erin pushed herself away from her desk and stood, rounding the corner to join Adele on the other side. She plopped down in the chair next to her secretary and sighed. "You've always been so put together, Adele. You've got it all figured out, so I don't expect you to understand this, but I'm feeling really lost."

Adele was quiet, but she nodded for Erin to continue.

"It's not just Ethan, although that's a big part of it. I sent him away, I know, but I didn't really want him to go. I wanted him to stay."

Adele treated her to a disapproving frown. "It's not like you to play games."

"Come on! I didn't even realize I was until after," Erin defended. "And it wasn't really a game, at least not the way you mean."

"Alright then," Adele conceded.

Erin bit down on her lip. "Like I said, I don't expect you to understand. I'm not even sure *I* understand completely, but I've had some time to think about this. I'm still trying to figure it all out, but . . ." She hesitated and played with her glasses. "I've told you about my mother."

Adele wrinkled her nose in distaste. "Jillian? Yes."

"And I've told you about Seth."

She scowled. "He's another one on my list."

Erin smiled. Leave it to Adele to be protective of her. She loved her for it. "I was *ugly* that night with Ethan, to use one of Sarah's words. Deliberately ugly. I was mad, sure, but there was more to it. The things I said were just . . . over the top. I knew it at the time, but I didn't really know why. I still don't." She paused. "But Adele, I do know I wanted him to fight for me. I wanted him to claw his way back into my good graces. I wanted him to stay, and I wanted him to—"

"Love you?" Adele suggested.

Erin felt her face contort as she worked to keep her composure.

"Adele, all it took was one time seeing me like that—irrational and ugly and emotional—and he up and left. Just like that. And I think the reason is because—"

Erin choked back a sob and looked into the sympathetic eyes of her friend. She was at a loss for words, but she knew Adele would have them. She had the kindest, warmest eyes. They were the color of coffee beans, complimenting the rich dark brown of her skin.

Adele reached for Erin's hand. "Because?"

Erin didn't answer. She shook her head instead, not trusting herself to speak.

"Because you're unlovable? Is that what you were going to say?"

Erin took a deep breath and blew it out slowly to regain her composure. "I don't know. Maybe."

Adele shifted closer. "You listen to me, now. Your mother is abnormal, and that's the truth. The way she is, it has nothing at all to do with you and everything to do with her. Think of Erica Daniels. Do you blame her for the neglect she's experienced at the hands of her father?"

"Of course not," Erin muttered. She knew where Adele was going with this, but it wasn't at all the same. Erica's dad was an abusive scumbag.

"Of course not," Adele repeated. "Because it's not her fault. But that sweet girl might grow up, just like you, and think that something must be wrong with her because her daddy couldn't love her. But she'd be wrong. Just as you are wrong."

One fat tear escaped from the corner of Erin's eye, and she wiped it away. Why was the world so cruel sometimes? "What kind of parent hates their flesh-and-blood daughter?" she asked.

Adele didn't hesitate. "A very, very flawed one," she answered, observing Erin quietly before adding, "You are loveable, Erin Hennings."

Erin nodded, looking down at her lap.

"And you love Ethan, right?"

She nodded again.

"Then you need to tell him."

"I don't know how."

"You just speak the words, child!" Adele said in exasperation.

Erin laughed. "No, I mean, well, yes, that too, but I meant I don't have his number. His old number has been disconnected."

Adele smiled. "Where there's a will, there's a way."

Erin knew she was right. It might take some real effort on her part, but she had enough information to track Ethan down—if she really wanted to. "Thanks, Adele."

Erin stood, but Adele wrapped a hand around her wrist and tugged. "Sit down. We're not done yet."

She sat. Adele was just about the only person who could stop Erin in her tracks like that. "We're not?"

Adele gave her a pointed look. "You said it wasn't just about Ethan."

Warily, Erin returned her gaze. She was no longer sure she wanted to open this can of worms today, but Adele was like a hound on a scent, and she wouldn't let it go until Erin dished. "You're too shrewd for your own good, you know that?"

"There's no such thing," Adele remarked matter-of-factly. "Now, start talking. And this better not be about that Jason Bender."

She spoke his name with such distaste that Erin chuckled.

"No. Believe me, I'm not wasting any more time worrying about that guy, but listen, what I'm about to tell you, it can't get out to anyone, okay?"

Adele sniffed. "When have I ever shared one of your secrets? I don't even tell my Thomas the things you tell me in confidence."

"I know, I know, and thanks for that." Erin took a deep breath. "Lately I've been thinking."

"Hmm. Very dangerous."

"Knock it off. I've been thinking of making a change."

Lifting her brows, Adele asked, "Are we talking hair color here or something more substantial?"

"You're impossible. I'm talking a career change."

Adele looked as scandalized as if she'd just seen a streaker run past the window. "You want to leave administration? Erin, you can't!"

"Why not?"

"Because you're so good at it! You love these kids! You love this school!"

"I do, but I feel like I want to get back to basics."

Adele eyed her up. "What does that mean?"

"It means I don't necessarily want to leave education. But I need a change. I'm burning out, Adele. If I'm not crunching numbers or busting my tail to meet state requirements, I'm on one end or the other of a yelling match with a student or parent, or sometimes even a teacher. I can't keep everyone happy."

"But since when do you care about all that? I'm always telling Thomas what a ball buster you are. What happened to that mentality?"

Erin shrugged. "I don't know. It didn't use to get to me. Now it does."

"So, what are you thinking?"

"I thought maybe I'd get back into the classroom or something."

"Here?"

"If you mean Nicolet, then yes, but not necessarily here at the high school. That might be weird. I could work in any building. I'm actually certified K–12, and even though I taught high school math and science, I did my student teaching in a fourth-grade classroom and really loved it."

"Hmm." Adele steepled her fingers under her chin.

"What?"

"Well, now. I don't want you to go thinking I'm not trustworthy, but I feel this moment warrants the breaking of a confidence. I'll let her know I've told you about this out of fairness to her, but you have to promise that what I'm about to say won't go any further."

"What are you talking about?"

Adele rolled her eyes. "Just promise, Erin."

"Fine, cross my heart. What?"

"Gladys Fisher is a good friend of mine."

Erin squinted her eyes. "Why is that name familiar?"

"She's the secretary over at Lakeview."

Lakeview Elementary School was Nicolet Public Schools' most beautiful building. It was located on a high bluff on Ridge Street and overlooked Lake Superior, as the name suggested. Originally, it had been Nicolet's high school and was one of several historic buildings in town. Everything about it was lovely and quaint. It even had a beautiful auditorium where musical events took place and a large stone fountain in the courtyard at the front. Ann Lundquist had been the principal over there for the last ten years and had done an amazing job.

"Alright, so?"

"She told me Ann's husband has taken a job in Anchorage. She's staying here one more year so her daughter can graduate with her class, and then she'll join him over there."

Erin's pulse picked up. "What? No way!" This was amazing news! All the principals within their district were in their forties or younger, and all had ties to the area. Erin hadn't even allowed herself to consider putting in for a principal at another local school because nobody would be leaving those positions for years.

"She isn't going to announce this until just before Christmas, according to Gladys, but if you're waiting in the wings when she does . . ." Adele smiled happily. "This might just be the kind of change you're looking for if the negativity is getting you down. High school students run *from* their principal, but elementary students run *to* them. They adore them."

Erin sighed. "Adele, you have no idea how good that sounds."

Adele patted her hand. "There. That will give you something to look forward to. You'll be a shoo-in. And in the meantime, you just work to find that boy's phone number." She paused in the act of standing. "Who knows? Maybe I'll just help you with that too." She winked. "But not until Monday."

Erin stood alongside her secretary. The older woman towered over her. She was large-boned and quite tall. Thomas was the exact opposite, and yet somehow they managed to be one of those couples who just *fit*. "Adele, you have no idea how much you've helped me today. I feel about fifty pounds lighter."

Adele reached for her, pulling her into her arms for a warm hug. "Honey, you deserve all the happiness in the world. You'll come out of this just fine. You won't be the same as before, and that's a good thing 'cause I think now that maybe some of that toughness was just for show. Now you're learning how to be vulnerable, and that means some of life's arrows will hit their mark. They'll sting, but they won't take you down."

She gave Erin one final squeeze before stepping back. "And when you need her, you've got Mama Adele to help you through. Jesus too, if you care to know it. I keep telling you to try my church with me, and the offer stands."

Erin smiled. "Thanks, but I'm pretty sure I'm not Jesus material. I wouldn't make the cut."

"Child, how many times have I told you? There are no tryouts. If you want to be on the team, you're on the team, and that's that. Easy as pie."

"I'll keep that in mind," Erin said noncommittally. It was interesting, but lately she'd come to realize that the majority of the people in her life were either Bible-thumping Jesus lovers or well on their way to becoming one. Olivia and Sean were for sure, but so were her two running partners, which had surprised her. Even Sarah and Nadia had begun attending mass at the cathedral with Benny and his family. Maybe there was more to it all than Erin had previously thought.

Adele gave her a critical once-over.

"What?"

"Speaking of pie, you'd better start eating some. You are far too skinny, girl."

"Let's go out to dinner then. How about 906 Pizza?"

"Can't. I'm on a diet." Adele patted her butt. "Thomas mentioned I'm carrying a little extra in my tush these days."

Adele's tush was carrying more than just a little extra, but Erin made all the right noises and said all the right things to reassure her friend that she looked just fine.

"I told him he'd better watch it. A recent study has found that women who carry a little extra weight live longer than the men who mention it." She raised one eyebrow, and Erin burst out laughing.

She was still chuckling when she got into her car to leave ten minutes later, and true to her word, Adele watched her drive away.

Chapter 28

T hey were in the middle of a run of cool temperatures, and even though September was still more than two weeks away, Sarah found she was already looking forward to the changing of the seasons. This cool spell wouldn't last much longer. By the looks of it, they'd be back into the eighties by the start of next week.

It was early Friday evening, and Sarah was having a picnic of sub sandwiches with Nadia and Benny down at Nicolet Harbor. Erin was off on a run somewhere, which meant she'd be in decent spirits in time for the movie they were going to see together later that night. Running seemed to improve Erin's mood unlike anything else could.

Sarah had just finished filling Benny and Nadia in about the meeting she'd had that day, and she ended her storytelling by taking a dainty bite out of her dill pickle spear.

"Tell it again," Benny demanded with a satisfied grin.

"I can't hear it enough times, either," Nadia chimed in from the other side of the picnic table. "Now I wish I'd been there."

The noises of the harbor floated around them: the squawking of seagulls and the squeaking of park swings and the laughter of children, as well as the intermittent sounds of people walking and biking along the path a few yards from their table.

Sarah was glad Nadia hadn't been there. If she'd been a part of the video call Sarah had joined at her lawyer's office that afternoon, any remaining hopes or illusions that Bruce cared even a little bit about either one of them would have been destroyed forever. A young girl deserved to have that fantasy prolonged for as long as possible.

Maybe a few weeks ago, it would have bothered Sarah to look into the cold eyes of her father and listen to him try to cut her and Nadia out of his company and out of his life, but she'd been strangely calm and detached. Mostly, she'd let her lawyer do the talking, chiming in only occasionally to ask a question or respond to one.

Her father had tried to lowball her, as she and her lawyer had known he would. She'd declined his offer and told him she wouldn't consider anything less than her asking price of 1.6 million dollars apiece for her and Nadia's shares. Both Ethan and her financial advisor had assured her it was more than a fair price, and she trusted them, which was good because Bruce was a master businessman, and he knew how to manipulate a sale.

When she'd told him she'd be happy simply to hold on to the shares and receive the dividend payouts, a process she still didn't quite understand, he'd attempted to call her bluff and failed. He'd told her she would be required to participate in the day-to-day operations of the company to receive those dividends. She'd told him that would be fine. He'd mentioned that she'd have to move from Nicolet to make that happen, and she'd calmly replied that she wouldn't mind the excuse to leave the snowy north and return home to a milder climate. When he'd pointed out that she'd have to give up teaching, she lied to him with a straight face and claimed that she was really only continuing on as a teacher for something to do. She could just as easily learn the business as she could teach.

Sarah was so glad she'd practiced these responses in advance because she'd played the part of indifferent heiress beautifully. In fact, she'd nailed it, and she could see the glorious moment Bruce knew he'd been bested. It was brief, and if she'd blinked, she would have missed it completely. Although he'd maintained his cool demeanor, the slight flaring of his nostrils and the reddening of his cheeks gave him away. He'd lost, and he knew it. For Sarah, it was enough.

In the end, he couldn't abide the thought of having his daughters interwoven in his life and in his company, and he'd agreed to the purchase under her terms. Sarah Josten, English teacher, had stuck it to Bruce Josten, CEO and multimillionaire, but that wasn't the best part of the video conference. The best part for Sarah was looking into the cold eyes of her father and realizing that she didn't need his love or affection to be whole.

It didn't hurt her like it would have if she had been all alone in the world, as she'd been even just last year. New to town with no friends to speak of, she'd literally gone to work and gone home day after day until she'd met Olivia that night at the homecoming football game. That was the moment when things began to look up for her. That was the moment she'd begun to put down roots.

Her father didn't love her. He didn't even like her. And she may not ever be close to Lydie Mae, whether her mother was sober or not. But she had the beginnings of a solid relationship with her sister. She had a wonderful man in her life who loved her and made her feel safe and protected and special. She had good friends and a place to call home. She really didn't need anything else.

She snuck a look at Benny. Well, okay. Maybe she did need something else. And looking into his eyes, she knew she'd have them all in good time. There would be a ring one day. And babies. Lots of babies.

It was Sunday night, late, and Erin sat out on the patio wrapped in Sarah's wool blanket. It was clear, as it was most nights out there on the basin, and Erin found the Big and Little Dippers. Then, having exhausted her knowledge of stars, she turned her attention to the moon. It was a tiny sliver in the sky, but somehow it still cast an oversized reflection off the small ripples of the water.

Try as she might, she hadn't been able to sleep, so a little after midnight, she'd left Marvin in her room and tiptoed downstairs and out to the patio. The gentle lapping of the lake, along with the occasional loon call, were the only sounds to be heard, and they lulled her into a state of quiet introspection.

It had been a nice weekend with minimal time spent on work. She'd been active, taking two runs with Heidi and Leila and four walks with Marvin. On Friday, she and Sarah had gone to see the new Matt Damon movie, and last night, she'd played a round of mini golf with Leila. They'd bumped into Jackson Lang out on a putt-putt date with some female who couldn't have been a day older than twenty.

The two of them had been turning in their clubs at the same time she and Leila were picking theirs out, and when Leila caught sight of Jackson, her hands began to shake so violently that Erin reached out and took her putter. They'd stopped to converse briefly, although technically only Erin and Jackson carried the conversation while Leila stared down at her feet and the pony-tailed blonde chomped on her gum.

Sarah had once described Jackson as *salacious*, and after she'd looked up the word, Erin whole-heartedly agreed. The man oozed testosterone. He wasn't at all Erin's type, but she'd always liked him in the platonic sense. Leila, as it turned out, didn't like him in any sense, platonic or otherwise. She'd snubbed him outright that night, even though he'd tried to engage her multiple times before he finally shrugged in defeat and walked off with his date.

"So, I take it you're not a fan?" Erin had remarked once he was out of earshot.

Leila pursed her lips together as she followed Jackson's retreating form with narrowed eyes. "No," she'd answered darkly before quickly replacing her frown with an overly bright smile and changing the subject.

Erin had felt a surge of disappointment. She hated being left in the dark about things, especially when she knew the details would be juicy. And this story would definitely be a doozy. She could sense it. If she knew Leila better, she might have pushed for more information, but she consoled herself with the knowledge that she'd find out eventually. Because while she might not know Leila real well yet, she would in time. She was going to be a close friend. Sometimes you just knew that about a person.

The resident beaver on the lake smacked its tail down into the water a few yards off the shore, making Erin jump. Once the adrenaline surge had calmed, she chuckled to herself. That beaver had been swimming back and forth in Sarah's bay all summer long. He was busy doing *something*—building dams, presumably. Hilariously, Nadia had dubbed him "Justin Beaver." She was clever, that one, and Erin had to admit, she was going to miss her when she moved back home.

She turned her head in the direction of the cabin next door. It had gone up for sale last week, and for a few glorious minutes, Erin had let herself imagine living out here right next door to her best friend. She didn't want to leave the basin to go back and live in town, but at the same time, she was ready to be in her own space again. The best of both worlds would be to have her own place right out here on the bay, but reality hit when she found the asking price after a quick internet search. They wanted over five hundred thousand for the place. For a small cabin!

To say it was out of her price range was an understatement, but she was still disappointed. At least she could visit Sarah out here. This spot had become extraordinarily special to her. In fact, it felt more like home to her than her own house did. Maybe one day, if she scrimped and saved, she could buy a place on the water in her retirement. Or maybe she'd get lucky, like Sarah, and some rich relative would leave her an inheritance. Too bad she didn't have any relatives. Only Jillian.

Erin had come to love sleeping with the windows open and hearing the sound of the water through the night. She loved being able to jump in for a quick morning swim before work. And she loved sitting out and staring at the night sky. She never did that at home. She wondered why.

Undoubtedly, some of her warm, fuzzy feelings about being out here had to do with Ethan. She felt close to him here on the basin, even though she had no idea where he was. Earlier today, she'd told Sarah she wanted to find him. She told her about her conversation with Adele and how she was pretty sure she loved him.

It had been a bombshell moment for Erin, but Sarah's reaction had been underwhelming, to say the least. To be fair, her friend had been busy cooking in the kitchen, with Benny due for dinner within minutes, but still. All Erin had gotten was a vague smile and Sarah's half-hearted promise to help her find him.

Pulling her knees to her chest under the blanket, Erin sat for several more minutes, letting her thoughts roam wherever they wanted. She was daydreaming about a reunion with Ethan when she heard a noise from the other side of the house: a thump followed by a slow hiss, another thump, and then a curse.

Someone was out there.

Erin stood up slowly, bundling up the blanket and leaving it on the chair. She quietly lifted another chair and carried it to the sliding glass door. Carefully, she climbed onto it and grabbed the decorative wooden canoe paddle Sarah had displayed just above the door. It was about three feet long and had an anchor etched into it.

Erin brought the paddle down with her and listened. Mostly, it was quiet, but if she really concentrated, she thought she could still hear that intermittent hissing. Carrying the paddle in both hands like a bat, she walked around the side of the house to the back. Benny's truck came into view. She hadn't known he was staying over, and she instantly felt better knowing he was still there and just inside the house. She glanced at Sarah's bedroom window. It was open.

As she finished rounding the corner, she held her breath. She could hear something moving around on the porch. Quietly, she took a few more steps until it came into view. A shadowy figure was standing, facing away from her and towards the house, with one arm raised up high. Something glinted in his hand.

Realization hit all at once. It was Jason Bender, and he was holding a can of spray paint and going to town on Sarah's front door. The punk was vandalizing her friend's house! An anger unlike anything she'd ever felt fueled her next steps, and she covered the remaining yards between them at a run with the paddle held high above her head. Jason turned and had just enough time to let out one startled yelp before she brought the paddle crashing down on his skull with a loud thud. He went down like a tall, straight tree onto the floor of the porch. Quickly, she took in the words written on Sarah's door.

He wasn't very original.

"Who's the bitch now, Jason, huh?" she yelled at his prostrate form.

The porch lights flicked on a second later, and Benny filled the doorframe with Sarah peeking out from behind him. Benny looked from Erin to Jason, his expression of alarm fading as a slow smile curved his lips.

"Erin, what in tarnation?" Sarah asked, unable to see Jason laying there at Erin's feet. Benny moved to the side so she could take in the scene, and she blanched. "Oh, my lands!"

"Sarah, go call the police and bring me some rope or something," Erin ordered calmly.

Sarah turned and ran inside.

"Hurry up, I don't know how long he'll be out!" Erin called after her. She stood over Jason, holding the paddle at the ready in case he came to, and she needed to beat him over the head again.

Benny came out, stepping around Jason, and reached out a hand. "May I?"

Happily, Erin relinquished the paddle to him. They both stood guard in silence for several seconds before Benny whistled and shook his head.

"What?" she asked.

"You really clocked him a good one."

Worry furrowed Erin's brow. What if she'd really injured him? "Do you think I hit him too hard?"

Benny chuckled. "No. I think you hit him just hard enough."

It was the talk of the town for the next week. The story had even made the news, and Erin spent at least a few minutes each day fielding questions from teachers who were slowly returning to school to get their classrooms ready. They popped their heads into her office and asked for details, and they all left wearing smiles.

Adele was eating it up. "Everyone loves a good story where the idiotic villain gets taken down by the puny little damsel," she said.

According to Officer James, who had promised to keep Erin in the loop every step of the way, they were charging Jason with aggravated stalking, a felony offense in the state of Michigan that could carry as many as five years in prison, but he'd warned her that Jason may not serve much (or any) time if convicted. It was altogether possible that he'd pay a fine, be placed on probation, and be required to undergo psychiatric counseling.

"We'll have to wait and see, young lady," he'd said. "But either way, you won't have to worry about him bothering you again because just as soon as he can, that boy'll turn tail and run out of town. He's a laughingstock here now, and he knows it."

Happy as she was to have the Jason saga behind her, Erin was disappointed to have her time at the basin come to an end. There was no reason to stay now, and the truth was, she'd probably worn out her welcome weeks ago, not that Sarah would ever let on that she had.

Leaving was painful, and she had to remind herself over and over again that she wasn't going far. Lifting the last of her boxes into the Yukon, Erin closed the hatch while Marvin stared at her with doleful eyes. It was as if he knew his life was about to get much, much worse. He ran free out here, something he wouldn't be able to do at her house. After tipping his head from one side to the other, he whined.

"I know, boy." Erin crouched down to pet him. "I don't want to go either, but it's not over yet. How about one last hurrah, huh?"

Sarah was throwing another party. It was a dual-purpose send-off party for Erin and a welcome party for Nadia, who still hadn't met most of their friends. It was only supposed to reach a high of seventy-two degrees that afternoon, but Erin figured they'd still play in the water anyway.

As if on cue, the first car arrived, and Erin held Marvin's collar to keep him from running in front of Heidi's two-toned Mini Cooper. She called out a greeting to Heidi and Steven after they killed the engine and stepped out of the car.

"There she is, the woman of the hour!" Steven looked around, as if he were searching for something. "I hope there aren't any more canoe paddles lying around. I hear you're ruthless with those." He smiled widely.

"Better not let down your guard," Erin teased and then looking at Heidi, she asked, "Can I let Marvin go? He wants to say hi."

"Of course," Heidi replied, though it was Steven who reached down to scratch the rollicking dog behind the ears. Heidi was tied up. She held a beach bag in one hand and a bottle of champagne in the other.

"What's that for?" Erin asked her.

"I figured we'd have a lot to celebrate today."

"Like?"

"Your single-handed takedown of that crazy teacher, for starters."

Steven trailed Heidi and let out an amused chuckle. "This place sees more concussions than a hockey rink, that's for sure."

Erin took the wine from Heidi's hand and treated Steven to a saucy look over her shoulder. "You're so funny!"

Heidi shook her head definitively. "No more concussions here today. Sarah's finally recovered, and besides, statistically, it'd be almost impossible."

Raising one dubious brow, Erin added, "Knock on wood." She lifted the bottle of champagne. "And thanks for this, by the way. I'll stick it in the fridge."

Once inside, Heidi went to the small bathroom off the garage to change. Steven looked out the windows and down at the dock. "Boat's not here yet?"

Erin closed the fridge. "Not yet. They should be here in a few minutes. Olivia texted when they left the launch."

This party would be well attended. The same crew from the last time would be there—minus Nora—and Sarah had also invited several of their work colleagues, including Adele and her husband, as well as Leila and her cousin, Elena. It didn't take long for the driveway to fill up with cars of various makes and models.

Together, Erin and Nadia greeted each guest as they arrived. Although the party was mostly made up of friends and acquaintances of Erin's and Sarah's, Nadia had invited a small group of young college students who had just started their freshman year. Erin wasn't sure when Nadia would have met them, but she seemed comfortable enough with them, and Erin was happy for her. She hoped she would hit it off with Anna and Jess too. Time would tell.

The start of a party always felt a little forced and uncomfortable to Erin, but it didn't take long for everyone to relax and get into full party mode. Floaties dotted the shallows, and the paddle boards saw near-constant use. A rowdy game of cornhole had drawn a small crowd near the retaining wall, and even the sauna was seeing some action. Country music played in the background, mixed with the sound of Sean and Olivia's boat engine as they came and went with new groups of people on board each time. Benny manned the grill, cooking up brats and burgers, while Sarah rocked her job as hostess, making sure everyone had just what they needed. Marvin raced back and forth between the shore and the patio, not quite sure where he wanted to be.

Erin and Nadia chit-chatted with one another between guest greetings from their spot on the edge of the patio, and Erin had to marvel at how far they'd come in their relationship. Gone was any hostility, having long since been replaced by a mutual respect for each other and a love for Sarah. While she wouldn't go so far as to say that the Nadia of today was unrecognizable from the Nadia of a few weeks ago, Erin acknowledged that the young girl had undergone a major transformation, both on the inside and on the outside.

She never would have guessed that the skinny, haunted, stringy-haired girl she'd helped move in three short weeks ago could be so pretty. Her face had filled out, and her hair looked soft and healthy. She glowed with an inner happiness that hadn't been there at first. Erin hadn't even been aware of the changes as they happened, but looking at Nadia now, it was obvious that the U.P. agreed with her.

The boat pulled up to and away from the dock with the regularity of a New York City subway train, and Sean and Olivia were in their element as they showed everyone a good time. Erin laughed and visited with her friends, retold the Jason Bender story a time or two, and helped Sarah serve up food and drinks, and although she was genuinely enjoying herself, something was missing. Some*one* was missing.

Several days ago, Sarah had knocked on her bedroom door and slipped her a piece of paper. Somehow, her clever friend had managed to track down Ethan's new phone number. After shrieking and smothering Sarah with hugs and kisses, Erin had closed herself back up in her bedroom and called the number. Her heart had felt ready to leap out of her chest as she dialed and then listened to ring after unanswered ring, and she could nearly taste the disappointment when his voicemail picked up. It was the automated kind, so she wasn't even able to hear his voice.

With a sinking feeling, she'd left him a message, apologizing lamely and telling him how much she missed him. That night, she'd slept with the phone beside her in the bed. He hadn't called back. That had been three days ago. Whenever she asked Sarah what she should do, her friend advised her to give it some more time.

"But should I call again? Or maybe leave him a text message?" she'd asked.

"Just give it some time, Erin," Sarah had repeated.

"What does that even mean?" Erin had demanded just that morning. "How much time?"

But Sarah hadn't answered her. Instead, she smiled that same vague smile she always wore whenever Erin brought up Ethan's name these days.

Working side-by-side with Sarah briefly in the kitchen, refilling the bowl of potato salad from the last container in the fridge while Sarah opened up another package of brats, Erin was tempted to bring him up again, but she feared she might be becoming the most pathetic version of herself to date. "They're hitting the potato salad pretty hard," she remarked instead.

"A summer party just isn't a summer party without loads of potato salad, if you ask me," Sarah replied happily.

"I guess." Erin threw the empty carton in the trash and followed Sarah back out to the patio. It was a day much like the day of the last party, even though it was a little cooler. The sun shone brightly, and the water was nice and calm—perfect weather for being on the Steele River Basin.

Erin placed the bowl of potato salad on the table and turned to take in their surroundings. "I wish Ethan was here," she admitted. So much for holding back.

Sarah smiled sympathetically. "I know." She glanced at her watch.

"Why do you keep doing that?"

"What?"

"Looking at your watch. You've checked it a hundred times in the last hour. What are you waiting for?"

Sarah flushed. "Nothing. I just like to know what time it is when I'm . . . hostessing a party."

Erin raised her eyebrows. "Must be a southern thing."

"Hey, Erin!" Nadia's voice called from the center of her group of friends down by the water. She wore a white bikini and held a stick in her hand. "Watch this!" She threw the stick out into the deep, and Marvin, wearing a red doggy life vest, jumped through the shallows and began to swim out to retrieve it.

Erin couldn't believe what she was seeing, and she cast a surprised glance at Sarah. "No way—he's swimming!"

Sarah laughed. "I know!"

"When did you teach him that?" she shouted back at Nadia.

"Yesterday!" Nadia laughed gleefully.

Erin shook her head with an incredulous smile. Turning to Sarah again, she asked, "How did she get him to swim with her?" Erin had tried countless times over the summer, and lifejacket or not, Marvin would never go beyond where he could touch.

"I watched her do it. She just got in the water, went out deep, and called him."

"That's it?"

"That's it."

"Damn."

"What?"

"He loves her more than me."

Sarah shook her head in denial. "No. You're his mother. She's his litter mate. He loves you both, just differently. And you owe me a quarter."

"Shut up." Erin grinned.

The sound of a slamming screen door echoed through the trees. At first, it didn't quite register, but slowly, Erin's smile faded. "Is someone next door?"

"Oh!" Sarah exclaimed, clapping her hands together. "The new neighbors must be here. I heard they were coming today." Her voice sounded oddly breathless when she added, "I baked that peach cobbler for them. Could you run it over and let them know I'll be by after the party is over? I don't want to leave my guests."

Erin stared at her. "Now? You want me to run it over right now?"

"Yes, please."

"That's stupid. Why don't you—"

"Please, Erin. I'd like you to go now. It's important to make a good first impression."

Then why didn't she go herself? Erin wasn't even going to be their neighbor after today. And could Sarah be more insensitive? Erin hadn't been next door since Ethan left, and the last thing she wanted to do was go over there and be reminded that she'd lost him forever. And to add insult to injury, she'd seen that cobbler on the counter earlier and just assumed Sarah had made it for her as a parting gift. She knew it was Erin's favorite.

"Fine. I'll go, but for the record, this is weird."

"Duly noted."

"Ugh. Whatever." Erin grabbed the cobbler with both hands and turned on her heel. "I'll be right back."

Walking the trail between the two properties, Erin grumbled to herself. This was so bizarre. Love had made Sarah completely clueless about anyone else's needs but her own. She was so caught up in her little romance with Benny, she couldn't even see Erin's pain, and it was really, really disappointing. Erin would never have thought she was capable of being this thoughtless.

She was almost to the small porch when she heard voices talking. As she drew closer, she slowed down, listening to some of the conversation.

" . . . can't believe this! You get to live here, you lucky duck, and we get to come for visits."

"You come anytime you like," a deep, familiar voice said.

Erin would have recognized that voice anywhere, and so she wasn't in the least bit surprised when the screen door opened a second later and Ethan walked out. He spotted her immediately, still holding the door. Instead of letting it slam, he closed it gently, never taking his eyes off hers.

Erin's hands began to shake and her feet felt like they'd been cemented in place. "Wh—what are you doing here?" she finally asked.

Ethan stepped off the concrete slab and onto the grass. He walked towards her confidently, without hesitation. "I bought it."

"You . . . bought the cabin?"

He nodded.

"Why?" Her hands were shaking so badly that the cobbler was in danger of falling to the ground.

Ethan took it from her hands and walked it back to the slab behind him, where he set it down carefully. He came back to stand in front of her. "For you," he said artlessly. "I bought it for you."

Erin felt like she was dreaming. She felt weightless, without a body. This was all so surreal. Ethan was standing in front of her and telling her . . . what? That he'd bought a house for her? Erin had so many questions, the least important of which came out of her mouth next. "How did you even know it was on the market?"

He chuckled. "Sarah told me."

"You've . . . been talking to Sarah?"

He nodded sheepishly.

"Why?"

"At first because I needed to keep her in the loop about my resignation from the company, but also because I wanted her to be able to find me in case . . ." He left the thought unfinished.

Erin waited, but he didn't continue. "In case?"

He took a step towards her, their toes almost touching. "In case you needed me," he said, his voice husky.

In her ears, the beat of her heart was almost deafening. She almost couldn't hear her own voice when she admitted, "Ethan, I've needed you for the last month."

He grinned. "I haven't even been gone a whole month."

She couldn't joke yet. "Why didn't you call me back?" she demanded.

He moved even closer. "I wanted to surprise you."

She was surprised, alright. And torn between being angry that she'd worried and suffered for nothing and being overjoyed that the love of her life was back, seemingly for good. But then he touched her, and it was no contest. He caressed her face, and she leaned into his hand, closing her eyes.

"Erin," he whispered.

"Hmm?"

"Please understand. I needed to give you some time."

"Time to what? Miss you to the point of insanity?"

She heard the smile in his voice when he answered. "I'm glad you missed me, but no. I needed to give you time to be sure of your feelings. Because, you see, the thing is, I love you."

Her eyes fluttered open, and her lips parted in surprise.

"You love me?"

He nodded.

"Even after all the things I said that night?"

He lifted both of her hands in his and shook his head. "Erin, there's nothing you could say or do that would change how I feel about you. Nothing."

Voices from inside the cabin floated out through the screen, but Erin hardly noticed. This was the most important moment of her life, and she wanted to savor it. He loved her! Suddenly, she felt painfully shy and awkward, but she forced and fought her way through those emotions and broke through to the other side. This wasn't a time for holding back. This was a time to lay everything on the line. To bare her soul and be vulnerable. "I love you too, Ethan. And I'm so sorry—"

He pressed a finger to her lips, hushing her. "It's all in the past. We're starting fresh, from this moment. You and me."

She kissed his finger and repeated her declaration.

"I love you too," he whispered, drawing her to him.

She'd only known Ethan for one short summer, but on a soul-deep level, Erin felt like she'd known him forever. After a swift grin that left her light-headed, he lifted her off the ground so that her eyes were level with his, and as their bodies molded against each other, like two hands pressed together in prayer, he kissed her.

It went on and on and on, a glorious duet of give and take that Erin wished could last forever. But it wasn't to be, and her eyes flew open at the intruding sound of the screen door opening, its spring creaking as it stretched. Three craning heads peered out at them from inside the cabin, and all three wore wide smiles that stretched across their happy faces. Already plenty flushed, Erin felt even more heat creep into her cheeks as she smiled shyly back at them. She tried to wriggle free of Ethan's arms.

Chuckling, he reluctantly lowered her back down. "Alright," he called to them, "show's over." He looked at her and winked. "How about a rain check?"

"Deal," she answered immediately.

He took her by the hand. "Come on," he said, leading her over to the threesome and stopping just short of the concrete slab. "Erin, this is my family. Guys, this is Erin."

Sarah stood on the patio biting her nails and staring unseeingly at the various activities going on around her. Her mind was elsewhere, and she turned to look at the trees off to her right. What was happening over there at the cabin? She was dying to know.

She heard Benny's approach before she saw him. A sympathetic smile played on his lips as he pulled her hand from her mouth. "You're nervous," he stated unnecessarily.

"I'm second-guessing myself. Maybe this wasn't such a great plan. Erin might just have my head after this."

"Maybe," he conceded, "but only after she showers you with kisses first, which is exactly what I wish I was doing right about now." His lips curved in a slow, sexy smile.

Sarah felt a quickening of her insides. The fact that her body could respond to him, as tense as she was, was a testament to him and his supreme hotness. She reached out and stroked his arm for a brief moment, and then—without thinking—began to chew on her nail again.

Benny chuckled. "Have I ever told you what *I* do when I'm nervous?"

She cocked her head and thought back. "I don't think so," she finally answered.

"I flex my toes."

A surprised giggle escaped before Sarah could contain it. "You what?"

He smiled sheepishly. "Weird, hey?"

Folding her hands together to keep her nails far away from her mouth, she agreed with a nod and added, "Weird, but much more hygienic than nail-biting."

He grinned. "I used to have a lot of different tics. They started out big and obvious, and slowly one replaced another until I was left with the most inconspicuous one." He pointed at his right, bare foot. "That's the one that stuck."

Sarah was still looking at his foot when it stepped towards her. Wrapping her in a strong, protective hug, Benny spoke against her hair. "I've flexed my toes a lot over you, Sarah."

"Oh dear." She craned her neck so she could look at him. "I've caused you tense toes. I'm so sorry."

He gazed at her with a soft smile and a look of such unabashed adoration, she felt the pleasure of it all the way down to her own toes.

"Before I met you, I never knew what it was like to smile for no reason," Benny said, and then he kissed her.

With his lips pressed against hers, Sarah felt a bloom of emotion grow in her chest—an intensity of happiness she had never experienced before. She was loved.

It took another half hour, but eventually Erin and Ethan made their way over, along with Ethan's family. He'd mentioned to Sarah that they'd all be coming up. His parents had never been to the U.P., and he wanted to share it with them, but he also wanted them to meet Erin.

Sarah didn't know when it would happen, but she did know Ethan was carrying a ring in his suitcase. He'd asked her what she thought of that. Honestly, she wasn't sure. Maybe it was too soon, but maybe it wasn't. Only they could be the ones to make that call. She'd told him he'd know when the time was right and that his secret was safe with her in the meantime.

There was a lot of back-slapping as the guys all said their hellos. Erin made the introductions to the people Ethan had never met, holding his hand all the while, and when it came to be Adele's turn, the woman wrapped him in a bear hug before pulling him and Erin aside and launching into some kind of lecture Sarah hadn't been able to hear from where she was standing. But she watched Ethan laugh good-naturedly as the older woman poked a finger in his chest, and the picture the three of them made—the smitten Erin, the proud Ethan, and the protective mama bear, Adele—made her eyes mist over a little.

Noticing, Olivia sidled up beside her. "These are the moments, aren't they?"

Sarah put an arm around her tiny friend who knew firsthand how ugly and how beautiful life could be. There would always be hills and valleys, and knowing that made the high points even more meaningful. "These are the moments," she echoed.

Epilogue

The autumn colors were magnificent this year. Last year, an enormous windstorm had ripped the leaves off the trees well before they'd had a chance to reach their peak color, not that Erin had been all that focused on the leaves. She'd had Ethan to distract her all last fall. The biggest distraction had come in October in the form of a solitaire, princess-cut diamond.

So much had happened since then. A staggering number of engagements and weddings in their small circle of friends, two new jobs, one graduation, and one home renovation. Erin turned back from her spot in the gazebo Ethan had built near the shore and surveyed the house behind her. It wouldn't be long, another four weeks or so, and the addition would be finished.

They'd have to stay with Sarah and Benny for the final two weeks. It would be a little tight at Sarah's with five people staying there, not to mention a dog who now weighed in at a buck fifty, but Erin was kind of looking forward to it, and she already knew Sarah was. "It'll be just like last summer, Sarah had gushed." Then rubbing her growing tummy, she added, "Well, maybe not *just* like last summer."

Benny had proposed to Sarah at Christmas, two months after Erin and Ethan's engagement, but much like Sean and Olivia, they hadn't wasted any time getting married, and by February, Sarah was already expecting. She'd been six months along and absolutely glowing when she'd stood as Erin's matron of honor in her own wedding this past August.

Ethan and Erin were taking things much more slowly than their neighbors. They wanted to savor everything, and as much as Erin knew she wanted a family with Ethan, right now she wanted her husband all to herself.

Her phone buzzed on the table beside her, and she picked it up. She expected to see a text from Ethan, ready to fill her in on his day, but it wasn't Ethan.

Sarah: Meet me on the dock?

Erin: Sure!

Sarah: Come grab a mug of hot cider first. Nadia made some for us.

Erin: Yum! Be right there.

"Come on, Marvin," Erin called, standing up. He opened one eye, but he didn't budge from the dog bed she kept for him there in the gazebo. "Let's go boy!" she tried again with no success. She sighed. "Fine, let's go see Nadia."

At Nadia's name, he hopped up, all one hundred fifty pounds of him, and beat her to the door.

He raced ahead of her on the trail, and Erin laughed to herself. Gone were the days where she worried that Marvin might love Nadia best. She was just glad he'd found not one, but two loving homes with people who cared about him. He divided his time pretty equally between the two houses, so much so that he now had dishes and food at both places.

Nadia had already let him in by the time Erin arrived, and the two of them were long gone upstairs to her room.

"Looks like there might be another sleepover happening tonight," Sarah said with a laugh. She nabbed the mugs with one hand, giving Erin the thermos to carry, and stopped to grab the wool blanket on their way out the door. As she lifted her arm, her green maternity sweater hiked halfway up her midriff. In the kitchen, Erin had already noticed that it was extremely snug around Sarah's burgeoning belly, and now, apparently, it was also too short. Sarah gave it a quick tug.

"Didn't that fit you just last week?" Erin asked with an amused smile as she followed Sarah outside.

"Shut up. I'm as big as a hippopotamus, and I still have another month to go."

"At least you're a beautiful hippo, even if you do walk more like a duck now than anything else."

"Oh my gosh, I hate you!" But Sarah cast her a smile over her shoulder.

Slowly, they made their way down to the dock, not speaking until they were both seated in the Adirondacks. Sarah spread the blanket out over them both, lap to toes, before asking Erin to pour the cider.

"What do you think the boys are doing right now?" she asked, while Erin unscrewed the lid of the thermos.

"I don't know, baiting hooks, probably." Erin shuddered. "Do you know Ethan just pulls those nightcrawlers apart? He doesn't even cut them!"

"Hmm. I don't think I could do that."

"I *know* I couldn't." Erin handed Sarah her steaming cup. "Here."

Sarah blew gently over the top of the rim. "Thanks."

"I wonder if they'll make this an annual thing," Erin mused.

"I hope not. Benny already does that trip with the dudes in his family."

Erin snorted. "The *dudes*, huh?"

"At least they've shortened that trip to just *one* week now. Two weeks is too long. *This* trip is just right. A four-day weekend is plenty of time to fish, if you ask me." Sarah took a tentative sip of cider and looked out over the bay. "Isn't it funny, though, that our husbands are off fishing somewhere in Canada when they could be fishing right here for free?"

Erin nodded. "Yeah, but it's good for them. Every now and then they need to get together without the women around so they can spit and fart and be, you know, manly."

"Spitting and farting are your definition of being manly?" Sarah laughed.

Erin grinned. "Anyway, Ethan was really looking forward to it, so I'm glad they went. We should get together with the girls tomorrow, have dinner out somewhere."

"I'll text them," Sarah said, reaching for her phone in her back pocket. It took her a few tries to secure it in her hand. Even the little things were getting harder for her friend to do. With all that weight she was carrying out front, her center of gravity had shifted. It must be getting uncomfortable, but she rarely complained.

Sean and Steven had wanted to go on this fishing trip too, but their work had taken them out of town for the weekend. They'd already begun making plans for next year's trip, however. To the delight of their wives, the four guys had become pretty good friends, especially Steven and Ethan since they now worked together.

A few months after Ethan's return to Nicolet, Steven had approached him with a job opportunity. He was the president of a local company in Nicolet called Chester Biotechnologies. He'd started as an engineer there long ago and had slowly climbed the ranks. It turned out their CFO had retired at the end of last summer, and Steven had wondered if Ethan might be interested in applying. The rest was history.

As she somehow always managed to do, Sarah read her mind. "How is Ethan liking the job? Still a good fit?"

"He loves it. And he loves that it's allowed him to help his family. He's still working on getting them to move up here."

"I'm surprised he's having to work so hard to convince them," Sarah admitted. "I've been to Flint."

So had Erin. It was sad to hear Ethan's parents talk about what it used to be like down there. But like a lot of people, they still felt pride in their hometown, despite the downward turn it had taken.

Sarah sipped her hot cider and then rested her cup on top of her belly. Erin wrapped both hands around her warm mug and looked at the sky. The sun was about to dip below the tree line.

"I sure am glad you live out here, or I'd never see you. I miss not having you at the high school. It's not the same. And with Adele gone now too . . . it's like the wild, wild west over there."

Erin tried really hard not to smile at that. She'd heard from a few people in the know that Gabe had a new appreciation for just how valuable Erin had been to him in her old position.

"There's talk of hiring an assistant principal, you know."

Erin did know. The same sources had told her that her replacement, Eric Chase, a seasoned high school principal from down in Traverse City, had stormed into the superintendent's office and demanded help, or he was going to walk. Gabe pointed out that Erin had done the job all alone for years, to which the new guy had said something along the lines of, "It's no wonder she left, then, because she did the work of two people all that time."

It was all the thanks she needed, which was good, because it was all the recognition she was ever going to get. "I hope they do hire somebody."

Sarah perked up, nearly spilling her cup of cider in the process. "Hey, maybe you could do it!"

"Right," Erin said sarcastically. "I'm going to give up the best job I've ever had to be demoted back at the school that nearly did me in. You know what assistant principals do, right?"

"Discipline," Sarah conceded.

"Exactly. Whoever they hire will get all the jobs Eric doesn't want to do himself. No thanks. But I do miss seeing you and Olivia every day. That was definitely a perk, working with you two."

Sarah studied her. "So, you really are happy then?"

Erin shook her head with a smile. "I can't even tell you. Adele was right. When I walk around Lakeview, the kids all shout at me, and not four-letter words, either. They want to show me things, like the pictures they've drawn for me or the muffins they baked me."

Sarah slanted her head. "They bake you muffins?"

"Yeah. At the beginning of the year, the kids who put out the school newsletter gave me a survey. One of the questions asked about my favorite food, and I chose muffins."

"What were your other choices?"

"Hamburgers and broccoli." She patted her stomach. "I should have circled broccoli. Turns out, there is such a thing as too many muffins." She laughed.

"Don't even pretend you're in danger of getting fat," Sarah warned, patting her own stomach. "Look at me."

"You're growing a human inside you. You get to eat all the muffins your little heart desires. I'll start bringing them over."

"Don't you dare!" Sarah gasped in horror.

Erin chuckled. "Anyway, I love everything about that place. You walk in, and you just can't help but smile. Elementary school teachers are the happiest people on the planet. Plus, I have a view of the lake from my office, and I get to leave and go home while the sun's still up. I'm not stuck at basketball games or football games, or whatever else kind of game five nights out of the week anymore. I'm sold, Sarah. I'll never leave this job. It's too perfect."

Sarah smiled at her. "I'm really happy for you, Erin."

"Thanks." Erin eyed Sarah up in all her maternal glory. "I'm really happy for you too."

Sarah reached out a hand, and Erin held it and squeezed. "How did we get so lucky?"

Erin thought for a moment and shook her head. "It's not luck. It's a blessing." She discovered the truth of those words as she spoke them, and she found herself suddenly overwhelmed with such a feeling of intense gratitude, her limbs tingled with it.

Erin looked at her friend, this woman who had come into her life so quietly, so unassumingly—whose constant and gentle presence had softened Erin enough to open herself up to receive all the good things in life. "You know, when I count my blessings, I count you twice," she told Sarah.

Sarah turned her head and beheld Erin with a smile of delighted surprise. "That's the sweetest thing you've ever said to me!" she marveled. "You know I love you too, right?"

Erin swallowed. "I know." She gave Sarah's hand another squeeze before letting go and resting her head against the back of her chair. Sitting there in the chilled autumn air with her best friend beside her and a hot mug of cider in hand, Erin knew she was right where she was supposed to be.

Next In Series

Erin isn't the only one who's curious. What is going on between Jackson Lang and Leila Molina? Find out in book four, *A Time and a Season*.

https://books2read.com/A-Time-and-a-Season

About Author

For Charlotte, few things are more relaxing than an escape into a cozy, little story, and that's what she hopes you'll experience within the pages of her books. An author of contemporary women's fiction, Charlotte writes about small-town women and their families, sprinkling in just the right amount of romance for all the feels. She lives on the Lake Superior shore with her husband and three children, and like most of her characters, she can't image living anywhere else.

Visit her website or follow her on Facebookand Instagram. You can also join Charlotte's monthly newsletter to receive bonus material and other news.

Website: charlotteeverhartbooks.com (You can join the newsletter from there!)

Facebook: facebook.com/CharlotteEverhart.Author

Instagram: https://www.instagram.com/charlotte.everhart.auth
or